THE DEVIL INSIDE HER

A British Murder Mystery

THE DEADLY WOLDS MYSTERIES

JACK CARTWRIGHT

CHESTNUT PRESS

ALSO BY JACK CARTWRIGHT

The Deadly Wolds Murder Mysteries

When The Storm Dies

The Harder They Fall

Until Death Do Us Part

The Devil Inside Her

Secrets From The Grave

The Wild Fens Murder Mysteries

Secrets In Blood

One For Sorrow

In Cold Blood

Suffer In Silence

Dying To Tell

Never To Return

Lie Beside Me

Dance With Death

In Dead Water

One Deadly Night

Her Dying Mind

Into Death's Arms

No More Blood

Burden of Truth

Run From Evil

Deadly Little Secret

The DCI Cook Murder Mysteries

A Winter of Blood

A Secret to Die For

THE DEVIL INSIDE HER

A Deadly Wolds Mystery

PROLOGUE

It was strange, Lily thought, how everything could change in the blink of an eye — her marriage, her life, the weather.

The fog had descended abruptly, swaddling her like death's embrace, unwelcome and bone-chilling. It was the same fog they had spotted from the bottom of the hill, falling like a spectre, its long arms reaching, begging for touch.

Finally, it had enveloped them all.

She had only just reached the road, breathless with adrenaline. Marie was still behind her somewhere, or maybe to the side, or up ahead, she thought, twirling on the spot, abandoning all sense of direction. She needed to find help. Someone. Anyone. Marie needed her. She shouldn't have left her alone, not in that state.

But she couldn't be too far away, surely.

"Marie?" she called, her voice swallowed by the fog.

As Lily stared into the ivory veil, a fresh fear gripped her, a vision of headlights emerging like the mirrored shine of a predator's eyes in the darkness, growing larger and closer. And just as her fear escalated, it manifested. Lily heard the growl of an engine, and before she could even react, a dark car sped past on the other side of the road, a menacing, ebony shape in the darkness, its headlights on full beam only just penetrated the gloom. The snarl of its engine dissipated in the thick, sound-consuming fog. She doubted it had even seen her.

She felt exposed, alone on the road. She spun, no longer knowing which way was up, let alone the right way to go.

"Marie?" she cried again, panic rising like mist off a lake. "Cecelia? Franky? Violet?"

She longed for the sound of Violet's derisive comments, Cecelia's angry retaliation, and Franky's sarcastic replies. She longed for the sound of Marie's ragged breathing as she struggled with the slight incline. But more than anything, she longed for that deep, safe voice in her ear that had always told her everything would be alright.

"Jordan," Lily whispered, as she often did in times of need, as an atheist might utter a prayer in desperation. "Help me." She knew he couldn't help her, not anymore, never again. But she begged for him anyway. "Jordan, please."

She felt her way along the tarmac, aware of the steep drop to one side of the road, the way one might tentatively feel for the bottom stair in the darkness. Until a few seconds ago, the long, steep slope into the forest they hiked alongside had offered an unparalleled view of their serene surroundings. The height from the ridge had been a gift, a vantage point from which to take in the valley, the crisscrossing hedgerows, ripening leaves, and gliding kites that soared above the Wolds.

Then, the morning fog had been an aesthetic detail, an aspect of beauty adding drama to the scene.

Now, it was damn well dangerous.

Of course, a sheer drop in the Wolds was nothing compared to other areas of the country. Few places in the Wolds fully allowed for treacherous pitfalls. That's why they'd chosen this place, they thought it would be smooth sailing, a long week of easy hiking. Well, that and Franky had wanted to show off the outstanding natural beauty on hers and James's newly bought doorstep. But they had underestimated the erratic nature of British weather, a deceptively cruel and unforgiving mistress. The drop along which they had been walking had been significant enough to want to avoid, offering a fifty feet tumble to the bottom that would, at the very least, break an ankle. That's why they had crossed the road: to follow the hiking path on the bank on the other side.

"Marie?" she called out, hearing the fear in her cry.

Gone were the days when she would face danger head-on, when she and Marie would walk home across London after midnight and accept free cocktails and lifts from strangers into the city.

"Marie, are you alright?"

But the fog was too thick to carry sound.

She tapped the ground with her foot but struggled to identify the material beneath it. It didn't feel smooth, like tarmac, but many of the smaller roads nearby were stony and muddied by the wheels of tractors and four-by-fours. It felt similar to the hiking path on which they had been walking. But she couldn't be sure that such a vehicle was not about to run her down. Lily held up her hand, hoping to find something, someone to ground herself, a tree, a fence, a friend, but her fingers only moved through a wispy, white nothingness.

She felt like she could be dreaming, so disorienting was the greyness surrounding her. She yearned for the crisp, white skies they had enjoyed only a few moments before, the promise of the sun behind the clouds. She yearned for the yellow Viking helmet logo they kept an eye out for on signposts, the one showing them the way forward.

Then, a stick broke, not a flimsy twig but a solid stick beneath a heavy hiking boot. It *cracked*.

Lily spun. "Marie?"

A figure emerged through the fog, slowly, carefully, feeling its way towards her.

"Oh, thank God," she said. "Marie, you're walking. Are you okay now? Where are the others?" The figure continued its trajectory, more certain than Lily — she could see that now — of where it headed, with stronger, more decisive steps. "Careful now," she said. "That drop is here somewhere. We're back on the road."

She turned around, searching for the edge of the drop, squinting through the wisps. But ever-so-slowly, the fog was clearing, she could make out strange shapes, although she could not yet identify them. She thought she could see the slope off the road, a safe distance from where they stood, metres away. She sighed with relief.

But her breath was cut short.

From behind her, the figure had lurched. She felt it step up behind her, uncomfortably close, and wrap an arm around her neck. She laughed at first, thinking it was a game, a childish prank to scare her. But when that laugh soon dissipated and doubt cast its shadow over her mind, the grip tightened as if in response.

"Marie?" she choked.

But it wasn't Marie. It couldn't possibly be.

"Stop," Lily said, panicking, gripping the arm that held her tight. Her nails scraped against a raincoat's nylon sleeve, creating a sickly, squeaky sound. "Please."

But with each protest, the grip only tightened, so that she couldn't speak or breathe. She tried to pull at the fingers wrapped in thick gloves that held fast. The figure's breath grew ragged and exerted in her ear, quickening like a lover's as she fought back. She tried to scratch but found no bare skin. She tried to scream but found no air. She tried to stamp on the feet of her assailant, but her efforts were too weak to penetrate their heavy, leather boots. Her vision blurred and darkened, and the blood drained from her face as though her fear was a fever. She blinked, and warm tears of dread dropped onto her cold cheeks.

Dreamy images merged with reality. The trees seemed to tremble like cold commuters on a train platform. The sky swelled like a snowy tidal wave about to consume her. Whether she imagined it or not, she believed the fog was lifting, and through it, the drop grew clearer, closer. Suddenly, that drop seemed like a haven. A promise of reality. A sheer fall to shake her from this spectral grip around her throat. If only she could reach it and throw both of them forward. Maybe then she'd have a chance.

She felt life slipping away, falling into a panicked sleep.

So Lily lunged forward with what little strength she had, and caught off-guard, the figure's grip weakened for the first time. She managed to thrust them forward a few metres closer. The drop was within reach. A single step. If only she could...

"Cecelia!" she screamed, using what little breath she had. "Marie, Franky, Vio-"

But the figure pulled her back by the throat, its grip increased ten-fold. Its fingers squeezed around her windpipe, focusing its impact, knowing time was running out. The fog was lifting. Its cover would soon be blown. The figure moaned in her ear, a genderless, inhuman moan, exhausted with the exertion of killing her.

Then, in the chaos, Jordan's face swam across her vision. Lily reached out to touch it, and instead of her fingers falling uselessly through the wisps, she felt his skin beneath her fingerprints, the stubble of his cheek, the bone of his jaw. A new will emerged, a yearning that surpassed fighting for her life — the desire to join him, to lie beside him one more time.

She stopped struggling.

She closed her eyes. The figure continued to squeeze, and deep within Lily Hughes's ebbing consciousness, she sensed herself turn limp. She sensed a final breath escape her lips. She sensed herself dying. She sensed herself being pushed forward, then flying, falling, tumbling, rolling, breaking, splintering, falling.

She didn't reach the bottom. The pain faded, as did the light, and she was lying in her husband's arms — warm, calm, and at peace with the world.

CHAPTER ONE

The house on the outskirts of Hagworthingham was the kind of cottage featured on tin chocolate boxes that were sold in old-fashioned sweet shops. Hagworthingham was by no means bustling, though compared to George's tiny village of Bag Enderby, it was almost cosmopolitan. Ivy didn't need much. A post office, pub, and shop would suffice. Peace and quiet was exactly what she wanted.

She looked through George's window at the white house with its porch entrance, iron garden gate, and symmetrical chimneys. A proud cherry tree took up most of the front garden.

"It's almost sickeningly sweet, isn't it?" Ivy said.

George didn't reply. He seemed to be lost in his own little world.

She often caught him staring into space these days. But he followed her lead as she climbed out of the car, shaking himself back to reality, and as they had done hundreds of times before, they walked together up the garden path to a stranger's front door.

Ivy knocked and then turned to him. "You didn't have to do this, you know, guv?"

"Please," he said, straightening his jumper that bore a baked beans stain on the sleeve. "It gets me out of the house."

"You should be at home," she said. "Resting."

"I'm not dying, Ivy," he said, wincing.

"You're grieving. You should give yourself time."

"To do what? Stew?"

"To rest. You just lost your wife."

"I'm aware of that, Ivy," he said sadly, only because he didn't have the energy to be angry.

Ivy turned back to the door. It seemed everything she said since Grace had died had been the wrong thing. For the hundredth time in the last two weeks, she told herself to stay quiet. George wasn't looking for advice, she knew that. She just didn't know what he *was* looking for or what she could offer to help him find it.

Ivy coughed in the silence. They had stood on a doorstep like this so many times, but never for this reason. Usually, the conversation on the other side included tears, shock, and the beginning throws of grief. It was highly unlikely that would be the case today.

When the door opened, Ivy resisted the urge to pull out her warrant card and introduce herself as Detective Sergeant Hart. Perhaps it was because her boss was with her and that they spent much of their time knocking on doors.

"Ivy?" asked the woman who answered, a smart, smiling forty-something-year-old who swung the door wide in a welcoming gesture. In one hand, she held a clipboard holding notes and a booklet — about the house, no doubt. The other, she held out for Ivy to shake. "I'm Ella Alexander. We spoke on the phone?"

"Nice to meet you," Ivy said. "This is my friend George Larson."

"Pleasure," George said, shaking her hand with a smile that faded as quickly as firework dust.

"Please, come in," Ella said as though she owned the place.

They stepped into the hallway, and Ella immediately began her real-estate spiel. "Good thing you could come this morning. It's our only empty slot," she no doubt lied. "This one is very popular." Ivy smiled, humouring her, and George looked on with a stare she'd seen him use in interview rooms. "Please," she said, holding up a hand and nodding at their shoes. "If you wouldn't mind."

"Of course," Ivy said, kicking off her boots while George knelt to undo his shoelaces.

She could understand why it was necessary as soon as Ivy stepped onto the new, fluffy carpet. It felt like fresh snow beneath her feet. However, she also knew that taking off their shoes was a sales technique to make them feel at home. At least Ella hadn't gone so far as to bake fresh cookies.

"Cherry Tree Cottage," she declared, leading them through the house. "Three-bedroomed detached family home. Large living room, cosy kitchen and gardens to front and rear. Views across farmland. Parking for at least two vehicles. Space to work from home. Six miles from Horncastle and five from Spilsby, so a full range of amenities and schooling. Both are accessible via bus, on the route from Skegness to Lincoln—"

"Thank you," Ivy said, smiling but cutting her off, nonetheless.

As detectives, she and George knew when someone was selling a story. It was a pleasant story of a cosy little house in the Wolds, but a story all the same. Ella tried to lead them into the living room, but Ivy beelined for the kitchen, asserting a dominance that truly made her feel at home. George followed, opening and closing cupboard doors and checking the pipework beneath the sink.

While Ella raved about the marble counters, apron sink, farmhouse-style cupboards, and local stone tiles, Ivy noticed her own promising details. She saw the vegetation-heavy view through the picture window and noticed the morning light that cast a long, narrow shadow across the kitchen floor and a rainbow prism against the dishwasher. She spotted the ageing trampoline in the back garden. It was a slight on the view, she thought. Anyway, Hattie and Theo already had one at home. They didn't need another when they visited Mum every other weekend.

Only when they had explored the entirety of the downstairs did Ella excuse herself, receiving an urgent phone call.

"Cue the fake call from another prospective buyer," George muttered, grinning. "So, what do you think?"

Ivy shrugged. "I think it's sweet. Feels less like a step back than the others."

"What do you mean?"

"Well, the one in Louth." George gave a low whistle. "With the shower off the kitchen? Felt like I was moving back into the studio flat I had when I was twenty."

"I think it's useless to think about our lives that way."

"What way?"

"Linearly," George said. "Backwards, forwards."

"You mean it's more of a circle?"

"Hmmm, no. A meandering, perhaps."

"Well, this is one hell of a curve," Ivy said, sighing. "You know, I haven't lived alone in fifteen years?"

"You get used to it," George said bitterly, his usual gentle tone gone. He turned to the wall dividing the kitchen and the hallway, held his ear to it, knocked twice, then nodded, reassured of some secret concern. "You sure about this?" he said, talking to the wall.

"About what?"

George rubbed the paint with his palm, not meeting her eye. "All of it. The divorce. Living without the kids."

"You think I should stay married to a man I don't love?"

He turned to face her. "Of course not." He sighed. "It's just...if Grace's death taught me anything, it's that life is short, and we shouldn't waste time not being with the people we love. Hattie," he clarified. "Theo."

"Exactly, guv," she said. "I feel the same. That poem you read at Grace's funeral. Her favourite. How did it go?" She closed her eyes. "*Doesn't everything die at last, and too soon? Tell me, what is it you plan to do with your one wild and precious life?*" She opened them to see George's gaze glazed with tears. "Life is precious. And I've wasted too much of it being unhappy." The longer she looked into George's eyes, the more she felt her own grow moist. "And I know that as a mother, that should mean spending more time with my children. But the truth is, it doesn't. The truth is, I want to spend more time on my own, living *my* life, working through *my* desires." She shrugged. "It's not like I'll never see them again."

George smiled, briefly, a shadow of a smile, and lowered his gaze to the skirting by his foot. He kicked it once, then nodded in satisfaction. Ella's smothered footsteps sounded in the hallway. "Here we go," he muttered.

She stood for a moment in the doorway, then held up her phone.

"I'll be honest with you. That was another interested buyer. I don't want to pressure you, but I can't imagine this house will still be on the market by the end of the week."

Ivy smiled, again humouring the woman without biting. "Can we see upstairs?" she asked.

"Of course." Ella blinked, then smiled sweetly. "Follow me."

The upstairs was just as charming, with three spacey bedrooms off the landing, one for herself, one for Hattie and Theo, and one she could use for a multitude of purposes — an office, a library, a gym. The possibilities felt endless.

But when Ella began selling the arched, double-hung windows and the view beyond them that, Ivy had to admit, was gorgeous, she felt grateful for the buzzing in her pocket. She held her phone for George to see and sensed him watch her as she left the room.

"DS Hart," she answered, closing the door behind her.

"Ivy, it's Tim Long. How are you?"

She hesitated. She wasn't sure he had ever asked her that before. "I'm fine," she said, then paused. "How are you?"

"Very well." He coughed. "Look, I need you over in Tealby.

Caistor Lane. There's a body. A hiker, by the looks of it. Middle-aged woman. Possibly a nasty fall."

"Tealby? Up north?" Ivy joked. So far, she and George hadn't conducted any investigations further north than Ketsby, firmly in the south of the Wolds. "I can be there in thirty minutes. I'll call the team."

"They're already there. Maguire was the one to call it in."

"Oh, well, I'm on my way then, guv."

"Good. And erm... you'll be alone, will you?"

Ivy paused. "I can ask him?"

"No. Well... if he wanted to..."

She rolled her eyes. She was tired of being the go-between for George and Tim as though they were shy schoolboys passing notes. It had been going on for weeks now. "I'll see what he says."

"Alright," Tim said. "And Ivy? Thank you."

On the other side of the bedroom door, Ella was still prattling on about the windows. George wordlessly stared at the woman as though held hostage.

"I've got to head off," Ivy explained from the doorway.

George turned to her. "Still being overly nice, is he?"

"Strangely so, yes."

"What's the gig?"

"Middle-aged woman. Nasty fall when hiking."

"In these parts? Unlikely."

Ivy nodded gravely. "That's probably why Maguire called it in."

"Where?"

"Over near Tealby."

"Up north? That's a change."

Ivy smiled, shuffling awkwardly. "I could drop you home first, guv."

"Thanks."

"Or you could come with me?"

He shook his head with closed eyes as though even the idea was an ugly, intrusive thought. "No."

"I just—"

"No, Ivy," he said, stronger this time.

"I understand, guv, I do. I just... I'm not sure I can do it without you."

He smiled a warm, kind smile reminiscent of the man he used to be, the tension in his face breaking like a wave. "I'm not ready, Ivy," he said softly. "Not yet."

Ella looked between them, her mouth open and brow furrowed, lost in their cryptic conversation. But then she caught herself and, in an attempt to ease the tension, said, "I was just telling George about the windows. Arched, double-hung. Newly glazed. They—"

Ivy held up a hand.

"With all due respect, Ella, you can stop selling." She smiled at the dismayed expression on the woman's face, then looked around once last time. "Draw up the paperwork. I'll take it."

CHAPTER TWO

Perhaps it was that the Lincolnshire Wolds were so pretty that Ivy's reflection led to the conclusion that all of the crime scenes in the last few months had been particularly eye-catching. A fairy tale cottage, a bygone church, a charming watermill — but the scene that met Ivy as she rounded the corner was particularly idyllic. She had followed the Wolds' meandering lanes, enjoying the churn in her stomach as she crested hillocks and the expansive views offered like sweet treats between the hedgerows. The air remained hazy, as though she watched the world through a misted-up window. Following Tim's instructions, she headed towards Tealby, then eventually slowed to drive beneath the police tape lifted by a local officer who recognised her car.

After three months of near anonymity, it seemed that she and George were finally becoming noticed.

The view offered from the road stole her breath. It was screen-saver worthy of a scene synonymous with the Wolds, of drooping, well-worked fields, singular lines of tall trees and larger clumps of forest, and lush fields the colour of fresh peas, disturbed only by the occasional hay bale or slowly chugging tractor. Along the bottom of the valley, a wave of fog crawled away like a fleeing ghost.

As soon as Ivy climbed from the car, she heard a raucous melee of female voices disturbing the peace, not high or bickering, but low and growling like a pack of threatened lionesses. To the side of the road was a dirt track on which stood two people she recognised and four she did not. One woman — tall and strong-armed with dark, curly hair — pointed a finger at another woman — small and mousy with short, bright purple hair — between the hands that held her back.

The two people Ivy did recognise, Maguire and O'Hara, looked on in despair, evidently unsure whether the argument fell under police responsibility. She walked up and stopped beside them, attempting to decipher the chaos.

"You did this, Violet," yelled the pointing woman in a thick East London accent. "You and your petulance."

The purple-haired one reeled. "What, you think I killed my own sister-in-law?" Ivy couldn't identify her accent, but it sure wasn't local.

"If you hadn't stormed off like a bloody *child*, we wouldn't have been separated in the fog."

"She was at the back! We would've got separated, anyway. I couldn't see my own hand."

"Rubbish," spat the curly-haired woman, tears like phlegm in her voice. "Rubbish."

Ivy was unsure whether she was calling the purple-haired woman's excuse rubbish or the purple-haired woman herself rubbish. Either way, she felt it was time to step in. She did so before anyone could retaliate, even though all of their mouths had opened, full of something to say.

"Good morning," she declared in the way a teacher might enter a squawking classroom. "My name is Detective Sergeant Ivy Hart. Can someone tell me what's going on?"

The women hushed like schoolchildren, glaring at each other, on the verge of deflecting the blame. There was a long silence that stretched out like a highway along which they all shuffled. Suddenly, nobody wanted to say anything.

Eventually, someone spoke.

"Lily's dead," someone said in a voice thick with grief.

Ivy turned to her. She looked exhausted. The bags under her eyes reminded Ivy of shadowy hammocks bearing too much weight. Her blond hair was thick with sweat, highlighting her silver roots, and her skin was as grey as the fog Ivy had seen crawling along the bottom of the valley. "We don't know what happened."

"And what's your name?" Ivy said gently.

"Marie," she answered.

"Marie, can you tell me what happened?"

She took a deep, gusty breath that threatened to knock her over. "We were hiking along this path, and it suddenly got dark. No, not dark. Foggy. We couldn't see anything. I mean, it was a foggy morning, anyway, but for a few minutes, it was so thick—"

"What time was this?"

"About eleven?" she said, turning to her friends, some of whom nodded in support, and Ivy gestured for her to continue. "And when it lifted, Lily was gone. I went to find her, and I..."

Ivy waited, then, "Yes?"

"I did," she croaked. "Find her, that is. At the bottom of that slope. She must've lost her footing in the fog and fallen. We didn't know if she was... So we called you. But she is, isn't she?"

Ivy didn't answer. She didn't know the answer yet. She offered what she hoped was a reassuring smile, although she doubted it, and turned to the others.

"And who are you?"

The woman called Marie continued to speak for them, perhaps not wanting to give them a voice that could escalate into an argument once more. "This is Franky." Marie gestured to the woman still holding her friend by the arm on a tight leash. She nodded gravely at Ivy. She was the opposite of Marie — fresh-faced and caramel-skinned, with long, recently bleached blonde hair and glistening brown eyes. "Cecelia," she continued, pointing to the hefty, dark-and-curly-haired woman who still panted with anger. "And Violet," she finished, neglecting to raise a tired arm to acknowledge the last member of the group, the only one who could have been named such — the woman with violently purple hair.

"What brings you all out here?" Ivy asked.

"A hiking trip," Marie said. She looked around, then pointed to a nearby signpost on the trail beside wooden steps that would lead ramblers further uphill. Ivy noticed a yellow logo on the sign that looked like an acorn wearing a horned helmet. Below was some writing she couldn't decipher from this distance. "The Viking Way," Marie clarified. "We're here with our husbands."

"*Your* husbands," Violet muttered.

She was met with eye rolls, moans and a sharp "Shut *up*, Violet," from Cecelia.

"Very well," Ivy said, moving them along. "My colleagues will speak to you, and we'll get an idea of what happened to your friend."

"Lily," Marie said weakly. "Her name is Lily."

Ivy stepped forward and placed a gentle hand on her shoulder. "We'll find out what happened to Lily," she whispered, then frowned. Up close, the woman looked positively unwell. "Do you want to sit down?"

"Please," she replied, nodding.

"PC O'Hara, take her to your car for a rest. Then I want you two to interview everyone in turn."

"Interview?" Cecelia snapped, her vitriol directed now at Ivy. "You think we had anything to do with this?"

"It's procedure," Ivy explained flatly. "To find out what happened." She looked around. "Where's..." She hesitated, almost saying *the victim*. "Where's Lily?"

"Over the road," O'Hara said, nodding to the edge of the tarmac. With one last look around the women, allocating their faces to memory, Ivy turned and walked over to it. She didn't bother checking both ways before she crossed the road. It was closed off and empty.

"Can't go down yet, sarge," Maguire called, following. "We're still waiting on CSI."

It was odd, she thought, how out of place his thick, southern Irish accent seemed in the English countryside, yet, how warm it was compared to her own.

Ivy nodded to confirm she had heard him and bent to peer through the trunks and leaves that blocked her view of the bottom of the slope. It did not look treacherous enough a drop to kill a woman, but Ivy knew full well that was no accurate measure of danger. She'd heard cases of victims drowning in puddles or fatally banging their heads on garage doors. Anyway, the leaves that littered the slope looked wet, and she imagined they held the same hidden hazard as black ice. Precarious, broken roots stuck up here and there like wooden shards, and the steep degree of the slope itself was enough to cause a nasty tumble.

At the bottom of the hill, wrapped around a tree, was a body. From this angle, it looked like the kind of rag doll dummies she'd seen used in car crash simulations. The limbs were limp and at nauseating, uncanny angles. Her neck, too, was at an impossible angle.

Ivy swallowed and looked away. "ETA on Katy?" she asked Maguire.

"We called her about thirty minutes ago, so any minute now."

"You called this into Tim?"

"Yes, sarge. I was called in with the ambulance."

"Why?"

He stuck out his lip. "What do you mean?"

"I mean, why call it into major crimes? Why didn't you think we're looking at a regular, albeit tragic, hiking accident?"

"In Tealby?" he said with raised eyebrows.

"Stranger things have happened."

She paused, waiting for him to answer her question.

He sighed. "I guess it was something about her position... wrapped around that tree." He swallowed, just like Ivy had. "Like she hadn't even tried to catch herself. Even with a drop like that, I don't get how it happened. I don't know," he finished, shrugging. "I suppose it was instinct. Police intuition, maybe? Why?" he said, suddenly looking panicked. "You think I was wrong to do so?"

"No," she said, watching him carefully. "I think your instinct was exactly right."

Over his shoulder, she watched a car pull up and stop outside the police tape on the road. Two dark-haired men in raincoats and clean hiking boots climbed out, glanced around with pained expressions, and then opened their arms to embrace the women who ran into them. "What's this then?" Ivy muttered.

"Their husbands, I think," Maguire answered. "The one you were talking to, Marie, she said she'd called them."

Ivy strode over, ready to hear the answers tumbling from the men's mouths.

"Are you alright? What's going on?"

"Where's Lily?"

"What the hell happened?"

They held their wives in tight embraces as though sheltering them from storm winds. The older and shorter of the two, a beer-bellied man with thinning hair and large, kind, blue eyes, had his arm around the dark-haired woman who had been confronting Violet when Ivy had arrived. Cecelia, Ivy remembered her name. The younger, taller man comforted the ill-looking woman, Marie, who already looked a little rosier in his company. He was strikingly handsome, with neat, salt-and-pepper hair that only served to bring out the colour of his eyes. They were also blue, but unlike the other man's, his glistened with a polished boyishness.

21

The attention of his glance alone as Ivy walked over was enough to stir a reaction in her chest.

But before she could answer any of their questions or express her own, she was interrupted by another woman, the good-looking one, Franky, who swooped over like an unexpected bird in Ivy's peripheral. She wore a complex expression that changed throughout her features. Her raised eyebrows showed concern, her flicking eyes worry, and her thin lips scathing.

She looked between the two men, who appeared to shrink a little.

"Where the hell is James?" she asked.

CHAPTER THREE

The fog had fully lifted, burned off by the sun, allowing Ivy to fully appreciate her surroundings. The narrow country road was jam-packed with officers, husbands, and wives on the verge of exploding into another bickering row. The crisp air was electric. Katy Southwell's van, along with Ivy's car and the cars of Maguire, O'Hara, Peter Saint, and one of the new-arrival husbands, blocked the tarmac. Ivy left Southwell and Saint to discuss the job at hand, watching them, along with the rest of Katy's team, inch down the slope towards Lily's body, Saint offering a gentlemanly hand on the way down.

The women had scattered, split off into pairs or on their own, throwing glares over their shoulders. The two husbands spoke quietly between themselves, and when Ivy looked their way, they straightened, smiled as well as they could considering and adopted the polite mask expected of a certain class of Englishman. Franky DeSilver was pacing back and forth further up the hiking path with her phone to her ear. When the men had been unable to answer her question, she had stormed off to call her husband again.

But even without the fog, Ivy felt no more clarity. The details were hazy, to say the least.

She walked over to Maguire, who interviewed the purple-haired young woman Ivy remembered was called Violet. She spoke with a high, squeaking voice, offering barely discernible words. In fact, Maguire was not writing in his notebook but squinting at her face as though trying to decipher what she was saying.

"I can't believe this is happening," Violet repeated, wringing her hands. "First Jordan, now Lily."

Maguire bent his head, catching her eye. "I understand, Miss Hughes, I really do. But right now, I need to know what happened in the minutes before Lily's death."

She nodded, swallowing her sobs with great effort.

"Can you tell me what happened?"

"We were just walking," she whispered. "Then the fog seemed to get thicker, and we were separated. I couldn't see anything. I could barely see my own hand in front of my face. I walked on for a bit, then stopped and looked behind me, and the others had disappeared behind this... well, this wall of cloud."

"So, you were at the front?"

"Yes," she said. "I was leading the way. The others barely know how to read a map."

"You're following the Viking Way, no?" interrupted Ivy.

Violet turned to her, only now noting her presence. "Yes."

"Don't you just follow the symbols on the signposts?" Ivy nodded to one nearby, the cowboy-looking logo indented into the wood. "I mean, it must be difficult to get lost around here. Do you really need a map?"

Violet narrowed her eyes. "You can get lost anywhere."

"Before the fog fell," Maguire said loudly, bringing both women back on track, "did you see anyone? Anyone aside from the five of you? Any cars on the road? Any other hikers?"

"Like I said, I was looking ahead," Violet said. "I like to look forward," she added quietly.

Ivy found her demeanour terribly attention-seeking but struggled to ignore the bait.

"And why's that then?" she asked, biting.

"I think society has been stuck in the past for too long."

"And you like to symbolise your futuristic thinking in your hiking patterns, do you?"

"We're all on a path. I, for one, like to be at the front of the pack."

"Leading the way," Ivy said.

"Exactly."

"And what happens to those at the back?" Ivy said.

At this, Violet looked nauseated. "What are you saying?"

"Just that—"

"I'm not saying Lily *deserved* this. How dare you insinuate—"

"I did not insinuate anything," Ivy said. "I'm merely trying to understand what happened to your friend."

"My *sister-in-law*," Violet spat. "Lily was my sister-in-law."

"Did you see anyone or not?" Maguire said impatiently.

"No," she said, turning on him. "I didn't see anyone up ahead. Maybe there was someone behind us. I don't know."

"Alright," he said, flicking through his notebook and rubbing his forehead, clearly overwhelmed at what should be the relatively simple task of taking a statement. "Let's start at the beginning again. What time did you leave the campsite this morning?"

With one last look, Ivy moved away, hearing the words, "Around eight a.m.," drift away on the same breeze that had carried the mist.

She wandered over to where O'Hara had begun interviewing Franky. With stress, her beautiful, put-together appearance was faltering but not at all failing, as though her put-togetherness came from deep within. Her hair still fell straight and bouncy, her skin was still flawless, and her clothes were still well-pressed and expensive. She appeared shaken but only beneath a brave face. If anything, she seemed more concerned about her husband than she was about the friend who lay tangled at the bottom of a nearby hill.

"I've called him," she insisted, "but he's not answering."

"I'm sure he's fine, Mrs DeSilver. You get plenty of dead zones around here. He probably doesn't have a signal."

"Isn't there anything you can do?" she said, sensing authority and turning to Ivy, who came to stand beside O'Hara. "Can't you put a search out for him?"

"I think that's a bit presumptive at this stage," Ivy said.

"You saw what someone did to Lily," she said shrilly. "How do we know they're not doing the same thing to James right now?"

"You think someone did this to Lily?"

Franky gaped wordlessly for a second, then said, "I mean, look at her. I saw her. We all did." She hesitated and leaned in as though sharing a secret. "That's no accident."

"I agree," Ivy whispered back.

Franky straightened and pulled at her clothes as though uncomfortable with mockery.

"Please," she said. "My husband?"

"Look, I promise you," O'Hara took over, "if we find any reason to suspect that your husband might be in trouble, we will do everything we can to help him. But the likelihood is that he's locked up in a pub without signal on his phone. For now, we have to focus on what happened to Lily."

She spoke clearly, Ivy thought, and confidently, with the remnants of her West Country heritage clinging to the tail of each sentence.

Franky silently mouthed her friend's name and nodded.

"Can you tell me what you remember before the fog came down?"

Franky took a deep breath, compartmentalising her anxiety, placing the worry for her husband into one box while she moved her attention to grief and short-term memories. "We were walking," she started, "just as we had been all morning. We were just warming up to it, slowly climbing," she said, looking at the hill, up which they were only halfway. "We could see the fog coming down from the top, but we didn't think it would be a problem. It's not like we're hiking Ben Nevis, is it?"

"Is this something you often do as a group?" asked O'Hara. "Hiking?"

"Not really," Franky said, shaking her head as though she couldn't believe anything that was happening. "I mean, we always go on trips, the four of us. James and I just moved to the area. So we thought a hiking trip could be something different. Beats drinking mojitos all day by the pool in Greece."

Ivy looked around at the bleak weather and refrained from stating the obvious, that sitting beside a pool would be far more preferable.

Franky read the message anyway, and she shrugged. "Lily needed the fresh air for a bit. This is more her type of thing. Time in nature. She likes being outside. She likes the English countryside."

"An old soul?" asked Ivy.

Franky smiled sadly. "She always was."

"Why did Lily need fresh air?" O'Hara asked. The same question was also on Ivy's lips, along with one other.

"She's grieving," Franky said softly, looking over at the drop. "Her husband died. Six months ago."

"How?"

"Car accident," she said, matter of fact.

O'Hara made a note in her notebook but, for now, did not ask for more information. Instead, she stuck to the task at hand. "Then what happened, Mrs DeSilver? When the fog came down?"

"We got separated," she said. "We were walking in a line, but when the fog descended, I could barely even see Cecelia, who was right beside me."

"So, you were with Cecelia in the fog?"

"Yes. We stayed together."

"So you and Cecelia were at the front..." O'Hara said, and over her shoulder, Ivy watched her draw a small diagram of five women walking along the footpath, establishing their positions.

"No," Franky cut in, "Violet was at the front. She had stormed off just before the fog descended. Then it was Cecelia and me. Then it was Marie and Lily at the back."

As she spoke, O'Hara updated her drawing, adding little scribbled names above the stick figures.

"Were you all evenly spread out?" asked O'Hara, an interesting question Ivy hadn't considered.

"Marie and Lily were a bit behind. Marie's not been feeling well. She was struggling with the hill last time I looked back."

"And Lily? Was she struggling?"

"Lily?" Franky's face lit up. "No. She's the fittest of all of us. She just likes to stay at the back. We call her the sheepdog. She herds us all together. Keeps us as a group. Even when we're driving each other crazy." For the first time, she showed grief, her eyes welling with tears. "I don't know what we'll do without her."

"You said that Violet stormed ahead before the fog descended," O'Hara said, using the moment of weakness to pry, a trait that Ivy admired. "Was she angry about something?"

Franky laughed. "Try the whole world. Find something she's *not* angry about."

"Specifically this time," O'Hara said flatly.

Franky ran a hand through her perfect hair, somehow making it look even bouncier. "I suppose Cecelia and I just ran out of patience. Violet was complaining."

"About what?"

"About everything. About the hill. About the path we were taking. About our speed. About our conversation."

"Your conversation?"

Franky sighed. "We were talking about our nails," she said,

exasperated. "One of Cecilia's had chipped that morning when putting on her hiking boots. I offered to take her to the salon I discovered recently in Market Rasen. We were talking about going there this evening after the hike. Then Violet pulled a Violet."

"What's pulling a Violet?" O'Hara asked as though it was a new verb she was learning.

"It means you freak out about nothing," Franky said dismissively.

"What did she say exactly?"

"She said that overhearing our conversation was a feminine cliche, that we were... Oh, let me think how she put it. That's right. *Caricatures of the patriarchy.* That we didn't even realise our own brainwashing, that getting our nails done was an inflammatory act."

O'Hara paused and, without bias, said, "And you don't agree?"

"No. I don't think that getting my nails done is an inflammatory act, making me a caricature of the patriarchy."

"So then? What did Violet do after she said this to you?"

"Further words were exchanged," admitted Franky, picking at her own nails, which did not look broken at all.

"What words?"

"Like I said, Cecelia and I lost our patience. All that woman does is complain. Do you know how exhausting that is to be around twenty-four-seven? I've never known someone so negative and jaded, as though the world is out to get her. I don't know how she bears to move through it."

"And you said this to her, did you?"

"Something like that," Franky mumbled.

"So she stormed off ahead?"

"Yes."

"You said earlier," Ivy stepped in, "that the four of you often go away together on holiday. Am I right in assuming that Violet is the fifth wheel?"

"You can say that again," Franky said. "No one wants her here. Lily invited her. God knows why."

"You told us that Lily's husband recently died. Violet also mentioned that Lily was her sister-in-law. Am I right in assuming it was Violet's brother who recently passed away?"

"Jordan," Franky said, nodding. "Violet's brother. Lily's husband."

"Last name?" asked O'Hara, making a note.

"Hughes."

"So that's why Lily invited Violet," Ivy said. "Because she's grieving?"

For the first time, Franky looked guilty. "Yes, I suppose that's why." Then, her face darkened. "But if that's how a woman behaves when she's grieving..." She stared across the road towards Violet, who stared right back with dark eyes. But Ivy could not tell where Franky's stare fell, on Violet or just past her, to the drop, at the bottom of which her friend lay broken and beaten — dead. "Then no wonder nobody liked her."

CHAPTER FOUR

The slope wasn't particularly steep, not like a Welsh mountain. But the going was tricky. The ground was uneven with rocks, and even the bare patches were damp and slippery. Only when Ivy was descending did she fully appreciate how such a fall, at such an angle, could break the body of a woman.

Near the tree line, rogue roots threatened to catch Ivy's firmer steps, and the loose soil meant that seemingly solid footholds were little more than an illusion. One wrong step could cause the kind of head-over-heels tumble to which Lily had fallen prey.

Behind her, carried by the wind but muffling as Ivy descended, came the echoing growls of Lily's friends at the top of the hill. They had turned on each other again despite O'Hara and Maguire interviewing them separately. Accusing yells and persistent bickering disturbed the peaceful surroundings, the way a chainsaw might tear through the forest calmly.

She did her best to avoid CSI's yellow markers as she descended but struggled to fully control her steps. At the bottom of the slope, Katy Southwell watched with eagle eyes, whether concerned about Ivy's safety or the preservation of evidence, she could not be sure. When she finally reached the bottom, Ivy felt the kind of relief that had not been offered to Lily Hughes.

She settled on the flat ground and greeted Katy with a weary "Good morning," which Katy reciprocated. A friendlier welcome, however, was offered by the man over her shoulder, who threw out a long arm to shake Ivy's hand.

"No sign of George this morning?" Peter Saint asked.

As the region's Forensic Medical Examiner, Peter Saint had earned tremendous respect. Ivy had always considered him a man who had never stopped growing. He was far taller than anyone she knew, and each extremity, his limbs, ears, and nose, seemed oversized. His socks were always on show, as his trousers were nearly always too short, the sleeves of his cagoule stopped a good two inches short of his wrist, and his ears were things of wonder, cavernous. Yet had nature deemed it fit that his extremities be in proportion, she doubted his character would have developed as it had: peaceful, gentle, and empathetic.

"Afraid not," Ivy said.

"He needs more time," he said, nodding, understanding in the way that only men of the same demographic can understand each other.

"How's he holding up?" asked Katy.

"He's holding up," Ivy said, shrugging. "I saw him this morning. He can leave the house. He seems quite philosophical about it all, really." Ivy looked between the two of them, doing all she could to delay the time when she would have to turn her attention to the dead body not far from her own two feet.

"I heard Grace was a lovely woman," said Saint. "I'm sad I never got to meet her."

"Me too," Katy said. "I don't think I've ever heard someone spoken of so highly. Even at their own funeral. You knew her, didn't you, Ivy?"

She nodded. "For the last five years."

"And how are you holding up?" asked Saint.

It was the first time anyone had asked her that. Even Jamie, who had come to the funeral with the kids, hadn't asked her that. She hadn't even asked herself. "Fine," she said non-committed. "I mean, Grace was lovely." But she saw in their eyes that they expected more. "It's a tragedy that the loveliest people are always taken from this world."

She didn't even mean what she was saying. It wasn't only lovely people at all. Murderers, rapists, dictators — they all died too. But when it came to expressing grief, comforting George, or thinking about Grace, all she could rely upon in the darkness was the neon-like pull of a cliche.

"Philosophical indeed," said Saint, frowning. "I can see why you and George spend so much time together."

Ivy smiled, but her reluctance to continue the topic caused her to turn her attention to the body and ask, "So what have we got?"

Saint, too, turned his concerned eyes to the woman wrapped around the tree.

"Well, I wouldn't rule out accidental death," he said, just as a particularly shrill accusation echoed down from the top of the hill. He looked up towards the bickering friends who remained out of sight and added darkly, "But I wouldn't put money on it."

Ivy followed his gaze and remembered her own treacherous descent. "You don't think she fell?"

"Oh, she fell alright," Saint said. "She's got a broken leg, two or three broken ribs, not to mention a broken neck. But none of those seem to be the cause of her death." He looked into Ivy's eyes as she waited for him to drop the ball. "She was strangled." He knelt down and pulled a pen out of his inner jacket in a manner similar to the forensic pathologist, Doctor Pippa Bell, who often used a pen for the same purpose in the mortuary. "Strangulation marks," he said, pointing to the faint bruises on Lily's throat. It took all of Ivy's willpower not to focus on the twist of the dead woman's neck. At least her eyes were closed. "No finger marks that I can see. I wouldn't testify to this, but in my opinion, her attacker was wearing gloves. Without them, the bruising is far more defined, you see?" Ivy nodded, following as best she could. "But this," he said, circling the air over her eyelids, "is petechiae. Pinpoint haemorrhages in the skin. Her tongue is swollen, too. And look..." He bent closer, ran his pen along the soil beside Lily's face, then held it up to show a thick liquid dripping like a dark treacle.

"Blood?"

Saint nodded. "From her ear. It's an infrequent sign of fatal strangulation but not unheard of." Ivy heard something akin to pride in his voice as though he'd come across a rare find.

"So you suspect foul play?"

"You can say that again. Your man was right to call this in."

"I agree," Katy added, looking between her two colleagues. "You can see the path of the fall," she said, pointing at the yellow tags sticking out of the soil. "With analysis and some models, we could probably pinpoint exactly which bone was broken at which point in her fall. But none of that explains the marks on her throat."

"So she fell down the hill," Ivy said, "then a passer-by saw her and took the opportunity?"

Katy hesitated. "Maybe."

"You don't think so?"

"We need to do more analysis of the—"

"Come on, Katy."

"This isn't official," she said, biting her lip. "We can't be sure."

"But?"

"But," she said, looking up the slope, "if I had to guess, I'd say she was strangled and then fell down the slope."

"Fell?" Ivy repeated.

"Was pushed," Katy clarified.

"What makes you say that she was killed before she landed here?"

"She fell like a rag doll," Katy said simply. She stepped up behind Ivy and placed both hands on her shoulder blades. "What would you do if I pushed you now?"

"You won't, though?" Ivy said sternly.

"Just answer the question, Ivy," Katy said playfully.

Ivy imagined it, the force from behind and how she might react. "I'd hold my hands up, try to regain my balance."

"Right," Katy said, coming back around to face Ivy, satisfied. "Or to catch yourself. It's human nature. Instinct."

"But Lily didn't do that?"

"No, she didn't. See usually, when someone falls down a slope like this, you'll see slide marks from where they stood for a second before falling again with the momentum. You'll see signs of them grappling with the ground, trying to grip it or regain their balance. But there's none of that. There are only the impact marks of where she fell heavily again and again with no resistance."

Peter Saint nodded as Katy relayed her theory. "I concur," he said. "Her body has a few broken bones, but I would guess that if she had been alive when she was pushed, the damage would be far more serious."

"More serious?" Ivy said. "How so?"

"As Miss Southwell said, it's human instinct to throw out your arms to catch yourself. To tense up. But it is a rather badly designed instinct. In truth, it would be better if we went limp and let gravity do its work. Roll with the punches, as it were. That's why many a drunk man has walked away unharmed from a fatal car accident. Because his reactions were slow, and his body failed to tense before impact."

"So what does that mean?"

"It means that Lily Hughes was dead before she reached the bottom of this hill."

Ivy looked again at Lily's back, which was bent unnaturally around the tree trunk, and she felt a smidge of gratitude that the woman did not have to experience the pain of her spine curving at such an angle. She bent to look closer, swallowing the sickly saliva that erupted in her throat. From the positioning of Lily's head, one wouldn't guess that she had mangled limbs. With her eyes closed, she looked peaceful even, her lips set in a slight smile, as though in on a secret to which the rest of them were ignorant. Her splayed, auburn hair matched its earthy surroundings, and a few ants had already mistaken Lily's curls for mossy wood or perhaps a mallard feather, and they crawled freely upon it. She lay on her front, one cheek pressed into the cold soil and the other exposed to the forest air. Ivy kneeled to look closer. There was a redness not unlike subtle acne on her exposed cheek.

"What about this?" Ivy asked, pointing to it.

"Ah," Saint said. "*That* is a slap mark."

"A slap mark," Ivy repeated. "I thought you said the attacker was wearing gloves?"

"That's exactly what I said."

Ivy stood up, her joints sore from the dampness. "She was slapped before the attack?" she clarified.

"From the swell of her cheek and the way the blood has already risen, I would confidently say so."

"So, time of death?"

"An hour at the most," Saint said, checking his watch. "Just after eleven a.m."

Ivy sighed. "At least that fits their story. She was killed when the fog descended. And the slap?"

"At a guess?"

"The best you can."

He examined her cheek again. "The redness has begun to darken, which means the blood vessels have broken. Blood has started to leak into the surrounding tissue—"

"Peter..." Ivy said patiently.

"Two or three hours ago." He sat back on his heels, satisfied with his answer. "Between nine and ten a.m."

"What does that mean?" asked Katy.

"It means that that lot," Ivy said, looking up towards the bickering from atop the hill, not unlike the incessant chattering of Amazonian birds, "are not telling me what I need to know."

CHAPTER FIVE

The climb up the slope to the road was no less treacherous than the way down had been. Ivy's feet kept slipping beneath her, and the wet leaves threatened to slide her all the way back to where Lily Hughes had met her end. More than once, she smashed a knee into the cold earth. She had to dig her fingers into the harsh soil, gripping for dear life like a stranded cat in a tree. It didn't help that she was wearing her black, heeled boots and a rather restrictive suit jacket. At the top, just after her right leg slipped suddenly and just before she tumbled backwards, a strong arm reached out, which she grabbed gratefully, and it pulled her up the final metre until she stood once more on solid ground. His grip was surprisingly firm and warm.

"What are you doing here?" she said, wiping the dirt from her trouser legs.

"Maguire called us," Byrne said, brushing some loose soil off Ivy's shoulder. It shamed Ivy slightly to think that, when she and George had been assigned PC Byrne and Campbell, she had judged him, belittled him, and perhaps made life difficult for him. But, it had to be said that he and Campbell had proven themselves on more than one occasion and that her faith in the more experienced of the four PCs they had been allocated was growing with every investigation they undertook. During those first few weeks, he seemed aloof, immature even. Perhaps some deep part of her psyche had favoured Campbell purely because she was female. Whatever it was, she was grateful he had caught her before she made a fool of herself.

He nodded over the road at Campbell, who was talking to Marie Entwhistle and her husband in the back of O'Hara's police car. "He said they might need the backup."

It seemed that in the time it had taken Ivy to climb the fatal slope, the women had once more dissipated, perhaps exhausted by their own arguments. They had separated into twosomes and onesomes. "What were they arguing about?" she asked. "While I was down there?"

"It was hard to tell, to be honest," Byrne said with a grimace. "But they were all basically blaming each other, saying Lily shouldn't have been left on her own. Lily is the victim, I presume?" he said, turning to Ivy, who nodded. "They shouldn't even have been here in the first place, that one said," Byrne relayed, nodding at Cecelia. "And why were they hiking in the middle of nowhere anyway instead of sitting on a beach in Greece?" He nodded at Violet next. "They all turned on that one and said she shouldn't have stormed ahead. Then *she* blamed that one," he said, nodding at Marie in the back of the police car, "saying that she was the last one to see Lily and that they should've stuck together."

"Quite the circus," Ivy mumbled. Nudging his hand away, which still hovered at her side in case she needed it again. "Well, make yourself useful."

"I'd just started interviewing Mr and Mrs Adams," he defended himself. "Saw you needed help."

She met his defensive gaze. His voice was slick with the growing confidence Ivy had witnessed in Byrne recently. Especially in George's absence, he had stepped up with boldness and clarity, and it was impossible not to notice that his body was filling out daily. He seemed to be filling out as a teenage boy might, undergoing a very late stage of puberty.

"Well, let's get to it, then."

The woman with the dark, curly hair who had been shouting at Violet when Ivy arrived had now settled down. She was removing her hiking boots with great pain, wincing as she pushed one boot's heel with the tip of the other's toe while her husband rubbed her back sympathetically. Ivy and Byrne approached just as she was peeling off a long, thick hiking sock. Plasters covered her toes, and she was lifting them to poke at the blisters underneath. Hiking was a pastime that Ivy had never understood. Why would one walk so far and so relentlessly that one's feet literally started bleeding?

"Don't touch them, love," Cecelia's husband was saying to her.

Just as she began to reprimand him for unsolicited advice, she looked up to see the two detectives blocking the sun.

"Cecelia Adams?" asked Ivy.

"Aye, that's me," she said.

"And I'm Bob Adams," said her husband, standing with a cheery smile to shake their hands enthusiastically. Then, as though only just realising the solemnness of the situation, he sat back down slowly, avoiding his wife in his peripheral vision.

"We're just trying to get an idea of what happened in the minutes before Lily's death," Ivy began. "I believe my colleague was just talking to you."

"I was telling him about Violet storming off, leaving us to fend for ourselves in the fog."

"I thought you were with Franky?" Ivy said. "That's what she said."

"Sure, Franky and I were together," she said quickly. "But what about Lily? She was left alone. Even Marie didn't look out for her."

"Did Lily need looking out for?"

"No, you're right," Cecelia said darkly. "Lily didn't need looking after. That's why she's wrapped around the bottom of a tree right now."

"I just mean—"

"I know what you mean. No one expected this. No one knew that a few minutes of fog could've caused this to happen. But we're friends. We look out for each other. That's what we do. Or that's what we *should* do. But some of these girls don't know the meaning of friendship. We're only bloody here for Lily in the first place. What was she doing on the road on her own anyway?"

"She was with Marie, wasn't she?"

She laughed a sharp, cold laugh. "Marie couldn't look after Lily. She can barely look after herself."

As she spoke, she went to touch one of the blisters on her toes. Once more, her husband reached out to stop her. "Don't," he said. "It'll get infected." She slapped his hand away. "You heard what Lily said."

"What did Lily say?" asked Ivy.

"Oh, just about the blisters," Bob said, waving a hand.

"What about the blisters?"

Cecelia rolled her eyes. "I love the woman, I do. But Lily was always doing this."

"Doing what?" Ivy asked, her patience wearing thin.

"Taking an everyday health ailment and telling us it could kill you. Jordan, her late husband, was a doctor. Someone told you about Jordan, didn't they?"

"Yes."

"So she told this horror story over drinks the other night," Bob said, leaning forward.

"Don't bother, Bob. It's always the same story," Cecelia said. "But what people don't tell you is that ninety-nine per cent of the time, everyone's fine." She looked over the road at the drop beyond which her friend had died. "The problem is the other one per cent of the time, isn't it?"

"Yes," Ivy said. "That is what I've found to be the problem."

Cecelia's eyes welled and she turned to her husband suddenly and said, "I want to talk to the kids."

"They probably shouldn't know about—"

"I'm not going to tell them about Lily," she said. "I just want to talk to them. I need to hear their voices."

"Alright, love," he said, tugging his phone from his pocket and handing it to her. She grabbed it, stood, then limped further up the hiking path in only one sock.

"How many children do you have?" Ivy said, watching her go.

"Three." He sighed, but it was not an unhappy sound. "Two girls and a boy."

"What about Lily? Does she have kids?"

"No, she and Jordan never wanted any."

"Did you know Jordan well?"

Bob Adams smiled and shrugged. "He was more my wife's friend's husband than anything else. The girls are all friends. They've known each other for years. To be honest, us men just kind of tag along."

"Tag along how?"

"Well, this trip, for example. They're the ones hiking. We just drive ahead, do our own thing, and sometimes sit in the pub until they turn up at the end of the day. I know everyone's husbands, of course, but I can't say we're close. Not like the women are."

"The women are close?" Ivy scoffed. "That's not the impression I've got."

"They're in shock," Bob said. "This is a strained situation. But believe me, Sergeant, those women would do anything for each other," he said, meeting her stare with his ocean-blue eyes. "*Anything.*"

Ivy allowed the comment and its intensity to sink in for a moment before changing tact. "So you know Franky's husband? James, was it?"

"Yeah," he said. "I know James."

"Do you have any idea where he might be?"

Bob shrugged. "He left this morning saying he was going home to sort something out."

"And you saw him leave?"

"Yeah. I saw his car drive onto the road."

"What time?"

Bob squeezed his eyes shut dramatically. "Quarter to ten," he said. "About."

"That's all he said, is it? He was going home to sort something out?"

"Yeah, he didn't give any details. But he doesn't live far away. He shouldn't be long."

"But no one has heard from him?"

"Not yet," Bob said casually, "but I wouldn't worry. He's probably holed up in a pub somewhere." Then he wrung his hands as though overcome by some sudden anxiety. "Honestly, I'd give the man as much time as possible before telling him about Lily. It will break him."

"They're close?"

Bob exhaled a laugh that had little humour in it. "You can say that again."

"James and Lily were—"

"Friends," Cecelia said quickly, walking back up the path toward her husband. She held up the phone. "Signal is bad. I can barely hear the kids."

"We'll call them back later, love," Bob said soothingly.

"Look, I know what you're thinking," Cecelia said to Ivy. "About James and Lily. But that's not what it was. He would never cheat on Franky." She said, leaning down to slap her husband on the shoulder. "And certainly not with Lily. Their relationship is more complicated than that."

"Complicated how?"

"Deeper. They've been friends for years. Decades. Franky met James *through* Lily."

"But tell her what you told me," Bob said, nudging his wife, encouraging her to gossip. "Go on."

"Tell her what?"

"What you said about Lily and James the other night."

"I don't know what you're talking about."

Cecelia played dumb, but in her eyes was a desire for him to stop talking. She knew exactly what he meant.

Bob looked between his wife and the detectives with a harmless grin. "You said that if James had never met Franky, then he and Lily would probably have married."

Cecelia rolled her eyes. "That's not true. That's not what I said. If James and Lily had wanted to get married, they would've done so a long time ago. They're just friends," she said to Ivy. "I'm telling you."

"Well, they didn't seem very friendly the other night," Bob said, leaning back and stretching.

"What do you mean?" asked Ivy.

"Saturday night," Bob clarified. "Our second night of the trip, James and Lily were—"

"It was nothing," muttered Cecelia. Any affection between the married couple had gone. She was fuming, and he acted ignorant of her mood.

"Hmmm, it was something," Bob said playfully.

"This isn't a joke," Cecelia snapped.

"I know, I know," he said, sitting up. "I'm sorry, love. I don't mean to be insensitive, but you have to admit..." He puffed out a breath of air. "It was one hell of a fight."

CHAPTER SIX

The Red Dragon was not the sort of establishment that Bob Adams was used to frequenting. In his opinion, a decent pub had to have three things — a dartboard, a jukebox, and London Pride on tap. But so far as he could see, this pub had none of those things. In lieu of a dartboard, vintage mirrors and overpriced artwork adorned the walls, although Bob could never understand why someone might spend hundreds on a pointillism painting of Prince William playing polo. Instead of eighties rock classics emanating from a battered jukebox, soft folk songs that made Bob feel sleepy played in the background. And rather than a dark pint, he nursed a single-malt Macallan in an ornate, crystal tumbler.

Still, he had to admit, the whisky was exactly what he needed — full-bodied and oaky — and he could certainly get used to resting beside an open-hearth fireplace in a comfy Chesterfield armchair with a belly full of a gourmet slow-braised beef pie. He could see why James and Franky had moved here, and he was sure that was the exact reason for being invited up to the Wolds.

If only the conversation matched the classy surroundings.

Opposite Bob, sharing the long sofa with Violet and Franky,

Lily continued her story. In the firelight, her auburn hair caught the flickers of light, and despite the content, she kept their attention like a beacon in the night.

"So he comes to Jordan a week later, and now they're the size of marbles," she said, holding her fist up for dramatic effect.

"He continued running on them?" asked Cecelia, who shared the loveseat to Bob's left with James.

"Yep," Lily said. "Every day."

"Why?" asked Franky.

Lily shrugged. "He had a running schedule to be ready for a marathon in two months, and he had to stick to it."

"Even with blisters the size of marbles?"

"Even so."

"That's stupid," Violet said, sipping her own whisky.

"Some people have ambition," James said pointedly.

"Some people have a death wish," she countered.

"Anyway," Lily continued, keeping the peace as always, "Jordan gave him the same advice as before. He prescribed him an antiseptic ointment, told him to bandage them and take a week off running."

She let the sentence hang there.

Eventually, Bob was the one to ask, "And? Did he do it?"

"Nope," Lily said. "He kept running every day. The blisters became infected, he nearly got sepsis, and no exaggeration, he could have died," she finished, piling the words together as though they all held the same weight.

"Wait, what?" James laughed.

"Yep."

"Very reassuring," Cecelia muttered, touching the socked feet she had pulled beneath her on the sofa. She had taken off her wet boots and placed them by the fire. Nobody judged her for it. They were the only ones staying in the pub and it had a distinct homely, living room feel to it. Anyway, her blisters needed to breathe.

"But I'm sure that won't happen to you," Lily added lamely.

"Do you remember every case Jordan worked on, Lil?" asked Franky softly.

Lily laughed. "Pretty much," she said, swirling her whisky glass and staring into the treacle-coloured ripples. "The interesting ones, at least. Funny thing is, they're all coming back to me recently. All of his stories, all of his cases. As though my mind is finding a way to remember him whenever possible."

They sat in silence for a few moments, processing the story and their friend's grief, the tired mood disturbed only by the rogue crackling of the open fire.

Eventually, James yawned loudly.

"Reckon those two will be finished yet?" he asked, nodding to the ceiling.

"Did you see them after dinner?" Cecelia laughed. "Toby couldn't get her upstairs fast enough."

"I don't think Marie was complaining," Lily added.

"I wouldn't either," Cecelia added with a sheepish grin at Bob, who merely tutted.

"Well, I wouldn't complain about a good night's sleep," James said, stretching.

"If yesterday's anything to go by, they'll be at it all night," Cecelia warned.

"I don't know how they have the energy," Franky said, and James looked at her, his face falling as though a secret hope had just been extinguished.

"They're newlyweds," Bob said and winked at Cecelia. "We were the same, weren't we, love?"

"Cut it out," she said but smiled.

"Well, they'll get over it," Franky mumbled.

This seemed like one dig too many for James, and Bob had witnessed enough of them in the last two days alone. The drunker Franky got, he had noticed, the punchier her jabs seemed to become.

"I'll just risk it," James said, pushing himself up from the seat. "I'm going to bed." He turned to Franky. "You coming?"

"In a minute," she said, holding up her half-full glass.

"Good night, all," he said with a heavy, whisky-laden wave.

"I think I'll call it a night, too," Lily said soon after. "That whisky's pushed me over the edge."

"I'll come with you," Violet said, standing, and she walked out of the room without another word.

Lily offered a playful eye roll at her sister-in-law's social misgivings and said her goodnights, giving Cecelia and Franky a kiss on the cheek and the men a gentle touch on the shoulder.

The three of them were left sipping their whiskies, listening to their friends heading upstairs and saying goodnight to the lone bartender as they passed by the bar.

"She's a right one, that one, isn't she?" Cecelia said as soon as the two women's footsteps on the pub's stairs faded into the night.

"Lily?" Bob said, surprised to hear his wife talk about her best friend in such a way.

"Have off," she replied. Then she whispered, "*Violet*."

"Oh," Bob said. "She's alright, isn't she?"

"She's a piece of work," Franky concurred.

"Did you hear her at dinner? Talking about Kimberly what's-her-face and..." Cecelia pushed fake glasses up her nose. "*Interfractional feminism*."

"Intersectional," Bob corrected.

But she ignored him.

"*You can't possibly understand the nuanced oppression of disabled women of colour,*" she imitated in a mock high voice that Bob felt did not properly match Violet's huskier tone.

"So pretentious," Franky said.

"She's just young, that's all," Bob said. "And idealistic."

He wasn't sure what the fuss was about. He'd found the girl to be fine, a little abrupt, sure, but harmless all the same, and not bad on the eyes, he had to admit. He had quite admired the soft-punk look back in his day.

"It's going to be a long week," Cecelia said, leaning back and clutching her whisky glass as though it were a cup of Yorkshire tea. "That's all I'm saying."

Franky sighed, whether at the thought of another five days with Violet or at the thought of leaving the warm, cosy bar, he couldn't be sure. "I suppose I'd better head up too," she said, as though she found little joy in the thought of sharing a bed with her husband. Then she downed her whisky as though it was no more than apple juice. "Goodnight."

And with a kiss on both of their cheeks, Franky headed upstairs, leaving Bob and Cecelia alone. By now, the whisky had well and truly gone to his head. He felt pleasant, warm waves rippled through his body and the kind of lightheaded sensation that reminded him of dreaming. But all of a sudden, he felt the need for something more, something he didn't realise he had been missing, and as soon as the thought crossed his mind, he suddenly wanted it more than anything else in the world.

"Hey, come here," he said, standing up suddenly and holding out a hand to his wife.

"What are you doing?"

"Come with me."

"Why?"

"Just trust me, will you?"

She sighed and let herself be pulled up from the sofa. Hand in hand, he led her around the corner to the bar, where the lone bartender on the night shift was putting away glasses. He was a young man, no older than nineteen, with thick, dark hair gelled into a neat side parting.

"Hey, bud," Bob called, getting his attention.

"Evening, sir."

"You don't have a ciggie, do you?"

"*Bob*," Cecelia scolded.

The barman laughed politely. "I might have some out the back," he said, and ever the host, he went through a door behind the bar.

"We can't," Cecelia said. "What about the kids?"

Bob laughed and put a hand around her waist. "What about them? They're not here."

"What about staying alive long enough to watch them grow up?"

He rolled his eyes. "Please. One drunk cigarette isn't going to give us lung cancer, love. Lighten up," he said, then laughed at his own accidental pun. "Light up, that is. Get it?"

She rolled her eyes. "God, you always get like this when you drink whisky."

"Like what?"

"*Silly*," she said. "And handsy," she added, removing his hand that was moving down her back.

The bartender returned with a scruffy, half-a-pack of cigarettes and handed them to Bob.

"Customer left these a few days ago. Yours if you want them," he said.

Bob took them, shook the young man's hand in gratitude, and held them out to his wife.

"Look," he said, "do you want one or not?"

Cecelia looked between the bartender, her husband, and the cigarettes, biting her lip.

"Yeah, go on then," she said.

Outside, the cold spring air only added to Bob's experience when he lit the cigarette between his lips, took a deep inhale, and exhaled in relief.

Cecelia took her own drag and laughed in disbelief. "What the hell am I doing here?" she asked the stars, throwing her head back to watch the cigarette smoke disappear into the night.

"Oh, it's not so bad," Bob said, having grown to very much like the posh pub that, now he had spent some time there, he found met his every need.

"No, I mean *here*," she said. "On this holiday. In the middle of bloody nowhere, in my bare, blistered feet, hiking every day in the rain and fog when I could be on a beach in Greece."

"It's not so bad," Bob repeated. "If you ask me, people are too quick to leave the country these days. Don't appreciate what's on their own doorstep. When I was a kid, a weekend in Margate was peak holidaying and did us just fine."

"Shush," Cecelia said suddenly.

"I'm just saying, just because you get on a plane doesn't mean—"

"Bob, shut up," she hissed moving along the wall of the pub towards the alleyway that ran alongside it and led to the car park. "Do you hear that?"

"That's not what I'm saying," came a loud voice, and Bob instantly recognised it as James's.

"You can be so bloody insecure," came Lily's voice soon after. What was usually a soft and soothing sound was now harsh and no doubt whisky fuelled. "You know that?"

"Well, you make it damn easy," he spat back. "Going out of your way to avoid me."

"I've not been avoiding you."

"You have. You barely looked at me all night. You've barely talked to me since I moved. You don't write me back. You don't return my calls."

"Jesus, James, in case you forgot, my husband just died. Sorry if I've been distracted."

In the silence that followed, Cecelia caught Bob's eye, her expression half concerned, half elated at overhearing such drama.

Eventually, James retaliated, his voice low and cautious. "Is this about...you know?"

"About what?"

"You know what."

"Don't be ridiculous."

"At least don't lie to me, Lil," James said, the hurt evident in his voice. "At least tell me the truth. You owe me that much."

The scoffing sound that followed was so loud it reverberated against the alley walls.

"I owe *you*?" Lily said, and Bob had never heard his wife's calm, quiet friend speak so loudly. "*I owe you?* You owe *me*, James! Or have you forgotten?"

"So..." James said, "it is about that."

"I'm not talking to you like this," Lily replied, her voice growing quieter as though she was walking further away, and Bob was suddenly very grateful for the backdoor entrance to the pub.

"Like what?"

"You're drunk, and I'm tired. Goodnight," she said sharply, and Bob heard the scuff of her shoes on the alley's uneven paving as she walked back inside.

He waited until he heard James's footsteps follow shortly after, and he peeked around the corner of the pub to make sure they were both gone before turning to his wife, who frowned in the orange glow of the pub's outdoor lighting as though undergoing her own inner processes of interpretation.

"What the hell was that about then?"

"None of our business," Cecelia replied, and she gave him a warning look. "And that's how it's going to stay."

CHAPTER SEVEN

"Well?" Ivy asked. "What does he owe her?"

Bob shrugged and picked at the grass by his feet, clearly conflicted over telling a secret that wasn't his to tell. "No idea."

He looked at his wife, who mirrored his confusion, shrugging alongside him, although admittedly with less conviction, as though she might have considered it more than her husband, and now several possibilities ran through her mind.

"All I know," Cecelia said, "is that I've never heard Lily speak that way before."

"What way?"

"So... *passionately*, like James had brought out a frustration in her that no one else could. A different side of her."

"Like a lover can?" Ivy tested.

"Like a sibling," she said firmly.

Ivy eyed her, the defiance in her dark features. "Why are you so sure there's nothing between them?"

"Because Lily is the best friend I know," Cecelia answered quickly, her voice breaking. "She'd never do that to Franky. You don't know her, but I do. We all do. Don't we, love?"

She turned to her husband, who, this time, matched her certainty.

"Aye," he said. "She's one of the good ones."

"Very well," Ivy said, but she had been around long enough not to blindly believe the grief-stricken biases of a victim's loved one. She turned to take in the road, wondering where her attention was most required, and spotted a white-suited shape that needed a hand. "I'll leave you with Byrne to finish up your statements."

With that, she walked over to the familiar face struggling up the slippery, steep hill. Just as Byrne had offered his support, Ivy did the same to Katy Southwell, gripping her hand to pull her up the last few metres.

"Thanks," Katy said, straightening. "God, compared to this, the other crime scenes were a doddle. At least we didn't have to endure a Tough Mudder obstacle course each time."

"I've had easier crime scenes," Ivy admitted. She nodded a few metres to her right, where Katy's team had cordoned off a piece of the road beside the drop. "That's where you think she fell?"

Katy brushed herself down despite her clothes being covered in a full-body forensics suit. "No."

Ivy frowned, then, "That's where you think she was pushed?"

"Exactly," Katy said with a stony grin, and they walked over to the space together. "I asked my team to cordon it off as soon as I got here. Look," she said, pointing at the mud tracks in the middle of the road. "Signs of a scuffle. These are heavy footprints. Someone was shuffling or struggling, two people even. There's only so much we can tell from footprint analysis, but this is the *middle* of a road. You wouldn't usually have such obvious prints going across it, especially when there's no footpath on the other side."

Ivy bent to get a closer look at the scuffs in the loose gravel. She could barely decipher tyre tracks from footprints. Everything was trodden down, imprinted into the ground over and over again, and not for the first time, she admired Katy's ability to note anomalies in what appeared to be an extremely everyday sight.

"Look at this," Katy said, bringing Ivy's attention to the side of the road. She pointed down at a slip mark that curved over the edge of the drop.

"She could've slipped?" Ivy said weakly.

"Sure," Katy said. "She could have. She could have accidentally walked onto the road, accidentally walked across it, accidentally slipped on the wet soil and accidentally fallen over the edge. We can't rule that out yet."

"But she didn't, did she?"

"You know my interpretation, Ivy. Saint said she was strangled. I'd say it happened here, hence the scuff marks. And I'd say she was pushed from here, too. Hence, the slip mark. Then, like Saint said, I'd guess she was dead before she reached the bottom."

"I see," Ivy said, looking out at the small forest.

But in truth, she was struggling to see the wood for the trees. All she could see was the evidence in front of her, but there was no narrative. No story slowly formed in her mind. When George was there, she could usually see it. She could see him kneading an idea like a piece of dough in his mind. He'd roll it out and shape it into a basis for an investigation. But all Ivy could see were scuff marks on the road, the women spread out along the lane, and the one tangled at the bottom of the hill.

But she had no idea how it all linked together.

"You alright, Ivy?" she heard Katy's voice penetrate the thick fog of her mind.

"Fine," she said, shaking her head. "I'm just trying to process everything."

"I'll write up my report," Katy said, taking a step back, "and send it over to you later today."

Ivy nodded. "Thanks."

Katy offered a warm smile, and as though knowing what Ivy needed better than she did, she walked back towards her van and the team that had gathered at the back of it, leaving her alone. Just in front of them, Campbell interviewed Marie and her husband. The rest of her team did the same, interviewing each of her friends. Then, as though they all sensed her stare, each of them looked up and nodded in her direction. A request for guidance gleamed in their eyes, a desire to be told what they should do next, a need for Ivy to take charge and understand the situation on some deeper level than they did.

But she abandoned their eye contact and turned to the drop. She preferred its expansive, relatable emptiness. She put her hands in her deep raincoat pockets and stroked her mobile phone. A comforting voice was just on the other end of it - a voice of reason, of guidance.

She could call him. He would know what to do next, would know what tasks to allocate and to whom, and what narrative they should follow. Yet he was grieving. He needed time alone. She knew that. She needed to step up. She needed to take charge.

But in truth, she felt utterly incapable of doing so.

"Erm, Sergeant?" said a soft voice behind her. Ivy startled and took a big step back from the drop, knowing that she was far too close. She spun on her heels. "I'm sorry," Franky said. "I didn't mean to scare you."

"You didn't scare me," Ivy said, doing her best not to sound defensive.

"I was hoping you had news about my husband?"

"Your husband," Ivy repeated with a blank stare.

"James DeSilver. He's not answering his phone."

"I'm sure he's just busy," Ivy said lamely.

"He always answers his phone," Franky said. "He runs a business. He's always on call. I never see him without it."

Ivy took a deep breath. "I'm sorry, but what exactly do you want me to do about it?"

"I don't know. Put out a search?"

"A search party?" Ivy repeated. "Do you know how many

resources I would waste if I put out a search party for every husband who isn't answering his phone?"

Franky's face dropped. She did not seem like a woman who was used to being told no. "My best friend has just died, possibly murdered. That's why you're here, isn't it? You don't think this was an accident. You think someone did this on purpose. And now my husband is missing. How do I know he hasn't been killed? How do I know this isn't part of something bigger?"

"Do you have any reason to believe that?" asked Ivy calmly.

Franky didn't reply.

"Is there anyone who might want to hurt your husband, Mrs DeSilver?"

"No," she said quietly. "Of course not."

"Then I'm afraid we can't start the search party quite yet," Ivy said, walking away, but not before turning to ask one last question. "Unless you have anything you want to tell me?"

Franky met her stare only for a second, then glanced around as though searching for a quick answer to her problems. If she did find one, she seemed to have found it in Cecelia's eyes, who watched like a hawk from the other side of the road. When Franky turned back to Ivy, her glistening eyes belied a new resolve.

"No," she said. "Nothing." A single frightened tear dropped. "I just want my husband back."

CHAPTER EIGHT

Ivy turned her back on a shaken Franky DeSilver and walked further down the road towards Campbell. She was talking to Marie and her husband, who both sat in the open boot of O'Hara's police Astra. Marie still looked sick, her skin a grey not unlike the clouds, although every time she caught the stare of the beautiful man beside her, a healthy rouge rose to her cheeks. He sat as close to her as possible. She was almost on his lap. He had draped one long arm over her shoulder and the other hand rested on her knee. Ivy and Jamie had been like that when they'd first got together: when they couldn't keep their hands off each other.

"You alright, love?" he kept asking, rubbing Marie's back as though talking about Lily's death was an act of labour.

"I'm okay, I'm okay," she kept repeating. "I just can't believe this... Lily... she was just behind me."

"I thought you said she stayed with you?" Campbell said, looking back at her notes. "When you had a funny turn?"

"No, she did. She stopped with me. I had to sit down for a minute. I thought I was going to pass out, honestly. Lily said she would go back to the road to find help. To find someone who could drive us into town to a doctor."

Campbell eyed her. "But you're feeling better now?" she asked.

"I feel better, but it's relative. These funny spells come and go, but this one was bad. Suppose I just haven't had time to think about it again since Lily..."

"And is this an ongoing health problem for you?"

"That's a bit personal, isn't it?" Marie's husband asked, pausing his rub of her back. "Do you really need to know her medical history?"

"It might be relevant," Campbell said flatly.

"They started a few months ago," Marie said, holding his hand. "Like I said, it's up and down."

"Have you been to the doctor?"

"Of course I have. It's... Look, it's a whole thing. Toby's right. I'm not sure I want to talk about this right now. The important thing is I thought I was going to faint. Lily said she should go back to the road to find someone, and that's the last time I saw her."

"So when Lily walked back towards the road," Campbell clarified, "the mist had been getting worse. Growing heavier. Is that right?"

"Yes."

"Did you see anyone else nearby before Lily walked away?"

Marie stopped to think, then said firmly, "No."

"There were no cars on the road?"

"No."

"Did you see any other hikers this morning?"

"No."

"No one walking the dog?"

"No. We started early. It's not exactly peak hiking season. Felt like we were the only ones out here, to be honest."

"And did you hear the sound of any cars after the fog fell? Even if you didn't see it, did you hear anything?"

"No, I can't say I did. But the fog was thick. I tried calling out to the others, but I don't think they heard me. It's like my voice didn't carry, like the sound was trapped in a vacuum."

"So there might have been a car? It's possible that somebody could have driven along the road during the thick fog."

"I suppose so," Marie said, looking at Toby, who squeezed her hand in reassurance.

Campbell flicked through her notes, closed the book, and looked at Marie. "Is there anyone you can think of who might have wanted to hurt Lily?"

Marie's laugh escaped like a surprised scream. It was, in Ivy's experience, the kind of shocked sound one could not improvise. "Lily? Of course not. Everyone loves her. There's nothing not to love."

Ivy stepped forward. "What about James DeSilver?" she asked.

Capturing both Marie and Toby's attention was an uncanny experience. They turned as one, as though a single organism with single movements. Again, his dazzling stare caught Ivy off-guard.

"James?" Marie repeated.

"Yes, Franky's husband, James. Would anyone want to hurt him?"

She grimaced and shook her head. "Not that I could think of."

"But more so than Lily?"

"What do you mean?"

"I mean, your reaction to someone wanting to hurt Lily was one of disbelief, much more so than your reaction to someone wanting to hurt James."

Again, Marie looked at Toby, who shared her discomfort, not meeting Ivy's eyes. "I'm not saying someone would want to *hurt* James," she answered.

"But?"

"He has more of a...prickly personality, let's say."

"And Lily was what, a smooth personality?"

"Yes," Marie said simply. "Easy going. Easy to be around. But James is..."

"Difficult to be around?"

"For some people," Toby chimed in.

"And for you?" Ivy asked him directly.

"Look, I like the bloke," he said, shrugging.

"Well, you haven't known him long," Marie said. "We're recently married," she added and held up her left hand, on which was a sparkling engagement ring next to a plain wedding band.

"Congratulations," Ivy muttered.

"Thank you," Marie said, looking down at her ring without noting Ivy's tone.

"But you don't like James?" Ivy said, more in tune with people's tones.

"It's not that I don't like him," Marie said diplomatically, "it's just that I think Franky can do better. Their marriage is based on being a perfect little power couple but behind closed doors, it's a very different story. They're all about money, all about status, buying this big new house in the Wolds and inviting us all here to show off where they live now."

"You're not local?" Campbell asked.

"No. We all live in London. We're just up here on holiday."

"What's wrong with a big new house in the Wolds?" asked Ivy.

"Nothing," Marie said. "I just mean...that's not what love's about."

She took Toby's hand in hers and looked deep into his eyes.

"You can't buy happiness," he said, planting a kiss on her cheek.

"And where was James this morning?" Ivy asked Toby. "Bob Adams said that you men have been going ahead to the next stop and waiting for the women to catch up that evening. So why wasn't James with you?"

"Well, we usually do our own things," he replied. "I was at the market when Bob called about Lily, so he came to pick me up in Walesby. James said he was going to the house for a few hours, that he had to sort something out."

"Sort what out?"

"He didn't say."

"Did you see him leave?"

"Yes."

"What time?"

Toby shrugged in a sloppy way only such an attractive man could make look charming. "Quarter to ten."

Campbell made a note in her notebook, although Ivy couldn't see exactly what she wrote.

"So you men go ahead in the morning," Campbell clarified, "do your own thing, and what? Set up the tents?"

At this, Marie and Toby burst out laughing.

"I'm sorry, did I miss the joke?" asked Ivy.

"Franky organised this. She wouldn't be seen dead at a camp-site." Marie squirmed as though having forgotten for a moment that a friend of hers was indeed dead, and that word would forever remind her of that day. "No, we're staying in pubs, B and Bs. Last night, we were glamping," she said.

"Where?" Campbell asked.

"Oh, what's it called? Just outside..." She looked at Toby for clarification. "Thoresby?"

"Thoresway," he corrected. "A glamp site called Wolds Grove."

"And what's the difference?" Ivy asked dryly. "Between camping and glamping?"

"The tent's already up," Marie replied with equal dryness. "It's big enough to walk around in and has a log burner and even an en-suite. They're more studio apartments with fabric walls."

Toby squeezed his wife's shoulder. "Only the best for the Devious Divas."

"I'm sorry?" Ivy said, with a glance at Campbell, that she quickly dropped to hide her smirk.

"That's what we call ourselves," Marie said without a shadow of shame. "Our little group of best friends. The Devious Divas. Cute, isn't it?"

"Adorable," Ivy said, already walking away and gesturing for Campbell to follow, unwilling to endure another second in their loved-up company, her stomach churning with an acidic concoction of jealousy, pathos, and plain old revulsion. "Absolutely precious."

CHAPTER NINE

Ivy stood with Campbell in the middle of the tarmac and caught her team's attention, silently telling them to finish up their interviews. Peter Saint had already left with the promise of sending his report later that day, and Katy was discussing the next steps with her own team further down the road.

She felt overwhelmed in George's absence but also grateful. A larger team made a huge difference. Three months ago, without George at her side, she would've had to navigate the social dynamics of four screaming women, their coddling husbands, and the mystery of a dead woman all on her own. But today, they had managed to do everything they needed to in only an hour. Ivy was not sure she would ever have been able to do it alone.

"They're a right bunch," Maguire said, his heavy Irish turning the sentence into just three syllables. "I just had to stop them from going at each other again."

"For a group of friends, they're volatile," Byrne agreed.

"Divas, you might say," Campbell added with a grin at Ivy.

"Tensions are high," O'Hara offered. "No one knows how they'll behave when something like this happens."

Ivy clapped, grabbing their attention, but for what, she was still not sure. She began talking without knowing what plan would develop at the end of it. "Anything stand out in the statements?" she asked, getting to the point.

The team seemed a little ruffled. The playful expression on their faces dropped. They tensed. If George was here, he would've let them finish their bits before jumping into action.

"Anything?" she asked, doubling down.

"Well, the fight between Lily and James last night," Byrne began. "One dead and one missing. I'd say that's something of note."

"Could be," Ivy said. "Could be just another argument between old friends. Anything else?"

Byrne did a kind of humble bow, jaw tensed.

"The argument between Violet and the others," Maguire offered. "I wouldn't say she's particularly liked."

"Cecelia said that no one wanted her here," Ivy said. "That Lily invited her as her sister-in-law. They probably bonded over their grief."

"Well, she's clearly rubbed a few of them up the wrong way," Maguire said.

"Yeah, I'd say she isn't one of the original Devious Divas," Campbell said.

"The what?"

"Don't get me started," Ivy said.

"It's their little name for their group," Campbell said with a grin.

"Christ," muttered Maguire.

"Anyway, they seem to want to blame Violet for separating the group," Byrne said, keeping them on track. "She, Franky, and Cecelia got into a fight just before the clouds rolled in properly. Violet stormed off ahead."

"But it was Marie who fell back," Campbell said, checking her notes. "She's been feeling ill. She had a funny spell. Lily hung back with her and went to find someone to help on the road. That's when she was separated. That's when the fog fell."

"The important thing is they were all separated," O'Hara said.

"Which means any of them could've done it," Ivy said, stating what they were all thinking, and the team lingered in the silence that followed, no doubt running through each possible scenario with each woman as Lily's attacker in mind.

"Cecelia and Franky were together," pointed out Byrne. "At least those two could hold the other accountable."

"Unless they're in it together," Maguire added.

"And Marie could hardly stand," Ivy pointed out. "Let alone kill someone."

Maguire scoffed. "So she says."

"So she looks," Ivy countered. "Not sure you can fake that kind of sickliness."

"Otherwise, there's the possibility someone just turned up on the road. Someone outside the group. A stranger, even."

"Or one of the husbands," Campbell said. "They would've known where they were, even in the fog."

"Would they?" Ivy asked. "Or would they just know that they were doing the Viking Way?"

"No, they have one of those apps," Byrne said. "Cecelia told me. It tracks where you are all the time. A lot of couples use them, you know, so you can see when someone's going to be home for dinner. So the husbands could see where they were along the hiking trail and when they'd turn up at that evening's accommodation."

"Who exactly had them?"

"All of them, I think," Byrne said.

"Not Violet," Maguire spoke up. "She doesn't even have a smartphone. She's against them, you know, data protection and all that."

"Well, have they checked it to see where James is?"

"Franky did," O'Hara said. "But there are so many dead zones in the Wolds. It hasn't been updated since this morning. He could be anywhere."

"Anyway, you can turn it off," Campbell said. "You can easily just pause it, and we wouldn't know if it was off on purpose or if they're in a dead zone."

"Alright," Ivy said, processing this new information. "Task one." She adopted George's habit of creating a mental to-do list. "Campbell, Byrne, get in touch with this app. What's it called?"

"G0247, guv."

"Okay, if that lot's movements have been tracked, I want to see it for all of them. Get a warrant if necessary. But first, I want you to find James DeSilver. Put out an ANPR on his car and find out where his phone last pinged. If James argued with Lily, that's the closest thing we have, so far, to a motive."

"Yeah, it seemed like everyone loved her," Byrne said.

"That's how it always seems."

"See, that's the problem," Maguire said. "All we have are people's words, and as we know, they don't go very far. We need more than stories. We don't know who to believe, or whose story we should follow up on."

"The guv would know," Byrne said.

Ivy raised her eyebrows but refrained from asking if he was undermining her authority in George's absence. She almost said it as a joke but knew it would only sound defensive. Anyway, it was true.

"I just mean, he's good with stuff like this," Byrne backtracked. "At seeing the story. You're more..."

"Yes?"

"Practical. You go where the evidence is."

"There is no evidence, Byrne."

"What did Saint and Katy say?" asked Campbell, throwing her a bone.

Of course, she should have relayed that earlier, straight away even, as soon as she'd gathered the team. She felt frazzled, off her game. She could only think about how George would have done everything she did better. "They both believe Lily was dead by the time she reached the bottom of the hill. No doubt, their reports will state as such. Saint ruled her death as strangulation."

"So, she was strangled on the road?" asked Byrne. "Then pushed?"

"Exactly."

"Fingerprints?"

"None. The killer wore gloves."

A long silence followed. The team looked to Ivy, expecting something that she could not deliver.

"So what else do you want from us, sarge?" asked O'Hara.

She blinked hard, finding it easier to concentrate with her eyes closed.

"Maguire, visit local houses. Ask if they saw anyone: other hikers, dog walkers, cars on the road. I can't imagine many come through here. Maybe they'd notice if one wasn't a neighbour."

When she opened her eyes, he was nodding. "Yes, guv."

"O'Hara, you stay here. Send that lot home," she said, nodding at the watchful group of friends and two husbands. "Stay with Katy and her team. Help them with anything they need and call me if they find anything else." She clicked her fingers at the PC, another task coming to mind. "What was the name of the campsite they stayed at last night?"

"Wolds Grove," Byrne said without hesitation. "They liked it so much they're staying there again tonight."

"Good. Byrne, you're with me." He had impressed her enough times today. "Campbell, are you okay looking for James DeSilver on your own?"

"Yes, guv," she said, sharing an impressed look with Byrne.

"Good. O'Hara, send Katy and her team over to Wolds Grove glamping site in an hour."

"I think they're almost done, sarge," she replied, "they could probably—"

"In an hour," Ivy repeated.

"Yes, sarge."

"Good. Let's meet in the incident room for a briefing when you're all done. Like Maguire said, there are too many stories being thrown around. This afternoon, I want facts. Evidence. You hear?"

"Yes, sarge," they said, not quite in the same unison as they would have replied to George, but together nonetheless — a similar sound to an orchestra warming up.

"Byrne, with me," Ivy said, strutting across the road with him on her heels.

"And where are we going, sarge?"

"You'll see," she said, unwilling to explain until out of earshot of the friends who still milled around, lost. It wasn't until they had climbed into Ivy's car, closed the door, and she had started the engine that she was willing to discuss it.

"You want Katy's team to go to the glamp site in an hour?" Byrne said, putting on his seatbelt. "Why in an hour?"

"Because Byrne..." Ivy typed *Wolds Grove* into the satnav. "I want a look around first."

CHAPTER TEN

The difference between a campsite and a glamping site became abundantly clear as soon as Ivy drove through the open gates of Wolds Grove. The atmosphere was entirely different to the camping trips she'd experienced with Jamie and the kids. While those holidays had been marred with stress, lost tent pegs, and lost tempers, this environment was one of peace. When they pulled into the dusty car park, zen music even played from a speaker outside the reception door.

The details were spectacular. Every line of the building was perfectly angled, every surface polished to a glossy finish, and every detail had been considered. Where possible, furniture had been made using bamboo, and if not bamboo, then local, distressed wood. But the highlight of the location was its surroundings. On a slight incline surrounded by rolling hills, it felt at once above the Wolds and nestled into its bosom. Wherever one looked, the views offered a serene, idyllic image of East Lincolnshire.

Byrne gave a low whistle as Ivy turned off the engine, and they looked through the windscreen. "This is fancy," he said. "I went camping a few times with my sister, and believe me, it was nothing like this."

"I know what you mean," Ivy said.

She climbed out of the car, and Byrne followed close behind as she entered the reception. The low dong of a sound bowl announced their entrance, and a woman in loose-fitting linen came out of the back office to greet them. She looked like a model for a Scandinavian spa, young and blonde with skin that practically glowed.

"Good morning," she said in a voice like silk.

Ivy, however, didn't have the time or patience to maintain the peace. She immediately displayed her warrant card.

"Detective Sergeant Ivy Hart," she said. "I'd like to speak to the manager, if I may."

For a few seconds, a panic disrupted the receptionist's fresh face. Her eyes flicked between Ivy and her computer screen, then settled.

"I see," she said slowly. "Would you excuse me for a second?"

When she returned, she did so with an older woman dressed in a shiny, black pantsuit. She was the yin to the yang of the receptionist, with dark hair and acne-scarred skin beneath a thick layer of make-up. "I'm the manager," she said, holding out her hand. "Sabina Anter. I can show you around. Is there anything in particular you need to see?"

Ivy shook her hand, getting straight to the point. "You had eight guests yesterday. They're also staying here tonight."

"That's right," the manager said. "So, how can we help?"

"I need to know where each of them is staying."

"We have a strict privacy—"

"I won't beat around the bush: I don't have time. One of your guests was found dead this morning, Mrs Anter." Ivy held up her warrant card again, saying nothing more.

The manager nodded as though she understood well enough. "I see," she said. "Follow me."

They walked silently through another door off the reception that led into a large, undulating field. At the centre was a grand, tent-shaped pergola carved with vaguely Asian-looking symbols that Ivy doubted originated from the same religion or culture. A clean, beige canopy draped over it, giving it the distinct feel of a wedding tent — luxurious and remarkable, merging the natural light and greenery of nature with the seclusion and warmth indoors. Beyond this eye-catching feature, as far as Ivy could see, were yurts, smaller versions of the grand tent scattered on the grass, with a generous amount of space between each one.

As they walked towards a cluster on the far end of the field, the manager said, "Can I ask what happened?"

"Not at this stage."

"Then, may I ask who it was?" she asked. "Perhaps I can help in some way."

Ivy considered the facts she knew, and those which she could reveal and provided a concise summary.

"Lily Hughes was found dead this morning at the bottom of a slope near Tealby. Not far from here."

"An accident?"

Ivy remained closed to the question.

"Well, where I come from, the police do not tend to investigate accidents."

"Mrs Anter—"

"Miss," she said sharply. "And are you here because you think that my establishment was involved in some way?"

"That's not why we're here, no. We just need to look at her tent. At this stage we're just trying to understand her last movements."

"Good," she said, "because I can tell you—"

"I assure you, we are not here to accuse your establishment of anything."

"Good," she muttered, mostly to herself. "Good."

They walked in silence for a little longer until Ivy asked a question of her own. "Whose is that?"

She pointed to the house that had just come into their line of view, positioned atop a mound overlooking the Grove. It stood just in front of a copse of trees that surrounded the outer walls as though their branches shielded a secret. In an enclave of other buildings, one could quite easily have confused it for a shed or shack with its one-story front and two-story back. Even from afar, Ivy could tell that it was rundown. The stout, crumbling chimney looked like a scab about to come loose from the skin, and dirty vein-like streaks on the exterior walls screamed damp, as though free-flowing blood ran through the old stonework.

"It's mine," Sabina said. "I live there."

"You live *there*?" Ivy said, then tried to salvage the derogatory tone. "I mean, on site?"

"It's my family's land."

"A farm?" Ivy asked.

"Yes. When my father died, I repurposed the land and built the Grove."

"Alright then," she said, and they walked on in a silence that Ivy, for one, preferred. Eventually, they reached a collection of yurts at the edge of the field, and Sabina pulled back the entrance to one.

"Miss Hughes was staying in the Harmony Yurt," she said.

"Has anyone cleaned it yet?" asked Ivy.

"We haven't had the chance yet, no," she said, her head bent with shame.

"Fantastic," Ivy said, going to enter.

"I'll join you," Sabina said.

"No need," Ivy said, turning. "I noticed a camera at the main gate. Could I ask you to email the CCTV footage you have of your entranceway and car park from yesterday?" Sabina opened her mouth to say something or perhaps ask a question, but Ivy spoke over her. "My colleague will give you our details. For now, you can show him where James and Franky DeSilver are staying." She went to enter the yurt and then turned again, remembering her manners. "If you don't mind?"

Sabina looked between Ivy and the open canvas slit as though debating whether she should allow someone to enter a guest's yurt without her, but she soon decided against any protest. "Of course," Sabina said, then gestured for Byrne to follow her. "Follow me."

Ivy nodded at Byrne, trusting him to remember what to do next, and she turned to enter the yurt in which Lily Hughes had been staying.

The unexpected beauty of the interior design stole Ivy's breath for a second. It was luxurious in a way that Ivy would never choose for her own home but would certainly appreciate for a night or two of relaxation. Various lamps along the walls bathed the entire room in warm, orange light. In the centre was a four-poster bed with floaty, white hanging curtains, and the slats of the roof were painted a bright, Grecian blue, spiralling together in a pattern reminiscent of the most intricate mandala. It was cosy to the extreme, with fresh, leafy plants spilling between the boundaries of inside and out.

Ivy explored the space, concluding that Lily Hughes had been a very clean woman. She had already laid out pyjamas she would never wear on the pillows of the bed she would never sleep in. In the Moroccan-tiled bathroom off the side of the main room, Lily Hughes had lined up her toiletries at right angles on the bathroom shelf, and she'd folded and packed her clothes inside a single Rimowa suitcase. Ivy only recognised the design because she'd once investigated a murder in which someone had locked a victim inside one. Such brands did not display their logo all over themselves but expected only an exclusive sliver of society to recognise it from quality alone.

In many ways, the yurt looked exactly how Ivy imagined it did when Lily had walked into it less than twenty-four hours earlier.

The only thing of note that had certainly not been there before was a six-by-four, gold-leaf-framed photograph on the bedside table. It was heavy when Ivy picked it up, and she stroked the decoration. It wasn't a cheap frame.

The photo was of three people, two of whom Ivy recognised. One was easily discernible from her bright, colourful hair as Violet. The other woman was much more alive than the last time Ivy had seen her. Both women wore summer dresses, although Violet's had a much witchier edge — long, laced sleeves and a tight bodice — compared to Lily's more conservative floral pattern.

In the photo, Lily was laughing, staring slightly above the camera, her mouth wide and features scrunched up, not in an ugly way, but far from flattering either, as though she'd been caught off-guard by something hilarious the photographer had just said. Lily had liked the photo not for its image, Ivy discerned, but for the memory it evoked. In between the two women, his arms flung over their shoulders, was a tall, slim man wearing a crisp white shirt over navy blue shorts and boat shoes.

They stood in a forest beside a lake that continued into the background, undisturbed by boats, beaches, or man-made creations of any kind. For that reason, and because of the great, redwood-looking trees that surrounded them, Ivy doubted they were in England. It looked like the deep wilds of North America.

"Who do you think that is then?" Byrne said over her shoulder.

Ivy's heart thumped, and she dropped the photo in surprise, causing it to fall on the walnut floor and crack down the middle. "Shit," she said.

"Sorry, sarge, I didn't mean to—"

"Did you get it?" she interrupted.

"Yep," he said, holding up a toothbrush in a plastic bag. "I chose the blue one beside the razor rather than the pink one beside the moisturiser."

"Good thinking," Ivy muttered.

"So who is it?" he asked again as Ivy bent to pick up the cracked photo frame.

"Jordan," she said certainly. "Lily's late husband. Violet's brother."

"Looks like they're in the middle of nowhere."

"It does, doesn't it?" Ivy muttered, then looked up at the PC. "So," she said, nodding to the yurt's doorway and lowering her voice, "what do you think?"

Byrne shrugged. "She just seems to care about her business," he started, then shuddered theatrically, "but fancy living in that creepy, old house. I mean, she could've done it up a bit."

"Maybe she didn't have the time," Ivy suggested.

"Or the money?"

"Have you seen this place?" Ivy said, gesturing to the mandala-like roof slats and ornate furniture. "A night here will cost a pretty penny. I can't imagine she's struggling financially."

"I guess," Byrne said and eyed Ivy. "What about you? Do you trust her?"

It wasn't like Lily Hughes would miss the keepsake. She opened the back of the gold-leaf frame, removed the photograph, tucked it into one of her deep pockets, then turned to Byrne and grinned.

"At this stage," she started, "I don't trust any of them."

CHAPTER ELEVEN

The house that, until very recently, George had called home had grown shabby, he thought from where he leant against his car bonnet. The weeds had spread, and the grass had erupted into an unruly micro-jungle from the lack of Grace's fair hand. The early perennials hung their heads as though weeping with grief, bees no longer buzzed happily between each petal seeking sweet nectars, and no birds flitted to the feeders she had topped up so diligently.

How easily things fell apart without her.

He sighed and took another sip of his takeaway coffee, postponing the inevitable. Under his right arm was a package of flatpack boxes he had bought on the way over. But the effort of putting them together was too much to think about.

Down the street, a woman pushed her stroller frantically, running for the bus. The driver was kind, waited for her, and even helped her lift it up the step while the buckled toddler giggled at the attention. George watched on with envy at the urgency of her run, the energy of it, the driver's small act of kindness. How could they all continue as though nothing had happened? How did buses still run on time? How did the weeds keep growing? How did the world keep turning now that Grace was gone?

The bus rattled past, and soon, George was alone again on the street. He took another sip and gave yet another sigh, exhausted by every tiny movement these days — getting out of bed, buying groceries, pushing himself off a car bonnet. But when he breathed in, it was the cool sea air that pushed him to take action, the same way it called to sailors and pirates of the past. It was time to reach the horizon. It was time to cross the threshold, whether the line in the sand, the sky, or the past.

Finally, he pushed himself off the car, his body a bag of bones, and walked up the root-filled garden path, careful of his footing. He took out his keys and placed them in the old lock, muscle memory telling him to pull the door towards him slightly and wiggle the key before it turned. Something clicked. The first time he had walked through that door, Grace had been in his arms. They had already been married for thirty years at the time. It was just a game, a joke, that every time they moved to a new place, George would carry her over the threshold as though they were newlyweds, as though they were about to begin a new life together again.

But this time, George was alone. And Grace was God only knows where. He struggled to feel her presence at all.

As he opened the door to their marital home, only a cold, gusty breeze met him on the doorstep. After three months without housing a living soul, the house was dusty and dense with silence, as though memories were the only inhabitants. The house looked exactly as he had left it all those months ago on that dark, stormy evening before he had driven out to the Wolds and been met with the ghosts of his past career. All plates and cups were still in the cupboard, although the door was now a little stiff to open. The books were on the bookshelf, although they had accumulated a thick layer of dust, and above the fireplace, the same outline of his favourite painting remained like a birthmark on the wall.

He threw the coffee cup and flatpack boxes onto the dining

table and slumped down into the old leather sofa. It felt stiff and cold beneath his thighs. He looked around, but still, he could not sense Grace within the walls. The house had a presence of its own now, as though it had grown used to being alone, and it felt unfamiliar to George.

"Where are you, Grace?" he said to himself.

No sooner had the words left his lips than he heard a knock on the door.

Of course, she wouldn't be, he knew that, but still, George half expected and fully wished, as he walked over, reached for the front door, and opened it, for his wife to be standing on the other side.

But it was not Grace. Of course, it wasn't. Grace was gone.

"Jamie?"

"George," Jamie said, nodding. "I hope you don't mind. I was driving past and saw your car outside."

"Of course," George said, holding the door open and stepping back. It was a reasonable excuse, that George believed, seeing as Ivy's family home was only a few streets away.

Jamie stood in the middle of the room and turned around to face George, who lingered in the doorway. He looked around for a few seconds, taking the scene in, then finally, his stare landed on George.

"I'm sorry," he said earnestly. George even detected a crack in his throat. "About Grace."

George had heard those words countless times over the last few weeks, even once already from Jamie at the funeral, and he still didn't quite know how to react to them. Sometimes he said, 'Thank you', although he was thankful for nothing. Sometimes, he said, 'Me too', but that seemed to elicit an unbearable look of pity. So these days, he had settled for a kind of humble bow and didn't say anything at all.

Jamie returned to gazing around the house as though it

brought him comfort. He placed his hand on the dining table that took up the centre of the large, open-plan room.

"Do you remember that time," he said, his face suddenly lighting up, "Grace made us play Pictionary after your birthday dinner?"

"Remember it?" George said, laughing and rubbing his head. "I still have the scar."

"Loveliest woman in the world," Jamie said, shaking his head, "with a fierce competitive streak."

"The only time she was unkind," George said. "When I couldn't guess her depiction of the Unbearable Lightness of Being."

"A bean floating through the clouds," Jamie recalled. "I mean, she was nothing if not creative."

"Yeah, far too creative," George said. "How was I ever supposed to guess that?"

"It's your favourite book, George, for God's sake," Jamie said, imitating her words at the time.

"If you think it's so easy here, why don't you have a go?" they said in unison, imitating throwing a pen aggressively.

She had run over to him the second the marker had left her hand, and George had yelped as it had hit his forehead. It was a memory he and Grace — and no doubt Jamie and Ivy — had relived and laughed about many times. But it was in the past. So much had changed since then. And when their laughter simmered, that same dense silence filled the house once more.

"Is that why you came here?" George asked. "To talk about Grace?"

"One of the reasons," Jamie replied. "I can't imagine how much you must miss her." He shook his head. "Or maybe I can."

"Look, Jamie," George said, resisting the urge to remind him that losing a spouse was not the same as separating, "if you want me to talk to Ivy, then I don't think—"

"No," he said quickly, stepping forward. "No, it's the opposite, actually."

"What do you mean?"

"I mean..." He hesitated. "You haven't mentioned it to her, have you? In the last few weeks, I mean?"

"I've been a little preoccupied."

"I know, I'm sorry. I just... Please don't."

"Don't what?"

"Tell her. What I told you."

"You told me a few things," George said.

"About her being the one to leave," Jamie said. "About me and the kids wanting her back if only she wanted the same." George remembered those significant words from only a few weeks earlier, just before all hell had broken loose. "She clearly had a reason for not telling you," Jamie continued. "For making you believe that I was the one to kick her out. I don't understand what that reason is. But I don't want Ivy to know that I told you. It wasn't my place. I'm sorry. I shouldn't have put you in that position."

George nodded, but the look on Jamie's face softened his resolve. His wide, wet eyes beneath a thick, blonde fringe reminded him of Jamie's youth when he'd first met the lithe, surfer-like young man. But the bags beneath them betrayed a different story. He had always been a handsome man, but the last few times George had seen him, Jamie looked exhausted, his skin greyer, his hair thinner.

"I think I have my own apology to give," George said. "I shouldn't have interfered, Jamie. I'm sorry."

"You were trying to do the right thing."

"I was trying to do what I thought was the right thing. But Ivy is going through her own process. I can't say I understand it. And I don't know why she lied to me either. But hopefully, one day, when she's ready, she will tell me the truth."

"Don't hold your breath, George," Jamie said bitterly, as

though he knew Ivy better than anyone else. He was hurt. George could see it in his eyes. He felt betrayed. And George knew that betrayal triggered the pendulum swing of love, forcing it in the other direction towards a feeling not far from hate. "Just...look after her, won't you?"

George questioned his theory. There was still love there. He could see that, too.

"Of course I will."

"She's not as strong as she seems. It makes me feel better to know that you're there. Every day. Beside her."

George nodded but felt a pang of guilt in his chest. Sure, he was there today to help her look around her new house, but would he be there tomorrow? And the day after that? And the day after that?

Again, he performed the kind of humble bow he had been practising when he wasn't sure what to say. Still, it seemed enough for Jamie because he turned back towards the front door, giving George's shoulder a gentle squeeze as he passed.

"You know, George," he said, stopping with his hand on the door handle. "This might sound crazy, but I felt her the other day. Her presence, that is."

George frowned. "Ivy's?"

"Grace's," he said, with the softest smile George had ever seen on such a rugged face. "I was in the garden, just watching the kids play, making sure they were safe, and this robin flew over and landed on the chrysanthemums right next to where I was sitting. And it just stared at me. They don't usually come so close, especially with the kids screaming and yelling. On the chrysanthemum, George. Do you remember? She brought over the saplings for Ivy's birthday?"

"Yeah," George said and laughed. "She rolled her sleeves up, went outside, and planted them for you right there and then."

"Exactly," Jamie said. "I mean, I don't know if it was her or just a robin, but I *felt* her like she was right there in front of me. You know?"

"Yeah," George lied and smiled in an attempt to hide his jealousy. Because that was the only feeling Jamie's story evoked. He had not felt that way at all, not once since Grace's death. She just felt gone. So very much *not* here. So very much somewhere else.

"Thanks, George," Jamie said before he left. "For looking after her."

Then he smiled once more and left.

Yet again, George was left alone with the dense silence. It was the Dead Sea of silences, full of salt, painfully finding its way into the crevices of George's heart. He wished the silence was made of water so he could fall back and float on it. He wanted it to carry him away on its tide, beyond the horizon, to wherever it was Grace was waiting.

Instead, he unpacked the flatpack boxes and pushed one of them into a box shape, struggling with the configuration of the flaps. It was the only thing he could think to do, lest he spend all day staring at the wall again, lost in memories. He walked over to the bookshelf and picked up the first book in his eyeline, an old hardback, a second edition signed by the author. But he turned to the title page, which bore a far more valuable signature.

"My George," he read aloud. "Happy thirty-fifth birthday, you handsome, lovely man. I'm assuming this is still your favourite book after all these years. I hope you enjoy the re-read. I'm with you always. Your Grace."

He reprimanded himself as a heavy tear dropped onto the page and smudged her precious writing. He closed the book and studied the title on the front cover, but through his tears, all he could make out was the word *unbearable*.

"If only you were," he said aloud. "If only you were with me."

CHAPTER TWELVE

The whiteboard was as busy as she'd ever seen it. Ivy wasn't sure they'd ever had so many suspects so soon into an investigation. She felt as though she was juggling a collection of new names and only just catching them before they slipped through her fingers. Still, the whiteboard helped to organise her thoughts. Behind her, Byrne and Campbell sat at their desks, one eye on the board and its smattering of information, the other on the tasks at hand.

On the left-hand side of the board, Ivy wrote seven names. By all accounts, every single one of them had the opportunity to kill Lily Hughes.

Lily's friends — Cecelia Adams, Marie Entwhistle, Franky DeSilver, and Violet Hughes — had been mere metres from her in the fog. Bob Adams had been at the glampsite, unaccounted for. Toby Entwhistle had been at the market, unaccounted for. James DeSilver had been at his house, unaccounted for. The investigation would be a process of elimination more than anything. Ivy could see that from the get-go.

Beside James DeSilver's name, Ivy wrote two notes. The first simply read, *Missing*. The second read, *Argued with Lily*. It was the closest thing to a motive they had as of yet.

But beside Marie Entwistle's name, Ivy added one more thought: *Last to see Lily alive.*

Along the bottom of the whiteboard, Lily drew a long, single line from left to right. About three-quarters of the way along, she drew a cross and wrote, *Lily's body found 11:17 a.m. Tuesday,* and she left a space after this event, for all her years as a detective had taught her that finding a victim was often not the end point of investigative events.

She added two more crosses just before the first, and above one, she wrote, *08:00 Set off hiking*, and above the other, *08-09:00 Someone slaps Lily*.

Ivy stepped back to admire her artwork — 'Lily Hughes's Death on White Canvas'. It was like an abstract design, all lines and monochrome, like a Franz Kline painting. In such pieces, the white spaces themselves often held meaning, the parts without paint, lines or words, and Ivy found that to be true of her own work. There were plenty of gaps. Too many. She stared at it, filling the space with hypothetical answers, and by the time Maguire and O'Hara walked into the incident room, their entrance declared by the squeak of the floorboard and swing of the door, Ivy was ready and waiting.

She clapped once, the way a maestro might grab the attention of an orchestra.

"Huddle up," she said. "Let's talk through what we've got." She looked around the room, quiet on a Tuesday afternoon with only a few spare PCs milling around. "Where's Ruby?"

"Haven't heard anything," Byrne said, turning his chair around to better face the whiteboard.

His desk was the closest to Ivy, whereas Campbell, Maguire, and O'Hara had to either pull their desk chairs across the room or borrow one close by. An unspoken etiquette of the incident room usually prohibited such borrowing, but what the officers didn't know wouldn't kill them.

"I thought the guv was giving us that space," Maguire said,

yanking over a chair with a broken wheel. He pointed to the very back of the incident room, a dark, shadowy place rarely ventured into.

"It's in process," Ivy said flatly. The truth was that Tim's promise to convert the old, useless storage space into an office for major crimes was progressing slower than Ivy's divorce.

"Aye, well, a glacier moves faster than the decision-making in the force, so let's not get our hopes up, eh?"

"Never mind that," Ivy said. "Does anyone know where Ruby is?"

"Probably working from home, sarge," Campbell spoke up, settling down in her seat. "She's been doing that a lot recently."

"Sounds nice," O'Hara said, opting to lean against a nearby desk. She often appeared to prefer standing. In contrast to Maguire, who struggled to sit still without tapping a leg or rearranging his long limbs, O'Hara's stouter figure allowed her the grounding to stand as firm and full as a mulberry bush. "Didn't know that was an option."

"For you, it's not," Ivy said, ignoring the sarcasm.

"Well, as a researcher, it is," Campbell said. "Anyway, if she gets the job done, which we know she does, I, for one, don't care where she does it from."

"Well, I do," Ivy said sternly. "She's a part of this team. She should be here."

"You want me to call her sarge?"

"No," Ivy said. "No, not now. Let's focus." She tapped the whiteboard, beginning the briefing the only way she knew how — by mirroring George's movements. "Campbell," she said, deciding to draw from the most reliable well of information. "What have you got?"

"I've been in touch with Go247 and told them we're investigating the murder of one of their users," she said.

"And?"

"And they've given me access, sarge."

"Okay," Ivy said, frowning. "That was easy."

"Too easy," Campbell said. "So much for data protection. They're sending over the access today, sarge. Shouldn't be more than an hour. I'll let you know when it comes through."

"Don't bother. I trust you. Just go through it straight away. I want to know their movements over the last three days, if they were always together, and if not, who was with whom."

"Yes, sarge."

"Good. What about DeSilver?"

"Still no word," Campbell said. "I'll check his movements on the app as soon as I get it. But otherwise, Bob saw his Audi A4 leaving Wolds Grove and turning right at about quarter to ten."

"I can confirm that," Byrne added. "From the CCTV of Wolds Grove's car park that Sabina Anter sent over. It shows DeSilver leaving at nine forty-six and Bob driving Toby to the market at ten-fifteen."

"Exactly. Nine forty-six. That's when James DeSilver's phone last pinged, too," Campbell added.

"And then?"

"Then nothing, sarge. Those country lanes don't have cameras, not until he'd reach the Orford Road into Binbrook."

"Okay, and?"

"He never does reach it."

Ivy stared at Campbell. She'd driven that route herself less than an hour ago, from the glampsite towards the Orford Road along Spring View. She couldn't remember any major turnings, limited pullovers, nothing much at all, in fact, she wasn't sure they had even passed another car on the way.

"Any turn-offs?" she asked.

"Only dead ends," Campbell said. "A few farms, some private driveways, but no through roads."

"It's less than two minutes from Wolds Grove to Orford Road," Ivy recalled.

"Yes, sarge," Campbell said, showing off her research. "Zero point six miles. Takes about one minute and twenty-five seconds."

"So somewhere in that zero-point-six-mile stretch of road, James DeSilver has disappeared?"

"Yes, sarge."

"You said his phone pinged. Do we have access to his messages yet?"

"We do, as it happens. Not that it's much help."

"What was his last message?" Ivy asked, dismissing the sentiment. "Who was it to?"

"A pay-as-you-go number. Unregistered. Couldn't track it back to anyone, and all messages before then had been deleted. But we do know it came from a house near Stenigot."

"Get Ruby to track that pay-as-you-go," Ivy said. "I want to know who James DeSilver was meeting."

"It's unregistered," Campbell replied. "I don't think it's even possible to—"

"Tell her to use the time she saved by not coming into work."

Campbell hesitated but relented. "Yes, sarge."

"Stenigot," Ivy repeated. "Why is that familiar?"

"It's where the DeSilvers live, sarge," Byrne spoke up. "They just moved there a month ago. According to Cecelia, they were all going to stay in their house on the last night of their trip."

"And has anyone been to the house?"

"He's not there, sarge," Campbell said surely. "ANPR would have picked him up."

"Yes, but whoever sent that message might still be," she said, impatience rising in her tone. She was angry at herself, she knew, for not sending someone to the DeSilver house earlier. But, while she tried to practice George's self-awareness and accountability, it did not come naturally.

"Franky DeSilver might have gone there," O'Hara said. "I told them all to go back to Wolds Grove in case we needed to talk to them, so they were all in one place. But she was fretting about him. She could have gone to check if he was at home first."

"Call it in," Ivy said urgently. "I want an officer there as soon as possible." She looked around at the team, seeing which one of them would step up and decide it was their responsibility. Their inaction inspired an impatience in her that she knew it never would in George, and that realisation only added to her mood. "*Now*, please."

CHAPTER THIRTEEN

Byrne placed the desk phone back into its cradle and turned back to Ivy and the whiteboard, his demeanour calm and collected in the face of a storm. "Done, Sarge," he said. "Two officers are on their way to the DeSilver house now."

"Good," Ivy said, her impatience dissipating now she knew action had been taken. Still, it worried her that her frustrations could swell and disperse as easily as an uncertain tide. Usually, she could keep them to herself, but as a leader, she displayed them openly, projecting them onto the world, or, more specifically, onto her team. "What about DeSilver's work?"

"He's a businessman," Maguire said, checking his notes. "Owns a business in Lincoln. Just moved here from London."

"What kind of business?"

"Property management systems and software," Maguire said, frowning at his notes. "Not one hundred per cent sure what that means, to be honest,"

"For hotels," Ivy said, writing *PMS Business* beside James' name on the board. "Helps reception check guests in and out, allocate rooms, calculate costs, et cetera. What's it called?"

"VavaRoom," he said, enunciating the syllables with a chuckle, and Ivy wrote *VavaRoom* in brackets. "That's pretty good, to be fair."

"Byrne, pick up that phone again," Ivy said, clicking at him, copying the endearing manner in which George did it, but somehow coming across as demanding instead. "I want officers at DeSilver's office in Lincoln too. Find the address."

"Tentercroft Street," he said, having already looked it up. "I'll pass them the details."

He picked up the handset once more, and in the absence of his attention, Ivy turned to Maguire. "What about the locals?"

Maguire rifled back through his notes and stabbed his finger on a page. "Only a handful of people live along Caistor Lane, before it reaches the main road anyway. Luckily, they seem the type to look out their windows to see who's coming and going, you know? Most of them saw the lasses walk along the road."

"All five of them?"

"Yes, sarge."

"And when the fog fell?"

"Well, then they couldn't see much."

"Maguire—"

"One of them saw a car," he said quickly, checking his notes. "A Mr...Evans. Just before the fog fell, heading in the direction the women were walking."

"Timings, Maguire. What time?"

"Just after eleven," he said. "That's when the fog rolled in."

"And what kind of car was it?"

"He didn't say. Or more, in his words..." He followed the quote with his finger like a school kid learning to read. "I'm not Jeremy bloody Clarkson."

"And that was just before the fog fell?"

"Seconds, he said. It's not usual, apparently, for someone to drive down that way. That's why he remembered. He assumed someone had gotten lost. There's not much down there, just a very long detour to the main road."

"Do any of them have doorbell cameras?" Ivy asked. "Neighbourhood watch, that sort of thing?"

"No, this old codger didn't, but some of the fancier ones looked like they might."

"Good. Head back over there. Get whatever footage you can of this car that passed by just before the fog fell. Let's say from ten-fifty onwards."

Maguire looked beyond the incident room windows at the downpour outside and the drops that dragged heavily down the windows, then back at Ivy. "Now, sarge?"

She grinned. "Might as well get ahead of it, Maguire."

"Yes, sarge," he muttered, rising from his chair.

"And while you're there," Ivy added. "Head over to Spring View Road. Drive down the dead ends and driveways between Wolds Grove and the main road. Knock on doors. Ask if they have seen James DeSilver or his car since this morning. You're looking for a black Audi A4."

"While I'm there?" Maguire said, mouth agape. "That's miles away."

"You better get going then," Ivy said, and with a sarcastic thumbs-up from O'Hara, he pulled the collar up on his coat and left the room. "O'Hara," she said, turning to the PC, who quickly dropped her hand and her grin. "Did any of Lily's friends say anything when you sent them home?"

"No, sarge. They all looked emotionally exhausted, except Franky. She seemed eager to leave. That's why I assumed she was going home first, to look for her husband. Then I waited an hour, like you asked, and sent Katy and her team over to Wolds Grove."

"Good," Ivy said and went to turn away, but O'Hara wasn't finished.

"Sarge, I hope you don't mind, but I had some time, you see when I was waiting to send Katy over to the glampsite."

Ivy turned back to face her. The last time O'Hara had acted on her own accord without approval she'd almost had to call in bomb disposal at a local train station but had decided to risk the lives of numerous civilians instead. "Okay?"

"So I looked up the places the women said they'd stayed over the last five days and called them up to check their bookings."

Ivy watched her with narrowed eyes, then began to nod. "Now *that*," she said slowly, "is the kind of police intuition I *do* appreciate." O'Hara's face lit up, and Ivy turned back to the board, pen poised. "What did you find?"

"So the first place they stayed on Friday night was a B and B in Barton Upon Humber. Blueberry Cottage. Cute, upscale kind of place. They booked five rooms."

"Makes sense," Ivy said. "Three doubles and two singles for Lily and Violet. Anything of note?"

"Nothing," O'Hara said. "Owner said they were pleasant guests. Got a bit loud over dinner, but she blamed herself for the complimentary wine."

"Okay," Ivy said, writing *Friday Night: Blueberry Cottage* at the beginning of the timeline on the bottom of the board. "Next?"

"Next night was a pub in Caistor. The Red Dragon. Again, nothing of note. The guy I talked to at the bar said they knocked back their fair share of whisky, but that was about it."

"I'm starting to see a pattern here," Ivy said.

"Hike by day, drink by night?" Campbell offered.

"Seems like it."

As Ivy wrote *Saturday Night: The Red Dragon*, O'Hara continued, "Then Sunday night was at a hotel in Normanby. Wildflower Escape. Again, it's a nice place. Five stars, three rosettes." She looked up at Ivy. "They booked six rooms."

She stopped in the middle of writing *Sunday Night: Wildflower Escape* on the board. "Six rooms?"

O'Hara nodded slowly. "Bob Adams booked a room for himself at the last minute. Came downstairs around 11 p.m. apparently and asked if anything was available."

"A late-night tiff?"

O'Hara shrugged. "Could be, but could be something—"

"Believe me," Ivy said, cutting her off. "I know a late-night tiff. That's what happened."

O'Hara shared a loaded look with Campbell but said nothing more.

"Good," Ivy said, stepping back. Her artwork was becoming less and less abstract, and it looked all the better for it. She added *Monday Night: Wolds Grove* to the timeline, and her vision was complete. "O'Hara, print a map of the area to put here," she said, gesturing to the small amount of leftover space beside the whiteboard. "I want every place they stayed at marked, and I want to see the route they took this morning while hiking, and, of course, where they finished."

"Yes, sarge."

Ivy tapped the names on the left of the board. "We need to eliminate all of these people, but while we do that, I want to make progress on the third-party theory. Maguire is helping with that as we speak." She nodded at the rain outside. "But I want any nearby road cameras, dash cams, anything that might have captured other hikers, dog walkers, or any other cars that might have driven down Caistor Lane in the hours before Lily was killed." She looked around at her team, who were already laden with tasks. "For that, we need—"

"A researcher," Campbell finished, nodding at the door, outside of which a floorboard had just creaked loudly.

"Sorry I'm late, sorry I'm late," Ruby said, twirling into the room like a small tornado that hadn't yet touched the ground. Her coat was loose and flapping, her hair flattened and dripping with rain. "My dad's car broke down, and I had to drive him to work, and then *my* window wipers started playing up. It was a nightmare. I—"

"Ruby," Ivy said, becoming the fire to Ruby's frying pan, "get a briefing from Campbell. We're trying to build a picture of the hours before Lily's death."

"Lily?" Ruby mouthed.

"Hughes," Ivy said flatly. "She's our victim."

"Yes, sarge," Ruby said sitting down and immediately taking out her laptop before even removing her soaked-through raincoat.

"One more recap," Ivy said with a sigh, aware that Ruby had no idea of the briefing she'd spent the last hour conducting. "Lily Hughes, our victim," she said pointedly, "has been on a hiking trip with four friends and three of their husbands since Friday. They stay at a different place each night. The women hike all day while the men go ahead to the next location. Last night, they stayed at a glamping site, Wolds Grove in Thoresway. This morning, at eleven-seventeen a.m., Lily Hughes's body was found by her friend Marie Entwhistle. When a dense fog fell, it appears she was strangled and then pushed down a steep drop. Coincidentally, James DeSilver, the husband of Lily's friend, Franky, has gone missing and hasn't been seen since nine-forty-five this morning."

"So, what does it mean?" asked Byrne, squinting at the board as though it might be a secret magic eye poster.

"What?" Ivy asked.

"I mean, what's the narrative?" asked Byrne.

"The narrative?"

"Yeah, like the guv, he always—"

"James DeSilver," Ivy said quickly before she could be compared with George again and consequently feel inadequate. "He has the motive of arguing with Lily the night before. If he owed her something, perhaps he didn't want to give it to her. He has the means. It wouldn't be hard for a man to overpower a middle-aged woman as small as Lily. And he had the opportunity. If he left Wolds Grove at quarter to ten, which was confirmed by both Bob Adams and Toby Entwhistle, plus the CCTV, then he had plenty of time to kill Lily." She took a breath, a little overwhelmed by the review. "And on top of that, we don't know where the hell he is."

"So you think he did her in then ran?" asked Byrne.

"With a few more details in between," she said. "But yes. You all wanted a narrative? There's your narrative. Now go find me the evidence."

Ivy turned around to ponder the whiteboard, hearing only a lethargic scraping of chairs. When she turned around, she caught Campbell shaking her head, sharing a look with Byrne.

"Yes?" Ivy asked.

A pink flush rushed to Campbell's cheeks, but she stood her ground. "It just doesn't make sense, sarge. James DeSilver's car would have been caught by ANPR if he'd driven to murder Lily, surely."

"Not if he didn't pass a camera. And I agree, it doesn't make sense yet," Ivy agreed. "But it will. That is why we need to build the evidence. It doesn't matter how meaningless it might seem."

"But, sarge—"

"We are following procedure, Campbell, by eliminating suspects through MMO and—"

"I get that, but shouldn't we at least get the women's DNA? I mean, surely we're branching off too quickly. They all have the opportunity. As you said, Marie was the last to see Lily alive, and she was found out of breath metres from where Lily was killed. Franky and Cecelia only have each other as alibis. And Violet had stormed off in a rage. How do we know she didn't direct that at Lily? One of those women had slapped Lily already that morning. We should be finding out who. We should—"

"*Campbell*," Ivy said sternly, eerily reminiscent of her mother. She closed her eyes and breathed out. "I appreciate your concerns. But I am not going to demand the DNA of four grieving friends before we even know they're involved. Now, please, get back to the tasks assigned to you."

"Yes, sarge," she said quietly, standing up. "Will do."

"I want to know every single thing about James DeSilver," she said, watching Campbell move to her desk, "and I want it by tomorrow morning." The air in the room held its own dense fog, a hanging tension that stifled their voices and caused them all to breathe uneasily. Before Ivy could move away to her own desk, she stopped and looked down at the latecomer. "Oh, and Ruby?"

"Yes, sarge?"

"Next time you're late," she said seriously, "call me."

Ruby continued to look only at her laptop. "Yes, sarge."

"We need you here," Ivy said, with one last warning look, and Ruby finally looked up from the screen. "You're a valued member of this team," she said, but her voice sounded more threatening than sincere. "Remember that."

CHAPTER FOURTEEN

George was stirring the second batch of sauce and adding a few pinches of salt when he heard the front door open. He went to greet Ivy. He had spent all day alone, and although he had enjoyed the solitude, he found himself craving conversation. She ran through the front door of the house and peeled off her rain-drenched coat. The moody danger of navigating the tiny lanes of the Wolds during a downpour after dark was not one she had yet gotten used to, and she seemed exhausted by the drive home. It would still be her home for the next week or so until Ella Alexander finalised the paperwork on her new house.

He dipped back into the kitchen as he heard the sound of spluttering over the sound of the popular radio station, an unusual choice for George, who usually preferred the sound of silence or, if not, Classic FM on low. But he had wanted a rest from the noise of his thoughts.

"I'm beat, guv," Ivy said, walking to the kitchen and throwing her coat onto a chair. "Fancy a takeout for...oh."

George looked around. His usually tidy and homely kitchen had been transformed into something that resembled a family kitchen at Christmas. Sauce-lined utensils, torn packaging, and empty containers littered each countertop, and a different-sized pot or pan occupied every hob on the stove. The sink was filled to the brim with dirty dishes and cutlery. Spots of red, white, and green dotted the floor like tile decorations, whether rogue juices, dustings of flour, or loose basil leaves. Between it all, like a let-loose spinning top, he flitted between each surface, managing — only just — the chaos.

"Welcome home, Ivy," he said, reaching to turn off the radio so he could be better heard above the sounds of boiling water and splatting sauces. "I found an old recipe book of Grace's in Mablethorpe," he said, holding up a tattered, spineless, old hardback that looked like a firm breeze might destroy it completely. "Thought I'd give it a go."

"That's great, guv," she said, eyeing a crusted frying pan left on the side with a melted handle.

"How was work?" he asked, frowning between the recipe and the spluttering sauce he stirred on the hob.

"Fine," she said, crossing her arms and leaning against the doorframe.

"Come on, Ivy," he said. "Give me more than that."

She sighed and rubbed her forehead. "Middle-aged female found at the bottom of a steep drop. Peter and Katy agree she was strangled and then pushed. She was hiking with four friends when a heavy fog rolled in, and they all separated. That's when she was killed."

George whistled. "So all the women are suspects?"

"And their husbands. Three of them, anyway. They probably knew where the women were hiking and can't yet be accounted for. Plus, one of them is missing."

"Missing?"

"A James DeSilver: local businessman and old friend of the victim. He hasn't been seen since nine forty-five this morning."

"Sounds like a doozy," George said, holding up a spoonful of the sauce, walking over and raising it to Ivy's lips. "Here, try this."

She winced but struggled to avoid his insistence and sipped at the hot liquid. "Mmmmm," she said noncommittally, which seemed enough to please George. She grabbed a scrunched-up tea towel and wiped her mouth. George tried it. It tasted like seawater. "Sounds like a doozy?"

"Yeah, sounds like a tough one."

"That's all you have to say?"

"What do you want me to say, Ivy?" he said, adding some lime juice.

"Something," she said. "Anything! You're our DCI, for God's sake, give me some input."

"I'm on leave," was his only reply.

"So?"

"So, I don't know the full story. I'm not at liberty to give advice."

"Not at liberty?"

"It's not my case, Ivy. Anyway, I'm sure you have it under control."

Ivy stared at him, horrified by his passivity. "Guv, look at me," she said. "Look at me." He sighed, put the wooden spoon into the sauce, and turned to face her. "You need to come back," she said simply. "The team needs you. They're lost without you."

"Lost how?"

"They need your leadership."

"They have you."

"I know," she said quietly. "But they need your...that quality you have...a...."

"*Je ne sais quoi?*" George said, grinning.

But Ivy only looked at him without smiling, her face earnest and a little sad. "Kindness," she said seriously, "your gentleness and patience, guv. It's a quality they can't learn on their own. And they need it."

George frowned. "I don't understand what you mean, Ivy. Are the team being unkind?"

"No, it's just that..." She shrugged. "Well, I don't know. Maybe." She slumped against the counter. "Ruby has been working from home like she doesn't want to even be in the office. And I can see why. The atmosphere in the incident room is..." She struggled to find the right word again, as though every word today was hard to find. "Different."

"They'll get used to it," he replied with a smile that only served to infuriate her.

"No, guv, they won't," she said flatly. "They need you. They're lost without you."

"They'll find their way."

"Find their way where? Look, some people are born to lead. Some people are born to follow. We've had enough experience with... ineffective leaders to know that when you're one of the good ones, you've got to step up. In that incident room is where you belong, guv," she said, "not here making outdated recipes with too much salt."

At this, George only frowned and sipped the sauce on his spoon.

"Tastes fine to me," he said.

"You don't get it," she said, and George noticed the petulance in her voice, the strain, as though even her vocal cords were tightly strung. "The team needs you. They need you to come back, guv. Back where you belong."

He put the spoon back in the pot and leaned heavily on the counter.

"I'm grieving my wife, Ivy. Don't I get some time? Some grace?" he said. "Or have you decided that I've had enough by now?"

She stared at him with her arms crossed. "I think you're stalling."

"Stalling?"

"Yes. Postponing getting back to reality. To what you're good at. To where you should be."

"I told you, I'm not ready, Ivy. Just because you think I am—"

"It's not about you!" she cried, throwing her hands up. "That's what I'm trying to tell you. It's about the team. *They* need you. *They're* lost without you. And every day you spend here making terrible meals is another day that *your team* grows further apart. Can't you see that? Or do you just not care anymore?"

He looked at Ivy, at her furrowed brow and heaving chest, her tell-tale signs of frustration. He could see in her tense body all the things he didn't miss about the job — the stress, the pressure, the strain. Then he looked at the simmering sauce in the pot below him, which symbolised all the things he missed about Grace — the comfort, the homeliness, the flavours, and the zest of life. He wasn't ready to give that up. Not yet.

"Look, Ivy..." he said slowly, turning to face her. "Are you going to eat this ratatouille with me or not? Because the recipe says I really shouldn't let it simmer for more than fifteen minutes before baking."

Before he had even finished talking, Ivy had turned on her heels, grabbed her coat, and headed for the front door. He thought he heard her mutter something on the way out. It sounded like the word *delusional*. Then, the door closed behind her with a slam that rattled the entire house.

George shook his head. He and Grace had never had kids, so he couldn't be sure, but he imagined that this feeling was what it felt like to live with a teenage girl. Still, he felt guilty until, that was, he looked down at the simmering pot, closed his eyes, and inhaled, allowing the herbs to waft through his sinuses and the steam to dampen his skin. Then he only felt relief and, of course, the feeling that never left him — an ache for Grace.

Soon enough, just as the house had settled back into a peaceful quiet, it was disturbed by a rapping at the front door.

"Forgot your key, did you?" he said to himself, grinning, and he looked out the window at the pouring rain. It wasn't exactly the best weather for a teenage-like storm out of the house. He walked out of the kitchen and through the living room to the front door. "I knew you'd be back," he said, swinging it open and wearing his best smug expression.

But it wasn't Ivy.

"Campbell?"

"Heya, guv," she said shyly, standing on the porch, allowing the rain to drench her. She jabbed a thumb behind her. "I saw Sergeant Hart leaving a minute ago. Sorry to bother you."

"No bother, no bother," he said. "Come in, why don't you? You're getting soaked."

"I can't be long, guv," she said, not budging. "I just...well, I needed to tell you something."

She had to speak up over the pouring of the rain, and the trickles running down her face must have been cold, but it didn't seem to bother her. The look on her face was a determined one, even more so than usual.

"Look, I know what this is," George said. "Ivy just told me. The team is lost without me," he said with a chuckle. "But you'll get used to it, I promise you. I'm just not ready, I need—"

"It's not us, guv. The team's just fine." At his raised eyebrows, she added, "I mean, we miss you, of course we do. But no..." She took a deep breath as though about to reveal something — or perhaps betray it. "It's Ivy. *She* needs you, guv." Campbell looked up at him with eyes that shone through the rain. She reached into her coat, pulled out a single Manila folder she had been protecting from the downpour, and handed it to George. "She's the one who's lost."

CHAPTER FIFTEEN

Despite having newly taken on the cooking duties of the household, which was usually Ivy's responsibility, George also kept to his old task of making the morning coffee, so by the time Ivy came downstairs and flurried into the kitchen, he was just washing out the espresso machine's filter after having made her a fresh brew.

"I'm late," she replied, checking her watch. "Oh, Christ." Then she turned to him. "Morning, guv. Look, about last night—"

"It's fine," he said with a casual wave of his hand. "Let's say no more about it."

She smiled, but something on her face lingered, a resentment or dissatisfaction of some kind.

"What's on the agenda for today then?" he asked, sitting back in his chair and watching as she flitted around the kitchen looking for her travel mug. George knew it was hidden under the multiple pots and pans on the drying rack, but he stayed silent. He was buying time.

"Find James DeSilver," she muttered, opening and closing cupboard doors. "Have you seen my travel mug?"

"No idea," he said, shrugging. "What about the women? Lily's friends?"

"What about them?"

"Well, are you going to follow up? Check their statements? Get DNA?"

Ivy slammed the cupboard door closed a little too hard. "Priority is finding DeSilver," she said. "He's our main suspect. And hopefully, Maguire and Ruby will have made progress on the third-party theory."

"Why are you so fixated on DeSilver?"

"I'm not *fixated*," she snapped, rifling through the drying rack and finally finding the travel mug. "He's the only one with an MMO, and I don't think it's a coincidence he's disappeared. I'm just following procedure."

"Remind me of his MMO again?" George said, taking a sip of his coffee.

"Have we got any bread left?" she asked, opening the bread bin.

"Sorry," he said with a grimace. "I used the breadcrumbs to top a casserole."

"Of course you did," she said, slamming it shut. She moved to the sink to wash out the mug. "He argued with Lily the night before her death," she said, answering the question. "That's his motive. He's a strong guy, by all accounts, and very able to kill someone as small as Lily. That's means. And he told the other husbands he was going to his house in the Wolds while Lily was killed, but there's no evidence of him going there. Opportunity."

"But he and Lily are old friends? That's what you said."

"I did?" she said, looking over her shoulder. "When?"

"Last night. You said he was one of the husbands and an old friend of the victim."

"Well, yeah."

"So, it's not a motive, is it? An argument? Old friends have them all the time. We should know," he said with a smile.

But Ivy ignored the friendly allusion, instead focusing on the jab at her detective skills. "It's the closest thing we have to a motive for now."

"What about the slap?" George said. "If someone had slapped Lily only hours before her death, that would indicate some kind of altercation, surely?"

"The slap?"

"Yes, that Saint identified."

"I didn't tell you about the slap, did I?"

George immediately realised his mistake. Ivy had not told him that much at all. It had been part of his late-night reading after Campbell's visit. "I'm sure you mentioned it, yes."

"When?"

"Last night, when you were telling me about the case."

Ivy stared at him for a few seconds then shrugged. "God, I probably did. Sorry, guv, I'm knackered."

"No problem," he said, swallowing. "So, will you follow it up?"

"What up?"

"The slap."

"Oh, yeah," she said. "Of course, right after we find DeSilver."

George took a big sip of coffee, allowing the liquid to burn his tongue to prevent him from spilling any more mistakes or offering more unsolicited advice. But he couldn't help himself. "I thought you wanted my input, Ivy."

"I do," she said. "I mean, I did. Last night. But this isn't the best time, guv. I'd rather find something to eat, to be honest, so I can make it to work at all."

"There's leftover ratatouille if you want it," he said, not without a hint of mischief in his tone.

"I'm good, thanks," she said, stilling moving to the fridge to check its contents.

George took another sip of coffee and decided to take a leap, perhaps catching her off-guard was the way to gather some honest information. "Have you heard from Jamie?" he asked.

Ivy laughed. "Where did that come from?"

"Just asking," he said. "You haven't mentioned him in a while."

"I'm trying to move on, guv," she said, bending to check for breakfast in the vegetable drawer. "I have to."

"I know. See, I was just thinking..." George said, watching the back of her head for any indication of a reaction to what he was about to say as she moved some Tupperware around. "What if I talked to him?"

Ivy stopped in her tracks and stared blankly into the fridge. "What?"

"Jamie. What if I talked to him?" he repeated. "You know, man to man?"

She closed the fridge door slowly and turned to face him, her voice softer as she said, "No. No, guv, you don't have to do that."

"It might help."

"It won't," she said. "Trust me. He's made up his mind. He doesn't want me back. He's made that very clear." George nodded, but Ivy wasn't convinced. "You won't talk to him, will you? It'll just make me look desperate."

"If you don't want me to," he said earnestly, "then, of course, I won't."

He couldn't remember the last time he had lied to Ivy. In fact, he wasn't sure he ever had before, but he justified it by reminding himself of one simple fact: she had lied to him first.

And clearly, she was going to continue to do so.

Ivy closed the fridge door and settled for coffee, which she poured into her takeaway mug. "I should get going."

"Of course," he said, rising from his chair in an old-fashioned gesture. "Hope it goes well."

"Thanks, guv," she said with a brief smile. Then, travel mug in hand, she left the kitchen and, in a series of identifiable sounds — coat, keys, shoes — she headed out the front door.

George sat back down and counted to two hundred after the door closed behind Ivy. Then he calmly rose from the kitchen table, cleaned his coffee mug in the sink, placed it on the dryer rack, headed to the front door, grabbed his keys and coat off the hook, and left the house, feeling some morsel of purpose for the first time in three weeks.

"God help me, Grace," he said on the porch as he pulled up his coat collar and looked down the driveway at the bend in the road, around which Ivy had only just driven, "because she is *not* going to be happy."

CHAPTER SIXTEEN

The drive from George's house to Lincoln Hospital was one Ivy was still growing accustomed to, so wildly different was it to the unperturbed stretch of coast that made up Mablethorpe or the hidden nooks of the Wolds that reminded Ivy of an old, wonky bookshop set in nature with an earthy, woody, secret to find around every corner. Instead, expansive flatlands made up the Fens. Where the sea might be in Mablethorpe, here were miles and miles of wetlands, reserves, and fields to the horizon, disturbed only by the waterways crisscrossing the grassy grounds and the deep dykes along the side of the road. While the Wolds offered her an anonymous haven, a place to hide and get back to herself amongst the comforting hills, the Fens offered perspective, a viewpoint inland towards new possibilities, and she always enjoyed driving along a road that led to somewhere new.

It was a beautiful journey, and she already felt calmer after navigating George's still chaotic, if at least cleaned, kitchen and his emotionally charged questions, the answers of which she didn't want to face so early in the morning, especially not before coffee.

Yet, even in a state of awe, one name showing up on her

buzzing phone could take it all away. She closed her eyes and took a deep breath, the way a cliff diver might before launching themselves into a rough ocean.

"Jamie," she said, pressing the green button on her phone. "What's up?"

The harshness of her tone triggered a memory of their first years together when his name on her phone had inspired fluttering in her chest. The way she had answered him then had been with soft, cooing sounds and terms of endearment. He had been *my love, dear, darling*. Never Jamie. How far they'd grown apart, how very far those days were behind them.

"You okay?" she added, trying to be better.

"Not really," he said. He'd long stopped pretending to be fine, to be coping. He wore his sorry-for-himself on his sleeve, just like his heart and just like his disappointment. "I won't be home until late tonight. I need you to watch the kids."

"Well, I can't," she said, then chewed the inside of her cheek. "Sorry."

"Why not?"

"I'm on an investigation," she said as calmly as she could. "You know how it is. Late nights, last-minute meetings."

"Oh, believe me Ivy," he said darkly, "I know how it is. But the kids need you."

"Well, where's their father going to be?"

"I told you. I won't be home until late."

"Where will you be?" she repeated, using a similar tone to the one she used during interrogations.

"Busy," he said, with such venom that she imagined that if he were in the car with her, she would have to brush his spit from her face. "I would call your mother," he said, "but you told me to stop asking her—"

"I told you to stop *relying* on her."

"So you want me to call her?"

"I want you to give me more than twelve hours' notice, Jamie."

"Look, Ivy, can you watch them or not?"

"Not," she said.

"I see," he said. "Don't know why I asked."

"George is off, Jamie," she said. "Maybe you forgot but Grace just died. He's on leave. I'm taking on his role. So—"

"Fine."

"I'm sorry, I can't just drop a murder investigation at the drop of a—"

"So what, you're trying to take George's job now?"

Ivy sucked in a breath that hurt her chest as though hit by a particularly wild wave. "Excuse me?"

"Using Grace's death to—"

"Don't you dare finish that sentence, Jamie," she growled, and the line filled with a silence in which Ivy sensed at least a little shame. "Am I thinking about my future? About the future of Theo and Hattie? Of course I am. This is my chance to show Tim what I've got so that when George *retires*," she said pointedly, "he knows I'm ready to step up."

"Don't pretend this is for them, Ivy, for the kids. It's for you. It's always for you."

"This is my chance, Jamie. Don't ruin it for me like you've ruined everything else."

"God, you're unbelievable," he cried over the phone. "What have I *ruined* for you? I gave you a house by the sea, two kids, a nice life—"

"*We*, Jamie. We did that. Not you."

"So you see us as a team now, do you? Because you sure have a funny way of—"

"Is it a date?" she asked suddenly. The Fens passed by in a blur, and Ivy checked her speedometer. She was way over the limit, her foot pressed down to the floor as though her entire body had locked in place. But she didn't slow down.

"What?"

"Tonight. Are you going on a date?"

"What business of that is yours?"

"We're *married*, Jamie."

"You really are ridiculous, Ivy. We're separated."

"So what's she like?"

"Who?"

"Your date?"

"Oh, right, my fake date, my date concocted from your paranoid imagination?"

"Blonde, long legs, big up top. That's your type, isn't it, Jamie?"

"It *was*," he said and scoffed but held the harshest, most obvious insult on his tongue, perhaps saving it for an even darker moment sometime in their future. "If you must know, I'm meeting my lawyer."

"What?"

"My lawyer. My divorce lawyer, Ivy."

"You're meeting your lawyer for dinner?"

"Believe it or not, you're not the only one with a job. I'm at work all day. I only have time in the evenings. You know, somewhere between bringing home money for my kids and feeding, bathing, and putting them to sleep."

"Well, you know what, Jamie, no," Ivy said, easing off the accelerator only because the turn to Lincoln Hospital was coming up soon. "I don't think I will come and watch our children while you're deciding with your lawyer how best to take them away from me."

"Oh, please, Ivy. I don't need to decide that. You decided it for yourself," he said, his voice breaking at the end, and he hung up. It was all she could do to keep her eyes on the road, but her tears blurred the city ahead and the other cars. Whether they were tears of anger or sadness, she could not be sure.

Still, she knew the turning into Lincoln Hospital well enough by now to take it smoothly even when her sight was compromised, and she pulled into the car park, found a space, and turned off the engine. She brushed away the mascara lines under her eyes as though they were no more inconvenient than a rogue fly on her face and climbed out of the car.

It was the last thing she needed, she thought, as she approached the double sliding doors to face the people in Pip's mortuary, dead or otherwise. But as she navigated the hospital and started down the long, windowed corridor towards the morgue, her eyes dried, and her heart settled. She was on the job, and the job gave her a focus like nothing else in life. It provided a purpose stronger than motherhood or being a wife or a friend.

It was life and death, she thought, as she pressed the buzzer to the mortuary, and it demanded her attention.

"Ivy?" Pip asked as the door swung open. Doctor Pippa Bell was a force to be reckoned with. As the county's leading forensic pathologist, her reputation was without flaw. But as an individual, she had earned the nickname, the Welsh dragon, with the ability to make the brightest of detectives question their abilities. She was in full pathologist attire — scrubs, latex gloves, mask and all. But even beneath a hairnet, strands of her bright orange hair peeked through. It was not a subtle orange, not the orange of a sunset or a cinnamon roll. It was a bright, garish orange, the colour of a traffic cone.

"Yes," Ivy said slowly. "Why? Were you expecting someone else?"

Pip grinned but didn't answer the question. She held the door open for Ivy to enter. "Full PPE," she said, nodding to the inbuilt cupboards. "You know the drill."

Pip entered the morgue and left Ivy to pull herself into the papery scrubs, hairnet, and shoe covers. As she got ready, her heart fluttered with nerves. She had never had to do this alone. She'd always had George to lean on, quite literally sometimes, when she felt faint at the sight of a corpse. He usually took the lead while she offered comments from the corner, there but just barely containing her nausea.

Still, it was her job, and she would continue to do it while she could still stand.

She pushed open the door to the morgue, and suddenly, Pip's strange welcome made sense, the surprise at Ivy's presence and the knowingness of her grin. For once, Ivy had no problem walking into the middle of the room because her attention was far from the dead body lying on a gurney to Pip's right and much more focused on the live one to Pip's left.

"Guv?" she said, looking George up and down. Beneath his PPE, he was in his work outfit — a smart, white shirt under a woollen vest with an earthy-coloured tie and no baked bean stain on his sleeve. He'd shaved, too, his face no longer stubbly with a sign to the world that he had no wife to hold him accountable anymore. "What are you doing here?"

George turned from his conversation with Pip to welcome Ivy with his most pleasant smile. "Ivy," he said as though they were acquaintances passing on the street.

"I thought you weren't ready to come back?"

"So did I," he replied, shaking his head humbly. "So did I."

CHAPTER SEVENTEEN

"What about needing time?" Ivy muttered, walking around Pip so that she and George stood on either side of Lily Hughes's body. "About having space to grieve?"

"I thought about what you said," he replied over the gurney as though Lily was no more than a car bonnet. "About the team needing me."

"We do," she said. "I mean, they do. But a heads-up would've been nice." She felt blindsided, ambushed, left in the dark — but why? "Why didn't you tell me this morning?"

He shrugged but didn't meet her eye. "I didn't know this morning."

She eyed his pressed shirt and shaved face, the look of a man who had woken up prepared for his day ahead. "Sorry, guv, but I find that hard to—"

"Not to disturb your little domestic," Pip said from the foot of the gurney, her Welsh accent belying the meaning behind the statement, "but I have a job to do and don't have all day." She nodded down at Lily Hughes. "Maybe you can save your disputes for somewhere other than over a recently deceased. Not exactly respectful, is it?"

George nodded solemnly. "You're right," he said and seemed to genuinely catch himself out on his behaviour, looking down at Lily and perhaps imagining somebody acting in such a way over Grace's body. "Sorry, Doctor Bell."

"Sorry," Ivy muttered.

But she couldn't bear to bring herself to look down at Lily. She would never usually stand so close to the body, but she felt a stronger need to prove herself than usual. She kept her gaze locked instead on a plug socket on the opposite wall the same way a twirling ballet dancer might practice spotting to stop their head from spinning.

"As I was just telling George..." Pip stared, and Ivy felt a wave of irritation. She had been the one to arrange the briefing with Pip and yet it had started without her. "The most obvious cause of death on initial examination is a broken neck." Pip's hand moved in Ivy's peripheral to gesture, no doubt, to Lily's twisted neck. "But on closer examination, her neck was broken after she was killed."

"How do you know?" Ivy asked, more to distract herself by talking than anything else.

"Blood vessels in the eyes, bruising on her neck, and a broken trachea," Pip said simply. "The finger marks are quite evident."

"I thought the killer was wearing gloves?" Ivy asked. "That's what Saint said."

"Finger *marks*," Pip reiterated. "Not prints. The killer *was* wearing gloves, but even so, it takes a lot to strangle somebody, Sergeant Hart, physical strength as well as emotional. The killer had to not only strangle Lily but force her to succumb. She would have struggled. That much is clear."

Again, Pip's hand moved to the edge of Ivy's vision, pointing at a particular mark or set of marks on Lily's neck.

"Adrenaline would have been pumping, giving her a surge in resistance. Now, if the victim was already vulnerable, say unconscious or tied down, it could take a minute, maybe a little more.

But in this case, I'd say it was minutes. If she was struggling, it would have been harder for the killer to press against the carotid arteries and evenly compress the windpipe."

"And that's necessary, is it?"

"Very," Pip said. "You don't just take hold and squeeze. Not if you really want to kill someone. You have to know what you're doing." She looked between the two detectives and then settled on Ivy. "Come here, Ivy."

"Why me?" she said, knowing what was coming.

"It was a tough choice, I won't lie," Pip said, rolling up her sleeves. "You look like you're about to pass out, but he..." She nodded at George. "He looks like he's just woken up or not gone to sleep. One of the two." At this, George actually snorted out a laugh.

"Great," Ivy said, stepping closer to the pathologist, who turned her around and stepped up close behind her.

"Now I'd say the killer used a combination of both compression of the carotid arteries and the trachea. The carotid arteries run along either side of your neck. Here," she said.

Pip stroked from just below Ivy's ear down to her collarbone, and Ivy squirmed at the intimacy.

"Applied pressure to both sides of the neck like this," she continued, placing her fingers gently on either side of Ivy's neck, "will stop blood flow to the brain, cutting off the oxygen supply and resulting in hypoxia. While this can lead to unconsciousness and brain damage, the killer *intended to kill* Lily, which is why they also applied pressure to the windpipe."

Pip stroked the middle of Ivy's throat, from just below her chin down to the top button of her shirt. Once more, Ivy winced. She couldn't remember the last time someone had touched her neck.

"This is the windpipe. When it's compressed," Pip said, stretching her fingers around Ivy's throat so that they pressed lightly into the front, "organs shut down as the body is starved of oxygen. This led to Lily's death, I'd say within three to four minutes."

They stayed in position for a few seconds longer — Pip with her fingers closed around Ivy's neck, Ivy standing at her mercy until she spoke up. "Are we done?"

"For now," Pip said with a wink at which Ivy rolled her eyes.

"So the killer knew what they were doing?" asked George. "As in, they had done it before?"

"Possibly," Pip said, shrugging. "Or they simply looked it up online beforehand."

"But there's a big difference," George said, "between researching and actually carrying it out."

"Oh, don't get me wrong, they were committed," Pip said. "It looks like they didn't hold back. They had a window, and they used it. The fog had obstructed the view of any witnesses for... how long did you say?"

"Five minutes," Ivy said. "Lily's friends estimated five minutes at the most."

"Then they did it in no more than four," Pip said, "leaving a minute to come and go." She whistled. "It's close. It was a risk. As soon as the fog lifted, they could be seen. I'd say they were desperate. There are easier ways to kill someone. Slower. Less easily detected ways. But for whatever reason, Lily Hughes *had* to die that morning at the first opportunity that presented itself."

Ivy and George allowed this analysis to settle.

"You'd do alright as a detective, Pip. You know that?" George said eventually.

"I'll leave that to the professionals, thanks, George."

Ivy stole a glance at Lily's body. Just one second was enough time to cause a wave of dizziness and for her to notice that the red mark on the woman's cheek had faded. "Saint said she'd been slapped," she said quickly, preferring to omit the banter if it meant leaving the morgue earlier. Her legs were starting to shake. "There were broken blood vessels when we found her."

"That's right," Pip said. "I read Doctor Saint's statement, but by the time I got her, the signs were far more subtle. Of course, I picked up on it..." she said, never one to hide her talents under a bushel. "I can tell you, though, it was a hell of a slap. The skin was traumatised, but it never had the chance to develop into a bruise. Her blood stopped circulating long before that."

She pointed at Lily Hughes as she spoke, but Ivy couldn't bear to follow her gestures.

"What about toxicology?" she said, staring once more at her trusty plug socket.

Pip picked up on the urgency. "A routine drug screen noticed the presence of Fluoxetine, which is—"

"Antidepressants," George and Ivy said at the same time.

They met each other's eyes, ignoring the sarcastic comment that clearly hung on Pip's lips.

"And Estradiol," Pip continued without comment. "Which is a...." She looked between the two detectives. "Anyone?"

But Ivy and George looked at each other, then shrugged.

"An HRT. Hormone Replacement Therapy," she said. "Boosts oestrogen levels. For menopause," Pip said. "Popular in women this age. In fact, these two drugs are often taken together."

"What about alcohol?" Ivy asked, starting to feel a build-up of saliva in her mouth, the tell-tale sign that she was running out of time. "By all accounts, their group are big drinkers."

"0.08% BAC," Pip said knowingly.

"She was still intoxicated?"

"Alcohol was still in her system, yes. Must have been a big night out the night before."

"What about the time of death?"

"Well, once more, Saint's estimation was accurate. She'd been dead less than an hour when he saw her, and my examination says the same. The difference in body temperature between Doctor Saint's examination and mine, along with the progress of rigor mortis, would suggest she died sometime between ten and twelve yesterday."

"Matches the witness statements," Ivy said. "They said the fog got heavier around eleven when they were all split up."

"What do you mean, the fog got heavier?"

"Well, it was foggy, but then it grew thicker for a while. Like a heavy cloud rolled in or something."

It was hard not to look at Lily when she spoke, hard not to imagine what she had endured, but the effects of her empathy drove her bout of nausea home. Ivy grabbed the metal handle of the gurney to stop herself from falling, so overcome and light-headed was she. The gurney rattled as she pressed her weight onto it. Her vision transformed into a series of waves, and even when she shook her head, she couldn't find a focus. It was all she could do not to let her knees buckle beneath her.

"Let's not take the dead down with you, Ivy, eh?" Pip said, calmly moving closer to grab Ivy's elbow and remove Ivy's weight from the gurney. "She's been through enough."

George looked on with his stoic stare. "You alright?" he asked.

"I'm fine," Ivy lied, her mouth thick with saliva. "What about DNA analysis?" she asked quickly.

"I've swabbed her for DNA and sent it to the lab already," Pip said. "You should get the results today. That is if Katy has anything to match it to. I only saw one sample in the report."

"Don't worry. That DNA belongs to James DeSilver," Ivy said, gently removing herself from Pip's grip, forcing herself to stand straight, and heading for the door. "I'm certain of it."

CHAPTER EIGHTEEN

"I thought you wanted me to come back?" George called after Ivy, who stormed across the hospital car park. Whether she was running for the promise of sitting down in a cool car far away from a dead body or because she was angry, George couldn't be sure, though he imagined it was a combination of both.

"I did," she said once they reached her car. "I do. But why didn't you just tell me? I felt ambushed. Like you and Pip knew something I didn't. If I'm running this investigation guv, I need to know. And if I'm not, I need to know that too. Either way."

He settled beside her, leaning on the car and craning his neck to check that colour was returning to her cheeks. "You've got the lead on this one, Ivy," he said. "I'm just catching up."

"So why didn't you tell me this morning you'd be here?"

"I didn't know," he said. "Really. But I thought..."

Ivy opened the car door, left it open, and sat down in the driver's seat as though her legs hadn't yet recovered. "You thought what, guv?"

He climbed into the passenger seat and made himself comfortable.

"Honestly?"

"Honestly."

"I thought you'd want the support," he said. "You know what Pip's like."

"Translation," Ivy said. "You didn't think I could do the post-mortem on my own."

"I mean..."

"Well, thanks a lot, guv."

"Come on, Ivy, you could barely look at the victim. You almost wiped out and brought her down with you."

"So that *is* what you're saying. That I can't handle the job?"

"No," George said, "I'm saying we both have our strengths." He smiled. "And our weaknesses. We work better as a team, don't you think?"

"Yes, guv," she said, "that is what I think. Which is why I asked you to come back yesterday morning."

"And you were right," George said, nodding. "I should have."

"So what changed?"

He performed his best nonchalant shrug. "I listened to what you said. About the team needing me. And you're right. It's where I belong, in that incident room, out in the real world, doing a real, meaningful job. Not locked up at home cooking... What was it again? Terrible recipes with too much salt?"

"Outdated," she said with a grin. "Not terrible. The ratatouille was pretty good in the end." At his raised eyebrows, she explained, "I tried some when I got back last night."

"I thought there was some missing," he said, sharing her smile.

"So that's it?" she said. "Just an overnight change of heart? And now you're back?"

"That's it," he said.

He sure as hell wasn't going to mention Campbell turning up on his doorstep, handing him a copy of the case file, and telling him that Ivy was lost without him. It would do nothing for the team morale. And it would do nothing for Ivy's self-confidence.

"So, what do we do now?" she said.

"I follow your lead," he said. "What was the plan for today?"

"To find James DeSilver," she said simply.

"Then let's do that."

Ivy breathed in and out as though her racing heart might have settled back to normal, and George was glad to see that a little colour had returned to her cheeks. "Let's call the team. If Pip's analysis told us anything, it's that James took the opportunity to kill Lily as soon as he could, which means he was waiting for it, which means he was following them all morning, waiting for the perfect moment to get Lily alone."

"Sure," George said slowly and added quietly, "unless it wasn't James DeSilver."

"I thought you were following my lead?" Ivy snapped.

George held up his hands. "I am. I just think it's too soon to narrow our focus to one suspect. *Four women* were there with Lily. All unaccounted for. Any one of them could've been waiting for the right moment to get her alone, as you say."

"This is *your* style, guv, *your* way of doing things. To form a narrative. To see where it gets us and what evidence it brings."

"Right, and I'm flattered," he said jokingly, holding a hand to his heart. But Ivy was in no mood for jokes. "But that's not to say that we should dismiss any other lead."

"I respect that, I do," she said. "But do I have the reins or not?"

George held his hands up as though letting go of the reins, and Ivy took out her phone to call the team. As usual, she answered within seconds.

"Campbell, it's Ivy," she said, then looked up at George. "The guv is here too."

"Guv?" she said.

"Morning, Campbell," he replied over the loudspeaker.

"Welcome back," she said. "It's nice to hear your voice." But George didn't return the compliment, noticing Ivy's clenched jaw as she no doubt interpreted the relief in Campbell's voice as a personal slight on her leadership. "Sarge, I've been looking into DeSilver, like you asked," she said, efficiently filling the tense silence. "But nothing of note. He hasn't used any cards in the last twenty-four hours or made any ATM withdrawals. He hasn't sent or received any more messages, other than from his wife, although he did receive five missed calls from the same unregistered phone he'd texted just before he went missing. In the days before, all his messages were in the group chat about what time to meet for breakfast, et cetera. But I did find a text sent to James from Lily. It was sent early Tuesday morning, but he'd deleted it."

"Something dirty?" asked Ivy.

"Possibly," Campbell replied. "But there's no way of knowing what it said."

"What about him as a person?" Ivy asked. "Bank records, criminal history, anything?"

"No criminal charges. I can request a warrant to look at his bank records, though?"

"Do it."

"Yes, sarge."

"Good. What about the scope of his house and work? Did Byrne... You know what? Gather the team round, would you, Campbell? I'd like to hear from all of them."

"Yes, sarge," she replied, and after a minute or so of muffled voices, squeaking chairs, and rumbles from the other end of the line, Campbell picked up the receiver once more and said, "We're here guv."

"Ivy's leading this one," George reminded Campbell. "I'm just catching up."

"Sorry, guv, I mean sarge."

"Byrne," Ivy said, ignoring the detour, "did you hear back from the officer who went to the DeSilver house?"

"Yes, sarge," came his voice over the phone. "He wasn't there, which figures. No sign of any disturbance either."

"And his workplace?"

"Same thing. No sign of DeSilver or anything suspicious. He has an office there but none of his employees have seen him since Friday. They said he was on holiday until next week."

"Where's Maguire?" Ivy asked.

"Here, sarge," came his rough yet melodic accent.

"Did you follow the dead ends and driveways off Spring View Road? Any sign of DeSilver?"

"Nothing, sarge," he said spiritlessly, "no signs of a black Audi A4, and nobody remembers seeing anything. There's only a handful of turnings, mostly driveways to houses far back off the road and a few leading to farmer's gates. There's plenty of fields and some woodland beyond that, but we'd need a whole search party to—"

"Never mind that," she snapped, clearly frustrated by the dead end and unafraid to make her frustrations clear to the team. "What about the neighbours on Caistor Lane? Did you find any footage of the car that drove past before Lily was killed?"

"Aye, I got doorbell footage from a few houses down from Mr Evans, and I've been looking through them this morning. I can't identify the car. Sorry, sarge. It's too far away from the doorstep. But I see it go past at exactly eleven."

"What colour is it?" George asked over Ivy's shoulder.

"Guv?" Byrne said his voice higher than Maguire's and more excitable. "Is that you?"

"Hello, Byrne," George said with a smile, as though the team could see him through the phone. "I'm just catching up on the investigation," he added, eying Ivy.

"Well, good to have you back," Byrne said, and George waited for Ivy to continue the phone call.

"Maguire, answer the question," she said.

"I'm not able to give a definite colour, but it was dark. I'd guess a black saloon."

"Okay, keep looking at the footage," Ivy said. "I want to know when that car reaches the main road. And keep trying to identify the colour, even the number plate if possible."

"The car doesn't reach the main road, sarge."

"It's still there?"

"Or it turns off the main road before it reaches the next camera. You know what the Wolds are like. We're not in the middle of the city. Cameras are scarce out here."

"Well, get any footage from other nearby roads. Speed cameras, whatever you can. Again, try to identify the number plate. Ruby, can you help with that, please?"

But she was met with only silence on the other end of the line.

"Ruby?" Ivy repeated.

Nobody replied, and amongst the silence that lingered, George imagined them all sharing anxious glances, neither one wanting to tell Ivy the truth that Byrne eventually shared.

"She's not here, sarge."

"Where the hell is she?"

"Well..." He cleared his throat, and then admitted, "I have no idea."

CHAPTER NINETEEN

"It's no secret," Campbell said quickly. "She's just working from home today."

"And who authorised that?" Ivy asked, her voice tight.

"It's in her contract, sarge. I'm pretty sure DCI Long authorised it originally."

Ivy met George's stare as though O'Hara had proven her point.

"Fine," she said eventually. "Call her. Tell her to help you with this, Maguire."

"Yes, sarge," he said.

"She did send over a report early this morning," Campbell said in defence of her colleague. "She's doing a bit of background work on DeSilver and the rest of the group. She said she might have a couple of lines of enquiry."

"Fine," Ivy said, unwilling to praise Ruby's hard work if done at a distance. "Is she following up on them?"

"Yes, sarge, I believe so." Ivy went to speak, but before she could, Campbell continued to offer accolades. "I also sent her the G0247 data to see if she could correlate anything I couldn't. But it's useless. All their locations jump around depending on whether they have a signal or not, and the men have clearly turned theirs off altogether."

"Probably don't want their wives to see them sitting in the pub all day while they're out hiking in the fog," Maguire said.

"Exactly. We can't take much from it, sarge."

"Just great," she said, to George's surprise, and he imagined Campbell slumping in her chair. It wasn't her fault Ruby was at home. "O'Hara?"

"Yes, sarge?"

"How's the map going?"

"It's already up, sarge, next to the whiteboard. I've already marked the places they stayed over the last five days, and I'm just marking their route from the morning before Lily's death."

Ivy looked at George, and he nodded back. He was impressed. They seemed to have been getting on productively enough without him, although by the sounds of it, productivity wasn't Campbell's reason for asking him back.

"Very good," Ivy said tersely, her tone immediately undermining the praise in her words. "Now, I'd like to go over Pip's report. Are you all ready?"

"Yes, sarge," came a symphony of accents over the phone, most punctuated by Maguire's and O'Hara's, the only ones that were not local and stood out like the deep timber of a cello in a string piece.

"She identified the cause of death as asphyxiation from pressure on Lily's windpipe. Not a broken neck."

"Okay," Campbell said, her voice growing smaller as though she was walking away from her desk. "To be expected, from Katy's analysis, no?"

"Right. And, alongside the alcohol, there were two lots of pills in her system. Fluoxetine and estradiol: treatments for depression and menopause respectively."

"Again, that figures," came Campbell's voice, now distant from the phone. "She was fifty-six and recently widowed."

All of a sudden, an ache pulled at George's chest in the same unexpected way the ocean withdrew before a tsunami. The mention of the word *widow* hit George like a heavy wave, not so much because it reminded him of Grace — she existed in the forefront of his mind anyway — but because he knew that whenever a dead spouse was brought up, the team would pity him. He could see it now in Ivy's eyes as she avoided looking his way.

"What about the time of death?" came Campbell's distant voice, and George realised she was standing at the whiteboard, making notes, taking over from Ivy, who had taken over from George.

"Doctor Saint's analysis was accurate," Ivy answered. "Late morning."

"Fits the witness statements," Byrne said.

"And the timing of the car that went past Mr Evans's house," Maguire added.

"Good," Ivy said, "things are starting to make sense. Pip said she'd sent DNA swabs to the lab already, so they should be in touch today. Be ready. I want to know as soon as Katy makes the connection to DeSilver."

"Sarge," Campbell began slowly, "should we take DNA samples from the friends?" From the tone of her voice, George could tell that Campbell knew it was a sensitive topic. She spoke tentatively as if the question had already been asked. "Just so we have more DNA, something to compare the results to."

"I told you," Ivy said, her voice calm with only a slight tremor of frustration. "Once we have found James DeSilver, then we'll see where we are."

George took a breath, and then took the moment he'd been waiting for.

"Hold on," he said, ignoring Ivy repositioning herself to glare at him. "That's not a bad idea—"

"They're grieving, guv."

"So we'll need to show some sensitivity."

"We risk getting their backs up at a time when we need all the help we can get. I get that we will eventually need to take it for the purposes of elimination and to provide a full investigation for the CPS, but—"

"We can at least start the process of elimination while we look for DeSilver. And maybe we can get an idea of who slapped Lily yesterday morning. You heard what Pip said. There was a struggle. The killer had to exert physical energy. It's possible they left DNA traces, sweat, spit perhaps. I think we should go for it - sensitively."

"Every minute we waste on other lines of investigation, the further we get from finding DeSilver, allowing him to get further and further from the area," she said to George, then turned back to speak clearly into the phone. "I want all hands on finding him. Do you hear me?"

"Ivy, it will take less than a few hours," George pushed. "This is the whole point of having a bigger team." He moved closer to the phone, making a bold choice. "Campbell, I want you on it. Be tactful. Everyone else, focus on James DeSilver."

Confronted with two different sets of instructions, Campbell remained quiet for perhaps ten seconds as though weighing up her options, hearing the two voices on the end of the line and deciding which instructions to follow. In the end, she seemed to go for the voice that held the higher rank.

"Yes, guv," she said, looking for some kind of acknowledgment from Ivy but received none. "I'll get onto it."

A terrible silence followed, and then Byrne cleared his throat.

"Right then," he said. "Let's erm...let's go on with it, eh?"

Ivy ended the call, sat back in her seat and turned away from George to stare out of the window.

"What was that?" she asked.

"That was following process, Ivy, that's all," he said.

"How the bloody hell are they supposed to do as I ask, if you step in and override my decisions?"

"We need the DNA, Ivy."

"I know, but now? Now? When our lead suspect is still missing, and the only witnesses we have are all grieving. You speak of tact and sensitivity, guv, and I get that. But timing, timing is crucial. I've got limited resources, and my primary suspect is missing. I can't afford to lose twenty per cent of my team to an errand we can conduct at a later stage, and I can't afford to...to piss the witnesses off."

He wondered how much of the outburst was genuinely fuelled by his intervention and how much was a result of the challenges she was facing personally. A good boss would have sought to understand, but a good friend would let the layers peel away and be there when the root of the problem is aired.

"You're putting too much on James DeSilver," he said.

"Guv, are you actually back?"

"Sorry?"

"Are you back officially, or have you just come to check up on me?"

"Ivy, you are more than capable—"

"I'm not referring to my competence. I'm referring to my state of mind."

"You're going through a lot."

"I'm going through a divorce. I'm not burying my husband," she said, then exhaled to control herself. "Sorry, that's low."

"It's fine," he said. "I supposed I deserved it."

"Guv," she said as if struggling to find the words. "Guv, get some sleep. Don't cook. Don't work on the house. Just... just sleep."

"I don't need to—"

"DCI Long told you to get your head together, guv," she said a little harsher, shaking her head as if battling conflicting feelings. "Just go home."

CHAPTER TWENTY

When George pulled up in front of the police cordon on Caistor Lane, he imagined he was seeing the scene for the first time, even though he had pictured it a hundred times in his mind already that morning. The previous night, he had spent rifling through photos, staying up into the dark hours, studying each image. Of course, he had been spending most nights like that in the last three weeks, rummaging through shoe boxes for old 35mm film prints taken with Grace's point-and-shoot camera and analysing each one — the curls of her hair on their wedding day, the blue of the sea on their honeymoon, the look of unadulterated joy on his own face. But last night had been the first night he hadn't spent lost in his memories.

Although he had spent it lost in CSI documentation.

He'd studied the site of Lily Hughes's death so meticulously that he already knew it inside and out. He'd even walked down this very road in his dreams once he'd finally fallen asleep. Still, he wanted a fresh perspective, and for that, he needed to pretend he'd never been here before. Not even in his imagination.

George grabbed the manila folder in the passenger seat and climbed out of his car. There was a single unlucky constable on duty. He rubbed his hands with the cold and blew into them, eying George as though excited for the promise of an interaction.

"Now then," he said as George approached.

"Morning," George replied brightly. He showed his warrant card to the officer, who nodded him through with only a glance at his face and lifted the police tape for him to duck beneath. It seemed that, after three months, he and Ivy were finally getting recognised in the Wolds. "Anyone been through?"

"Nothing," the officer said. "Not even a dog walker. Seems like a quiet road."

"Sure," George said. "Or people are avoiding it."

With that, he smiled at the officer and walked further down the tarmac.

The scene looked just as it had in the photos — a quiet country lane with a hiking path on the left and a steep, forested drop to the right. He walked to the first little yellow tag and saw that Katy and her team had left it in the middle of the road. He checked the notes in the folder. *Signs of a struggle*, it said, and George bent down to inspect the scuff marks on the tarmac. If there were signs of a struggle, they were no more discernible than on the mud on the road. As usual, he would place his trust in Southwell's judgement.

Like a studious reader, Campbell had scribbled handwritten notes in the margins of the report as though analysing a poem. On this photo, she'd drawn an arrow to a tree at the back of the picture and written, *Marie Entwhistle found here (five metres)*. He studied the image for some kind of missed detail but to no avail. Between where he stood beside Katy's yellow tag and the tree beside the hiking path, it did indeed seem to be five metres.

Certainly close enough to attack Lily. And certainly close enough to notice a struggle, George thought.

Surely?

He walked over to the drop at the side of the road. It was a sheer slope that started quite suddenly, and George admired the fearless drivers who drove regularly alongside it. However, he knew only too well that it was exactly because of precarious road-side drops like these that around sixty per cent of fatal car accidents occurred in rural areas. Beside a slip mark that even George could see was out of place was another of Katy's yellow tags, clearly identifying where Lily had fallen.

Planting his feet firmly on the ground, he leaned over to look down the slope. The steep fall dizzied him and stirred a feeling akin to dread in his chest, just as it had, no doubt, inspired the same dread in Lily Hughes when she had been thrown over its threshold. There was only one thing for it. He had to, rather without dignity, lower himself to a sitting position and scoot down the hill. It was the only way.

"Lord help us," he muttered to himself as he shimmied down the slope.

He wondered what Ivy would think if she could see him now. Her instructions had been very clear — *Go home, guv*. And yet here he was, scooting down a slope on his own.

"Go home, guv," he heard her say,

Those three words had held a multitude of messages: *You're confusing the order of things. You're undermining my authority within the team. You're not ready to come back.*

There was nothing for him at home but empty walls at which to stare and become lost in a slideshow of memories. No, his time would be better served being productive. But surely there were less arduous ways of doing so.

Descending a steep hill in leather-soled shoes without breaking a limb required his utmost concentration. The ground was sodden and slippery from the downfall, so by the time he reached the bottom of the slope, he already knew it had been a waste of time. Whatever evidence had remained in the soil where Lily Hughes's body had lain, whatever hair traces and blood spots Katy had managed to notice in her eagle-eyed expertise, had been washed away by the rain. All that remained was an ominous puddle of water that reflected the spectral branches above like the dusty glass of an old mirror.

He caught his breath and looked between the soil and the evidence in the folder. How the team had jumped from the scene and evidence before his eyes to their current main suspect was a mystery to him. All they had to go on were scuff marks and the tall tales of old — and therefore biased — friends. Yet Ivy seemed so very determined in her approach. It was as though she had a personal vendetta against the suspect, or more likely, a personal vendetta against her own faults, a determination to prove herself, whatever the cost.

George looked up the slope that had led him to nothing but a muddy-watered dead end. He took a deep breath and then began his ascent, hoping for clarity, as any person does when they climb uphill, whether a mountain or a garden slope.

He focused on the tasks at hand. The immediate task was the slope, followed by the investigation. But the underlying task was finding a way to fill the gap that Grace had left in his heart. He mused on the fact that each of those tasks required a similar technique: put one step in front of the other and don't look back.

By the time he had crested the slope, reached his car, and sat inside, unsure where to go next, George found that for all that was unclear, he had only one very clear thought in his mind, a resolution that grew stronger and stronger the more he considered it. Ivy was wrong to focus entirely on James DeSilver. The question was, how could he change her mind when it was as fragile as his own?

CHAPTER TWENTY-ONE

The day was overcast but mild, a typical spring day. The previous day's rain still hung in the air in a light haze-like spray emanating from a waterfall, cold and damp enough to cause a chill to run down Campbell's spine. She stood outside the final yurt, watching the canvas lift slightly in the breeze, collecting herself. Gathering the DNA from the first three women had not been difficult, although each experience had its disarming elements. Still, from her brief interaction with the fourth friend of Lily Hughes at the crime scene, Campbell had a feeling this one was going to be trickier.

Even though they were only holiday lets, each yurt seemed to have taken on the distinct personality of its occupants, at least in Campbell's mind.

The Adams' yurt had felt like a family room, even though they were holidaying without their children. It was as though they felt most at home in a slight state of chaos. Their suitcases had been open and overspilled with the amount of clothes necessary for three weeks away, not one, and empty Coke cans, sweet wrappers, and loose toiletries littered the few sideboards beside abandoned shoes kicked to the sides of the room. The bed was unmade and in disarray, as though young feet had recently been trampling and jumping all over it.

They had both given their DNA freely to Campbell, who decided it best to get Bob's too, if he was willing. Cecelia had been on a video call with her children. She had not even ended it as Ivy ran a cotton swab along the inside of her cheek. Their young voices had shrieked at the sight of it over the phone, and this appeared to relax Cecelia in some strange way Campbell could not relate to. Both Cecelia and her husband seemed to want the process to be finished as quickly as possible so they could return to their family.

Once Campbell had placed both their swabs in separate sterile containers, she had moved on to the next yurt.

In contrast, Marie and Toby Entwhistle's room was neat and orderly, with the lighting on low, candles and incense lit, as though they were making the most of their extended holiday. When Ivy knocked on their door, and they invited her to enter, she witnessed them tangled in each other's arms in bed, fully dressed, as though she'd caught them exchanging sweet nothings. That wasn't to say that they didn't seem traumatised by their friend's death. Their eyes were wet with tears, and Campbell guessed they had been sharing their grief in some kind of quiet, loving ritual.

They, too, offered their DNA freely, as though happy to help. In fact, that was exactly what they had said to her.

"We're happy to help. Is there anything else we can do?" Marie had asked.

"For now, no," Campbell had replied. She held up their swabs, which she had packaged in small plastic bags. "But this will help us move forward in our investigation."

But that had seemed to do little to ease their tensions. They looked at each other with concerned stares, and for a moment, they reminded Campbell of two lambs caught in fresh snowfall, so pure and innocent were their interactions. She tried to remember the feeling of being newly in love, how it softened the world and made life seem precious. But again, she struggled to relate to their behaviour, and her cynical mind was yet to be convinced of its sincerity.

"If you could just stay put for now," Campbell said, dampening their helpful spirits and reminding them that they were, in fact, suspects. "We'll be in touch."

With that, she had left and headed to the DeSilver's tent, which bristled with uncertainty. When Campbell entered, Franky was pacing back and forth as though overwhelmed at the space available in a room designed for two people but held only one.

"Have you heard anything?" she cried, rushing forward as soon as Campbell entered. "Have you heard from my husband?"

"I'm afraid not," Campbell said, explaining that she was merely there to collect DNA to help with the investigation and that Franky would know if and when they received news of James.

"Let me go home," she said. "Please. That's where I should be waiting. That's where he'll go."

"You are not a prisoner here, Mrs DeSilver," Campbell reminded her. "But we are currently investigating the murder of your friend, and it helps our investigation if you stay in one place." As though reinstating her point, she led the restless woman over to the bed and sat her down on the end of it. "For Lily," she finished.

"For Lily," Franky repeated, then her face crumbled like dry soil, and she wept into Campbell's shoulder. Such intimate forms of comfort were not particularly encouraged in the force, but she considered it a means to an end. Only ten minutes later, when Franky had stopped sobbing, could Campbell conduct the necessary buccal swab and make her escape.

And still, Campbell remained outside the fourth yurt, gathering her senses. Only after a deep breath did she knock on the wooden pole that held up the canvas door and was told to enter. Immediately, she was met with an icy welcome.

"Do you realise that it is against our human rights to keep us locked up in here?" Violet said.

She stood in the middle of the room with her arms crossed, wearing a dark expression, as though Campbell was precisely the person she had been expecting but the last person in the world she wanted to see.

"Nobody is keeping you locked up," Campbell reminded her. "You are free to go, but we do ask that you aid us in our investigation. You could find another hotel. We just ask that you stay local."

"How long for?"

"Well, that depends on—"

"Will you be reimbursing us?"

"I don't—"

"Do you know how much it costs a night to stay here?"

"I'm not in a position to make financial decisions," Campbell said. "But I would've thought you would want the best for your sister-in-law, Miss Hughes?"

"How dare you," she spat, her youthful face scrunched into an ugly snarl. "Of course, I want the best for Lily. But keeping us locked up here isn't going to bring her back."

"Well, if you truly want the best for Lily, for her killer to be brought to justice, then I'm sure you understand the need to stay local."

Violet didn't reply directly, but the snarl on her face remained. "I want an update. It's my right."

"Actually, Miss Hughes," Campbell said, growing tired of the tirade of emotions she'd already faced that morning, "it isn't. We do not have to update you about the case if we—"

"I'm a relative of Lily's, that gives me the right to—"

"It gives you no such right at all. We are not obliged to provide any updates to relatives, especially if it might affect the integrity of the investigation or a suspect's legal rights."

It was all Violet could do to gape silently before whispering, "A suspect's legal rights?"

"Yes," Campbell confirmed. "Like the presumption of innocence."

But she knew that was not what Violet was asking. The young, purple-haired woman continued to gape at her. "I'm a suspect?"

"Yes, Miss Hughes," Campbell said, pulling out a new swab packet. "Until we can eliminate you, you all are. Now..." she continued, pulling on a fresh pair of latex gloves. "I'm here to collect your DNA. Just a basic cheek swab. Open up." Violet didn't move. "If you wouldn't mind," Campbell said, moving forward with the swab.

"Actually, I do mind," Violet said, stepping backwards, a horrified look on her face.

"It doesn't hurt."

She rolled her eyes. "It's invasive."

"I'm sure you got used to it in the pandemic, Miss Hughes, and I promise it's far less invasive than—"

"Do you have a warrant?"

Campbell hesitated but could not lie. "No."

"Then you do *not* have my permission to stick that in my mouth," Violet said loudly, pointing her finger. "Do you hear me?"

"I'm not doing this for fun," Campbell said. "It is to further our investigation, to find justice for Lily. Surely you understand that?"

"I understand my rights."

"Well, actually, you don't seem to—"

"I have *privacy* rights. I don't want my DNA on some police database. God only knows what you do with it, who you sell it to."

"I can promise you that nobody is making a profit from the police DNA database," Campbell said, her patience razor thin. "Believe me, you're not that important."

"Don't come near me," Violet said quietly.

Campbell lowered the swab and took a deep breath, hoping the extra oxygen might bring more patience.

"I'm sure you understand, Miss Hughes, that you are in a compromised position."

"Oh?" she laughed. "Is that right?"

"Yes, it is. Not only were you one of the last people to see Lily alive, but you have a history with the victim."

"That is not evidence. It is purely circumstantial."

"Oh, I'm sure you've done your research watching true crime documentaries and ITV dramas," Campbell said, "but in the real world, circumstantial evidence is exactly what we build a case upon. Direct evidence," she said, holding up the swab kit, "is what proves it."

"Whatever helps you sleep at night," Violet muttered. "But you do not have my permission to take my DNA. Is that clear?"

"Crystal," Campbell said, placing the swab kit back into her coat pocket. "In that case, Miss Hughes, I would like you to accompany me to the station for an interview. Now, would you like to come voluntarily? Or do I have to arrest you?"

CHAPTER TWENTY-TWO

In the empty lobby, George searched the reception desk for the metal bell that every reception desk had for such occasions. Instead, he found only a small gong beside a laminated note that said, *Ring me if you need attention*. He found the note rather alluring, picked up the small, knob-like stick that sat beside it, and tapped the gong with a firm *dung*. Its dull ring echoed throughout the minimalist space.

He looked around for any sign of Ivy or the team, aware of declaring his entrance to the entire Grove. But there was no sign of anyone at all. The whole place felt quiet, eerily so. He wondered if the news of a guest's recent death had spread by now amongst the local Wolds gossip mill.

Then came movement from the door behind the desk, and a beautiful, smooth-faced young woman emerged wearing a flawless, pressed beige outfit.

"I'm so sorry. I was on my break," she said, head bowed with a shame undeserving of the fact that she had merely been eating what George assumed was a well-deserved lunch.

He smiled. "It's no problem."

"How can I help you?" Her voice sounded so silky one could reach out and stroke it.

"I just have a few questions," he said, keeping his cards to his chest. "Are you the manager here?"

"No," came a much firmer voice from behind him. If the receptionist's voice was silk, this voice was granite. "I am."

George turned to see a dark-haired woman who could've been anywhere between thirty and forty-five standing in front of soundless, gliding glass doors. She wore a dated but not unflattering pantsuit and heavy make-up. George wasn't exactly a feminine beauty expert, but even he knew that she was wearing too much.

"I'm the owner, actually," she continued. "Who's asking?"

"My name is Detective Inspector Larson," he said, finally taking out his warrant card. The woman glared at the receptionist as though she'd betrayed an agreement, no doubt, to warn her if any other police officers entered the establishment. "Can I ask who I'm talking to?"

The uncomfortable tension demanded a British politeness that riddled their conversation.

"Sabina Anter," she said, holding out her hand, shifting into a well-practised professional mode. "I assume you're here about the Lily Hughes investigation?"

"And why do you assume that?" George said sweetly.

"I've become acquainted with your colleagues already."

Imagining the stern interactions between Ivy and Sabina, he grinned. "I bet you have."

"So how can I help?" she said, moving behind the desk, perhaps to reinstate her position of authority.

George leaned on the counter casually, but there was no doubt he was invading her space.

"I am not here to disturb your business, Miss Anter. I can assure you. I just have some questions."

"Your colleagues have already asked me plenty of questions."

"Well, I have a few more," he said. "For one, what was your relationship with Lily Hughes?"

"My relationship?" Sabina laughed, sharp and fast, the sound of nails hammered into granite. "She was a guest for God's sake."

"So?" George said, leaning further. "You must've interacted with her, even a little?"

"Perhaps I said hello to her when they checked in?" Sabina said, raising the ends of her sentences into a question, paving the way for doubt. "Maybe again when they came for dinner? But that's all. I barely recognised her name."

"You seem very defensive, Miss Anter. I can assure you I'm merely making enquiries."

"Yes, well. It's very hard to stomach spending every penny you have building a luxury business only for you lot to roll in and take over.

"And you didn't know anyone else in Lily Hughes's party?"

"No," Sabina said, looking down. "I didn't."

A more pseudo-scientific man than George might have interpreted her eye movements as indications of deceit, but he knew that such body language analysis was difficult to prove in a court of law. Still, he followed her gaze to the reception desk, where a pile of papers lay haphazardly beside the keyboard.

"Like I said, they were guests at this establishment, Inspector, and we have hundreds of guests every year..."

She continued to reel off statistics about her business as though it was something she was used to doing in times of stress, perhaps in board rooms or before a table of investors. But George was only half-listening, his stare drawn to the collection of documents on the desk. His eyes focused on a single word in the header of one paper and the torn envelope of another, a rare yet familiar word prominent like a friends face in a crowded pub.

VavaRoom.

He turned over the syllables on his tongue silently, and just as a smell might inspire some elusive childhood memory, the word rang just as elusively in his mind, but he was at a loss to place it.

"Megan," Sabina said suddenly, watching George, her eyes wide as though realising the entire thought process going on behind his eyes. "Why don't you tidy up the desk? Bring these papers into the office while I finish here, will you?"

His head snapped up as the receptionist, Megan, busied herself, cleared the desk, and rushed into the office.

"Where were you, Miss Anter?" George said. "Yesterday morning?"

"I was working," she said firmly.

"All morning?"

"Yes."

"So you saw the women leaving for their hike?"

"Out the window," she said. "I think so. I'm not sure."

"And what time was this?"

"Eight a.m.," she said quickly.

"But you're not sure?"

Sabina laughed in the way people do when they don't find something funny but don't know how else to relieve the tension in their chest. "My God, Inspector. You speak as though I'm a suspect."

George didn't reply.

He allowed his grey, expressionless eyes to do the talking. Then, eventually, he broke the stare with one of his warm smiles. Grace always said that's what made him so attractive to her and such a good detective to his peers — his ability to consciously switch from stoic and mysterious to warm and friendly in a heart-beat. Grace often said he was like a coin in that way, easily flipped.

"Thank you for speaking to me, Miss Anter," George said, realising where he recognised the word, or rather the name, Vava-Room, suddenly popping up in his mind the way so many inspired thoughts do — at random. "We'll be in touch."

He did all he could not to rush outside but to slowly walk across the lobby and exit the way he'd come, pulling out his phone casually even though he was eager to find the not-so-recently-called contact. He looked back through the glass to see Sabina watching him, then turned his back on her as a dependable voice answered as usual.

"Guv," she said.

"Campbell, I need you to do something for me. Where are you?"

"Look to your right," she said, and like a love interest in a romantic comedy, she waved from across the car park.

George grinned, hung up, and walked over to Campbell's car just as she opened the door for a young purple-headed woman who might have passed for a younger Doctor Pippa Bell, only without the tattoos and heavy metal clothing. Campbell slammed the door closed on her and turned to face him.

"Present for Ivy?" he said, nodding to the woman.

"You could say that." She frowned. "I heard she sent you home, guv?"

"She did." He grinned, as a truanting schoolboy might. "Campbell, I know you've already put yourself in the deep end this morning to follow my word, but I need you to do something else for me."

The news was not well received, but she bore the burden well and shrugged.

"Well, I'm in it now, guv," she said. "Go on."

"I need you to look into Sabina Anter, and specifically her connection to James DeSilver."

Campbell looked confused and peered over his shoulder at the reception. "Anter?" she said. "The owner?"

"Yes. Isn't she on your radar?"

"No, she isn't," Campbell said, shaking her head slowly. Not in such a way that she found the idea foolish, but in such a way as though she couldn't believe she hadn't considered it earlier. That was the problem with shake-ups in the team. It clouded judgement. "Why do you think they're connected?"

"VavaRoom," George said, and Campbell's face lit up with recognition.

"James DeSilver's PMS business? Why?"

"Because," he said slowly, "there was a letter from his company addressed to Sabina Anter on her desk." He flicked his eyebrows knowingly. "And I'll bet it's not a love letter."

CHAPTER TWENTY-THREE

As she and Campbell stood side by side, staring at the closed interview room door, Ivy recalled the first time she had taken the lead in a suspect interview. It was five years ago when George had allowed her to do so. He'd been the first DI she'd worked with who had been willing to take a step back so that she could take a step forward.

Her harsh words to him induced a pang of guilt. But there was little use in dwelling on her mistake. She would just need to do better. Five years ago, his actions had been a turning point in their professional relationship. Such a simple thing, she thought.

"Set the tone from the beginning," she said to Campbell, who nodded her understanding. "Let her know that you're in control but there to get the truth and nothing more."

"Yes, sarge," Campbell replied. Then, in a surprising show of vulnerability, she turned to Ivy and added, "Are you sure about this?"

"Don't you think you're ready?"

"*I* know that I am."

"Look. I'd put you in there alone if I could, Campbell, but you know I've got to be there with you until you get the exams under your belt. So, if you say you're ready to take the lead, then you're ready to take the lead. She's *your* suspect. You brought her in. Now let her know why."

"Yes, sarge," Campbell said, returning to focus on the door.

"Stick to the facts," Ivy continued. "Be empathetic. Try to create a connection with her. See if she opens up."

At this, she turned again to Ivy. "Have you met her?"

Ivy grinned. "She's more likely to open up if she feels heard. So let her speak. Ask questions and avoid interrupting. Avoid leading questions. Avoid rushing. If something feels off, ask the question again in a different way for clarification and see if the answer changes."

"Yes, sarge."

"Observe her body language but remember that I'm there too. That's what I'll be doing. So you focus on the questioning." She turned to Campbell and noticed that, unlike Byrne, she hadn't changed much in the last few months. Her back was still straight with confidence, head high, eyes focused, just like she had been when Ivy and George had first met her. "Give her the chance to tell the truth."

"Yes, sarge."

"You're ready," Ivy said, reaching to open the door. "Right, let's go."

When they entered the room, it was under the scrutinising gaze of Violet Hughes. She sat in the chair, her arms crossed, eyes wide and unblinking. She was a striking sight. She wore large, white-rimmed glasses and a garish, rose-print shirt, with her purple hair. It was not the look of somebody who preferred to blend in.

Campbell dropped the case file on the desk and sat down without a word. Ivy followed suit, following the prospective detective's lead.

"Good afternoon," she began jovially. "I am PC Alice Campbell, and this is Sergeant Ivy Hart. Violet Hughes, you are not under arrest. This is a voluntary interview. You are free to leave at any time. Do you understand?"

"Yes," Violet muttered.

"You are under no obligation to say anything, but anything you can tell us will be greatly appreciated."

"Fine."

"Please answer my questions truthfully and to the best of your ability. If you do not understand a question, let me know, and I will rephrase it for you."

Violet hung her head back. "Can we just get on with it?"

Ivy shuffled in her seat. She had to agree that doing things not quite by the book was a little exhausting.

"Alright then," Campbell continued. "Can you explain to me what happened on Tuesday morning? Walk me through the hours leading up to Lily's death."

Violet looked between the two women, ready to be offended or incredulous at the very first question. "*Everything* that happened that morning? Do you want to know what toothpaste I used? Or what I had for breakfast?"

"If you feel it's relevant," Campbell said flatly.

"Colgate," Violet said. "And granola with fresh fruit."

Ivy chuckled as though she was in on the joke, and Violet glanced her way nervously.

"What time did you all wake up?" asked Campbell.

"So we really are doing the whole morning?" She sighed. "Seven a.m. We agreed to meet for breakfast at seven-fifteen."

"And that was on site, was it?"

"Yes, in the restaurant. A buffet breakfast. I can tell you what the others had if that's what you want to know."

"That won't be necessary. And over breakfast, how was everyone?"

Violet shook her head. "I don't understand the question," she said. "What do you mean, how was everyone?"

Again, Ivy laughed, a little louder this time.

"How were people's spirits?" Campbell continued.

"People's spirits?" Violet repeated.

"Well, on day five of a hiking trip, people are feeling tired and losing motivation. Or was everyone raring to go?"

"People were...fine," she said, shrugging.

"Is that your analysis?" asked Campbell, looking up from making a note. "Or were you just not paying attention?"

"Look, I don't know what to tell you," Violet said, leaning forward. "They're not exactly people with a wide range of intellect. We talked about the food. Bob was happy they did a full English. Franky complained about the coffee. We talked about the hike ahead and what pub we could stop for lunch at, and we agreed when we would meet the men at the end of the day. It wasn't exactly stimulating conversation."

"Including Lily? Would you say she didn't have a wide range of intellect?"

"Lily is..." she started, shuffling. "Lily *was* a lovely person. But no, I wouldn't say she was intelligent, exactly. She didn't question people's beliefs. She didn't have strong opinions. She wasn't a big personality. She was a people pleaser. I guess some people are just like that."

"Like what?"

"They prefer being nice over being interesting."

Campbell let the comment linger in the air for a moment before moving on.

"How would you describe your relationship with Lily?"

Again, Violet shook her head, but not so much out of incredulity but as if the situation was only just hitting her.

"She was my sister. Not by blood, sure. But Jordan loved her so much, and I loved him so much. That love kind of passed on to Lily without me even trying. She's the only reason I'm here. She's the only reason I put up with those breakfasts, with those people, with those bloody hikes. She's the only one who knows what I've been through since

Jordan's death. I just wanted to be around someone who understood."

"I'm sorry for your loss," she said in a clear attempt to empathise. But it fell flat. It felt forced. Campbell reminded Ivy of herself, unable to naturally solace others, unlike George, who could have carried the words as though saying them to someone he loved. He had a natural empathy, a rare and useful talent for a detective.

"And after breakfast," Campbell said, quickly moving on, "what did you do next?"

Violet's face remained unchanged, displaying only bitterness. "We went back to our tents and freshened up, then began the hike and left the husbands behind."

"What time was this?"

"Eight," Violet said. "Every morning, we left at eight a.m."

"And then what?"

"And then we walked," Violet said, as though it was obvious. "Like we did every day. We followed the signs and walked to our next stop, which was going to be Donington."

"On Bain?"

She shrugged. "I guess."

Ivy decided to assume that the other Donnington, in Newbury, was almost two hundred miles away, and it seemed the women were only averaging about fourteen miles per day. "And how was everyone feeling? How were—"

"Their spirits?" Violet said with a smug grin.

"Moods," Campbell alternated. "Was there any tension? Any altercations of any kind?"

"No," Violet said, frowning. "Why?"

"So everyone was getting on, were they?"

"Yes," Violet said, then muttered, "as well as they could."

"What does that mean?"

She sighed. "I prefer hiking earlier in the morning before everyone has woken up before their coffee has kicked in, before they feel the need to start talking about this, that, and everything."

"Why?" asked Campbell. "Because it leads to arguments?"

"Sometimes," she said. "But they're harmless."

"Harmless?" Campbell said. "Is that why Lily had a slap mark on her cheek?"

Violet's entire body stiffened. "What?" she said quietly.

It was Campbell's turn to act innocent. "Oh, somebody slapped Lily that morning. Surely you noticed?"

"I don't know what you're talking about."

Ivy allowed herself to grin once more, and she was sure Violet must have seen her expression change in her peripheral vision but chose to avoid her silent stare.

"Let's move on," Campbell said, no doubt remembering Ivy's advice — not to sound accusing. "Let's move forward to when the fog rolled in. Can you tell me what happened in the minutes leading up to that event?"

Clearly ruffled, Violet rearranged herself on the chair, then readopted her nonchalant positioning and breathed out in exasperation, as though she had better places to be.

"We were walking along the ridge. A few minutes earlier, we decided to cross the road to the hiking path on the bank beside the road because it was safer. We were walking in a line. It was a narrow path. Then the fog fell and separated us."

"Cecelia mentioned an argument between you, her, and Franky minutes before the fog fell. She said you stormed off ahead."

"Stormed off?" she said. "Is that the language she used?"

"The exact words," Campbell said, meeting her stare.

"We had a disagreement," Violet said. "It wasn't an *event*. It's not exactly uncommon. We have very different views on life."

"In what way?" Campbell said.

"They're old-fashioned, let's say."

"Who?"

"Franky and Cecelia."

"They're older than you, aren't they?"

"Yes."

"Then, isn't a bit of old-fashioned behaviour to be expected?"

"I think that's a weak excuse," Violet said, the words sliding between her lips as though she'd used the phrase many times before. "Just because you grew up with certain views of how women should be, it doesn't mean you shouldn't adapt to the way things are now."

"And that's what you disagreed about, is it? The way women should be?"

"I just wanted some space," she said, "from the conversation. I find it depressing to hear fully-grown women complain about a broken nail."

"So you gave yourself some space," Campbell said, "and then the fog fell?"

"Yes."

"Can you describe what you saw?"

"I didn't see anything," Violet said. "That's the point. I could barely see my own hand. I looked back, or what I thought was back, but there was nothing there. Just this white wall."

"And did you hear anything?"

"Not really," she said. "Maybe some voices calling names."

"Did you hear anything other than voices? Any other sounds or movements?"

"No," she said. "Nothing at all." Ivy made a note. *Car?* This seemed to wind Violet up, as she added defensively, "Look, I told you all this in my statement already."

"What about in the lead-up to the fog falling?" Campbell continued, ignoring the protest. "Did you notice anything unusual or suspicious?"

"No, nothing," she spat, then sighed. "I mean, Lily and Marie had fallen back a little, but that's to be expected."

"What's to be expected?"

"Marie being slow," she said flatly.

Ivy looked up from her notes.

"Why is that to be expected?" asked Campbell.

"Because..." Violet looked between the two women, her expression confused, as though she wasn't sure if their ignorance was some sort of trick. "Wait...has no one told you about Marie?"

"No," Campbell said.

"No one told you about Monday night's dinner?"

"No," Campbell repeated, struggling to hide her frustration as to why she was the one now answering the questions. "Why don't you enlighten me?"

Violet sat back. "It's a long story."

Ivy matched her stance, leaned forward, and spoke for the first time. "Tell us everything."

Violet turned to her with raised eyebrows, clearly enjoying the power shift.

"Everything?"

"*Everything.*"

CHAPTER TWENTY-FOUR

As usual, Violet walked at the back of the group. Ahead of her walked couples, two by two like Biblical ideals, Bob and Cecelia holding hands at the front, James and Franky behind, his arm draped around her shoulders casually as a curtain might drape across the back of a sofa, and Marie and Toby just in front of Violet, with Lily in between. Violet had been left alone, as usual. Forgotten. Ignored.

One of these days, she would take the lead. They would see.

She would be right at the front.

The long summer sun lowered over Wolds Grove in rays of coral and buttercup yellow, streaming between the well-spaced yurts as though the site itself had been designed to present in harmony with the sunset. Birds or bats — it could've been either — flitted just below the blanket of the indigo sky, where a few stars had already broken through the darkness.

They headed to the central yurt, which was more of a circus tent in varying shades of beige, a large, air-filled structure in the middle of the field. The same woman who had checked them in at reception last night met them at the opening of the canvas, the woman in the pantsuit with dark hair and too much make-up.

The woman who'd insisted over and over again that she would do anything to make their stay more comfortable, to the point where Violet couldn't help but wonder how far exactly she would go to accommodate them.

"Sabina Anter," James said, making a show of introducing himself. He extended a hand and seemed to study her face curiously. "I've been looking forward to sampling your hospitality. You've made quite a name for yourself."

"Mr DeSilver," she said, slightly unsure of him. She cast a quick eye across the group, then adopted a more friendly demeanour. "For a party of eight?"

"It's seven, isn't it?" he said, turning around and then spotting Violet at the back. "Oh, sorry, you're right, it's eight."

Lily turned to give Violet a sympathetic smile, rolling her eyes to make light of the fact that, once more, she had been overlooked. But Lily didn't know all the times she hadn't been there to make light of it, or how long Violet had lived her life in the shadows.

Sabina led them inside to a table in the centre of the room, which had been impaled by the yurt's tall, central pole, dressed in ivy and fairy lights as though the designer had aimed to turn an inconvenience into a feature. All it meant, Violet thought, as they took their seats, was that James, who took the centre seat, could not see Lily opposite him. Perhaps that was for the best.

Of course, Violet sat at the end of the table, beside Franky and opposite Toby and Marie. On the far end sat Cecelia and Bob opposite each other, next to James and Lily at the centre of everything.

As usual.

Sabina soon returned with two ice pails of champagne, uncorked the bottles there and then, and placed one on either side of the table. "I'll leave you in Annie's good hands," she said, gesturing to the young waitress at her elbow with dark features in a pressed, white shirt. "Enjoy your evening."

Sabina returned to her welcoming position at the door, swaying between the tables, which were rapidly filling up. The room was already abuzz with conversation and laughter from locals and glampsite guests alike. Despite the location, it seemed to be a popular restaurant.

The waitress, who had introduced herself as Annie, proceeded to fill their glasses with champagne, and even before the last drop had been tipped, James assumed control by raising his glass to make a toast. "Here's to good friends, good food, good wine, and good money," he said. "Each makes life more bearable...except when we're splitting the bill with Bob."

"Hear hear," Bob laughed and went to down his champagne.

But just before everyone clinked their glasses, Toby stood up hesitantly. "If you don't mind, James?" he said, to which James gestured for him to go ahead. "I'd also like to raise a glass. To life," he declared and looked down at Marie, his handsome features accentuated by the soft candlelight. "This short and precious gift."

Marie, ever the oversensitive dramatist, allowed her eyes to well with emotion, and they all clinked glasses. Violet had already downed half of hers before clinking with Lily, the only one who bothered to include her.

Soon enough, Annie returned to the table with two other waiters who all stood to the left-hand side of each diner and set down their plates in synchronised union. "An amuse-bouche for you to start," she declared. "Chilled lobster mousse with lemon zest and a dill gel that pairs with your champagne to elevate the lemon tang and cleanse the palate. Enjoy."

"Delicious," Franky said beside her as Violet licked at the mousse on her fork, took a small mouthful, and struggled to keep it down, wondering when whisked fish had become fine dining.

They all, except Violet, lapped it up quickly, hungry after a day of hiking for the women and an afternoon of beer drinking in the pub for the men.

"Not going to finish that, Vi?" Bob yelled from the other end of the table, to which Violet shook her head. They proceeded with the fanfare of passing down her plate so Bob could finish it all in one.

"Take it easy, Bobby boy," James said. "You've got seven more courses to go."

"If they're all as small as that one," he said, dabbing his mouth with a monogrammed napkin, "then it shouldn't be a problem."

"Course one," Annie announced, returning with more plates soon after the first ones were cleared. "Tuna tartare with avocado, yuzu, and wasabi foam. Paired with a French Sancerre," she said, and at just that moment, their wines were poured. "To cut through the richness of the tuna while complementing the citrusy notes."

Amongst the — what Violet felt to be overplayed — *ooohs* and *ahhhs* when consuming the food, the conversation was sentimental and nostalgic, as though purposely designed to remind Violet that she barely knew these people and to leave her out of the conversation.

"What was his name, Lil?" asked James, swinging his head left and right to catch her eye beyond the indecently positioned yurt post. Finally, they met on the same side and grinned at each other as though their eyes hadn't met in years. Beside Violet, Franky stiffened and took her rather large sip of her Sancerre, even though Violet was sure the portions were so small because the tastes were supposed to be savoured.

"I don't know who you're talking about," Lily said.

"Come on, the guy who sat in front of you in English class. Harry someone. Floppy, yellow hair. Looked like a young Boris Johnson."

Lily laughed much harder than was necessary. "Harry Bennett?" she said.

James clicked at her. "That's the one."

"Now, what house was he in again, Lily?" Marie said, leaning forward, joining in the game.

James, Lily, and Marie had attended the same school and had known each other since sitting together on the red table in reception class. And didn't they love to remind everyone?

Lily thought for a second, closing her eyes in faux concentration, then said, "Joyce."

James and Marie laughed.

"How about...Mary Foster?" asked Marie.

"Shelley house," Lily said quickly. "Easy. Give me another." Then she looked up and down the table to include everyone. "See, the school's houses were all named after famous authors."

"Is that right?" muttered Violet, taking a swig of wine.

Lily looked at her and then did a double take at the expression on her face, as though only just noticing that this conversation wasn't particularly fun for anyone else, though Bob was chuckling along at the free entertainment. But Violet had found, getting to know him in the last few days, that he was an exceptionally easy man to please.

"How about Michael Thomson?" asked James.

"Brontë," Lily said, calmer this time, as though the fun was over.

James sat back, swirling his wine, which threatened to spill over the sides.

"It's a gift," he said with a huge grin.

"Course two," Annie proclaimed. "Seared scallops with pea purée, crispy pancetta, and truffle vinaigrette with a crisp, steely Chablis to pair with the sweetness of the scallops and the richness of the truffle."

"It's just the sheer number of them," Cecelia said while they ate. "Two, I can deal with. One for each eye, you know? But three is something else. You can't keep an eye on three of them at the same time. And now Niamh is turning thirteen, which means—"

"The teenage years." Franky whistled. "I don't envy you that, I must say. I think I gave my mother permanent migraines from how I behaved as a teenager."

"And then you've got the problem of Stephen," Bob said, pointing a fork at his wife.

"What's the problem with Stephen?" Toby said, listening on with his arm around Marie's chair.

"He was the youngest child until five years ago, and now he's the middle child, which means middle child syndrome," Bob explained. "I can already see it in him. He's acting out. Being a troublemaker. Trying to get attention."

"I was the middle child," Toby said, shrugging. "Didn't hurt me."

"That's because I give you all the attention you need," Marie said, stroking his close-shaven cheek in a way that made Violet feel quite nauseous for reasons aside from the pea puree, which, to her at least, resembled mushy peas.

"Well, I'm just saying," Bob said, turning his fork to Toby and Marie instead. "Think about it, you two. Before having kids, just think about it."

Cecelia leaned across the table to slap him on the wrist. "Don't say that! I wouldn't change a thing. It's the greatest gift there is, to have children."

"You just spent twenty minutes complaining about them," Violet pointed out.

But nobody seemed to hear her.

"So when are you planning to have little ones?" Cecelia asked the newlyweds.

For some reason, the question caused Marie's eyes to fill with tears again, and she turned her head to Toby's shoulder as he replied for both of them. "Well, let's just see," he said. "Let's see."

"Course three," Annie broadcast. "Foie gras terrine with fig jam, toasted brioche, and pickled cherries paired with a Bordeaux Sauternes, a classic pairing. The honeyed sweetness balances the richness of the foie gras while the fig and cherry components enhance the wine's fruitiness."

"No, we did think about it. Of course, we did," Franky was saying as they all finished off their fourth round. "We just decided to spend money on other things."

"Like a mansion in the Wolds?" Bob asked.

"Exactly," James said with a wink.

"Why didn't we do that?" Bob asked Cecelia.

"Well, you can do that with your second wife," she replied.

"You know," Lily said, "I read that it costs about two hundred thousand pounds to raise a single child from birth to eighteen?"

"Yeah, and the rest," Bob said. "In this economy, we'll be looking after the kids until they're retired."

"Well, you've got the government to thank for that," Violet added.

But again, as usual, as she had experienced her whole life, from so-called friends, so-called family, her own brother and now her sister-in-law and her snooty friends, she was ignored, and her words floated away like mist-wisps in the wind because, as always, no one seemed to be listening.

Nobody ever listened to Violet.

CHAPTER TWENTY-FIVE

"Course four," Annie stated. "A wild mushroom risotto with parmesan-reggiano and truffle oil alongside a Burgundy pinot noir. The earthy undertones of the wine and bright red fruit notes complement the mushrooms and truffle while its acidity balances the richness of the risotto."

"Oh, come on," Marie said. "I told the story a hundred times. You must be sick of it by now."

"Well, tell it again," Lily said gently.

"Yeah, come on, Marie. It makes me believe in romance," Franky said pointedly.

All eyes were on Marie and Toby, and he turned to her and said, "Go on then. You start."

The story of how they'd met had become a choreographed monologue. They knew when to bounce back and forth between the other and who delivered which line of the story best. They used the same phrasing each time. The same vocabulary. The same tones. It was a practised song. Violet had only known them for four days, and she'd already heard it enough times.

"I was in my favourite cafe," Marie started. "Cute little place where you can see St Paul's right outside the window."

"See, that's one thing I never understood," James already interrupted, his voice starting to slur after the fourth glass of wine. "What were you doing over by St Paul's when you live in Hackney and work in Ealing?"

Marie shrugged. "I just like it over there," she said. "I love that cafe. It's worth going out of my way for."

"Yeah, but multiple days in a row?" James said. "It's your *favourite* cafe?"

Marie looked at Toby, then back at James. "I don't know what to tell you." She laughed. "Like I said, I like it there."

"Okay," James said, holding his hands up before twirling them at the newlyweds. "Continue."

"I'd become used to the regulars and the staff there, so one day, I look up from my book, and there's someone I don't recognise. A man. Who catches my attention."

"Good looking, was he?" Bob said with a wink.

Marie shrugged playfully. "He wasn't bad."

"And I'm on my work break," Toby picked up. "So I go into this cute cafe and find an even cuter woman inside reading. So I change my takeaway coffee to a stay-in order."

"He looks up and catches my eye," Marie said.

"I get out my book," Toby said.

"Then he looks down at his book and back up at mine."

"And it turns out—"

"We're reading the same book!" the rest of the table said in unison, laughing and making Violet jump.

"What book was it?" Lily asked.

"It was the latest Kevin Banner crime novel."

"Oh, I like his books. He's from around here, you know. I'm sure of it."

"Anyway," Marie said. "He walked over, spun some line about fate, and asked for my number." She stared at Toby, clearly infatuated.

"*Spun some line?*" he said. "I think you'll find that it was a beautiful speech." He cleared his throat and held his chest the way a Shakespearean actor might. "I'm sorry to bother you. Look, I know you don't know me, and I don't know you, but I'm a man who trusts his gut and follows a sign when it's shown to me. And I can't help but think that fate has bookmarked us..." He gave a charming little laugh that made his eyes sparkle. "Because here we are, reading the same story."

Marie stared at him as he spoke, then looked back at the table and shrugged.

"I was smitten."

"Course five," Annie disclosed. "Lamb loin with herb crust, roasted root vegetables, and red wine jus paired with a Marchesi di Barolo, a bold structure matching the rich, savoury lamb. *Bon Appetit!*"

"Well, we said the same, didn't we, darling?" Franky said to James.

"What's that?"

"That we'd never leave London."

"Oh, yeah," he said. "We did."

"But things change," she said, spearing a cut of lamb. "We wanted a different lifestyle, a change of pace. It's just so peaceful out here. I think we would've moved out of the city eventually, even if it wasn't for James's business."

"So you're a country man now, James?" asked Toby with a grin.

"Now then," mimicking the local greeting. "I've got the tweed, the flat cap, the works. Even got a few shotguns locked up ready for the season."

"You'll be lucky if they let you beat," Bob said playfully.

"I do miss house-sitting for you in Richmond, though," Marie said sadly, then added, "not that I don't miss you two, that is."

Franky smiled. "You're welcome to housesit for us up here instead."

"Well, you'd never get me out of London," slurred Bob. "Born and raised in Lewisham and never planning on leaving."

"Here, here," Cecelia said.

Toby and Marie also lifted their glasses in agreement.

"What about you, Lily?" Franky asked. "Could you be convinced to leave London?"

Lily swirled her wine glass and stared into it. "I don't know," she said. "Maybe? If I've learned anything in the last year," she said, taking a large sip, "it's that you never know what's coming next."

"Course six," Annie informed the table, "is a pan-seared duck breast with cherry reduction and duck confit alongside a Willamette Valley pinot noir, the soft tannins complementing the meat while the wine's berry notes enhance the cherry."

It was only after that second-to-last course, when the tiny portions had finally filled them all, the wine had gone to their heads, and Bob had pushed his plate away with a soft burp, that was when Marie tapped her wine glass with a long nail. Looking back, Violet realised Marie had needed the Dutch courage. She'd known that the others needed it, too - they just didn't know it yet.

"Christ, another toast?" Cecelia called down the table. "Really?"

"Just a quick one," Marie said, her face flushed, whether with alcohol or nerves, Violet couldn't be sure. "Now, this won't be easy to hear, and believe me, it's not easy to say. But I have to tell you all something."

The merriment around the table stilled like a lake, its jolly ripples dissipating.

"What's going on?" Lily asked slowly.

Marie took a deep breath. "There's no easy way to say this, so I'll just say it," she said, and Toby took her hand, staring at her profile as though silently willing her strength. "Six months ago, I was diagnosed with pancreatic cancer."

If the table was still before, it was now positively frozen.

"I underwent a pancreaticoduodenectomy—"

"What?" Lily whispered. "When?"

"Soon after I was diagnosed," she admitted.

"Wait," Bob said. "What is that? Pancreata-what?"

"Pancreaticoduodenectomy," Lily explained. "They remove the head of the pancreas, part of the small intestine and gallbladder. To stop the cancer spreading." She turned to Marie. "Did it work?"

Marie held her oldest friend's gaze. And she shook her head.

"So what are the next steps?" asked Franky.

"What do you mean?"

"Well, chemo, radiation?" Franky asked. "Or what about immunotherapy? I hear that has some great results—"

"I'm not sure you—"

"What do you need? Can you go private? We can help, can't we, James?"

Mid-swallow, James startled and said, "Steady on, Franky—"

But Marie was shaking her head. "No. No next steps."

"What are you talking about?" Cecelia asked.

"It's terminal. They've given me three to six months."

A terrible silence settled like a night-time mist on the frozen lake.

James threw up his hands. "Everyone's terminal. The question is *time*."

"He's right," Lily choked, her voice dense with tears. "Jordan had a patient. A man not far off your age. He was given a year to live but ended up living *five* more. The treatments these days—"

"How long with medication? With the best treatment?" Franky asked.

Marie looked at Toby, then hesitated, but said. "Two years, but—"

"Two years!" James said. "Brilliant."

"Brilliant?" Lily scolded.

"Well, it's a hell of a lot better than three months."

"How can we help, Marie? What can we do?" asked Franky,

glancing at her wine glass. "I mean, Jesus, should you even be drinking?"

"You'll have to prise wine from my cold, dead hands," Marie said, but nobody laughed at the poor choice of words. "Look, I know it's a shock."

"That it is, love," Bob added.

"But we talked about it." She gripped Toby's hand, and he looked at her in a way that no man had ever looked at Violet, like a lover in a film, so visibly, unashamedly enamoured. "And we agreed." She took a deep breath. "I'd rather enjoy the next three to six months without the medication than take it and be miserable for the next two years."

"What are you talking about?" asked Lily.

"I'm not doing the treatment, Lil. I'm not spending my last years in and out of hospital, feeling nauseous, losing my hair, and God knows what else."

"Marie—"

"It's decided," she said, and Violet had never heard her sound so insistent.

"But love..." Cecelia said softly. "You never know what might change. You could be buying time before—"

"They're not going to cure cancer in the next two years, Cecelia."

Again, they all sat in that cold, misty silence.

"That's why you were over by St Paul's," James said quietly, looking up into Marie's eyes. "It's next to the hospital, the one where Jordan used to work. You were having treatment there?"

"Yes," Marie said quietly, as though he had solved a very sad puzzle.

"I feel sick," whispered Lily.

Even Violet felt a knot in her chest. She found Marie to be a bit annoying. In fact, she found her to be a simplistic, naive, overly infatuated fool. But she didn't want her to die.

"Why didn't you tell us sooner?" Lily asked.

"I didn't want to ruin your appetites," Marie said with a wry grin.

"Marie..." Lily said, her voice breaking.

"I suppose I was just waiting for the right time."

"Your final course," shared Annie, her enthusiasm landing on deaf ears. "Chocolate soufflé with raspberry coulis and vanilla bean ice cream. Paired with a Madeiran wine that contrasts beautifully with the rich dark chocolate, while its sweetness enhances the raspberry and vanilla tones."

Violet watched them all in turn, lost in thought, processing Marie's news. One by one, they set their spoons down on the table, unable to eat another morsel.

"I'm sorry," Marie mumbled, and Toby reached for her hand. "I just wanted you all to know."

CHAPTER TWENTY-SIX

"Cancer?" Campbell said.

Violet had set the scene so powerfully and in such detail that Ivy felt she had to adjust to the harsh interview room lights after being transported to a candlelit yurt twenty miles away.

"Yes," Violet replied. "Pancreatic cancer."

"What on earth was she doing on a hiking trip?"

"Don't ask me," Violet said. "She insisted. Everyone said we should end the trip early. Take it easy, go to a spa. But Marie said it's what she wanted: to pretend like everything was normal. She insisted she could do it. We just took it slow."

"Well, that explains why she looked like she was about to collapse," Ivy said.

"It was tough for her," Violet said in a rare show of empathy. "Of course it was."

"How did it make you feel?" Campbell said, jumping on it. "To hear about Marie?"

Violet frowned as though it was the first time somebody had asked her. "I don't really know her," she replied. But Campbell gave her the space she needed to elaborate. "Look, I find her a bit annoying, to be honest. And I find the innocent, young love display between her and Toby a bit pathetic, seeing as they're both in their forties." She paused. "But I felt sad. She's nice. I don't want her to die."

"When did you say she found out?"

"Six months ago. But when she found out it was terminal, that's when she stopped taking treatment."

"And when did she find out it was terminal?"

"About a week or so ago."

"So not long," Campbell said.

"No, I suppose not."

"That news must have hung in the air the next morning."

"Of course," Violet said. "But we did as Marie asked. We pretended everything was normal."

"So, nobody mentioned it?"

Violet shrugged. "Not that I know of. Not until after Lily..."

"Why was it mentioned then?"

"Because when the fog lifted, we found Marie on the road, almost passed out."

Ivy sat up. "On the road?" she asked, then remembered Campbell was meant to be leading.

"What was she doing on the road?" Campbell asked.

Violet, again, shrugged. "I don't know."

"Lily left her on the hiking path to go and get help when she was struggling. Did she follow her?"

"I don't know what to tell you," Violet said, her incredulity rising again just when she was starting to soften. "You'll have to ask her what happened."

"So you all found Marie on the road, then what happened?"

"She was on the verge of a panic attack. You know, breathless. We asked her what was wrong, and it was all she could do to point down the slope. That's when we saw Lily..." Her voice broke on her sister-in-law's name as though the memory alone caused agony. "At the bottom."

"But when the fog lifted, you were alone?"

"Yes," she said, seemingly grateful for the return to more logistical questions. "I had stayed where I was."

"And where were Franky and Cecelia?"

"Still behind me," she said. "But a little further down the path, as though they'd retraced their steps."

"To find Marie and Lily?"

Violet shrugged, and the movement was beginning to grate on Ivy. "I guess so."

Ivy leaned forward. Campbell was doing well enough, but they could get all of this information from reading the witness statements. There was one thing she wanted to know. "Why did you refuse to give us your DNA, Violet?" she asked.

"Privacy reasons," Violet replied flatly.

Ivy scoffed. "I don't believe you."

"Fine."

"Do you drive, Violet?"

"Yes."

"Do you go on holiday?"

"Sometimes."

"Do you walk down the street?"

"What are you—"

"So you're okay with the DVLA registering your information? You're happy for countries to share your data? You're happy to be caught on facial-recognition cameras?" Violet didn't reply. "But you're not okay with aiding the investigation of somebody you claim to have loved?"

"So, what?" Violet spat. "I should just throw my DNA away because we'll all be in the system anyway? I don't understand why you're focusing on me."

"We are not just focusing on you," Campbell said, taking back control, even though Ivy knew she was making that difficult. "That is why we asked all four of you for a DNA sample."

It was Violet's turn to scoff. "Of course. Of course, you're focusing on four women instead of the more likely suspect."

"And who's that?"

"A man. You know that ninety per cent of homicides are carried out by men?"

"Is that right?"

"It happens all the time, doesn't it? Some creep follows a group of women to a secluded space—"

"Actually," Campbell said. "It doesn't happen often at all. If you want to talk statistics, sixty per cent of homicides are carried out by somebody known to the victim."

"Yeah," Violet said. "A man."

"We don't discriminate," Campbell said.

"Well, maybe," Violet said, "in this case, you should."

"I don't think gender equality works that way, Miss Hughes," Ivy added.

"Look, check our statements. I was the furthest away from Lily. How could I get past the others to the road, kill her, and then get back to my original position in dense fog? Anyway, she was my brother's wife. I loved her. But I don't *know* her that well. Not like the others do."

"You mean her friends? You think them knowing her meant they wanted to murder her?"

"Decades of friendship," Violet said, leaning forward. "That's a lot of baggage: a lot of mistakes, arguments, miscommunications. That kind of thing builds up, you know. And then, one day, it all gets too much and collapses. It gathers momentum quickly and dangerously. Like an avalanche."

"You paint a powerful picture," Ivy said flatly.

"So you think that's what happened?" asked Campbell. "One of Lily's friendships experienced an avalanche?"

"No, not any one of them. Just one in particular. And I don't know why you're wasting time here instead of being out there looking for him."

"Who?"

"The man who did this."

"And who do you think that is?"

She looked between the two detectives. "It's obvious, isn't it?" She sighed. "You're the one who said murders are usually committed by someone the victim knows. Well, no one knew Lily better than James." Then she added in a mutter, "Probably not even Jordan."

"James DeSilver?"

Violet rolled her eyes. "Who else?"

"Why him?"

She chewed the inside of her cheek, then said simply, "They were having an affair."

Neither Campbell nor Ivy spoke straight away, allowing the information to sink in. The entire interview had been rather disarming. Try as she might, Campbell had failed to maintain control. Violet simply knew more than they did, and it kept coming back to bite them.

"James and Lily?" Campbell clarified.

"Yes."

"You mean James was having an affair." Violet merely glared at Campbell with a dark stare. "I just mean—"

"You mean my brother's dead, so Lily didn't have to be loyal to him anymore."

"I mean that James was the one who was married. Surely, Lily is free to—"

"Cheat with her best friend's husband?" Violet leaned forward, her expression impassive. "Tell me, officer, what percentage of murders are committed by the victim's boyfriends?"

Campbell hesitated, and then admitted, "That's not a statistic I can recite."

Violet sat back in satisfaction, and Ivy stepped in. "How did you find out about the affair, Violet?"

"I overheard Marie and Lily talking about it. They weren't exactly subtle."

"When?"

"On Tuesday morning."

"You mean in the hours before Lily was killed?"

She paused, then said, "Yes."

"And you didn't think this might be an important thing to mention in your statement?"

"Not really, no," Violet said. "It had nothing to do with Lily's death."

"You must have been angry."

Her expression was furious, but she replied, "It's nothing to do with me."

"So, you didn't feel like she was betraying your brother?"

"No."

"How long had the affair been going on?"

"I have no idea," she spat. "Why don't you ask James?"

"As you know, that's a bit difficult for us to do right now," Campbell pointed out.

"Because he's on the run?"

"Because he's missing," Campbell said, but Violet was only confirming Ivy's own suspicions, not that she would ever in a million years admit that to the woman. She found her abhorrent, misguided with strong opinions — a dangerous combination in Ivy's experience.

"Did you slap Lily?" Ivy asked suddenly, watching for a reaction.

But Violet revealed nothing as she turned to her with a sharp "No."

It was impossible to know whether she was lying or not, but one thing was clear — they didn't know enough about these people, their interpersonal dynamics, or the events of the last few days. Violet knew it and could well be using their ignorance to her advantage. Ivy wasn't willing to reveal anything more about their investigation than necessary. There was an intelligence behind Violet's eyes that worried her, a narcissistic self-righteousness that presented as obnoxious but hid a much more threatening sense that the world was wrong and that people like her should be the ones to change it.

"Violet, you do understand that once you are placed under arrest, we no longer need permission to take your DNA, don't you?" Ivy said.

Violet considered the statement.

"So, are you arresting me?" she asked. "And if so, on what grounds?"

Standing from her chair, Ivy collated her notes.

"Once PC Campbell has concluded your interview, you're free to go."

She turned towards the door, and just as her hand touched the handle, a niggling thought roused, and she turned to ask a final question.

"One thing I don't quite understand," Ivy said, and Violet grinned as though she thought there was far more than one thing. "Why were you at the front of the group?"

Violet looked up at her. "What do you mean?"

"I mean, it doesn't sound like you're connected to any of the other women. So why weren't you walking with Lily? The only person that you knew. The only person that you liked?"

She shuffled in her seat. "I don't like being at the back."

"Why not?"

"Like I said, I'm not a follower."

"I see," Ivy said, turning to the door, then once more back to Violet. "So, it wasn't that you wanted three people in between you and Lily that morning?"

The question hung in the air between them, and Violet's eyes grew darker.

"Like I said, I wanted to be at the front. I wanted to take the lead. If I was a man," she said, scoffing, "I'd probably call myself an alpha wolf."

"Would you now?"

"Yeah, I would."

"Then you would know that, in wolf packs, alphas lead from the back." Violet narrowed her eyes. "Perhaps you should've taken a leaf from Lily's book. Those who don't feel the need to push their way to the front..." Ivy turned, opened the door, and allowed it to slowly close behind her, adding, "They're the ones really in control."

CHAPTER TWENTY-SEVEN

Ivy marched straight upstairs to the incident room, her mind reeling with four of Violet's words, repeating over and over, patronising and annoying in tone but nevertheless true.

It's obvious, isn't it?

She allowed the squeak of the floorboard to announce her entrance, which was enough to grab the attention of her team and have them scurry to the whiteboard. Scurry was the right word for it. Whereas, when George was around, they might merely gather together as one. It was a difference she didn't particularly like yet didn't know how to overcome.

"Updates on James DeSilver," she said, tapping his name on the board. "Let's go."

"Still no use of his card and no updates from his phone," Byrne started, sitting at his desk close to the board.

"He's probably destroyed it by now," Ivy said. "What else?"

"The search warrant came through to look into DeSilver's bank account. Campbell just said it was interesting so far. Lots of moving around big money, but we assumed that's connected to his business. I can continue to look into it."

"Good. And get in touch with his business accountant or whoever can consent to us accessing their financial records."

"You want to look into his business?"

"James DeSilver murdering Lily might have been financially motivated. If there's nothing in his personal accounts, maybe he went through the business. We need to cover all bases."

Byrne hesitated as though he had more to say but settled on, "Yes, sarge."

"I've been talking to Ruby, guv," Maguire spoke up. "We've curated a list of cars and dog walkers seen in the hours before Lily was killed. Nobody of note. Just locals. But we're checking up on—"

"Let's pause on that," Ivy interrupted, causing Maguire to gape, and he redirected his energy to tapping his pen on his knee. "Could you identify the black saloon as DeSilver's car?"

"No, guv," Maguire said. "Not yet. There are no cameras on that main road for miles, and he could've turned off in any direction. Ruby's going through local cameras manually, looking for the number plate."

"Okay," Ivy said, not bothering to hide her disappointment. "What else have we got on DeSilver?"

But her question was only met with a tense, tight silence, the kind that comes before an eruption.

"Seriously?" Ivy said. "That's all we've got?"

"I was mapping out their hiking route," O'Hara defended, pointing to the unfurled OS map attached to a tripod easel beside the whiteboard and the neatly placed, colour-coordinated magnets dotted throughout the contour lines and topography.

"And Ruby and I were focusing on the third-party theory," Maguire said.

"Forget the third-party theory," Ivy snapped, then collected herself. "Look, I want all efforts focused on finding James DeSilver. Stop whatever else you're doing."

"What did Violet Hughes say?" asked Byrne.

"Many things," Ivy said dismissively.

"I mean, to make you so sure that DeSilver killed Lily?"

Ivy hesitated before admitting that she was following the intuition of a suspect, even if she did have the very same intuition. "She pointed out that James DeSilver is the most obvious suspect. And I'm loathed to admit it, but she's right. She told us that Lily and James were having an affair."

"Violet told you that?"

"Yes."

"And you believe her?"

Ivy didn't appreciate the tone, but answered calmly, "Yes. And that gives James even more of a motive than he had before."

"What other motive does he have?" asked O'Hara slowly.

"The fight," Ivy reminded her. "He and Lily argued a few days earlier, remember?"

"Right," O'Hara said.

"When Lily said he owes her," Maguire added, and Ivy had the feeling he was placating someone, but she wasn't sure if it was O'Hara or herself.

"Exactly," Ivy continued, "and in light of this affair, that might have been a bigger fight than we thought. What if she had called it off? What if she had threatened to tell Franky? Or what if *he* called it off? That could've been what he owed her. Time. Time to come clean to her best friend. Or loyalty, to not tell Franky at all."

"I don't know, sarge," Byrne began.

"Either way, Lily now being dead solved one of his problems," Ivy continued.

"From Bob's story, it seemed less...metaphorical than that, like he literally owed her something."

"I agree," O'Hara said. "I think we're jumping to conclusions."

"Well, in lieu of evidence," she said, "that's just what we'll have to do." A few of them went to speak, but Ivy held up her hand to show the matter was closed. They couldn't follow every avenue. She was picking a lane. "Until we know otherwise, we assume that DeSilver is on the run, not missing."

Byrne's desk phone began to ring. He looked at Ivy for permission to answer it, and she nodded.

"You think he's gone to ground, sarge?" O'Hara continued.

"Possibly. Look into residential records. Check if DeSilver has any other properties. Or any connection to one: relatives, parents, siblings. Send officers to each."

"Yes, sarge."

"Either that, or he's already on the other side of the country. Maguire, extend the search for DeSilver. Do what you can to use live facial recognition. Train stations, bus stations, ports—"

"Ports?" he interrupted.

"Yes, ports. Air and ferry. If he gets out of the country, we're screwed."

"How could he do that? His passport would be flagged, sarge. We'd be notified."

"Maybe he's got a fake one."

"A *fake passport?*" He laughed. "He's not bloody James Bond, sarge. I don't think—"

Ivy spun, her patience snapping like a rubber band pulled just a millimetre too taut.

"What bit is confusing you, Maguire?" she asked loudly. "Or are you simply incapable of following a direct order? Because if that's the case, I'd be happy to replace you with a PC who can." She clicked her fingers for emphasis, and the *snap* carried across the entire room.

It was at this point that Campbell entered, and her shoulders sagged as she approached the whiteboard, looking between Ivy and Maguire, deciphering the tension.

"I closed up the interview, sarge," she said slowly, "and sent Violet back to the Grove."

Ivy rubbed her face, her fury simmering to a steaming mixture of guilt and frustration in her chest. "Good," she said, quieter now and snatching her coat from the back of her chair. She didn't care where exactly she needed to go, she just needed to go somewhere. "Good."

In the awkward silence that followed, Byrne placed his phone's handset back onto the receiver and cleared his throat. "That was Katy, sarge, with the lab results."

"Go on," Ivy said.

"She identified three distinct DNA traces found on Lily Hughes and ran them against the samples we sent over."

"And?"

"They were mostly on her face, and they belonged to Marie Entwhistle, James DeSilver, and one unknown. Katy was able to identify James DeSilver's DNA on Lily's lips and Marie's on her cheek."

"The slap?" Campbell said.

"Not necessarily," Byrne countered. "Katy said the unknown could also be from the slap. It could be from a hug, a kiss on the cheek, or just from touching Lily's face. Or yes, from the slap. If they had been arguing, there's every chance some spittle..." He ended the statement there, letting them use their imagination to finish it off.

"An unknown?" Campbell repeated.

"They're not on the database, whoever it is."

"Well, if it wasn't the DNA of Marie, Franky, or Cecelia, there's only one left," O'Hara said.

"Violet," Campbell finished. "It's got to be her."

Ivy said nothing but pulled on her coat and straightened the collar.

"Where are you going, sarge?" Campbell asked tentatively.

"We don't know who slapped Lily. But I have a novel idea," she said, straightening her collar, again. "Ask."

"Who?" asked Byrne with similar caution.

"The women who were there for it. Campbell, you saw what state they're in," Ivy said, turning to her. "Who's the most... together?" She looked at the young PC, ignoring the glimmer of concern in her eyes. "Who would be the most likely to speak the truth?"

CHAPTER TWENTY-EIGHT

"Sergeant Hart," Marie said, pulling back the canvas at the entrance to her yurt. "What are you doing here?"

"I have a few questions," Ivy said, peeking inside. "I hope you don't mind?"

Toby appeared at her shoulder, smiling warmly at Ivy. Once more, his handsome features triggered an involuntary reaction in her stomach. She couldn't help but admire his thick, peppered hair, lake-like eyes, strong nose, and full, pink lips. It had been a while since she'd found somebody so attractive. She'd almost thought it impossible.

"No, no, of course," Marie insisted, and they both stepped back to let her through. "Please. Come in."

Their yurt was tidy and cosy with the lights on dim, even though it was a pleasant enough day outside, as though they preferred soft lighting to enjoy each other's company.

"How can we help?" asked Toby.

"Well, first of all," Ivy said, feeling somewhat awkward, "I'd like to pass on my sympathies."

"Thank you," Marie said, shaking her head. "She was my best friend. I've known Lily for forty years, I—"

"No," Ivy interrupted. "I didn't mean Lily. I meant you." She hesitated. "The cancer..."

"Oh," Marie said, her mouth forming a perfect circle. The limited colour drained from her face. "You heard about that."

"Violet told us," Ivy explained.

"It wasn't a secret, you understand?" Marie said. "I just didn't know if it mattered to tell you."

"Of course," Ivy said. "It's your business. I just wanted to say that I'm sorry. See, my uncle... he had pancreatic cancer. I just... well, I just wanted to say I'm sorry, that's all."

"And did he..." Marie swallowed. "Is he..."

"He passed away," Ivy said, braving eye contact. "Seven years ago now."

"I see," she said and gave a sad smile. "That seems to be the way it goes."

"So, is that what you wanted to talk to us about?" asked Toby with an air of defensiveness, as though he didn't appreciate a stranger walking into their space and reminding his wife of her mortality.

"No," Ivy said. "No, it's not." She looked around the room. "Do you mind if we sit down?"

"Of course," Marie said, gesturing to a collection of Moroccan pouffes to the left of the entrance.

They sat down somewhat awkwardly, not used to the low seating that is so common in non-Western countries. On the floor was a tray with a Turkish coffee pot and patterned cups, but nobody bothered to offer a drink.

"Look, I'll get straight to it," Ivy said.

She was strangely aware of wasting time. Far more than usual. The woman sitting in front of her had a limited amount of it. They all did, really. It was just that Marie knew precisely how long she had left. Three months. At least. That was about ninety days, Ivy quickly calculated, just over two thousand hours, and Ivy felt more guilty than usual to be taking up one of them.

"Firstly, I have some questions about James DeSilver. It's imperative that we find him as soon as possible."

"Please do," Marie said. "Franky is losing her mind with worry."

"Did James have any other properties?"

Marie thought for a second but replied with a firm, "No. They'd sold their house in London before moving up here."

"He has his office?" Toby offered. "Have you tried there?"

"We have," Ivy said. "No holiday homes, here or abroad?"

Marie looked at Toby, scrunching her face as though trying to remember. "Not that I know of. You could ask Franky, but, well... they're a couple who like to show off." She shrugged as though only telling the truth. "If they had a holiday house, we would have all been invited to it by now."

"What about family?" Ivy asked. "Siblings? Parents?"

"His parents still live in London. And his brother. I can't imagine they wouldn't have called Franky if he had turned up, though. She's been on the phone to them every day."

"Okay," Ivy said, deflated. "And Toby, to clarify, you saw James leave here at quarter to ten?"

"Yes," he said. "Yeah, not too long before Bob dropped me off at the market. I saw his car leaving the site."

"And no one has heard from him since?"

Marie and Toby shook their heads in solemn synchronisation.

"But he's alright, isn't he?" Marie asked.

It was one of those enormous, impossible-to-answer questions that people sought answers to from those in authority. Ivy had no idea if James DeSilver was alright. She highly suspected he was on the run from killing his best friend, so she doubted it. That's if he hadn't killed himself by now. But she replied, not with the truth but with what Marie was truly seeking — comfort.

"We're doing all we can to find him," she said. "I promise."

"Just, if he and Lily... I've known them both my entire life. I don't know what I'd do."

Toby put a long, strong arm around Marie's shoulder and held her in a tight embrace. "You heard what she said," he said softly, "they're doing all they can." Then he smiled at Ivy over the top of his wife's head, causing her stomach to drop as though she'd driven over a particularly steep hillock in the Wolds. He blinked slowly as though he was used to triggering such a reaction and recognised it in her eyes.

Ivy pulled her gaze away, addicted as she was to the flutter in her chest, and refocused it on Marie. "We have just finished interviewing Violet Hughes," she said simply, which grabbed the woman's attention.

"Is she alright? Is she in trouble?"

"Oh, she's fine," Ivy said. "Unshaken, believe me. But she told us that, after the fog lifted, they found you on the road."

"Yes," she said. "I was the one who found Lily."

"She told you that," Toby said, but Ivy resisted looking his way.

"I just mean, what were you doing there?"

"What are you trying to say?" Toby butted in once more, and Ivy closed her eyes when replying.

"I'm not accusing anyone, Mr Entwhistle. I'm merely trying to understand the timings." She opened her eyes and looked at Marie. "Did you go to the road before or after the fog fell?"

"After," she said calmly. "When the fog eventually thinned, lifted, or whatever, I couldn't see Lily anywhere. I was worried. I went to find her."

"Were you feeling better?"

"Not really. I was still breathless and light-headed. But I was working on adrenaline, I guess. I just... I had this bad feeling." She, too, closed her eyes, and the pressure caused a tear to roll down her cheek. "And I was right."

"Okay," Ivy said. "Thank you."

"So, is that everything?" asked Toby, moving to stand, clearly concerned by his wife's distress.

"No," Ivy said firmly. "The reason I'm here is that we know that Lily was slapped the morning she was killed. Two to three hours before she was killed, to be exact. We want to know what happened."

Marie took a breath and looked at Toby. They seemed to share an unspoken language. Silent words passed between each other's eyes. "You said you were talking to Violet?" she asked.

"That's right."

"And she didn't tell you what happened?"

"No," Ivy said. "She didn't."

"Violet gets a hard time of it," Marie said gently. "The others are quick to blame her, to put her in the wrong, but she's a sweet soul, really. She just lost her brother, her only sibling."

"That's nice of you to say," Ivy said, "but it doesn't answer my question."

Marie sighed. "Violet slapped Lily," she said simply.

Ivy nodded as though reassuring the woman that she was only confirming what they already suspected. "Why didn't anyone mention this in their statements?"

"Not everyone saw it. Only me."

"Why didn't *you* mention this in your statement?"

"I was in shock, I..." Again, she looked at Toby, who gave an almost imperceptible nod. "Honestly? I didn't want Franky to find out. She would be devastated."

"Franky would be devastated that Violet slapped Lily?" Ivy said. "Why?"

"No, she would be devastated to find out *why* Violet slapped Lily."

"And why did she?"

"Because of what happened after dinner on Monday night."

Ivy sighed and sat back, preparing herself for another long story. She looked at the Turkish coffee pot and held it up. "Does anyone know how this works?"

"Yeah," Toby said, "there's a kettle and coffee over there. Do you want one?"

"I shouldn't really—"

"Don't worry, I'll make it."

"In that case, yes, I'd love one," Ivy said, handing it to him, and he stood and looked at his wife, who nodded as though she was okay to be left alone on one side of the room without him. Then he busied himself with the kettle, filling it from the adjoining bathroom's sink. "Marie," Ivy said, staring into the woman's grey, dull eyes that she imagined were once blue and bright, surrounded by grey, sallow skin she imagined used to be rosy and plump, "tell me what happened after dinner on Monday night."

CHAPTER TWENTY-NINE

"You did it," Toby said as they walked across the dark grass beneath the midnight sky back to their yurt. There were so many more stars in the Lincolnshire sky than over London; they seemed to shine brighter, too, and as Marie looked up at them, she couldn't help but feel that in three to six months, she would be joining them. "How do you feel?"

Marie sighed, letting go of her existential musings and squeezing the hand of the man at her side, reminding herself that she was still alive, in this body, in this moment, by his side.

"Like a weight has been lifted," she said honestly. "I'm glad I told them, but I feel like I passed whatever I was carrying onto them. They're the ones who need time now to get used to it."

"I know this sounds wrong," he said, his shape formless and shadowed in the dark, "but all things considered, it was a pretty nice evening."

Marie laughed. "I know what you mean." She paused. "You don't think it was rude? To leave Bob and Cecelia there alone with Violet?"

"They can handle themselves." Toby laughed. "I'd feel sorrier for leaving Violet and Cecelia alone with Bob after seven glasses of wine. Anyway, half the table's gone to bed already. I think it's fine."

"You know what's crazy?"

"Nothing you say is crazy, my love."

She smiled and stroked his cheek, so smooth and cold beneath her finger, like a chiselled ice statue.

"I felt guilty," she admitted. "For telling Lily. I mean, did you see her face? She looked heartbroken."

"Of course she did," Toby soothed. "You're her best friend." He squeezed her hand in the darkness. "But of course, you don't need to feel guilty."

"It's just so soon after Jordan. And now she's losing me."

To Marie's surprise, Toby laughed, a loud, bursting laugh. She was so shocked she couldn't help but join in.

"Oh, you find that funny, do you?"

"I'm sorry," he said, turning to his wife and holding her in his arms. "I am. It's just unbelievable to me that even when you're the one with terminal cancer, you're still worrying about everyone else."

"You think I should be busy feeling sorry for myself?"

"I think *we* should be busy," he said, and she heard the grin in his voice as he took her hand, leading her off to the side of the field, "enjoying the life that we have left."

"*Toby*," Marie said, laughing and pretending to pull back while letting herself be pulled right along with him. "We can't. Not here. What if someone walks past?"

"That's all part of the fun," he said. "Anyway, it's pitch black out here. No one will see anything."

As he spoke, the moon broke through the clouds and glowed upon his seemingly ageless face. He was the most beautiful man she had ever met, let alone known or slept with. He was hers, her man, her husband, and for as long as her health allowed, her lover. How could she deny him? How could she deny herself?

"Well, you better not make a noise," she said.

"Speak for yourself," he replied, lowering his hand to her waist and leading her into the forest beside the field, just past the tree line where the shadows would offer them some privacy. His lips on hers, as always, was a breath-taking experience, and any resistance she had felt was lost in the sensation of his hands in her hair. But it was just as he was undoing her dress, his lips on her neck, her skin about to be exposed to the cool night air and his precious touch that she heard movement just beyond the trees.

"Stop," she said, and his hand stilled immediately. "Did you hear that?"

"It's nothing," he said, tugging on her zip, causing her to shiver to run through her that was quashed by the noise.

"It's voices," she hissed. "Quiet."

"Where you off to then?" came a deep, muffled voice.

"Sounds like James," Toby whispered into her ear, turning to face the on comers. And just as he said it, another voice spoke, along with a glimpse of auburn through the trees.

"I couldn't sleep. Fancied a walk."

"And Lily," Marie whispered, and like that, they stayed, pressed against the tree, Toby's hand on Marie's exposed back, as they listened.

"Same," James said. "Can you believe it?"

"No," Lily said. "No, I can't. I can't believe this is happening again, to be honest." She paused. "Am I cursed?"

"No, Lil," James said softly. "But you're not the one who's dying."

"I think this is worse," she said solemnly. "To endure life while the people you love fade away."

"Is that what you're doing?" he said, his words slurred as they had been over dinner. "Enduring life?"

"Do you have an alternative?"

"Yes," he said, stepping closer to her. "Enjoying it."

They were both visible through the trees now, caught in the same ray of moonlight that had captured Toby.

"How can I?" she said. "First Jordan and now Marie. How can I enjoy life without them?" She began to sob quietly, and James stepped even closer, putting an arm around her shoulders.

"What's wrong?"

"What do you think's wrong, James?" she said, pushing him away. "My best friend just told me she's dying."

"I know." He held her again, placing a hand on her hair and allowing her to burrow into his chest the way a wife might. "But I know you," he whispered. "You don't cry when you're upset. You bury into yourself. You cry when you're worried." He pulled back and looked down, still holding her, their faces inches apart. "When you're scared."

She shook her head. "I don't know."

"There's something else, isn't there? Come on, Lil. I can tell."

Lily wiped her eyes and pulled away. "Just something Marie said."

"About what?"

"About not taking the treatment. It reminded me of something."

"What?"

"A case Jordan worked on. Years ago. I can't remember..." Marie looked up at Toby in the darkness, who looked just as confused, and he shrugged. "I'm drunk," she said and laughed it off. "It's nothing. Really."

James hesitated. He went to step closer to her again but stopped himself.

"We're good though? You know, after the other night?"

"The other night?"

"You know, our argument. *You owe me*. All of that?"

"Oh." Lily laughed. "Yeah, of course. I was just being silly."

"So, you're not mad at me?"

"No, James. God knows I can't stay mad at you anyway," she said, and the moonlight caught James's wide smile. "I shouldn't have said all those things. It's not fair to you. You don't owe me anything. We don't work like that."

"I just need more time, that's all."

"I know. I was just being drunk." She laughed. "Again!"

"Well, that's what happens when you're around Bob," he said lightly, but Lily remained serious.

"I don't want to push you away," she said. "You're all I have left."

"I'm not going anywhere, Lil."

"You had better not," she said. "I don't know what I'd do without you."

James paused, and even from the trees, Marie could see the movement of his throat as he swallowed his fear.

"Do you really mean that?" he asked.

"Of course I do," she said. "You know I do."

"Do I?" he said quietly.

"James..."

"It's just... with Marie... it makes you think, doesn't it? It all goes so quickly. Remember when we were kids and thought we had all the time in the world? We thought we'd live a hundred different lives, but we've only got one, and we have to be sure that we're living it right."

He stepped closer to Lily, and Marie could almost feel his yearning to hold her again.

"You told me you'd be ready one day," he continued. "When I grew up. When I stepped up and got my life in order, and I have, Lil. I have the business, the house. Look where we are." He laughed. "Did you ever think I'd be able to afford something like this?"

"It was never about money. That's not the point."

"I know," he said, "I know it wasn't. The point is, I'm ready for *us*, Lil. And I think you are, too."

"That was a long time ago," she whispered, turning as though to push him away but really just placing her hands on his chest. "Before Jordan. Before Franky."

James looked down at her hands and chose to listen to her body language over her words, gripped her elbows with a soft passion, and leaned in to kiss her.

But she pulled away before his lips could touch hers.

"I can't," she whispered in his arms.

"Why not?"

"You know why not."

"Franky?" James scoffed. "I don't even think she'd care. I think she hates me."

Although Marie could not see so well in the gloom, she knew Lily well enough to assume she was rolling her eyes.

"Franky does not hate you, James."

"She pretends like we're this perfect couple in front of everyone else, but she barely talks to me. She barely looks at me. Let alone anything else."

"So, is that what this is? You're feeling neglected?"

"You know it's more than that." He took a deep breath, and Marie was surprised to hear that when he spoke, his voice was cracked with emotion. The whole time she had known him, Marie had seen James cry only once — at Jordan's funeral. "You know that I've loved you for forty years now. *Forty years*," he repeated. "I don't know anything else that has ever lasted that long. Not my dreams. Not my sense of self. Sure as hell, not my marriage. Nothing except my love for you."

This time, when he leaned down to kiss her, Lily did not pull away, and Marie gripped Toby's wrist in shock and something akin to excitement at the sight of her two oldest friends displaying a love she always knew lay dormant deep within each of their hearts. But the kiss lasted only a second, a single moonlit moment before Lily pulled away once more.

"No," she said, peeling herself from his arms and stepping back. "It's too late."

James stepped forward. "It's not too late."

"I can't do this...I..." Lily ran her hands through her hair, and it bounced like a flicker of fire in the darkness. "I think we should take some space."

"Lil—"

"I mean it," she said. "After this trip, don't contact me. You're up here. I'm in London. Maybe that's the space we need to..."

"To what?" James asked, his voice thick with tears.

"To finally move on," she said.

And before James could say anything, before he could fight, before he could declare any more of his decades-old feelings for his best friend, she disappeared into the night.

"What happened to not knowing what you'd do without me?" he called after her. "Hey? Lily?"

But her figure had already merged with the darkness.

"I'm not going anywhere, Lil," James whispered to himself before stumbling back towards his yurt, his wife, and a sleepless night filled with regret. "I'm not going anywhere."

CHAPTER THIRTY

"So, they were having an affair?" Byrne said.

Ivy marched up and down in front of the whiteboard, her agitation on display as she collected her thoughts. Where George would have stood still and stoic, the only sign of his anxiety would have been the occasional tap of the marker pen against his thigh, she paced like a dog in need of a walk. But Ivy wasn't George. She never would be. She had to do things her own way.

"No, it sounded more like Lily rejected James," she answered.

"A man scorned," O'Hara said. "Wouldn't be the first time that's a motive for a murder case."

"That fits with what Bob said," Byrne spoke up. "About James and Lily being old friends who might have got married if they hadn't met their partners."

"So, everyone knew?"

"No," Ivy said, "everyone knew they'd been friends since childhood, but that doesn't mean anything. Marie and James were friends since childhood, too."

"But Cecelia said that Lily and James had this deep connection," Byrne said. "So, everyone knew that, at least, right? That they were close?"

"I wonder what his wife thought of that," Maguire said.

"Franky?"

"Couldn't have been easy," he continued, "everyone knowing your husband has this *deep connection* with his best friend, especially when your marriage is on the rocks."

"Who said it was on the rocks?"

"Bob," Byrne said, "in his story, and James in Marie's."

"So maybe Franky slapped Lily?" O'Hara suggested.

"Or worse," Maguire added darkly.

"No," Ivy said, shaking her head. "Marie confirmed that it was Violet who slapped Lily."

"Marie told you this, did she?" asked Campbell.

"Yes," Ivy said. "All of it. About the slap, the kiss. She told me too much, if anything. I could've done without the details of her and Toby frolicking in the trees."

"She could be lying."

"Why would she?"

"Because the other DNA on Lily belonged to her. *Marie* could have been the one to slap Lily. We only have her word for it."

"What exactly did she say, sarge?"

Ivy finally stopped pacing, only in order to better recall the details.

"The morning after the kiss, Tuesday morning, the morning Lily was killed, Marie talked to Lily about it as they were hiking. She said they were walking at the back, out of earshot of the others. She told her what she'd seen the night before, the kiss with James, and that she was worried about her. They didn't realise that Violet was weeing in the bushes nearby and overheard everything. She came out and confronted Lily about the kiss. She accused her of cheating on Jordan. Then Violet slapped her, and Marie witnessed the whole thing."

"And what did Lily do?" asked Byrne.

"Marie said she just took it. As though she deserved it."

"And Violet?"

"She stormed to the front of the group and ignored Lily for the rest of the morning."

"Did she tell Franky?"

"I don't know," Ivy admitted. "I asked Marie, of course, but she doesn't think so. Franky hasn't said anything about it, at least."

"Well, someone should ask Franky," Maguire suggested. "Because that's a pretty solid motive."

"It also means Violet lied to us, sarge," Campbell said. "That's perjury."

"Not to mention the slap itself," Byrne said.

"That's motive," Maguire added.

"Well," Ivy began, "She wasn't under oath, so it's not perjury, but let's put Violet to one side for—"

"If she was angry enough to slap her sister-in-law for thinking she'd cheated on her brother," O'Hara said, "who knows what else she might do."

"Or what Franky might do if Violet told her—"

"I said put it aside," Ivy said loudly, then lowered her voice following a deep breath. "For now, I want updates on James DeSilver." They all slowed like a carriage that had lost its momentum, gradually rolling to a stop, but it was necessary to stop them from getting carried away. "Look, the more time we waste looking down dead ends, the further away James DeSilver gets," she added. "So, what have we got?"

"Still no use of his card," Byrne started, the first to adapt to the shift in focus, "but I looked into his account, and well... I thought James DeSilver was rich?"

"He's not?" asked Ivy.

"Not from the look of his account. Don't get me wrong, he's not broke, but he's certainly not swimming in it."

"Perhaps he has assets tied up elsewhere," suggested O'Hara.

"Like a new house in the Wolds?" Maguire said.

"Or a business?"

"Who's looking into his business accounts?" Ivy asked.

"We're still waiting on permission from the company's accountant," Byrne said. "He seems resistant without DeSilver's permission."

"Remind him we can get a warrant if he needs help making up his mind."

"Her," Byrne said. "A Miss Fletcher. But will do."

"Good. What else?"

"We sent local officers over to DeSilver's parents' house in London," Maguire said, checking the notes on his lap, his voice clipped and focused as though he had been unnerved. "But he's not there. Not at his brother's either." Ivy began to pace once more, her ideas of where James DeSilver might be slipping away like sand in an hourglass. "And he doesn't own any other properties."

"What about the ports?" she asked, stopping and staring at Maguire, daring him to question her.

"He's on the watchlist and would be flagged if he went through any airport or ferry port..."

"But?"

"But he hasn't been."

The silence that followed was long and heavy with indecision, and she knew that the team felt it too, which was why Campbell so tentatively raised her right hand to get Ivy's attention.

"This isn't school, Campbell," she said, not wanting her most capable PC to exhibit such childish behaviour.

"Sarge, maybe we should be looking closer to home? You know, around the last place he was seen?"

"The glampsite?"

"Yeah."

"Why would we do that?"

"Maybe he's closer than we think, that's all."

"I see," Ivy said. Campbell's longanimous tone grated on her patience. "So, you think DeSilver killed Lily Hughes and then stuck around to be caught?"

"No," she said flatly. "I think we're too narrow." Ivy bristled and opened her mouth to speak, but Campbell had started, and by all accounts, she was going to finish. "I think we should entertain the possibility—"

"Of what?"

"That his wife's fears are right. What if he's a victim in all of this?"

"What exactly are you suggesting, Campbell? Speak up." Despite telling Campbell that this was not school, she heard the same clip tone in her voice as her old headmistress's. "We have limited time."

Campbell stared Ivy down.

"I'm suggesting that we start looking for DeSilver. In a formal capacity, I mean."

"A search for what?"

"For his body or signs of a struggle."

"Absolutely not," Ivy said, dismissing the idea as soon as it left her lips. "That will take tens of officers, resources and time that we don't have. I'd just love to see Tim Long's reaction."

"Then let's ask him," Campbell replied, and Byrne's head turned sharply to give something akin to a warning look.

Ivy stepped forward. "James DeSilver is our lead suspect. He's on the run. Just because you're struggling to find me any leads on his whereabouts doesn't mean we should reorientate our entire investigation." She towered over Campbell but turned to address the rest of the team. "Any other bright ideas?" she asked. But when Campbell opened her mouth to speak, she added, "Relevant to the narrative of our investigation?"

Campbell looked down at her lap, where statements and reports balanced, plus what looked to be a legal document of some kind and several more pages of notes. Yet despite this,

Campbell shook her head and muttered, "No, sarge," along with the rest of them.

Ivy nodded, glad to see the PC was learning to prioritise the information she shared.

"Alright then." She clapped once, the way George did when he readied the team for action, but all her clap seemed to do was make them wince. "Byrne, I want access to James DeSilver's business bank account by the end of the day, by whatever means necessary. O'Hara, keep working with Ruby on facial recognition and monitoring of the ports. Maguire, keep looking at road cameras for any sign of DeSilver's car on Tuesday morning. And Campbell..."

"Yes, sarge?"

"Write up Marie Entwhistle's statement about what she witnessed between Lily and DeSilver on Monday night. I'll send you my notes. We'll need it for CID. O'Hara's right. *That's* his motive. Rejection. A man scorned. That's why he killed Lily Hughes," she said, then whispered almost to herself, "I'm sure of it."

CHAPTER THIRTY-ONE

George pulled his car into a lay-by in front of a closed farmer's gate, where, he imagined, the farmer often became annoyed by people like him who stopped to admire the incredible view beyond it. From here, one gained an ideal vantage point over the valley below. He'd spent all day in the depths of the Wolds, following blind corners and dead ends, travelling between the crime scene to the DeSilver house to the Grove to get an idea of timings and distance. But really, he had just been driving in circles. Finally, noticing the hill behind the glampsite, he longed to be at the top of it. To breathe the fresh air, and gain a new perspective, as Grace might have said.

That was why she loved the sea so much. It was always changing, pulling her beyond their little bubble of existence.

He climbed out of the car to stretch his legs. His knees groaned with the effort, an ailment faced by the tall. Cars and aeroplanes were the enemy, causing cramps on long journeys, and George felt like he'd been travelling for days.

He stretched. With the wind in his hair and the sun on his face, he already felt less claustrophobic. Straight ahead, he saw the extensive field that made up Wolds Grove. He could identify the bamboo-constructed reception and even the figures moving between the yurts. One moved quickly, left and right, as though pacing, maybe on the phone. He thought that might be Franky DeSilver. Two others he spotted walking close together, perhaps hand in hand, lovers on a stroll, the likes of which he had already seen in Marie and Toby Entwhistle. Violet was nowhere to be seen. Surely, he would have recognised her hair from here. After all, in the spirit of Alice Walker, one should notice the colour purple in a field.

To George's left, on a hilly outcrop, was a dark, decrepit house — a stain upon the landscape, a harsh but true impression. He could not understand why anyone wouldn't have improved the aesthetic of a house with such a view in such a place. Its dingy appearance was apparent even from a distance, all peeling paint and overgrown gardens, and a psoriasis-like roof with missing tiles, a black smudge on the Wolds' rich colour palette.

Perhaps it was just because he had been on a home improvement mission of his own in the last few months. Perhaps his standards were too high. But he also supposed that whoever owned that house didn't have a dying wife to impress or inspire memories in her fading mind.

Just before George's thoughts descended into a grief-ridden spiral, his phone buzzed in his pocket, and once again, the job's perk brought him back to reality. There was always a distraction. Always a ringing phone in a pocket, never far away.

"Campbell," he answered, "how are things?"

She sighed heavily enough that it blended with the wind that rattled through the earpiece. "I'd like to say fine, but I'd be lying. Where are you?" she added, as though hearing the rustle on the line.

"In a lay-by on a hill by the Grove."

"Have you just been driving around?"

"What am I supposed to do? I can't just go home, and..."

"And what, guv?"

"Well, I can't come in, can I?"

"I thought you were the boss?"

"I am," he replied. "But it's more than that. She needs a chance, and I... well, I'm not sure if I'm ready."

"Can she do that?" Campbell asked. "I mean, can a DS tell a DI what to do?"

"When the DI is technically on compassionate leave and interfering in a live investigation, then yes, there's probably some grounds there. Some leftie in the top brass would probably support her if she made a complaint."

"What would DCI Long say?"

"Tim has nothing to do with this," he said sharply, not wanting to engage with the idea of going over Ivy's head. "So, anyway, why the dark mood?" he asked, moving the conversation along.

"I don't like the thought of a killer on the loose when we were no closer to finding them yesterday than we are today."

"What's going on? Have we made any progress?"

He heard himself use the word, we, and although it felt disingenuous, he was compelled to let it be.

"Sergeant Hart is convinced that James DeSilver is on the run. She's got us looking into ports all over the country."

"She knows what she's doing," George said, not even convincing himself.

"Does she?"

"Ivy is more than capable," he insisted. "But her social life is... She's distracted," he said, then added, "and single-minded."

"Guv, call it what it is, won't you? She's *stubborn*," Campbell said. "She won't go back on her theory even when it's not working. It's like she doesn't trust us anymore. The mood is... well, it's not good."

"I know you don't know the whole story, but it's not about you or the team, Campbell. If Ivy questions anything right now, her entire life and recent marital decisions might unravel into uncertainty. So yes, she's stubborn."

"But there're so many moving parts," Campbell said. "We have to keep an open mind. Not send home the one person who might help."

George smiled at her compliment. He knew very well that Ivy had sent him home, not out of concern but because he had confused her theories.

"Well," he said playfully, "if I have to go rogue to help the investigation from afar, that's what I'll do. So, what about what I asked you to do? Have you done it?"

Again, Campbell sighed, but there was slightly less despair in it than before.

"Yes, guv, that's why I'm calling. You were right. The name you saw on the letterhead is James DeSilver's business. According to his website, Sabina Anter is a client of his."

"It's on his website?"

"Listed as a B2B of VavaRoom. For marketing purposes, I guess, to show credibility. Wolds Grove is a five-star establishment. It looks good."

"The document I saw didn't exactly look like marketing."

"Exactly," Campbell jumped in. "So, I did some digging."

"There's more?"

"You bet. Sabina Anter is *suing* James DeSilver's company." George let the news sink in as his eyes roamed the view of the Wolds. A new perspective indeed. "I found a court filing," Campbell continued. "She's suing VavaRoom for lost earnings resulting from a breach of contract. Allegedly, his software is full of bugs, resulting in cancelled reservations, double bookings, and wrongful payments. In the last few months, she claims to have lost up to fifty grand in revenue and complaint costs, lost bookings, the dent in positive reviews and so on."

"And?" George asked. "What's the judgement?"

"The case is ongoing."

"It's not been decided yet?"

"No, guv."

George's gaze soared across the valley like a hawk's might, subconsciously looking for anomalies in the perfect picture, the dart of a rabbit, the flit of a swallow, or... He squinted... A divergence in the tree line.

"There's something else, guv."

"Go on," George said, stepping forward to better identify the black object on the edge of the copse, a few fields east of the dark house and the Grove. But it was useless. He looked away, assuming it was a piece of farming equipment, perhaps a grain dryer or a disused tractor.

"I suggested to DS Hart that we put out a search party for DeSilver."

"And?"

"It didn't go down well."

"I bet it didn't if she assumes he's on the run."

Campbell huffed. "She thinks he's well gone by now."

"Yet his car hasn't been spotted on any ANPR?"

"Exactly."

But farming equipment was usually brightly coloured, wasn't it? To reflect the sun for temperature control and stand out in a field for safety reasons? George's gaze returned to the black mark by the trees. Something about it seemed too familiar to ignore.

"So, what do you think?" Campbell asked.

"About what?"

"About putting out a search party."

"I think it's a good idea," he said distractedly, his eyes fixed on the unidentified object.

"Right? I mean, how do we know he's not a victim in this?"

"Ivy's the one in charge of this investigation," George reminded her. "You should say that to her."

"I did. Word for word. And she shot me down."

"Why's she so sure DeSilver is on the run?" he asked distantly.

"For *no* reason. Except her own stubbornness," she muttered.

The reprimand was on the tip of George's tongue, but he felt it was better to let the young PC vent her frustrations. He found that a healthy silence was usually enough for people to say what they were really thinking.

"I thought maybe you could approve it," she said slowly.

But George was barely listening, his focus on the far-away object. Like the dingy house, it was a stain on the otherwise natural environment. It had no place being there.

"Ivy is in charge," he said. "For the time being, at least."

"I know that Sergeant Hart is in charge, but you hold the higher rank, guv."

"I did what you asked, Campbell," he said. "I tried to come back to the team, but Ivy needs this one. In all the years we've worked together, I don't think that she's had to lead an investigation from beginning to end. It'll be good for her."

George removed his glasses to see further, but there was little difference. He longed for the sharp vision he used to enjoy. Then, with that thought, something occurred to him. He'd had many hobbies in his life, short-term, minor distractions from the job that inevitably consumed all of his attention. But at least some of the tools from such hobbies remained. He turned and headed back to his car.

"I know but... Look, it's not like I want to go behind her back or anything," Campbell continued in his ear, "but at this rate, we're not going to make any progress. You know her better than anyone. Maybe you could talk to her?"

One such hobby, not too long ago, had been bird watching. He'd fancied himself a twitcher, taking long drives along the coast but rarely spotting anything more interesting than a seagull. Still, he remembered, reaching into his glove box and pulling out a chunky pair of Steiner binoculars, he'd kept the equipment.

"Guv?" Campbell said down the phone. "Are you still there?"

"I'm here," he muttered, returning to the vantage point, raising the binoculars to his eyes with his free hand, finding the black object, and immediately recognising the significance of what he was seeing.

"So, is there anything you can do?" she asked. "I mean, it's all well and good—"

"There'll be no need for a search, Campbell," George said, as sure as he could be, and as though he had finally spotted a rare bird, he slowly lowered the binoculars, his heart thumping in his chest. "I've found him. I've found James DeSilver."

CHAPTER THIRTY-TWO

As the paramedics pulled James DeSilver's body from the driver's seat of the black Audi A4, the birds in the surrounding trees sang as though a funeral choir, witnesses to a tragic fate.

As they lifted DeSilver's body onto a gurney with great care, Ivy came to stand beside George. He didn't recognise her from her voice. In fact, she didn't utter a word at first. Nor did he turn to face her. He recognised her from the distinct rhythm of her heavy steps, her oaky perfume on the wind, and the manner in which she stood beside him — comfortable and close.

They stood like that, in silence, watching the various factions perform their roles on James DeSilver.

Eventually, Ivy spoke, rousing him as if from a dream, so lost was he in the details of DeSilver's death.

"I thought you'd gone home," she said.

He cleared his throat. "I took a drive."

"How did you find him?"

"I was up on the hill there," he said nodding to his left. Ivy looked between the hill and the car, double checking that it would indeed have been in his eye line.

Deciding that his story added up, she continued, "So you called Campbell?"

There was no hiding the accusation in her voice.

"I was already on the phone with her," he said honestly.

She turned to face him fully, and he looked down to see an expression filled with frustration and, if he was not mistaken, hurt. "You're the one who said you weren't ready for this investigation, guv."

"I know," he said. "And I thought I wasn't, but I...I suppose I need something to do."

"See, that's what bothers me. Not that you're back. Of course I want you back. But I don't understand what changed overnight."

He didn't reply.

"It makes me feel like you don't trust me. Like you don't think I can do this on my own."

"*Nobody* can do this job on their own, Ivy. That's why we have a team."

She stared at him as though absorbing the words, but he wasn't sure whether they changed her opinion on the matter or not. But he wasn't about to tell Ivy that her husband had asked him to look after her and her subordinate had revealed concerns over her leadership. Silence was the better option, but still, Ivy walked away, clearly unsatisfied.

George followed, keeping his distance. He felt like a shadow, destined never to get close.

"What have we got?" she called to Doctor Saint, who stood in front of the car, wiping his brow with a handkerchief. Even though it was not a particularly hot day, George imagined that such an examination had been enough to break a sweat for other reasons. George, for one, had never seen such facial damage on a man.

"It was best to keep him where he was," Saint explained. "And I must be honest, I didn't have the heart to help move him. That poor soul deserves to rest in peace."

"Poor soul?" Ivy repeated. "He's the lead suspect in a murder investigation."

"That man was slammed into the steering wheel seven or eight times, from what I could tell. Maybe more. He would have suffered terribly. We give death row inmates more dignity."

"Eight times?" George repeated.

Saint nodded. "As though trying to cause as much harm as possible, wildly, over and over again, which screams of desperation to me. It was a traumatic brain injury, if not a haemorrhage. That's if shock and a cardiac arrest didn't get him first. Pip will be able to confirm."

"How do you know he was slammed into the steering wheel more than once?" Ivy asked.

"Did you see his face?" Saint asked, but the look on Ivy's face was clearly enough of an answer. "That type of trauma doesn't happen from a one-time collision." He looked at the car, which, though damaged, was not a write-off. "A man could walk away from that accident."

"Time of death?" Ivy said, having listened patiently to his analysis, but the need for an answer was clear in her voice.

"All I can say for now is that he's been here for over a day. Since yesterday. Not to mention that the blood on him was dry as a bone, but livor mortis is well-established, and the body had begun early stages of active decomposition, autolysis, putrefaction and the like—"

"What does that mean?"

"It means he has been dead for at least thirty-six hours, Sergeant Hart."

"Since Tuesday morning?"

Saint nodded. "At least."

Even from behind, George could sense the disappointment in the sag of Ivy's shoulders. This made nothing easier. It only complicated matters.

"It can't have happened long after DeSilver left the Grove," George pointed out.

"And he wasn't moved?" Ivy tried.

"Definitely not," Saint said, and he looked over their shoulders just as George heard the sound of a van pulling up. He guessed that it would be a white van containing forensic equipment and white-suited individuals. "Excuse me," Saint said, walking away to liaise with Katy Southwell. "I'll pass my report on to Doctor Bell."

"There," Ivy said quietly after a few seconds. "I was wrong."

She said it as though George had proved a point he had not made. "If you think this investigation is a matter of being right or wrong, Ivy," he said flatly, "then you're not in the right mindset to be conducting it."

"How did you know what time James DeSilver left the Grove?" she asked suddenly.

"What are you talking about?"

"You said that DeSilver couldn't have been killed long after he left the Grove. How do you know what time he left?"

"I..." A kind of panic rose from his chest. "I think you told me, didn't you?"

"No, guv. I didn't tell you."

"Or maybe Campbell told me then," he said, "when we were on the phone."

He sure as hell was not about to explain to Ivy that Campbell had given him a case file behind her back, nor that he knew as much about the investigation as she did, if not more. But he was also very aware of the Manila folder lying on the passenger seat in his car no more than ten metres from where they stood. All it would take is for Ivy to look through his window on the way back to her own vehicle.

"What were you talking about?" she asked. "On the phone with Campbell?"

George hesitated, then decided to be honest. They should

both be on the same page at some point during this investigation at least. "I asked her to look into something for me."

Ivy threw up her hands. "So other investigations have been happening while I've been leading just the one?"

"It was a small side project," George said. "I asked her to look into a hunch for me."

"She has enough to be doing, following my directions," Ivy said.

"Your *directions*, Ivy," George said, losing his patience, which, although it spanned a great distance, still had its limits, "would've had her going to every port in the country before you'd even checked within half a mile of where James DeSilver was last seen."

Ivy rubbed her face in her hands like an addict who had finally been called out on their behaviour. No longer enabled, her shoulders slumped forward, and she whispered, "You're right." She swallowed. "I'm out of my depth, guv. I don't know what I'm doing. I was trying to follow your style and your strategy of building a narrative, but all it's done is lead me down the wrong path. I don't know what I was thinking. We should've found him sooner. *You* would've found him sooner."

George placed what he hoped was a comforting hand on her shoulder. "I don't know what I would've done," he said. "It's not like, under my lead, we solve every investigation within a day, is it?"

She sighed. "What was the hunch?"

George straightened. "I saw a letterhead for James DeSilver's business on Sabina's desk."

"That's what Campbell was trying to tell me," Ivy whispered as though to herself. "I ignored her. So, there's a connection between Sabina Anter and DeSilver?"

"More than a connection. There's a rivalry. A lawsuit, in fact."

"You'll have to catch me up," she said.

"I plan to," he said with a grin. "If you'll let me back on the team?"

She laughed. "Let you back? You can bloody lead the thing. God knows I'm just making everything worse."

"That's not true, Ivy. You followed your instinct, and it was a good one. James DeSilver was missing. Everything pointed towards him having killed Lily Hughes. And quite frankly, you might still be right. If Saint says that DeSilver was killed on Tuesday morning, until we have a more accurate time of death from Pip, it's fully possible that he killed Lily then returned here, and someone killed him."

George began pacing, and he couldn't deny it, it felt good to be back in the driver's seat.

"Look, the way I see it," he continued, "we're looking at two options. Either somebody killed them both, or James killed Lily. Someone saw it and killed him in revenge. Either way, at least one person is lying to us. But, very possibly, two people are hiding what they know. The big question is, to help us strike a line through one of those options, who was closest to Lily? Who loved Lily Hughes so much that they would be willing to kill in her name?"

Ivy thought about it for a moment, but then she shook her head as though the answer was obvious.

"From the way they talk about her?" she said, looking over the field to where Wolds Grove nestled in the curves of the land. "It could have been any one of them."

CHAPTER THIRTY-THREE

He and Ivy stood in front of the closed yurt, biding their time before the inevitable.

"I hate this part of the job," George muttered. "The only thing worse than not being there for Grace when she passed away would have been a stranger turning up on my doorstep to tell me about it."

"Me too. Good thing you're back on the investigation, guv," she said, offering a cheeky grin. "I'll just follow your lead."

"I see..." George nodded, suppressing his own smile and knocking twice on the wooden pole that supported the entrance. "I see how it is."

Franky answered the door quickly as though she had been waiting on her haunches for the sound of news, ready to jump into action. Good or bad, he imagined, at this point, she just wanted to know what had happened to her husband. They say that not knowing is the true hell. Though George imagined that hearing her husband's face had been smashed into a steering wheel at least eight times would incite a hell of its own.

"Mrs DeSilver," he said when she whipped back the canvas opening, "can we come in?"

"Where is he?" she asked, looking over their shoulders as though they might be hiding his reveal behind the kind of sliding door that hid relatives on *This Is Your Life*. "Where is he?"

"Perhaps we should come in first," Ivy added gently, and George couldn't help but notice that her gentler tone of voice often came out when she was harmonising with his firmer tone. A lone harmony sounds off-key, he thought to himself. Or even a bit shrill.

"Just tell me!" Franky shouted, a different version now of the woman George had met only one day previous, a frantic, frazzled-haired lady with wide eyes and stressed skin.

Her cries drew the attention of Marie and Toby Entwhistle, who emerged tentatively from their yurt.

"Franky?" her friend asked, "What's wrong, darling?"

"It's James, isn't it?" She ignored Marie, eyes only for George and Ivy. "*Please*," she begged, as though they were torturing her. "Just tell me where he is."

George looked at Ivy, who gave a small nod, agreeing that prolonging Franky's suffering by forcing her inside and forcing her to sit down bordered on cruel. It was best just to tell her the truth.

"We found James's car this afternoon. I'm afraid James was inside," George said, sliding into the truth rather than avoiding the inevitable. Then he added, "There's no easy way to say this, but..."

Every part of Franky DeSilver seemed to shrivel. It was like watching a grape wither into a raisin, and if she was the fruit, he was the blaring light of the sun — blazing a hot, inescapable truth. Her soft, smooth skin crinkled as her face collapsed in agony, and her proud posture crumpled. Marie immediately rushed over, and even in her ill state, she was able to catch Franky just as she fell to the ground. In a crouched position, she held her friend in her arms and looked up at the two detectives as though accusing them of attacking her in some way with their words.

"I'm sorry," he said, believing that the sentiment would suffice.

"What happened?" she asked quietly.

"We don't know exactly. Not yet." He turned to Franky. "I'm sorry, Mrs DeSilver. We do need to formally identify him, but—"

"I knew it," she was whispering to herself. "I knew it." She clutched her chest. "I couldn't feel him anymore."

Marie Entwhistle stroked her friend's hair. The flawless, blonde locks had, only within the last day, begun to tangle and dry out.

"How did he die?" asked Toby, coming to stand beside his wife. He placed a hand on her shoulder, comforting Marie as she, in turn, comforted Franky. It was a Russian doll of comfort. They each stood at different heights, consumed by varying levels of grief.

George hesitated and then decided on a half-truth. "We're still investigating."

Franky released an animalistic moan.

"Where did you find him?" Toby asked.

"On the edge of a field half a mile away," George said.

"Half a mile away?" Toby repeated. "Jesus. How did it take you over a day to find him?"

"He could have been anywhere in the country," Ivy spoke up.

"But he wasn't, was he?" he said. "He was half a bloody mile away!"

Toby shook his head in disbelief, and for some reason, that seemed to affect Ivy enough for her to turn away.

"I'm afraid we can't share the exact details of an ongoing investigation, Mr Entwistle," George said, and it was at this moment, Bob and Cecelia Adams turned the corner and stopped in their tracks, their arms full of food shopping. Although it looked more like snacks than groceries, a family bag of ready-salted crisps and a bar of chocolate protruded from the open top. At the sight before them, they stopped, stilled, as though in shock.

"What's happened?" Cecelia whispered, her voice carried by the wind.

"It's James," Franky said, shaking. "They found him. He's... oh God."

"Love," said Cecelia, dumping her share of the shopping at her husband's feet. She ran forward and crouched on the other side of Franky, wrapping her arms around her friend's neck, who sobbed into the crook of her elbow.

They all stayed for a while like this: Toby with his hand on Marie's shoulder, Marie with her arms around Franky, Cecelia in a similar position on the other side, George and Ivy looking down upon them, and Bob to the side holding four bags of groceries, as though to relinquish his burden would only serve to invite another far more arduous responsibility.

Violet was nowhere to be seen.

"I appreciate this is a difficult time," George began, and all three women looked up to glare at him as one. "But two people have died in as many days. There's no evidence to suggest that the events are linked, but we do need to explore all possibilities. And to do that, Mrs DeSilver, I have to ask you some questions."

"Now?" said Cecelia. "For God's sake. Can you give her a moment?" She looked him up and down. "Who the hell even are you?"

"My name is Detective Inspector George Larson," he said, looking at Ivy, who once more offered a subtle nod. "And I am leading this investigation."

"I thought *she* was running the show," Cecelia replied, nodding at Ivy.

"I was," Ivy replied coldly, refusing to offer more information than necessary.

"DS Hart is the Senior Investigating Officer," George explained. "My job is to ensure procedures are followed. There's no change."

"But they haven't, have they?" Franky said. "They haven't been followed. If they had, you would have found him—"

"Look, I wish I could offer you more time, Mrs DeSilver, I do," he said, "but finding James has cast the investigation in a whole new light."

"So, what? You just tell me my husband's dead, and then you bugger off?"

"Actually, we need to ask some questions."

"Questions?" Toby said. "She's just heard that her—"

"It's fine," Franky croaked, holding her hand up to stop him. "It's fine. What are your questions?"

"Your husband's business, VavaRoom," George clarified. "Do you know if any of his clients are local to Lincolnshire?"

This appeared to be the very last question that Franky imagined he would ask. She shook her head incredulously, then said, "I suppose? I mean, most of his clients were back in London, but since moving here, I know that he's been marketing more locally. Why?"

"Were you aware that Sabina Anter is a client of your husband's?"

"Who?" she said.

"Sabina Anter," Ivy repeated. "The owner of Wolds Grove."

"The woman in the pantsuits?" she said hesitantly. "Why on earth would I know that?"

"Your husband never shared any part of the business with you?"

"It's *his* business, not mine. It's nothing to do with me. I don't get involved."

"So, you weren't aware of any ongoing lawsuits?"

Franky's head snapped up.

"What the hell are you talking about? What lawsuits?"

Only then did Bob finally come to his senses and lower the shopping bags to the ground. He cleared his throat, held up his hand like a schoolboy, and said, "Excuse me, officer?" George assumed Bob was talking to him, and he turned to face the man expectantly. "I might be able to help?"

CHAPTER THIRTY-FOUR

"So, did they say anything?" George asked Ivy from the kitchen table. She stood over the stove adding a light sprinkle of chopped basil into the sauce, then stopped to sniff. "When I was talking to Bob, I mean?"

"Not really," Ivy said, stirring the basil into the sauce. "Franky oscillated between sobs and simmering down, then it was like a fresh wave of grief would consume her." Even from behind, George could see her shaking her head. "I can't even imagine how she must've felt."

"Can't you?" asked George. "Haven't we seen it enough times by now?"

"Feels fresh every time, though, doesn't it, guv? Every time, they react in a new way that shocks you. It's the wild cries that always does it for me, like they're a wounded animal. It's like something inside us knows that those sorts of sounds are reserved for... for a pain I cannot comprehend."

"So, you believe her?" he asked, and Ivy turned around, one hand beneath the spoon she raised to her lips. She tasted it as though tasting his question, savouring the flavour and thinking upon it.

"I do, yeah," she said. "She didn't know he was dead."

"I agree," George said, nodding.

"So, are you going to tell me?" she said, turning back to the stove and adding over her shoulder. "Or are you going to keep me hanging?"

George exhaled loudly. He had spent the entire drive home processing the significance of what Bob Adams had said to him behind the yurt, only a few metres out of earshot of the women and Toby. Just before they had driven their own cars back home, George had promised to relay the details to Ivy over dinner that night.

"Bob said it was a few months ago now," George began. "When James and Franky had first moved to the Wolds. James had told Bob about the lawsuit. Sabina had been one of his first new local clients. He said it wouldn't be hard to fight back but that he needed to pay the legal fees, and he'd put all his savings into the house. He needed a few months to get back on track financially."

"Okay, that makes sense," Ivy said. "From what Campbell found in his bank account, for a man everyone talks about being the richest of all of them, he didn't have much to his name."

"It's a debt culture we live in," George said shaking his head. "I didn't have a credit card until I was thirty-six."

"Keeping up with appearances," Ivy muttered. "It's timeless." She pulled two plates down from a freshly painted, newly fixed cupboard beside the stove. "So DeSilver didn't have the money," she clarified. "I'm guessing he asked Bob?"

"Yes, and apparently, Bob struggled not to laugh in his face," George said.

"Bob didn't have the money either?"

"Far from it," George said. "It seems like that's always been a bit of a sore point in their friendship, that James and Franky don't seem to understand how expensive it is to have kids, how all their money is put into domestic problems, and they don't have ten grand to lend to a friend on a whim."

"That's how much the fees were?" Ivy said, spooning the sauce over two plates of tagliatelle. "Ten grand?"

"That's how much James asked him for." George shrugged. "When Bob said he couldn't lend it to him, James offered to sell him shares in the business."

"What difference does that make?" Ivy said. "If Bob doesn't have the money, he doesn't have the money."

"That's exactly what Bob said."

"So, he didn't get the money from Bob?"

"No."

"But he's still managed to pay the legal fees?"

George grinned. "Now you're getting it."

"I hope you're as hungry as you say, guv. I made enough to feed a family," Ivy said, carrying the two plates over and holding one out to George. "So, where did he get the money from?"

"That's exactly what I'm wondering," he said, accepting the dish and taking a deep sniff, rewarded with a scent of basil, smoky beef, and parmesan reggiano. "But I have an idea how we might find out."

Ivy raised her eyebrows and stabbed at a chunk of beef, reading his mind. "You'll have to get her to come into work first."

"I'm working on it," he said with a grin.

Then, with the kind of timing deserving of a playwright, there was a knock on the door. Ivy looked between the open kitchen door and George's feigned innocence, chewing slowly, an undeniable yet recognisable look on her face: *what have you gone and done now, guv?* Before he could move, she got up and stepped out of the room, trying to get ahead of his plans — pointless, of course. He was three steps ahead already.

George continued eating his meal. It was delicious. It tasted like success. After an exclaim of surprise and a few muffled pleasantries at the front door, Ivy returned not long later with somebody by her side George was genuinely delighted to see.

Somebody who represented his success in the Wolds, he supposed, and that at least made him pleased to see her. Somebody who hadn't quite been a big fish in a small pond with the competition issues to prove it, like Campbell. Nor somebody who had needed a chance and thrived under constant supervision, unwavering support, and more than one instance of intense, one-on-one motivation, like Byrne. Nor a pair of well-intentioned and well-matched but somewhat unambitious officers like Maguire and O'Hara. No, this somebody had been a rare gift from Tim Long, a sign that George's team was finally being taken seriously, a hint that they were no longer outcasts in the Wolds but a force to be reckoned with, who deserved the professionalism, experience, and firepower of the most efficient researcher Tim Long had to offer.

George positively beamed. After all, he hadn't seen her in three weeks.

CHAPTER THIRTY-FIVE

"Thanks for coming," George said, as though her company was a pleasant surprise, and stood from his chair as a sign of respect. "Please, please, join us. There's enough for the three of us, isn't there, Ivy?" he asked, knowing full well there was.

"Of course," she said stiffly, and after a moment of icy stillness, she thawed herself and walked over to the stove, plating up a third serving and placing it in front of Ruby, who seated herself at the rarely used third seat.

Ruby removed her hat and placed it on the back of her chair, commenting politely, "This looks lovely." Then she looked around the room and shuffled. "Feels strange," she said, turning to George.

"What does?"

"To be in your home, guv. I feel... I don't know. Out of sorts."

"Oh, please," he said, waving his hand dismissively. "We're all friends here."

Ruby raised her eyebrows, and George caught her giving a sideways glance at Ivy, but she didn't reply.

The three of them sat in silence for a few minutes, only the clanging of metal on porcelain disturbing the disquiet, Ivy eyeing

George, him responding with an innocent stare, their silent conversation of looks continuing, their expressions becoming more and more animated until Ruby couldn't pretend not to notice anymore.

She set her cutlery down and turned to Ivy.

"You didn't know he'd invited me, did you?"

Ivy cleared her throat. "I have to admit..." She glared at George. "I was surprised to see you here, yes. Had I known, then perhaps I would have made something gluten-free." She eyed George accusingly, unwilling to take the blame for what appeared to be an insensitivity.

"It's fine," Ruby said dismissively.

George dabbed at his mouth with a tea towel. "I just thought it'd be a good idea for the three of us to catch up, you know, get an idea of the lie of the land. Things have been a little up in the air recently." When neither of the two women replied, both in their own state of confusion at George's antics, he continued, "I heard you've been working from home recently, Ruby?"

"Oh," she said, as though the invite finally made sense. "Yeah, well, it's in my contract..."

"Of course," he said, "and that's your choice. It's just—"

"We need you in the incident room," Ivy said bluntly.

It was George's turn to glare at her for disrupting his gentle tact.

Ruby sat up as though ruffled. "Sarge, I've been doing everything asked of—"

"No, Ruby," Ivy interrupted softly, and to George's surprise, she reached over and held the researcher's hand. "We *need* you in the incident room. You're..." She searched for the right word and then found a good one. "Invaluable."

Ruby's dark skin turned rosy on her cheeks, like the colour of a fine wine or a sophisticated piece of cherry-wood furniture. "I appreciate that," she said. "I suppose I've just been feeling a little..." She searched for her own phrasing. "Out of place. In the team, I mean."

"Yes, well," Ivy said, taking her hand away to run it through her hair, "I'm sure I haven't helped. The atmosphere hasn't exactly been very welcoming, has it?"

"It's not just you," Ruby said quickly. "I mean..."

Ivy smiled. "It's okay."

"It's just... You know..." She sighed and looked between George and Ivy. "I'd heard a lot about your team before—"

"Our team," George corrected her, and she smiled politely before continuing.

"I heard about *our* team long before DCI Long asked me to join it. I heard about you taking on Campbell and Byrne: Campbell, who deserved a chance more than anyone, and Byrne, who nobody had ever taken a chance on. And I'd heard about you, guv, that you were nice and gentle, a different kind of leader. Too gentle, some of them said."

"Aye," George said, "I've heard that before."

"So, I was hopeful this time, I..." She sighed heavily. "I've worked in the force for a long time," she said simply, and that statement alone spoke volumes. George knew it held a career's worth of dealing with huge egos, anger issues, toxic masculinity, being talked down to, labelled, diminished, discriminated against, and stepped on to give someone else a step up. "I just thought that this time it would be different," she finished.

At this, Ivy stood and, without uttering a word, left the kitchen. For a panicked second, George thought his surprise had pushed her over the edge, that she'd become offended and stormed off. But then she returned from the living room with the decanter of whisky and two crystal tumblers she and George usually saved for after dinner. She handed one glass to George and one to Ruby, took an old enamel camping mug out of the cupboard for herself and then poured them each a generous measure.

"How about we make a toast?" Ivy said, holding up her mug. "A promise: for a fresh start?"

But Ruby didn't move, and her hands remained demure and still on her lap. She stared at the whisky glass as though it were a temptation that could also be a trap — either an offering or poison.

Half a minute passed, and Ivy slowly lowered her mug. Their team needed more than that to move forward.

"I wasn't a good leader," she said quietly, as though it was a confession. "I was scared of failing." She laughed at a private thought, probably to do with Jamie. "*Again*. And I copied the sergeants that came before me, their way of leading a team, with demands and force. I thought *that* was being a leader, being decisive. Not everybody has the guv's patience and kindness. It's a special thing in this job, and I'm sorry," she said, looking at Ruby, "to you and the rest of the team that I didn't do better to replicate it. I thought I was ready to step up," she said, turning to George. "But I still have a hell of a lot to learn from him."

He let Ivy's words sit there for a moment so they could be best absorbed, like perfume, into the skin, and finally, Ruby reached out, raised her glass, touched it against Ivy's mug, and smiled, nodding in agreement.

"Here, here," she said.

George did the same.

"Lucky for you," he said, offering Ivy a small smile that felt a little sad, "I'm not going anywhere anytime soon."

"Good," she said. "Because... well, if this is the time for honestly, then I have a few things I need to work on." She swirled her mug, took a large sip, and winced. "And I think I know where I have to start."

CHAPTER THIRTY-SIX

In contrast to the context of George's visit, the sun was shining. It was a glorious spring morning, and he strode across Wolds Grove with purpose. He knew the routes between the well-spaced yurts, and even the young girl at reception nodded him through without asking for his ID. But his reasons for being there were far from glorious. He felt a newfound sympathy for those he had to question so soon after the death of their loved ones. It had been hard enough to watch Grace die, but he couldn't imagine someone coming to ask him intimate questions about it the day after it had happened.

No doubt he would've kicked them out onto the street.

When George tentatively knocked on the correct yurt post, a tearful voice answered, "Yes?"

He peeked his head through the canvas opening to see Franky DeSilver sitting on the bed with Cecelia and Marie on either side of her, all three of them holding hands. They whispered to each other with an urgent type of female intimacy George had heard of but never experienced. He was of a different gender and a different generation, and when Grace died, the most sympathetic act even his oldest friends had done at the funeral was give him a stiff whisky and a pat on the back.

"I'm sorry to interrupt," he said, "but I hoped I could have a word?"

As one, the two friends looked between George and Franky and asked if that would be alright on his behalf, to which she nodded and dabbed at her eyes.

"Let's get it over with," she said.

They stood and gave their friend a hug before leaving the yurt and offering George a suspiciously polite, "Good morning," on the way out. He couldn't help but wonder what they had been whispering about.

He stepped forward and felt incredibly awkward with his hands behind his back. Usually, such interviews would take place in a loved one's home but in a neutral space like a kitchen or a living room. However, these yurts were basically just large bedrooms. It felt intimate. He looked around the room, if only for something to do, and only because his eyes landed on the bed did he ask, "How did you sleep?"

He didn't blame her for laughing. It was the kind of question asked at a hotel reception when they don't particularly care how you slept but feel the need to say something as you're checking out.

"I slept terribly," she admitted, although that was clear to see. The bags beneath her eyes were almost as dark as Marie's. "Can you imagine, Inspector," she said huskily, "sleeping beside someone for twenty years almost every single night, their breath permeating your dreams, waking up beside them, their face close to yours, and then one morning, they're just not there anymore, and you're alone in the darkness?"

She painted quite the picture. But George didn't need to envision it.

"Yes," he said simply. "I can imagine such a thing." He hesitated. It wasn't exactly procedure to share one's personal life with a suspect. "My wife recently passed away. I'd slept beside her for over forty years... I'm sorry, I didn't mean it to sound like a competition. I just mean... I do understand what you're going through." He stepped forward and caught her eye. "And I'm very sorry it's happening to you."

Her dark, accusing expression had softened, holding traces of guilt.

"Thank you," she whispered.

"I have to ask you some questions, Mrs DeSilver. Would that be okay?"

"Shoot," she croaked.

He looked down at her, trying not to seem so intimidating, then decided to pull up the armchair in the corner so they were on the same level. He sat down and leaned forward as though they were merely sharing a casual conversation.

"First of all, we are aware that James recently asked Bob Adams to lend him money," he began, causing Franky's head to shoot up. "Were you aware of this?"

"How much money?" she asked, answering the question for him with a question of her own.

"Ten thousand pounds."

"What?" she whispered. "Why?"

"For his business," George said, keeping it vague, not wanting to fill in the information before she could do so herself.

"And did Bob give it to him?" she asked, incredulous.

"I don't believe so, no." He shuffled. He never liked it when his questions turned into him offering answers, so he tried a new tact. "But we know that someone did. Do you know who might have lent James the money?"

The tears in Franky's eyes had taken on a new kind of angry shine. "I didn't even know that he was asking anyone for money."

"Why did you and your husband leave London, Mrs DeSilver?"

"We were sick of the place," she said flatly.

George didn't need more explanation. He could imagine how. He'd never liked the country's capital with its rat-like tube system and miserable screams of '*Stand on the right!*'

"And that's all? No other reason?"

"Like what?"

George waited for a second, then revealed his hand. "Do you know if your husband was experiencing financial difficulty?"

"Financial difficulty?" she scoffed. "We're in a better situation than we've ever been. We just bought a new house, for Christ's sake. Is that why you think someone did this? Did he owe someone money?"

"I don't know, Mrs DeSilver," George said. "Did he?"

"I don't bloody know, do I? Clearly, he didn't tell me anything. God only knows."

George bit his lip, then asked, "Is it possible that Lily Hughes loaned your husband money?"

"Lily," she said.

"Yes, would she have had money to give to James?"

"Lily," she repeated as though her name was a nervous tick. "I mean, maybe? I guess she must have got some money when Jordan died. I mean, he was a doctor... But Lily doesn't exactly talk about money. She didn't live an extravagant life."

"So maybe she would have ten thousand in savings?"

"I suppose?" Franky shook her head as though the image of her friend in her head and the image of her George was suggesting did not match up.

"Lily and James were close, weren't they? It's not a huge leap."

"Why do you assume that Lily lent it to him?" she asked, suddenly angered by a thought to which George had not been privy. "James has plenty of friends in the city who probably would've been able to lend it to him."

"It's a hunch," George lied. "I just mean, James and Lily had known each other since they were children. Maybe he felt more comfortable asking her."

"More comfortable than who?"

"Than his friends in the city," George clarified, then paused so the tension could settle a little.

"I suppose," she said eventually. "Maybe."

"Because they were close, weren't they?" George pushed gently. "James and Lily?"

Franky looked up, her stare hard. "What are you trying to say?"

"I'm trying to ask…" he said slowly. "How did you feel about James and Lily's friendship?"

"What do you mean?"

"Did it bother you that they were so close?"

"There's no need to beat around the bush," Franky said, standing up to pace the floorspace between the bed and George. "I know exactly what you're talking about." She laughed and ran a wild hand through her hair. "James and Lily," she said, as though she were the one revealing a secret to him, "I know about them. I know about the kiss."

CHAPTER THIRTY-SEVEN

"You know?" George asked, to which Franky scoffed.

"Violet wasn't exactly subtle when she slapped Lily that morning. She's never been one to keep her opinions to herself. Half of Lincolnshire heard what she had to say - that Lily had betrayed her brother by kissing my husband. She accused them of having an affair for years." Then she stopped pacing suddenly, the momentum causing her to sway. "And I've accused him more than once, but I know it's not true."

"How do you know?" he asked candidly, and Franky turned to face George so that she was the one now looking down.

"Lily would never do that to me."

"You're very forgiving."

"I know how it looks, but you don't know Lily. All you have is what's in your file. But she was so much more than that. She was the kindest person I've ever met. Sure, maybe she let my husband kiss her in some drunken state, but there's no way she would have carried on with him behind my back." She shook her head, stared at the far wall, and bit her lip as though tasting a flavour of doubt on it, but then she repeated, "No way."

"What about your husband? Would he do that to you?"

She laughed a short, sad laugh and slumped back down onto the bed. "Lily was a fantasy for James. Everyone knew it. But they had their chance to be together, and they chose not to." She locked eyes with George, her stare intense and almost feral. "Marriage is more than a fantasy. It's real. It's every day together, day after day after day. He wasn't the only one who fantasised about a life with someone else. Some idyllic alternative timeline. But he chose me, and I chose him. The day that he met me, the day that Lily introduced us, he had the choice of us in front of his eyes. He chose me. He chose me the day we got married. And he chose me on Monday night after he had kissed Lily. He came back to our bed. I know what he was like when he was drunk. I know how he could idealise Lily. But when he was sober, he was *my* husband, and he chose *me*."

For such a possessive speech, she didn't seem obsessive or unreasonable. George related to it, even as a married man. He understood where she was coming from, in theory at least. But he also knew that the subject of love rarely inspired rational thought.

"Forgive me," he said. "I just find it hard to believe you wouldn't have been angry at the idea of your best friend and your husband kissing, even if it was one drunken mistake."

"Oh," she said, her voice tumbling into a laugh. "Don't get me wrong. I was furious. James could be stupid and childish. But I'm an adult, Inspector. I know that one drunken dally doesn't outweigh a lifetime."

"So, you didn't confront either one of them about it?"

She shook her head and closed her eyes as a tear rolled down her cheek. "There wasn't exactly time," she said, her voice breaking.

George eyed her and considered the whole picture: the dramatic pacing, the forgiving attitude, the well-timed tear. She was exceptional either way, whether an exceptional liar or exceptionally forgiving.

"I know how it looks," she said quietly. "The jealous wife who kills her husband and her best friend for their betrayal. But life isn't that simple, is it? You say you were married."

"That's right."

"Then you know how complicated it all gets. We make mistakes-even the best of us. James and Lily were my two most beloved people in the world. Now they're gone. Whatever friend-ship they had and whatever jealousy it stirred inside me, I certainly didn't..." She took a deep breath. "I neither killed my husband nor Lily because of it."

"And I'm not accusing you of such," George said. "But I do have to ask... where were you in the fog?"

"The fog?" she said, blinking at the change of subject, no doubt trying to decipher whether he was being metaphorical or literal.

"The morning Lily was killed," George clarified. "Violet said that when the fog lifted, you were further down the path than you were before."

Franky rolled her eyes at the mention of Violet, even before George had explained what she'd said. "Of course, Violet would phrase it in such a way," she said. "I was with Cecelia. We retraced our steps a little in the fog to try and find Lily and Marie, but we soon gave up. That's all. No conspiracy."

"And there was no other point in your morning of hiking when you were separated? When one person went off on their own?"

"No," she said firmly, as though she'd had to answer the ques-tion many more times than once. "We were all together the whole time."

"From eight a.m. until the fog fell at eleven a.m.?"

"Yes."

"Very well," George said, placing his hands on his knees, ready to push himself up from the chair.

"Inspector," Franky said suddenly, and when he looked up, he saw the angry shine in her eyes had returned, and the wildness that had spread to her ruffled hair, wide eyes, and galvanised posture was stronger than ever. "You will find them, won't you? Whoever did this to James and Lily?"

"We will do our best," George said slowly.

"I want whoever did this to him." She used the word *want* in the way someone might use it to describe a deep, deprived hunger — or lust. "I want them to pay."

"I can make one promise," George said, gradually rising to his feet so as not to spook her, "that we will do our best to serve justice and ensure whoever is responsible goes to prison for a very long time."

From the hatred on her face, it seemed Franky DeSilver was seeking a far greater punishment. That was to be expected, but given time, emotions would numb.

He nodded his goodbyes and left her yurt, and she watched him from the bed as a dog might watch a stranger leaving its territory. Feeling restless, he walked to the far end of the field, where the ground swelled into a hill, from which he could see over the entire Grove. To his right, not too far away, stood that creepy house, quiet and disturbing in his peripheral, like a person he'd avoid on the street. His thoughts whirred, and images shot into his mind as intrusive thoughts — Franky's feral eyes, James's butchered face, Lily's twisted neck. He shook them away. They helped in no way. He needed to talk.

George pulled out his phone and didn't have to scroll down to find her number. It was at the top of his recently called list-along with Ivy's-and it was usually in that prime position, although recently, his contacts had been old friends and distant relatives, calling to check in and ask about funeral arrangements.

"Good morning, Campbell," he said when she answered.

"Guv," she said, probably surprised to hear him on her desk phone. "How are you doing?"

"I'm good," he said, closing his eyes to let the sun rest on his eyelids. "It's nice to be out and about, you know? I just spoke to Franky DeSilver."

"Oh," she said. "Would you like me to gather the team around?"

"Actually, yeah, that's a good idea. Are they all there?"

"Yes, guv," she said, and he heard some background noises as though she was waving at people across the incident room to join her.

"Everyone?" he checked.

"Morning, guv," came Ruby's voice over the phone, along with the scrape of a chair, and George smiled with relief.

"Morning, Ruby," he replied.

He listened to a few more seconds of footsteps and coffee mugs being placed down on the desk, alongside mumblings of, "Morning, guv."

Eventually, they settled, and Byrne asked, "So, are you back then? For good, I mean."

"Let's just take one day at a time," George said. "I wanted to call you all for an update. Has anyone heard from Ivy?"

"She isn't with you, guv?"

"No," he said with a knowing grin.

"I could call her," Ruby suggested.

"No, leave her," he replied. "I have an idea she's undergoing some professional development."

CHAPTER THIRTY-EIGHT

Doctor Pippa Bell opened the mortuary door with a surprised expression that slowly morphed into a sly grin as she looked over Ivy's shoulder and saw she was alone.

"Just you, Ivy, is it?" she said. "On your own, are you?"

"Yes," Ivy muttered, the smell of disinfectant already turning her stomach.

"Well, come on in then," she said and closed the door slowly behind her the way a hunter might close the door behind the prey that's walked willingly into their trap, and Ivy had the distinct impression she was playing with her food. "PPE," she said, nodding at the cupboards in the wall.

Ivy merely nodded, focusing on the breathing techniques she had learned long ago but often forgot to use. It had been a part of her police training, which she doubted had been offered to George's generation, part of the well-being movement for officers, helping them to maintain emotional resilience. Inhale for one, two, three, four, she remembered, taking a deep breath as Pip watched from the mortuary door. Hold your breath for one, two, three, four, five, six, seven, she said to herself as she put on the

PPE. And exhale for one, two, three, four, five, six, seven, eight. She repeated this cycle for three more rounds, and by the time she turned to face Pip, who had watched the entire performance, Ivy was ready.

"You good?" said Pip.

"Yes," Ivy replied.

But as soon as the smell of the formaldehyde hit her when Pip opened the door, Ivy stumbled to the left. She held the door frame for balance. If anything, she felt worse than usual, perhaps because she'd been there so recently. She'd had little time to mentally recover from having witnessed Lily Hughes's body. She wasn't ready for another one.

Pip walked to the gurney, where she waited for Ivy to make her way over. But Ivy only made it halfway across the room before she had to put her hands on her knees and lower her head to stop from throwing up. She hadn't even seen James DeSilver's body, yet the thought of it was enough to stir her breakfast.

"Sorry, Pip," she mumbled. "Just give me a minute, eh?"

Pip stepped over to her and placed a hand on her back. "It's no coincidence that George isn't here, is it?" she asked simply.

Ivy straightened, her head spinning. "I... I need to do this. I need to be able to do this without..."

Pip was so blunt and upfront that Ivy found it easy to be honest with her. Though she might kid around, she wasn't a judgemental woman.

"Even if it makes you ill?"

"Call it self-improvement," Ivy said, blinking hard and trying to focus. "I'm trying to work on my weaknesses."

"Why not focus on your strengths instead?" Pip asked, genuinely curious as to why Ivy was suffering in her morgue or perhaps more concerned about her passing out in it. "I mean, weaknesses are part of who we are. We all have them," she said wisely. "Spiders, heights—"

"Leadership," Ivy interrupted.

Pip smiled. "Well, we can't all be George Larsons, can we?"

Ivy laughed and shook her head. "You're right about that."

"Well, like I said, we all have our weaknesses."

"Yeah, and what's yours, Pip?"

"No, no, Ivy," she said, grabbing Ivy's elbow and leading her closer to the gurney. "We're focusing on *you* for now." Ivy's legs shook as she allowed Pip to take some of her weight. They stopped beside James DeSilver's body, but Ivy refused to look down at it. "Now then, do you know *why* you feel as you do?"

"Because it's not right. Because society has taught us to fear death."

Pip shrugged. "In a way, sure," she said. "Death and the unknown are two of humanity's greatest fears. But that's not about the bodies themselves." She paused. "Have you ever read Freud's essay *Das Unheimliche*?"

"Pip, please, can we just—"

"Have you?"

Ivy sighed. "No," she said, "I haven't. I suppose you have."

"Yes, I have actually." Pip moved around to the other side of the gurney to better command Ivy's attention. "See, it popularises the concept set out by Ernst Jentsch that we feel deeply disturbed by that which is familiar yet strangely foreign. Dead bodies make you feel uncomfortable Ivy, because they look like what you know, a living person, yet they are no longer full of life. The dead cannot move or smile or express themselves. Their chests do not rise and fall with even the most subtle of breaths. It's familiar, it's what you know, but something isn't quite right. It's *uncanny*. And that's why you fear it."

Ivy watched and listened as though she were a lecturer and Ivy the student, and she paid attention. Her gaze focused on Pip's face and the twitch of her piercings as she spoke, meaning that James DeSilver's body was now in Ivy's peripheral. She gulped down the rise of hot saliva at the back of her throat.

"Don't fight your discomfort, Ivy. It's okay to feel uneasy. Notice it, embrace it, but that's all. There's no need to judge yourself. In a second, I will ask you to look at him..."

Ivy's heart rate immediately quickened. She grimaced at Pip, who nodded reassuringly, and Ivy recognised her body's response.

But didn't fight it.

She allowed the adrenaline to pump through her veins as the inevitable moment drew nearer.

"And when you do, know that he is dead. He is not *supposed* to be alive. He is just an object. Remind yourself of it. Don't expect him to be alive. Don't create a valley between what is familiar and what is strange. That's where the uncanny lies." Pip paused. "Now...look at him."

Ivy closed her eyes, took a deep breath and counted to three, then turned to face James DeSilver, opening her eyes. Her vision swam, but less so than usual.

"He's dead," Pip said. "He's not going to jump out at you or suddenly his eyes. This is not a movie. This is real life. And death is a real-life process. It's as natural as being born."

"He's dead," Ivy repeated, looking down at his grey skin, sunken eyes, and slack mouth.

He didn't look as bad as she had imagined. She could tell he had a broken nose, split lip, and multiple bruises, but Pip had cleaned him up to such an extent that he might have had merely a rough night out and was sleeping it off. No doubt, the true damage was inside.

She didn't think about the fact that he was once alive, that he should still be, or how much he resembled a living body. She saw him as an object, neither strange nor familiar.

"How do you feel?" Pip asked.

Ivy nodded, still staring at DeSilver, feeling a new, un-nauseating feeling she thought might be curiosity. "Better," she said. "Much better, actually."

"Understanding fear removes its power."

Ivy frowned and looked at Pip. "That sounds familiar. Who said that again?"

The pathologist's eyes gleamed.

"I did," she said and pulled back the sheet to expose DeSilver's autopsied chest, no doubt to fully test Ivy's capabilities. "Now, if it's alright with you, Ivy, can I continue my briefing?"

CHAPTER THIRTY-NINE

Before that moment, James DeSilver might have been sleeping. The sheet had covered his body up to his chin like a duvet on a cold winter's night. But now his open chest was revealed along with his organs, the process of maintaining composure proved to be a little more challenging.

He's dead, she repeated in her mind. *He's dead, he's dead, he's dead. He's not supposed to be alive.*

"I know this is not easy to see," Pip said. "*I* don't *want* to see it. I've worked in this job for twelve years, and I didn't want to see it." She pulled a comb from her breast pocket and brushed a rogue lock of hair from James DeSilver's forehead. "Cause of death," she continued as if she was declaring the winner of a competition. Perhaps it was by accident, a side-effect of her accent, or perhaps on purpose, to undermine the severity of the moment. "Cranial trauma resulting in a calvarial fracture with subsequent epidural, subdural or intracerebral haemorrhage."

Ivy closed her eyes. "In English, Pip, please?"

"Blunt force trauma to the head, Ivy. His skull was fractured, and... well, to simplify the explanation, this led to swelling of the brain. He died slowly and painfully."

"Saint said that his injuries couldn't have come from one hit against the steering wheel."

"He's right."

"He said DeSilver must have hit his head against it seven or eight times."

"Try eighteen," Pip said quietly.

"Eighteen?" Ivy repeated quietly.

"That's not to blame Saint. It would be difficult to see on first inspection. See here?" She pointed at DeSilver's face. "See the pattern?" Ivy felt so focused on the pattern of bruises and abrasions on the corpse that she forgot to fear the corpse itself.

"It's a circle," she said.

"Or a wheel," Pip said. "The outline of the steering wheel's rim. Those kinds of deep bruises only come from repeated trauma in the same place over and over again."

"I thought it'd look worse," Ivy said, looking at the bruises that were still a subtle, light blue, the kind she probably had on her own shins from clumsily banging against George's coffee table.

"Remember, he died before the bruises could fully develop."

"Eighteen times..." Ivy whispered.

"Look, it's impossible to tell exactly how many times his face hit the steering wheel. But believe me, for this kind of internal damage, it's closer to eighteen than eight."

"Why would somebody slam his head against a steering wheel *eighteen* times?" Ivy said, not expecting an answer, but as usual, Pip had one anyway.

"To make sure he was dead," she said simply. "By my analysis, the killer was in a fit of rage." She turned to Ivy. "Have you ever been spooked by a spider or mosquito and hit it with a newspaper or perhaps the book you were reading?"

"I don't have time to read books."

"Ivy..."

"Look, Pip, I don't think a spider is quite the same thing as—"

"The chemicals released in your brain are the same. Answer the question."

Ivy rolled her eyes. "Yes. Of course, I have."

"And did you hit the spider once, your heart racing, your body in adrenaline mode? Or did you hit that spider multiple times, over and over again, maybe before you even caught what you were doing?"

"Multiple times," Ivy whispered, "but this *is* different. It's murdering a human being."

Pip shrugged. "When we see these kinds of injuries, we can assume the killer had gone into some adrenaline-fuelled mode, a trance if you will, in which their victim became no more human than a house spider. As I said, this was done in a fit of rage. It was an emotionally motivated murder, Ivy. That much is clear."

"So, it wasn't planned?"

"I wouldn't say so, no," Pip said. "The killer either panicked or got angry. Or both."

"What about their position? I mean, relative to James DeSilver?"

"From the pattern of injuries and hair follicle damage, they were sitting next to him," she said surely.

"His hair was torn out?"

"Clumps of it, yes," Pip said, "from the attacker yanking his head back to slam it forward again."

"Why didn't he escape?"

"After the first one, he'd have been dazed. Maybe that prevented him from doing so," Pip said, pointing to deep abrasions in DeSilver's right shoulder, "he had his seatbelt on."

"So, he was in the driver's seat."

"Very good, Ivy," Pip said, slapping her on the back. "The seatbelt crossed his right shoulder so we can tell he was in the driver's seat. You'll be a pathologist yet."

Ivy smiled. "Don't think I'm quite there yet, Pip. What about toxicology?"

She sighed. "It's hard to tell. Alcohol can be detected, but we can't say for certain it's not due to post-mortem bacterial fermentation. Other than that, nothing."

"No drugs?"

"No."

"DNA?"

"I've sent samples off to Katy. Take it up with her."

Just as she had with Saint, Ivy waited as long as she could to ask the question she most wanted to ask, knowing the answer would immediately derail her attention.

"Time of death?"

"Saint was right in that he'd been there for at least a day. My estimate is Tuesday morning. I can't be any clearer except to say that mid-morning would be fairly accurate."

"Between nine and eleven?" Ivy said, to which Pip nodded.

It took Ivy a moment to process the information. Once she had, it changed everything. The story around which her mind had orbited the last few days dissolved, like a believer in a debunked origin story, she had suddenly lost all faith. "You're absolutely sure?"

"Yes," Pip said, frowning at her face, which, had turned pale from the feverish feeling in her skin. "Why?"

"How accurate can your estimate be?" She turned to Pip desperately.

"It's the best you'll get," Pip replied.

"And you're *sure*?"

"Yes, Ivy, I am absolutely sure. I can show you my credentials if you like." But when Ivy walked across the room, lost in disbelief and regrets for how she had acted under her disillusioned, blind, callow faith, Pip grew serious. "Why?"

"Because," Ivy said, leaning against the far wall, not because she felt nauseous — for once in this room — but because she finally faced the truth in the reflection of her mistaken certainty. It hadn't been true faith. It had been the manipulation of a story for personal gain, the worst kind of belief, the selfish kind. "That makes it impossible that James DeSilver murdered Lily Hughes."

CHAPTER FORTY

"So, what did she say?" asked Campbell. "Franky DeSilver? Did she know about the money?"

"No," George said, bending into a crouch then easing himself down onto the grass so he could more casually enjoy the view that stretched out before him — the even distribution of the yurts like trees in an orchard, the sparse line of hedgerows at the far end of the field, the shifting shadows of light rolling across the curves of the Wolds, and beyond.

"And you believe her?" He could picture her face in the incident room, something he hadn't done before. He must be beginning to grow fond of her.

"Yes, I do."

"Did you ask her about Lily?" came Byrne's voice.

"I did," he said, pausing not without a tinge of drama. "She knew about James and Lily."

"What about them?"

"That they kissed."

"Violet told her?" asked O'Hara.

"Not as such," George explained. "Violet told the whole valley, apparently. She screamed it just after she slapped Lily. Marie was naive to think Franky hadn't heard."

"Naive?" Campbell said. "Or lying?"

"So that's a motive, guv," Ruby pointed out. "For Franky against both Lily and James. Betrayal."

"A woman scorned," O'Hara said. "Like we said, it wouldn't be the first time."

"No." Maguire's voice rattled like an old truck over the line. "We said that about James DeSilver. That *his* motive was Lily rejecting him."

"It's clear enough what James DeSilver's motive was, guv," Byrne said.

"A man scorned?" George said. "I know that's Ivy's reasoning, but I don't know. It takes a lot to spin from love to hate, in my—"

"Money," Byrne said quickly, and the team's murmuring stopped. "DS Hart asked me to get access to James DeSilver's business accounts by the end of the day yesterday, and I did. I found the transfer for ten thousand pounds for the legal fees. It was sent by Lily Hughes."

"So, she did lend him money," George said slowly.

"Exactly. And maybe he was never planning on paying her back."

O'Hara scoffed. "You think he would kill his lifelong friend and the woman he loved for ten grand?"

"Aye up, you were the one saying he killed her for rejecting a wee kiss," Maguire said.

"People have killed for far less money," Byrne said. "Anyway, she was starting to pressure him. Remember what Bob said in his story? She told James that he owed her."

"I don't know," O'Hara said. "From what Marie and Toby overheard, Lily didn't seem in a rush to get her money back. It seems like she only said 'you owe me' in the heat of the moment."

"Why are we even discussing it?" asked Campbell. "DeSilver

was killed on Tuesday morning. He couldn't have killed Lily Hughes."

George's phone began to buzz in his hand, and he looked down to see an incoming call. An overload of options prompted him to answer, decline, hold, or merge.

"Of course, he could," Byrne said. "He could've driven to kill Lily, then driven back to the Grove, but before he arrived, somebody caught up with him."

"He wouldn't have had time."

"How do you know? It's only a seven-minute drive between the two locations. He wouldn't have needed long."

"Why isn't he on any cameras then?"

"He was a local. He knew the area. Maybe he avoided the cameras. It's not like there's one on every road out in the Wolds."

George could practically hear the whoosh of Campbell's head over the line as she shook it back and forth. "There's no way he could've got there, killed her, and got back in time."

"Well, we won't know until—"

"Until we know his time of death," George finished for him. "Luckily," he said, having assessed the options and decided upon one, "I know someone who might have that information." He clicked the green button that indicated *merge*. "Morning, Ivy," he said. "You're on with the whole team."

"Morning, everyone," Ivy said brightly.

But amongst the unenthusiastic, murmured replies, only one voice rang out crystal-clear.

"Morning, sarge," Ruby said.

"Morning," Ivy repeated.

"How was Pip today?" asked George.

"Helpful, actually," she said, sounding sincere.

"But?"

"But nothing." Ivy laughed. "She even patted me on the back."

George raised his eyebrows at the kite he had been watching hovering overhead. "That's one for the books."

"I thought so."

"What did she tell you?"

Ivy inhaled deeply as though readying the team for a submergence of information, or perhaps a divulgence of something that might catch their breath. "She confirmed James DeSilver's cause of death as blunt force trauma to the skull leading to haemorrhage. Saint was right. This was no car accident. There were multiple impacts, multiple times. He probably hit his head once in the crash. But the other times were from someone grabbing his head and slamming it against the wheel on purpose."

"DNA?" asked George hopefully.

"Not yet," Ivy said. "Watch for a call from Katy, but let's not hold our breath. Most likely, they wore gloves again."

"Perhaps," George said, "if we're assuming the killer is the same."

"Katy said she'd send over the analysis from the car today," Campbell said. "That will give us more DNA evidence. If someone was in the car with James when it crashed, she should be able to tell us about it."

"Clothes fibres, maybe," Ivy said. "But I don't know about DNA."

"It's something," George said, a buoy of positivity.

"And maybe there'll be witnesses," O'Hara said. "Someone who saw the passenger in the car. I mean, it was a nice car. It would have stood out, wouldn't it? Expensive car like that—"

"Oh my God," George heard over the line, and the weight with which the voice whispered caused them all to silence. "Hold on."

It was Maguire who spoke, his voice hoarse and deep.

"You okay, Maguire?" he asked,

"There was..."

"There was what?" Campbell asked impatiently.

Maguire audibly gulped. "There was a black saloon at the crime scene."

"What are you talking about?" asked Ivy.

"A black saloon drove up to the police tape, and we turned it around."

"When?" O'Hara said. "I don't remember any cars coming up that lane."

"It was before you got there," he said. "It was just me and a uniformed officer. We were closing off the crime scene just after I called it in." The sound of a loud bang came over the line that could well have been the slam of the door, or more likely, the slap of a palm on a table. It was a frustrated sound. "Guv, I'm sorry," he said. "I had no reason to think of it until now."

"What the hell do you mean you had no reason to think of it until now?" Ivy said, her voice tight with the effort — and failure — not to scold the PC. "We've been talking about a black saloon car for days, Maguire."

"I know. But I was imagining it in the minutes before Lily's death going the opposite way from south to north, but this car was going from north to south *after* Lily's death."

"How long after?" George asked.

"Maybe five minutes after I arrived, and that was thirty minutes after they found Lily's body." His answers were quick and short, a first responder's dream. "I'm sorry, guv."

George heard Ivy take a breath but got there first.

"It happens," he said simply. "Our memories are not video footage we can rewind or prompt in a search bar. We can't remember everything all the time. We all know that well enough from witness statements. So why should we hold ourselves any more accountable than members of the public?" He allowed his words to sink in, then continued, "What do you remember, Maguire?"

"The uniform handled it mostly. They explained that the road was closed off, and the car turned around."

"Did they say where they'd been?"

"No," he said, and even just in his voice alone, George could hear the scrunch of his face as he struggled to remember details that he would never have imagined at the time might be so important. "The driver asked what happened, and uniform advised them to go the long way round."

"Then?"

"I walked over..."

George leaned his elbows on his knees. "Maguire, think..." He knew that pulling a memory was like resisting sleep after an all-nighter. "Did you see the driver?"

"I remember them rolling down their window..."

"Was it him?" O'Hara said urgently. "Was it James DeSilver?"

"No—"

"It couldn't have been," Ivy cut him off. "Pip gave me a time of death. James DeSilver was killed between nine and eleven on Tuesday morning. She was sure."

"So that means..." started Campbell.

"Yes," Ivy said slowly. "He was killed *before* Lily Hughes was killed."

There was guilt in her tone that reflected what they were all thinking, but nobody cared to or perhaps dared not to remind her of it: they had just wasted days focusing on James DeSilver as a lead suspect for a murder he could not possibly have committed.

"It wasn't a man," Maguire whispered, filling the silence.

"The driver wasn't a man?"

"No," he said slowly.

"How do you know?" asked Campbell.

"Because..." he said, his voice as even as a flowing stream finally settling into a lake. "I remember who the driver was."

CHAPTER FORTY-ONE

"Miss Anter," George said to the woman before him who wore a tracksuit in place of the pant suit and had clearly not made an effort that morning. "Detective Inspector Larson. We met the other day."

"I remember," she said, offering no more in the way of a greeting. "Your receptionist said we could find you here. May we come in?"

It felt odd to be standing on the doorstep of the old house which, until now, had served as little more than a stain on the otherwise luxurious property.

For a moment, the owner of Wolds Grove merely blinked into the low sun that blazed behind George and Ivy as though the daylight was too much for her to bear.

"It's my day off," she explained, looking herself up and down.

"And we don't want to take up too much of your free time," George said. "But we do need a word."

She looked between the two detectives, seemingly unsure whether their presence on her home's doorstep required a similar hospitality to that of her work. Eventually, she seemed to decide that it did. She stepped back and paced through the house for George and Ivy to follow.

It was like walking back in time, George thought. The house hadn't been decorated for decades, perhaps even not since it had been built, which George guessed to be the fifties at the earliest, due to the simple layout, the lack of central heating, and the damp that thrived in those corners that adjoined to an external wall.

They moved through the living room in a matter of steps, so small was the space. The kitchen, however, was vast even by modern standards, featuring butcher-block worktops and an old butler sink. The little table and chairs appeared to be hand-crafted, as everything was back then. Modern additions, such as the kitchen appliances and a laptop on the table, appeared grossly out of place. The house was not fit for habitat, in George's opinion, at least. It should have been either preserved for museum visits to invoke nostalgia in perpetuity or razed to the ground.

The smell of damp permeated the house, with black mould forming in the corners, stretching out to claim new ground. Those issues, however, were a result of time and could almost be forgiven. But the weeks' worth of dirty dishes, the breadcrumbs on the worktops, and the debris on the terracotta floor tiles were not.

Sabina Anter opened a cupboard door, and George dreaded the inevitable offer of tea. It was usual, he mused, for people to busy themselves under the circumstances, and Sabina was not one to break the mould.

"Milk, sugar?" she asked the detectives.

"Not for me," George said.

"I'm fine, thank you," Ivy added.

She eyed them suspiciously and lit the burner beneath the old kettle.

"Suit yourselves," she said. "So, how can I help you, detective?"

"We couldn't help but notice your car on the way in, Miss Anter," George began.

"My car?"

"Yes, it's the black saloon outside. Is it not?"

"Yes," she said, frowning. "Why do you ask? What does my car have to do with anything?"

"How long have you had it, if you don't mind my asking?"

Sabina laughed. "Is that why you came here? To ask me about my car?"

George smiled politely but said nothing and Sabina's expression faded a little.

"No, no, that's not why we're here," he said, shaking his head. "We're here to ask where you were on Tuesday between ten and eleven-thirty a.m."

He maintained a pleasant smile, which was always a sure way to invoke anxiety.

"What do you mean?"

"It's a simple question," Ivy added.

"You already asked me," she accused George, "the other day. I told you. I was working."

"And you stand by that statement, do you?" he replied.

She looked between the detectives incredulously. "You don't think I had anything to do with this? I didn't even know the woman. Why on earth would I have anything to do with it?"

"Maybe I should rephrase the question," George said. "Why were you driving down Caistor Lane at eleven a.m. on Tuesday morning?"

Once more, Sabina fiddled with her hair, pulling it into a bun, before catching herself and wringing her hands awkwardly instead. "I had nothing to do with that woman's death," she said simply.

"Then you should have no problem telling us where you were," George said. "It's a simple enough question, Miss Anter."

"I was...out," she said.

"We know that much. What I want to know is, why were you on *that* road at *that* time? Where were you going? We know you didn't go as far as the main road."

Sabina said nothing, and in her silence, the kettle, as if mirroring her thoughts, began the low whistle that would soon develop into a scream. She turned from them and switched off the burner before making her tea, all the while, in deep thought.

"Any thoughts?" George said.

"I can't recall," she said flatly, to which Ivy tried to catch his eye with what he assumed were raised eyebrows and a stern expression.

"By the way, we're sorry about the palaver yesterday morning. I sent an officer down to explain what happened. You heard the news, I suppose?"

Sabina blew on her tea, giving herself a moment to think, preparing for round two. "They only told me that another body had been found," she said quietly, "just outside the property."

"Yes, in the trees," George said, "Not far from here at all."

"A tragic accident?"

"Tragic, yes," George said, and he caught her eye. "It was James DeSilver, Miss Anter." Sabina spluttered into her tea and placed the cup down on the counter. "You know him, don't you, Sabina?"

"No," she said, dabbing her lips with a mangy tea towel. "I know *of* him. He was a guest only a few days ago."

"But you knew him already. I'm surprised you let him on your property at all." She studied his face, his eyes, and his mouth, reading whatever she could before replying.

"He booked our finest yurts with the full food pairing menu," she murmured. "Do you have any idea how much that costs, Inspector? It's not cheap. I'm not in a position to turn down money."

"Clearly," Ivy added.

"I'm sorry if my home isn't up to your standards..."

"Detective Sergeant Hart," Ivy reminded her.

"I've put everything I have into my business, just like my father did. It didn't hurt him to live simply, and it doesn't hurt me either."

"We're not here to judge," George said. "But there is the question of the legal battle between yourself and DeSilver's company."

She nodded as if his words had confirmed what she had wondered: how much they knew.

"It's true," she started. "I am in the process of seeking compensation from VavaRoom. It's an ongoing thing. But my dealings with the business were with his sales rep and technical staff. Until the other day, I hadn't even met him, and I was certainly unaware that he had booked the place."

"You didn't know he was coming?"

"Of course not. I don't examine the names of every guest who books," she said. "It wasn't until I was seating them for dinner that he introduced himself, and I realised who he was."

"And did you say anything to him? About the legal proceedings, I mean."

"Look, If James DeSilver wants to hand over thousands of pounds to impress his friends for a few nights, I wasn't going to deny him the privilege. But am I going to risk the enjoyment of the rest of my customers by airing my dirty laundry in my restaurant? No, Inspector. No, I am not."

"That must have taken considerable self-control," George told her.

Sabina smirked and shrugged. "It's in the hands of the lawyers now. It's not personal. It's business."

"How much have you spent suing James DeSilver?"

"I'm not suing James DeSilver," she said. "I'm suing his business. And rightly so. It lost me money."

"How much?" asked George innocently. "How much money did he cost you in lost business and legal fees?"

"You think this is all about money?" she said. "Do you

honestly think that I would kill a man over a standard business practice? Do you know how many businesses sue each other? I'll give you a clue. It's in the hundreds of thousands. It's common practice, Inspector. It is *not* common practice to kill each other over it."

"How much?"

She laughed bitterly and sipped her tea fast as if it was whisky on a cold night. "Seventy thousand."

George nodded and gave a low whistle. "Well, I can see now why you would accept James DeSilver coming to stay. Still, it couldn't have felt good. Could it? You serving him and his friends?"

"I saw any money I could take from that man as a win," she said darkly.

"It's a mind play, isn't it? To stay at the Grove?" asked Ivy. "Do you think he was playing games?"

"Well, if he was, I think I know who's winning."

"James DeSilver was killed early on Tuesday morning," George said. "An hour *before* Lily Hughes. We believe the deaths could be connected. Now, we know you weren't here when Lily was killed."

"Is that right?"

George turned to Ivy, eyebrows raised.

"Sergeant Hart?"

"Yes, guv," she said almost immediately, and then turned to ensure Sabina was paying attention to her. "We believe you were on Caistor Lane, the very same road where the accident took place."

"That's right," George added, to which Sabina slammed down her mug. "So, Miss Anter, I'll ask you once more. Where were you between nine and ten on Tuesday morning when the murder took place?"

She considered her response, then her face broke into a wry grin.

"Far away from here," she said. "Check the CCTV for yourself. You can see my car leaving the Grove around nine-fifty."

"Right," George said. "Just after DeSilver."

Sabina had not made the point she thought she had.

George turned and paced a few steps, then turned on his heels and returned slowly. "You can see how this looks, can't you?" he said. "You have a connection to James DeSilver and a volatile one at that. You believe that his software has cost you a considerable sum of money. And you're struggling to explain your whereabouts during both incidents. And to top it off, we have an eyewitness who saw your car at the crime scene. If I were to play devil's advocate, Miss Anter, I would suggest that James came here masquerading as a guest and witnessed the smooth operation of your business. I don't think it's beyond the realms of plausibility that, after checking into and dining in your... fine establishment, he felt quite confident that his legal team could win."

She closed her eyes, her nostrils flared, and she gripped her mug with both hands.

"Don't make this more difficult for yourself, Miss Anter," Ivy added.

George looked up at Sabina. "Just tell us the truth."

Sabina stared between the two of them, her eyes wide. For the first time, she looked scared.

"I was going to see someone."

"Who?"

She went to speak, then closed her mouth, frowned, and straightened, as though readying herself for a fight.

"I want to speak to my lawyer."

George looked at Ivy, who shrugged. He downed his tea, placed the mug on the counter, and pushed himself towards the front door.

"So be it," he muttered on the way out, but he stopped at the doorway, willing to offer one last piece of advice. "You see us as the enemy, Sabina. That's fine. Many do. But believe me, if you don't start talking, I'll have little option but to arrest you, and from what I've learned today, I have grounds to charge you. Then you're out of my hair. Someone else's problem." He shook his head. "I can't tell you where you'll be held. I can't tell you who you'll share a cell with whilst on remand. But I can promise you this: when that cell door closes and those lights go out, you'll be begging to speak to me." He nodded for Ivy to make the arrest. "Have a think about that, Sabina, eh? Have a good think."

She bit on her lip, as if dying to speak the words, but was fighting some kind of inner battle. Eventually, she calmed herself, finished her tea and slid the mug towards the pile of dirty crockery.

"I need to call my lawyer," she said, to which George felt a little disappointed. He caught her eye, offering her one more chance.

"You can do that from the station," he said, then turned to Ivy. "Inform her of her rights, Ivy." He glared at Anter. "Although, I'm quite sure she's already very aware of them."

CHAPTER FORTY-TWO

When Ivy and George entered the interview room, Sabina and her lawyer were busy whispering back and forth like two lone candles in a darkened room. They sat as close as conspiring spies or lovers sharing sweet nothings familiar in each other's company. She nodded along to his sentiments, and he listened hard to her concerns.

He was a grey-haired, clean-shaven, mature man wearing an expensive blue suit complete with a polka-dot pocket square. His nose was far too large for his face, but the confidence emanating from his firm, well-postured shoulders and focused eyes made it work for him as though there was little he couldn't spin to his favour, even his natural flaws.

"Sabina Anter," George said after he and Ivy sat down and began the recording, "For the purpose of the recording, I will make you aware of your rights. You have been arrested on suspicion of murder. You do not have to say anything, but it may harm your defence if you do not mention, when questioned, something which you later rely on in court. Anything you do say may be given in evidence. You are being interviewed in connection with the murders of Lily Hughes and James DeSilver. I am Detective Inspector George Larson, and I am conducting the interview along with..."

"Detective Sergeant Ivy Hart."

"Please state your name clearly."

"Sabina Anter," she said quickly.

"And your legal representation..."

"Stephen Ronan," the solicitor said, his high voice belying his confident posture. He laid his small hands flat on the table as he spoke. There was little doubt, the man had presence.

"Stephen Ronan," George repeated, processing the name and then placing it. His signature had been all over the public legal files Campbell had given him concerning Sabina's case against DeSilver. He had been Sabina's lawyer during the case, and since the investigation was still ongoing, he supposed he still was.

"That's me," Ronan said in his high yet intimidating voice, the same way the shrill whistle of a train warns of impending doom.

"Miss Anter..." George said, looking through the file his team had handed him when they'd arrived, then closing it and looking straight at Sabina. "Do you know why you're here?"

Just as she had been at Wolds Grove, Sabina remained professional and calm. She sat straight in her chair with her fingers interlocked as though she might have been conducting a job interview. Except her knuckles were white.

"I know that you are investigating the murders of Lily Hughes and James DeSilver, and for some reason, you think that I'm involved."

"For some reason?" George repeated, leaning forward. "I'm sure you know the reason."

Ronan leaned across to whisper in his client's ear. She turned her head to face him, nodded slightly, then turned back to George and said, "No, I don't."

"We brought you into this room today because not only have

you failed to confirm your whereabouts at the time of the two murders, but you have a clear motive for both – enough for me to charge you, I might add."

"Speculation," her lawyer whined. "What motive are you referring to, Inspector?"

George opened his folder again. "You were in the process of suing James DeSilver for income losses from using his software. Is that correct?"

"No," Ronan said before Sabina could speak. "My client was not suing DeSilver. She was suing his business, VavaRoom."

"My mistake," George said flatly. "Still, there is a link there that we cannot ignore simply because the language used to describe either party suggests otherwise. Perhaps you can explain exactly what happened?"

Sabina looked at her lawyer first, who gave an almost imperceptible nod of his head before she continued. "I don't mind telling you. There's nothing nefarious about it. I was using an old software at the Grove, a property management system from the early 2000s, and to be frank, it was crap. So I researched local software systems, and I found VavaRoom."

"Why were you looking locally?" Ivy asked. "It doesn't make a difference if a software is geographically nearby or not."

"We provide everything locally," she said. "I like to support local businesses. Alcohol, linen, furniture, bathroom supplies, marketing, food supply..." At this, Ronan flinched, swept across to Sabina, and whispered something, at which she grimaced and shook her head as though swatting off a fly. Or perhaps a stupid comment?

Sabina cleared her throat and continued. "I found VavaRoom. It had good reviews. They'd just expanded from London, a new business in East Lincolnshire but already with clout from the capital. The branding was good. They felt like a good fit. It was an easy choice, so I bought the software and..."

"What?"

"It was rubbish."

"In what way?"

"It would crash or freeze or need rebooting. Imagine checking someone into a high-class establishment and asking them to wait ten minutes while the software refreshes. It double-booked guests, so we had to cancel on people when they'd just turned up or compensate them. It rejected payments for no reason or didn't process them at all. Basically, it was useless. It's no exaggeration when I say I lost tens of thousands of pounds in lost business, Inspector. It is an entirely reasonable lawsuit."

"When did you enact this lawsuit?"

"Three months ago."

"And when was the first time you met James DeSilver?"

She laughed, but George didn't understand the joke. "Three days ago, when he checked in at Wolds Grove."

George sat back. "You're telling me that you hadn't even met the man that you were suing? Not at a mediation or a hearing?"

"That's what I'm telling you," Sabina said. "I didn't sue James DeSilver. I sued his business. The only contact I had was his legal team and, before that, his sales and services teams."

"Then why didn't you tell us that you had a connection to James DeSilver? When you knew we were investigating the murder of one of your guests. His friend?"

Ronan spoke in her ear before Sabina no doubt repeated what he'd told her to say.

"I didn't think it was relevant. I had no connection to Lily Hughes."

"Do you know how James DeSilver afforded to defend himself against your allegations?" asked George.

Sabina shook her head and widened her eyes. "How on earth would I know that? I assume he used his business' legal expenses insurance."

"I think we both know that you cannot always rely on timely

pay outs from insurance companies. He needed to bridge that gap."

"His in-house legal team, then."

"Nope."

"Well, I..." Sabina floundered. "How the hell should I know?"

"VavaRoom might have heralded from London, Miss Anter, but it is a small business. It would've paid its legal fees from their operational costs if that hadn't all been spent on moving the business to Lincolnshire."

"Do you expect me to feel sorry for a business that sells faulty software?"

"So DeSilver had to borrow the money from his personal assets," George continued, ignoring her question. "From a friend. From Lily Hughes, in fact."

Sabina's face dropped.

"Oh, come on, Inspector," Ronan said as though they were old friends in a harmless disagreement. "How does that give my client any motive at all for her murder?"

George leaned back and shrugged. "Cutting off his legal fees supply?"

"Oh, please—"

"Or I do have another theory," he broached. "Would you like to hear it?"

"Enlighten us," Ronan said.

But George had eyes only for Sabina. "You murdered James DeSilver out of spite. Lily Hughes saw the whole thing. So you murdered her, too. To cover your tracks."

She laughed and shook her head as though the very idea was so far-fetched, so disassociated from her reality that it was as comical an image as a cartoon.

Ronan, too, shook his head as though the thought disturbed rather than amused him. "My client had a private dispute with James DeSilver's company and went through the proper means to gain compensation through the courts, not through her own justice system." He threw his hands up. "A settlement hasn't even been reached. Why would she murder the defendant before receiving compensation from him? It makes no sense."

"I agree," George said. "It makes no sense at all. But do you really believe, Mr Ronan, that those who commit murder are of sound mind? That they behave reasonably?"

To this, for now at least, he had no reply.

"Whoever killed James DeSilver was *emotionally* motivated." George turned to Sabina. "He'd been playing games with you, hadn't he? Turning up at your establishment? Booking your services for him and his friends? That must've wound you up. That must have made you..." George leaned forward. "Emotional."

"I told you," Sabina snapped. "It is business. You may like to assume that every woman is *emotionally* motivated, but I can assure you, there was nothing personal about any of it."

"Nevertheless," George said, "that is only one of the reasons you are here in this room today. Motive aside, you still have not been able to tell us where you were at the time of James or Lily's death. You cannot provide an alibi. I have enough to charge you so your motives can be discussed in court, which is exactly where you will be if you do not start providing us with some answers of your whereabouts."

Sabina shared a worried glance with her solicitor, who jotted something in his file.

"Miss Anter," George continued, while Ronan remained preoccupied, "where were you between ten and eleven-thirty on Tuesday morning?"

"I was driving around," she said. "I like to drive around the Wolds when I get the chance. I don't get to see much of it walking between home and work, as you can imagine."

"That's not going to win you any arguments," George told her. "But why were you on Caistor Lane at eleven a.m.? It's a simple question. I fail to see why it's proving so hard for you to answer."

Ronan scribbled out whatever chess move he'd been planning and looked between George and Ivy with narrowed eyes. Sabina looked only at him, waiting for his council. He turned his back entirely on the detectives and leaned into his client where they returned to their conspiratorial stance. Eventually, she nodded as though understanding and turned back to the table.

"I was meeting somebody," Sabina said.

George wasted no time. "Who?"

"I can't say."

"Well then, you leave us no option..."

"Okay, okay." Sabina took a breath and looked at Ronan. "I was meeting somebody I used to work with. A friend."

"Who?"

"Someone I worked with at the Horizon Hotel. Before I founded the Grove."

"I need a name, Miss Anter."

She looked at Ronan, who nodded a defeated nod. "Tony Dunn."

Without a word, Ivy stood and left the room, leaving George to wrap up the initial interview.

"Interview ended at..." He checked his watch. "Two-twenty p.m. Is there anything you would like to add or say at this time?"

Ronan shook his head first, and Sabina mirrored his movements.

"I'll send somebody to escort you to your cell," George said, and he stood to catch up with Ivy. It was as he reached for the door handle that Sabina somewhat desperately called out behind him.

"Can't I go home?"

"I'm afraid not," George turned. He took little pleasure in detaining people until he knew of their guilt for sure, and in Sabina Anter's case, despite the facts, or lack thereof, there was doubt. "No, you're staying here until we've spoken to your friend."

He looked to the solicitor. "I suggest you stay local, Mr Ronan. We'll be conducting further interviews shortly."

"You have a little under twenty-two hours left on your custody clock," Ronan replied as if the battle was won or lost on the closing statements. "I suggest you prioritise locating Mr Dunn."

"My priority," George replied curtly, "is proving who killed Lily Hughes and James DeSilver." He nodded towards the front of the building. "There's a coffee machine in reception. Help yourself."

CHAPTER FORTY-THREE

"We need a Tony Dunn, who used to work at the Horizon Hotel," Ivy said, striding through the incident room before the team had even processed her arrival. "Ruby," she said, nodding at the researcher who was busy tapping away at her laptop, her fingers moving like a classical pianist's. "Work your magic."

Not long after George entered, he ambled across the room, picked up the marker pen and began to write the name of Sabina's alibi on the whiteboard. Ruby had already pulled up his LinkedIn profile and was ready to relay the information to the team, who had gathered around.

"Tony Dunn," she began, "worked as a kitchen porter at the Horizon Hotel from 2019 until 2021. There seems to be a gap between that and his next position..." She fell into a silence but muttered to herself while she worked.

"Suggesting he didn't have another job lined up?" George said.

"Suggesting that his departure was unplanned," Byrne added. "So, either he quit, or—"

"Was fired," Ruby said, sitting back in her seat. "He was arrested for theft at around the same time."

"Charged?" Ivy asked, to which Ruby shook her head.

"Doesn't look like it."

"Stealing what?" asked Maguire.

"Goods," she replied." That's all it says."

"Maybe they lacked sufficient evidence?" George said.

"Seems like it."

"When did Sabina work there?"

"2018 to 2021," Campbell answered for her, referring to her own laptop. "We outlined her past employment earlier when you wanted her file. The details should be in there."

"Good," George said.

"Who is he?" asked O'Hara. "This Tony Dunn?"

"Anter's alibi," Ivy said.

"Where does he work now?" asked George.

"An abattoir," Ruby said. "Out near Grimsby."

"Address?" asked George.

"I'll forward it to you."

"Good," he replied. "But I meant home address."

"Oh." Ruby frowned. "He's not on the public database. He might be renting. Sorry, guv. Give me a second."

"No problem. Meanwhile," George said, "Byrne and Campbell, prepare to leave. As soon as we have his home address, I want you to find him and confirm Anter's alibi. Timing is crucial. Her car drove down Caistor Lane at 11 a.m. Lily Hughes was killed between 11:05 and 11:10. We need proof, or at least a statement, that she was with Dunn during that window."

"Yes, guv," they said almost as one.

"O'Hara, Anter said she drove around the Wolds on Tuesday morning between leaving the Grove at nine-fifty and being on Caistor Lane at eleven a.m. Find out where she went, if you can. Be resourceful."

She opened her laptop. "Yes, guv."

"Maguire, recheck the Grove's CCTV cameras for a black saloon leaving around the same time."

"Yes, guv."

He took the rare moment of hard-working silence to walk over to the window and look outside at the uninspiring car park and red-brick buildings beyond. Despite the information overload, he felt no more the wiser.

Ivy came to his side and, as always, read his mind.

"You don't think it was her," she said. It wasn't a question.

George rubbed his forehead, feeling the wrinkles beneath his fingertips. "The timing is tight," he said. "Too tight. And the motives work, but..."

"But?"

"Why would Sabina Anter kill two people on the same morning she'd planned to meet someone? Especially when she must have known she would be suspected."

"For precisely that reason," Ivy said, "it's almost too obvious."

George shook his head. "You heard what Pip said. Lily was stalked. Followed. Someone waited for the fog to fall, for the perfect opportunity to get her alone that morning. If this alibi proves correct, Sabina Anter just didn't have time."

"It's a huge coincidence, guv, that Sabina happened to be driving down Caistor Lane just before Lily's murder."

"You know they say about coincidence."

"What's that?"

"Some rubbish about the universe at play."

"Beautiful, is that Keats?" She nudged him playfully. "Maybe in another timeline, she might have knocked down Lily's attacker before they could strike."

"Or Lily herself."

"There was no sign of blunt force trauma on Lily Hughes, guv. She was overpowered."

"No, there wasn't, but it's a playful universe indeed that Sabina Anter somehow missed her in the fog."

"Well, what about DeSilver?" asked Ivy. "Pip said that wasn't planned. It happened quickly. Desperately, she said."

"Impossible," came a voice that wasn't George's, and they spun to find Maguire approaching with an open laptop. "Look."

He pressed play on the video open on his laptop, and Sabina's motionless black saloon suddenly rolled into action, pulling out of Wolds Grove car park and turning left onto the country road. They could see her dark hair in the driver's seat and the unmistakable lapels of a grey pantsuit jacket. Maguire stopped the tape and pointed to the Timecode in the corner.

"Nine forty-six," he said, just two minutes after DeSilver. "But also..."

Maguire moved to another open window on his laptop, a grainier, older camera from a wider perspective of the B1225. He recognised it from going over and over the footage while looking for James DeSilver's car, which had never emerged from either end of that road. And when Maguire pressed play, he also recognised the black saloon that pulled out of the country lane and onto the main road, just as he recognised the grey pantsuit in the driver's seat. Maguire stopped the tape and once more pointed to the time stamp. "Nine forty-nine."

"Three minutes later," George said.

"That's how long it takes to reach the main road from the Grove," Maguire said. "I checked."

"She didn't have time to kill James DeSilver," Ivy whispered.

"No," Maguire confirmed. "She didn't. She also went the opposite way to him." He shook his head. "I can't believe I didn't see it earlier. As soon as I spotted DeSilver leaving, I stopped the tape. If I'd waited another minute or so, I would've seen Sabina too. I would've seen her car, and I would've remembered about the black saloon earlier. I'm sorry, boss. I feel like I've messed up."

George put a fatherly hand on his shoulder. "We are given less than a week to find out what happened to complete strangers using limited resources and questionable evidence," he said. "It isn't easy, and we make mistakes. The point is that we figure out the truth eventually. Sooner rather than later is preferable," he said with a grin. "But this," he said, tapping the laptop, "this is progress."

As they sat in the weight of their realisations, O'Hara declared her own findings. "An ANPR camera in Louth picked Sabina Anter's car up on Tuesday morning before driving to meet Tony Dunn. Then, a little while later, she must have passed a mobile unit, as there's a second instance. Hardly surprising, guv," she said. "If I lived a two-minute walk from where I worked, I'd probably want to drive around when I got the chance, too."

"Well, there's a breakthrough," George said with a little laugh. "Somebody in their investigation has told the truth about something."

"I found Dunn's address," Ruby announced, then looked up at George. "It's on Caistor Lane."

He grinned back at her, familiar with the sensation of a lead crumbling in his hands.

"It's not over yet," he said, staring out of the window. "She's not eliminated by any means. Sabina Anter's innocence still rests on her alibi for Lily Hughes's death. Like I said, the timing is crucial."

He gave Ivy a sideways glance and nodded for her to take over, who in turn addressed the two young officers with a reassuring smile, likely hoping to win them back.

"Well done, everyone," she said to the room, then addressed the pair. "Don't come back without him."

CHAPTER FORTY-FOUR

A determined Byrne and Campbell left the room, leaving the rest of the team to return to their positions, where they faced the dependable eighth member of their crew, the source of all ideas, information, and leads: the whiteboard.

"We're back to square one," Maguire said. "Do we need to go wide with this? More suspects, maybe?"

"No," George said, "we need *fewer* suspects." He sighed and stepped back to see the board in all its busy, chaotic glory. "This is a mess." He tapped at Ivy's artwork, the chart that showed the original seven suspects and each one's MMO. "We need to eliminate. We can't take this wider until every one of those names has a line through it. We don't have the resources."

Then, to a stifled yet dramatic gasp or two, he picked up the eraser, carved a white, blank smudge through the information-heavy board, and continued to rub out the rest. They needed a fresh slate. It wouldn't make a difference. The times of Lily Hughes's and James DeSilver's deaths would no doubt remain etched on the inside of his brain, like Hebrew symbols engraved into a tablet, forever.

"Let's develop this for CPS," he explained. "Whoever we eventually bring in, the case is never going to hold up unless we can prove why and how we've eliminated every other name." He turned to the team. "Give me a suspect. Even if we haven't followed up on them further."

"Violet Hughes," O'Hara said quickly.

"Motive?" asked George.

"Lily and James both betrayed her brother. At least in her eyes."

"Alibi?"

"She doesn't have one..." O'Hara said slowly. "Why did we let her go again?"

"Insufficient evidence," Ivy said from the window, her arms crossed. "She was at the front of the pack. She would have had to somehow find her back in the mist, avoiding everybody else, and locate Lily."

"She lied to us. She said she didn't slap Lily when Marie says she did," O'Hara argued.

"She said, she said," Ivy replied.

"And the DNA evidence?"

"Could apply to either of them," Ivy countered.

"Okay, in that case then, Marie Entwhistle is a suspect, too, no?"

George rolled his eyes. "We're meant to be *eliminating* suspects, not adding them." But he wrote her name down anyway. "Motive?"

But nobody replied.

"I'm not sure she has one, guv," Ruby said eventually.

"Then, alibi?"

"She hasn't got one of those either."

"Great," George said sarcastically. "We're really getting somewhere. Who else?"

"James DeSilver?" Maguire suggested tentatively. "For killing Lily Hughes, that is."

"Motive: rejection, alibi: he was already dead," Ivy said flatly. "Next."

"What about the husbands?" George suggested. "Toby Entwhistle?"

"No motive, no alibi," Ivy said. "Again."

"Bob?"

"Same."

"Except for some resentment at the DeSilvers having more money," George added.

"Yeah, money that James didn't have," O'Hara reminded them.

"Cecelia then?"

"Same."

"Franky?"

Ivy didn't reply. The team frowned as though puzzling over a shared maths problem, then came to what seemed to be the same conclusion voiced by O'Hara.

"Plenty of reasons why Franky DeSilver would have reacted badly and done something stupid," she said. "But she does have an alibi for Lily's murder. Cecelia."

George noted their findings and stepped back from the board. It didn't provide many more answers than before, but at least it was more streamlined. "The problem is the same," he said. "The lines between witness and suspect are blurred. We have to go where the motives are. If they don't have a motive, strike them." He went through each one, adding a single line through the names of Marie, Toby, Bob, and Cecelia.

"That leaves us with only two, guv," Maguire noted. "Violet Hughes and—"

"Franky DeSilver," Ivy finished.

"Just because we haven't found a motive," George reminded them, "doesn't mean they don't have one. We need to be sure." He pointed to O'Hara and Maguire. "You two, go through all the other names. Double-check everything, especially their alibis. I want evidence of Bob dropping Toby off at the market in Walesby. Look through Instagram, Twitter, Facebook, whatever you can find on each of their profiles. Better still, get access to their messages. Flag anything that might suggest they weren't the happy little friendship group they make out to be. If there's even a sliver of a suggestion that there was conflict, tell me. I want to know anything anyone might have had against Lily Hughes or James DeSilver. Hear?"

"Yes, guv," they said together, Maguire's Irish droll overpowering O'Hara's quieter, shorter vowels.

"Guv," Ruby said shakily, and George looked over to see her twitching with excitement. "I have something."

"Go on."

"The last number James DeSilver text. The pay-as-you-go."

"The unregistered number," Maguire said. "Jesus, I didn't even know you could track them."

"It's possible," Ruby said. "See, we'd already used phone masts to triangulate the location, so then it's a case of identifying the numbers that number had been in contact with to understand some kind of trend or common ground. That didn't really give me a lot, so I traced the phone's IMEI to its point of sale."

"You sound like you're building up to something, Ruby," George said, politely hurrying her along.

"It was bought by a female on Monday morning at a phone shop in Lincoln. I requested their CCTV, of course, but facial recognition couldn't pick up anything. She had her hood up and sunglasses on the whole time. She paid with cash, of course. The guy behind the counter remembered her, as she used crisp fifty-pound notes."

"Right?" Maguire said, intrigued as to where she was leading them.

"Crisp, as in un-used," Ruby said.

"An ATM," Ivy added, to which Ruby nodded. "She withdrew the money?"

"Very few ATMs dispense fifty-pound notes," she said. "I

found one that did, and after a few rather tense phone calls with the company that manages the bank's security—"

"You've got her?"

"Posy O'Keefe withdrew five hundred pounds in fifty-pound notes from that ATM on the morning she bought the phone."

"Hold on," George said. "Have we confirmed the name on the account with the bank? Presumably, the security firm who manage the cameras doesn't have access to accounts."

"That's a slightly longer process," she admitted. "They need warrants, documents, and all manner of red tape."

"So how do you know it was this Posy O'whatsit?"

"O'Keefe," she said. "Well, that's easy. She told me."

"Sorry?"

"She answered her phone, presumably her business phone, as she hadn't bought the pay-as-you-go yet."

"What do you mean *she answered her phone*?" Maguire asked. "I'm not following. And what makes you think it's a business phone?"

"She received a call while standing at the ATM," Ruby explained, and she mimicked answering a phone by placing her hand to the side of her head. "*Posy O'Keefe*."

"Jesus," Maguire muttered.

"Any good, guv?" Ruby asked, to which George simply smiled.

"Oh yes," he replied. "That'll do very nicely, Ruby." He turned to the younger officers, pointing at the researcher. "Now that is how it's done." He grabbed his jacket from the back of his chair and gestured for Ivy that they were leaving. "I want to speak to this O'Keefe character," he said. "We've got until tomorrow morning to find her."

CHAPTER FORTY-FIVE

Caistor Lane stretched on before them as breath-taking as ever, exhibiting the same variegated, expansive view that drew hikers to explore its wares. Fields of oilseed rape in bloom dashed the horizon, with squares of vibrant yellow and sprouting wheat in luscious greens dominating the rolling hills, reminding Campbell of lemons and limes in a bowl.

Without fuss or show, Byrne had not taken the road through Tealby but astutely chose the longer route, up Walesby Hill, from north to south, to avoid the crime scene that was still cordoned off. He sat with an elbow resting on the open window, one hand on the wheel. Even the way he drove these days exuded a new-found confidence, as though, no longer plagued with anxiety, he enjoyed the journey alone and the cold whip of wind in the hair he was growing out, which fell in windswept wisps around his forehead.

Campbell watched him and grinned. He was only in his twenties, she reminded herself, a prime age for a glow-up.

The beat of classic sixties rock played softly, and despite the rule against radios on duty, they felt comfortable enough in each other's company to ignore it. Even Campbell. Perhaps she was having her own glow-up. Not the same kind as Byrne. No, she'd had the same sense of style: the same haircut, natural make-up routine and body type since puberty. But a glow-up of personality? Of happiness? Her sense of accomplishment was indeed glowing more these days.

That was, at least, when the guv was back in charge.

Byrne slowed and turned down the radio, as everyone does when they're looking for a house number, as though the quiet will help them see better.

"There it is," Campbell said, pointing to a low, rectangular house on their right with a wide gate that opened into a large driveway. Byrne parked behind a white van, the only other car there, and pulled on the handbrake.

From the look of the buildings that enclosed the parking space, they were converted farm buildings - barn conversions, most likely adorned with climbing roses. Modern additions such as skylights and landscaped lawns made the buildings more attractive and no doubt more expensive. To their left was a pair of teal-painted doors to a garage that many might have considered a home-sized building of its own. But clearly, the main house was the building in the middle that began in front of them and continued in an L-shape around the corner. It was a charming structure with multiple French doors along both sides that opened up into the courtyard, allowing for an abundance of light alongside an impressive oak front door.

"Not what I expected from a kitchen porter, I'll be honest," Byrne said as he turned off the engine.

"I have a feeling he's a bit more than that," Campbell said.

They climbed from the car and strode up to the large front door, knocked, and waited. Up close, some signs of neglect revealed themselves: cobwebs tangled in the hinges of the door and the potted plants guarding the door — dry as a bone.

Before Campbell had time to notice any others, the lock turned, and the door opened.

"Tony Dunn?" she asked.

The man peered at them both quizzically before speaking.

"Who's asking?" His large glasses, which rested beneath a heavy fringe of curly, dark hair, magnified his sharp, intelligent eyes. From the shoulders up, he could have passed for a feeble nerd, but whatever lay beneath his tight tee-shirt was the result of many an hour in the gym. On first impressions alone, he looked like a man with ambitions beyond his current career.

"I'm PC Campbell," she said. "This is my colleague, PC Byrne." Beside her, Byrne nodded silently as if sizing the man up. "Can we come in for a moment? We just have a few questions."

For a moment, he merely looked between the two of them, searching their faces for an excuse. But, failing to find one, he finally feigned innocence and said, "Of course, come in."

The procedure was the same as it always was. He welcomed them inside, luring them into a false sense of normality. That was why, when Byrne and Campbell stepped into the impressive hall-way, it took them a second or two to process that Dunn had done a runner.

Byrne was the first to react. He tore the door open and powered across the driveway after Dunn.

Campbell stepped outside, her phone in hand, ready to call it in and report their error. She hesitated as Dunn skidded to a stop on the gravel when he saw Byrne's car blocking him in. He took an improvised detour, and, for a moment, he and Byrne played a game of chicken on either side of the van, peering through its dirty windows to find the other. Then, with a heavy crunch of gravel, Dunn made a run for the gate and the open fields beyond it.

"Gate," Campbell yelled, and Byrne sprang into action. He sprinted forward, stumbling on the gravel, and just as Campbell thought he was going to fall, he launched himself at Dunn, grabbing hold of his waist and dragging him to the ground, where they rolled in the dust. Campbell ran over to them, but Byrne needed no help. He manoeuvred himself on top of Dunn and dragged his arms behind his back.

"I didn't do anything!" Dunn cried into the stones. "Get off me. I haven't done a bloody thing."

"It's funny. We often find that innocent people run for no reason at all," Campbell said as Byrne caught his breath. She crouched before him, and he craned his neck to see her. "Needless to say, you are well and truly nicked, Tony. I'm pretty sure you're aware of your rights."

"What do you want?"

Byrne looked up at Campbell, and she nodded. He stood, taking his weight off the young man, who rolled over onto his back, gasping dramatically.

"We're investigating the whereabouts of Sabina Anter on Tuesday morning," she said.

Dunn lifted himself onto his elbows and squinted up at them. "Who?"

"Don't bother, Mr Dunn. We know that she came to see you on Tuesday morning."

"I don't know who you're—"

"She is...helping us with a murder investigation," she said. "She claims to have been with you on Tuesday morning."

"A murder—"

"In which you now find yourself implicated," Campbell continued. "What do you have to say? You can, of course, say nothing, and we'll take you back to the station. We can hold you for twenty-four hours, unless, of course, we see fit to request an additional twelve. You can request a duty solicitor or call your own legal team."

"Or?" he said. "Is all that really necessary?"

"Well, that depends," she said. "It depends on what you want to do."

He laid his head back in the gravel, closed his eyes, and gave his situation some thought.

"Was Sabina here on Tuesday morning?"

"Yes," he said, eventually.

"Time?"

"Late morning," he replied.

"Is that before eleven? After eleven?"

"I don't know. It was around then. She wasn't here long."

"Are you and her in a relationship?" Campbell asked.

"What? No, of course, not—"

"So why did she come over?"

He shrugged. "She came over for a cup of tea."

"You used to work together, didn't you?" asked Campbell patiently. "At the Horizon Hotel?"

He laughed. "Yes, she was front-of-house. I was a kitchen porter. What more can I say?"

Campbell moved her gaze from his sneering face to look around the courtyard. "You live here alone, do you?"

"Yeah," he said. "What of it?"

"It's a very large house for a young man like yourself to live in alone."

"It was my parents' house," he said. "I inherited it." In these three words alone, Campbell caught sight of the source of his anger: a young man on his own, living in his dead parents' family home.

She crouched again down to meet him at eye level. "I imagine it's hard to make ends meet."

"You could say that," he said through gritted teeth. "I get by."

"How do you think they would feel about you being arrested in conjunction with a murder investigation?"

"I told you, I didn't do anything!" he yelled, scrambling to get up before Byrne shoved him back down. "I don't know what you're on about. What murder?"

"A woman was killed on this road on Tuesday morning. You must have noticed that the lane was closed off."

"I don't get out much," he said.

"See, the problem is," Byrne replied. "For whatever reason, Sabina says she was with you on Tuesday morning, and although you've confirmed this much is true, neither one of you seems willing to tell us why. I mean, if you had said that you were in a relationship, fair enough. We may or may not have believed you, but it would have been *something*. But we've got nothing, Tony. Nothing but our imaginations." He leaned forward to ensure he had Dunn's full attention. "Are you involved, Tony?" he asked. "Is that why you've nothing to say?"

He looked between the two of them as though it was some kind of joke. Then, a look of realisation that they were not going to leave without a response hit him. Campbell could almost see the stakes being raised behind his eyes. He leaned back and muttered, "No comment?"

Campbell rolled her eyes and whipped the handcuffs from her belt in one smooth motion.

"Right, in that case," she said, "Tony Dunn, I am arresting you for—"

"Okay, okay," he said, banging the back of his head onto the gravel. "Jesus Christ. *Fine*. Sabina was here on Tuesday morning, okay?"

"What for?" Byrne asked, and Dunn finally relented.

"Take me to the garage," he said. "I'll show you."

CHAPTER FORTY-SIX

After an early dinner, George and Ivy had retreated to the living room, in their usual spots — Ivy on the armchair and George on the sofa, sipping at their daily oaky treat. Ivy read through the investigation notes for the hundredth time, and George squinted between his laptop screen and typed, one key at a time.

He tutted at the lacklustre results and muttered, "Derry, Donegal, Limerick." Then he threw up his hands. "Sod all in Lincolnshire. Sod all in England even."

"No offence, guv," Ivy said, not looking up from the file, "but if Ruby can't find Posy O'Keefe, I doubt you can. Just give her some time, and she'll have O'Keefe's BMI, NHS number, and Christmas list for you."

"We don't have a day, Ivy," he said.

"Why the urgency?" She looked up. "Has Tim been on at you?"

George removed his glasses and rubbed his eyes. "No. No, he's barely spoken to me at all."

"Is he avoiding you?"

"I think that he doesn't know what to say. You know, about

Grace. Some people do that when you're grieving, I've learned. They're scared to say the wrong thing, so they don't say anything at all."

"Do you wish he *would* say something?"

George laughed. "Right now, I'm enjoying the peace and quiet without him on our backs." He put his glasses back on and began prodding his keyboard again. "Anyway, I thought maybe Ruby could be overthinking it. That a simple approach could be best, you know, like good marketing."

"Well, you gave it a shot, at least," she said. "You know it's probably a pseudonym? You heard Ruby. If O'Keefe was so careful about concealing her face from the cameras, she's not going to have used her real name when answering the phone."

"You're right," he said but continued to search anyway.

Ivy returned to the well-thumbed pages, searching desperately for something they must have missed, a blazing motive or suggestion that Lily Hughes was not the embodiment of kindness her friends made her out to be.

"Surely, if the software was that bad, then Sabina Anter wasn't the only person upset with him," he said, which was enough for Ivy to look up from her notes, but with nothing to follow up with, she saw no reason to press him for more of his thoughts.

The buzz of a phone roused her from her musings, and without taking his eyes off the screen, George reached into his pocket and answered it.

"DI Larson," he said. Then, after hearing the voice on the other side, he exclaimed, "Campbell! Are you still at Dunn's house?" He listened to an answer to which Ivy was not privy. "What are you doing there?" He looked over at Ivy. "Wait, I'll put you on loudspeaker. Sergeant Hart is with me. Go on, talk us through it, Campbell. What was that about a garage?"

"When we got to Dunn's house," Campbell said without greeting Ivy, "he did a runner. Byrne tackled him, and we got him to talk. Eventually, he admitted that Sabina visited him on Tuesday morning. He said he had proof and showed us to his garage."

"What was the proof?" George asked, just as Ivy asked her own question.

"What was in the garage?"

"Videotape," Campbell said, once again reminding Ivy of her place in the team. "There're cameras all over his garage. We checked the tapes. Sabina was in the garage from exactly eleven oh-three to eleven forty-six, guv. She couldn't have killed Lily Hughes."

George looked at Ivy. From the blank look on his face, the news came as no surprise. They had assumed Sabina's innocence by now. She hadn't lied to them. She had omitted information, sure, but what she had told them had been the truth.

"What was she doing there?" asked George.

"Meat," answered Campbell.

"Excuse me?"

"Meat, guv. She gets her meat from Dunn."

A single jab of laughter escaped Ivy's lips.

"Wait, wait, wait. You're telling me she's using stolen meat for her eight-course, fine dining, paired food menu?"

"That's exactly what I'm saying, yes." Ivy rubbed her face. She couldn't help but laugh. She'd always found the fine dining industry a load of pretentious nonsense, but this level of irony was something else. She was a pub-food-with-the-football-on kind of girl, after all. "His garage was full of chest freezers, all filled with stolen meat from the abattoir," continued Campbell. "All sorts of stuff: lamb, steaks, even some venison guv.

"That's why he was fired from the Horizon Hotel?" George asked. "For stealing?"

"Exactly, we got Ruby to check in at the hotel. They gave us the whole story. Food went missing from the fridge bit by bit.

Dunn was sneaky and knew where the cameras were. So they couldn't prove it was him. But he would often be the last one cleaning up in the kitchen."

"So, he was fired," George clarified. "He got a job at an abattoir and went into business for himself, approaching his contacts in hospitality?"

"Looks like it, guv."

"It's kind of impressive in a way," Ivy suggested. "Kitchen porter to entrepreneur."

"Don't give him too much credit, sarge," Campbell said. "He's a sneaky little bugger."

"So, what are you doing at Wolds Grove?" asked George.

"Just finalising the evidence," she said. "Right now, I'm standing by the fridge in Sabina Anter's restaurant looking at about twenty polystyrene thermal boxes branded with the name of the abattoir."

"And I'll bet she doesn't have a single receipt," George said.

"I'm not sure if her tax returns are her main concern right now," Ivy added.

"So, what now guv?"

George removed his glasses, wiped them over with the sleeve of his favourite jumper, and placed them back on his nose, processing his words before he spoke them. "Hand her over to CID," he said. "She still committed a crime. We've got enough meat fraud issues in this country."

"Sure guv. But they'll close down the glampsite," Campbell said. "What about our guests?"

George paused for thought.

"We need them all in one place. Ask them to stay in the yurts, just for a little while longer. Tell them we're grateful. I think they've been living off snacks anyway, and it won't hurt them to do so for a bit longer. Bob has a car if they need a proper meal, and if they really want to leave, then, by all means, do not stand in their way. They've been patient with us so far. Let's not create enemies where we don't need them, eh?"

"Yes, guv."

"And Campbell?"

"Yes, guv?"

"Good job," he finished.

Ivy could practically hear her smile over the phone. She watched George's face soften. There was no doubt about it, he had a way with people that just did not come naturally to her.

"I'll pass that on to Byrne too guv, if you don't mind?" Campbell replied. "If he hadn't tackled Dunn to the ground, we'd still be chasing him over the hills."

George grinned. "Feel free to," he said and hung up.

"So that's Sabina scratched off," Ivy said, throwing the file down onto the coffee table and clutching her whisky in both hands. She ran her fingers over the moulding like it was braille, revealing a secret. "Only six more to go."

"Hold on, Ivy, here we go," George said, holding up his phone, which flashed and buzzed once more. "They're all at it tonight." He accepted the call and immediately put it on loudspeaker, holding it in the palm of his hand as though it was a carrot and Ivy a horse. "Ruby, you okay?"

"Meadow Drive, Binbrook," she said straight away. Even without context, they both knew exactly what she was talking about.

"I don't expect you to work late, Ruby—"

"I couldn't relax this evening. It wasn't easy, and I'm sure I've rubbed a few resources up the wrong way, but I got there in the end. Whether or not it's her real name, I don't know, but if you dig down deep enough, you'll find the lease is under a Posy O'Keefe Limited."

"Limited?" he said.

She paused and took an audible breath. "Posy O'Keefe is the

name of her business, guv," Ruby said. "That's why she was so hard to find. The lease is in the business name."

"And what is it that the firm does?" Ivy asked, calling out from the far side of the room.

"That's where it gets interesting," Ruby replied. "She's a private investigator."

CHAPTER FORTY-SEVEN

The house registered to Posy O'Keefe Limited was on a street with houses that varied from retirement-friendly bungalows to family homes with converted attic rooms. It was hard to imagine, George thought, a more quintessentially residential street, with the black bins out for collection, family estate cars parked in the driveways, well-trimmed bushes on well-mown lawns.

O'Keefe's house was one of a large semi with an extended double garage, a broad driveway, and an immaculate lawn home to a single apple tree. But, aside from the tree, the property lacked any details that hinted at the occupant's character — no knick-knacks or ornaments on the windowsills, no garden gnomes, or rogue children's toys. It was no more than an anonymous house in a row of houses. And something told George that was exactly what the occupant was going for - anonymity.

They pulled up outside the house, and Ivy's unimpressed expression seemed to mirror George's thoughts.

"It's like a show home," she said, rather unenthused.

"Really?" George replied, turning off the engine. "You've never heard of the term hiding in plain sight?"

He climbed out of the car and looked up at the house,

expecting the twitch of a curtain as they closed their car doors, announcing their arrival. But all the curtains were already open.

"Is she hiding?" Ivy asked. "Or is she simply blending in?"

They stopped at the front door, and George knocked twice. Through the frosted glass, he couldn't see as much as the outline of a coat stand, just a long, grey, empty carpet. Until a figure, wavy and formless, emerged from another room and approached.

"Oh, good morning," she said brightly when she answered the door. "Can I help you?"

His first thought was that she could be a model for some kind of outdoor pursuits brand. She was of medium height, trim, with strawberry-blonde hair pulled back into a tight ponytail that left only a few baby-hair wisps around her freckled face. Her freckles worked well to disguise the wrinkles on her forehead, which, despite her athletic figure, suggested she was closer to fifty than one might think. She wore black leggings and the kind of skin-tight, long-sleeved top that hikers wear, which suggested to George a level of fitness far beyond his own means.

"We're looking for Posy O'Keefe?" he said, to which she smiled sweetly, her intelligent eyes dancing between them.

"By which I presume you're referring to the person?"

It was as if her heavy Irish accent had been paired with her complexion like the wine at one of Sabina Anter's eight-course meals.

George held his warrant card up discreetly. There was no need to alarm the neighbours at this stage. "I'm Detective Inspector George Larson, and this is my colleague Detective Sergeant Hart. Can we have a word?"

"Of course," she said, inviting them inside. "Come on in, won't you?"

He and Ivy entered and, at her invitation, made their way through the living room, beneath an open archway, and into a lounge-kitchen area with double glass doors that led into a featureless garden. Even inside the house, there were no personal touches. The walls were bare, the counters clutter-free as though rarely used, or used and then immediately cleaned.

George and Ivy shamelessly studied the room, absorbing their surroundings. O'Keefe watched from the doorway, leaning playfully against the doorframe. She didn't offer them a cup of tea. Perhaps she didn't know where the teabags were kept.

"You're a difficult woman to find, Miss O'Keefe," George said eventually.

She crossed her arms and shrugged. "Really? I don't mean to be."

George laughed. "I don't believe that for a second," he said. "It took my researcher three days to find you."

"Well, maybe she needs to attend one of those training courses the force is always coming up with." At this, Ivy slammed shut the door of a cupboard she'd been inspecting. "Are you looking for something?" She directed her question at Ivy, but it was George who answered.

"We're investigating a serious incident that occurred on Tuesday morning," he said bluntly, watching for her reaction. However, all he received in return was a micro-expression, a lip twitch, a momentary reaction. "We're looking for somebody who could help us with our enquiries."

"Well, I'm afraid I'd love to—"

"James DeSilver," he said. "You know him, don't you?"

O'Keefe pushed off the doorframe and walked over to Ivy, opening the cupboard next to the one she had been investigating. "If you wanted a cup of tea," she said, pulling out a box of teabags, "you could have just asked."

She began the tea-making process, slowly popping three teabags into three cups, but her mind was clearly elsewhere.

"Inspector Larson, wasn't it?"

"That's correct," George replied.

"Despite what you might think, Inspector," she began, "I am

not hiding. I merely dislike being on every database in the country if I can avoid it. Off-grid, you might call me."

"Is that why the house is rented in your company's name?"

She turned to him. "That's my prerogative." George bowed, admitting that it was her right without interrupting her flow. "I've nothing to hide. And yes, I do know James DeSilver."

"How?" Ivy asked, but O'Keefe ignored the question.

"He was supposed to meet me on Tuesday morning at his house in Stenigot, but he never showed." She poured the boiling water from the kettle into the mugs. "That's why you're here, isn't it? Serious incident, you say? Involving James?"

"I'm afraid, I can't go into details—"

"Is he dead?" she asked, to which, despite George saying nothing, she was perceptive enough to derive an answer of her own. "How sad," she added. "Let me guess, I was the last person he contacted?"

Impressed by her intuition, George allowed another opportunity to develop her own narrative.

"Which means," she continued, "that you found me through his phone records despite me using an unregistered pay-as-you-go number." She opened the fridge for the milk, her eyes roving from side to side as though her mind considered every possibility but failed to find an answer. "That takes some doing."

George grinned. "Our researcher tracked your phone's point of sale. CCTV showed the new banknotes, which led us to footage of you withdrawing cash from an ATM last week." He grinned. "You made the mistake of answering your phone."

O'Keefe groaned and snapped her fingers. "Audio recording on an ATM camera. Well, whatever next. Even so, God only knows how you found my address." She walked over and handed George his tea, holding it up as though toasting. "I should give your researcher more credit."

George accepted the mug and toasted back.

"Why were you meeting James DeSilver on Tuesday morning?"

Ivy asked, unmoved by O'Keefe's charm, which George was rather enjoying.

"I don't know."

"Miss O'Keefe, we don't have time to—"

"I'm not being facetious," she said, holding up the hand that wasn't gripping her mug of tea. "He didn't tell me why."

"Is that right?" Ivy said flatly. "And did his wife know that you were meeting with him?"

At this, O'Keefe laughed out loud, a hearty, belly-full laugh. "Come on, missy. Use your imagination, at least. Do you think the only reason a man and a woman can meet in private is to have an affair?"

Ivy simmered. "Experience tells me that it's more common than not."

"Look, James was being very secretive about why he wanted to meet," O'Keefe continued. "And in the end, he didn't show up at all. I just figured he'd changed his mind. That's all I know."

"But why did he want to meet *you?*" asked George. "How do you know him?"

She looked into her tea, musing. "I've worked with James before."

"In what capacity?"

"He needed... assistance during a recent business dispute with a client."

"A recent business dispute with a client?" George repeated. "Would that client be Sabina Anter, by any chance?"

O'Keefe sipped her tea and held their gaze but didn't reply.

"Miss O'Keefe," George said, setting down his tea on the counter, "whilst I appreciate your right to client confidentiality and privacy, to stay off-grid, as you put it, my colleague is right. We don't have time to mess around here. Two people have lost their lives, and their killer or killers are still on the loose. We need to understand James DeSilver's movements on Tuesday morning and why somebody chose to kill him *just before* he was about to meet with you."

Still, she didn't reply.

"Perhaps you're not aware," he started, "but during a murder investigation, it is our job to gather evidence and eliminate suspects using a process of motive, means, and—"

"Okay, okay," she interrupted. "Please. You can save the speech."

It was O'Keefe's turn to set her cup down and turn to face the moment with both hands ready.

"Look, I know all about the procedures detectives must go through, Inspector Larson," she said, reaching into the zip pocket of her leggings and pulling out an ID of her own. She showed it to George. "I used to be one."

CHAPTER FORTY-EIGHT

There was no photo on the ID card, but simply her name, *Maeve O'Keefe*, above a nine-digit serial number, the pattern of which — seven numbers and two letters — George recognised immediately.

"Maeve?"

"My ma called me Posy, my da called me Posy," she explained. "After that, everyone called me Posy, which meant that everyone I met called me Posy. When I went my own way, people only knew me as Posy. It kind of works in my favour, so it made sense to call my firm Posy O'Keefe. Little Maeve goes unnoticed."

"Where were you based?"

"Right here in Lincolnshire," she said, nodding. "Not for long, mind. I doubt our paths crossed. I soon moved on to the RAF. I was there for twelve years. Loggie."

"Afghanistan?"

"And Syria."

George smiled. "Which is how you ended up in Binbrook?"

She whistled. "We're surrounded by RAF bases," she grinned. "How could a girl resist?"

"And now you're in the business of meeting married men in secret?" Ivy said dryly, to which O'Keefe rolled her eyes.

"Whatever James wanted to meet me for, believe me, it wasn't for anything mucky like that. He was tense on the phone. Agitated. He said it was urgent. That's why it surprised me when he didn't show."

"But you didn't bother to find out why?"

"In my profession, Sergeant Hart, you learn to let things go when a client falls through. Otherwise, God knows the kind of stuff you'd get caught up in. It's not like people call me when things are going well, is it? They don't call me for a wee natter. They call because they're at their wit's end."

"You say you worked with DeSilver before," George clarified. "He hired you to find dirt on Sabina Anter?" She made a show of not replying. "Look, we can find all this out, and we'll be back—"

"Yes," she said irritably. "For Christ's sake."

"And did you find anything?"

She tilted her head. "Did *you*?"

"Let's remember who's asking the questions."

She sighed, tired of the game. "I found some spotty teenager on Caistor Lane with a garage full of stolen meat," she said. "It was James's joker up his sleeve, if you like, in case he needed a way to get at her credibility."

"How did he get your number?"

She hesitated but then said, "His wife."

George blinked. That answer, he hadn't been expecting. "Franky?"

"Yes."

"She'd hired you before?"

"No."

"Miss O'Keefe, when we said we don't have time to mess around, we meant it."

She looked at him for a single, drawn-out moment, then downed her tea in one.

"Did you ever wonder why James and Franky moved to Lincolnshire?" she asked, carrying her mug over to the sink and washing it immediately.

"Franky said they were sick of London," George replied.

Instead of leaving it on the draining board, she grabbed a tea towel, drying the cup as she spoke. "Sure, but why Lincolnshire? Of all the counties in the country, why here? Why the Wolds? Cornwall's nice. Norfolk is glorious. Then there's Yorkshire, Scotland, Wales—"

"It's a beautiful place," George said, not wanting to hear an entire recital of the British counties. "Who wouldn't want to live here?"

She placed the mug in the cupboard. "There's one thing you might be overlooking." He leaned in, but what was offered was not a piece of information so much as a character assessment. "Franky has lived her entire life for her marriage. She has done everything for James. She's been the doting wife in London for decades now, there for him from the beginning of his business through the rise of its success."

"Okay..."

"But this is where she belongs. *This* is her home. Lincolnshire. Specifically, The Wolds."

"Wait, Franky's from Lincolnshire?" asked Ivy. "She doesn't have the accent."

"Well, she's a musical ear on her, eh?" O'Keefe laughed fondly, and then returned to the topic. "She adapts quickly. Anyway, London can beat the accent out of anyone. But believe me. She's a country girl. She never loved being in the city. She was there for James. That kind of life, living for someone else, living for their dreams and accomplishments, is unsustainable. Franky wanted to move home. To get back to herself and feel alive again without James dragging her down."

"So why didn't she do what the rest of us do?" asked Ivy bluntly.

O'Keefe raised her eyebrows. "Divorce?"

Ivy nodded.

O'Keefe shrugged. "I suppose they still love each other," she said, then closed her eyes, expressing the first sign of sadness breaking through what was surely a learned closure of feelings. "*Loved*." She swallowed and leaned back on the sink as though steadying herself and her emotions. "I've known James for a long time. Since he and Franky first got together. I was at their wedding, you know? And I'm sorry to hear about his death. Truly, I am."

"If you and Franky are such good friends, then why are you only finding out about his death now?" asked George. "Why didn't she tell you?"

O'Keefe smiled. "We're the kind of friends who see each other once a year and act like nothing has changed. I turn up on their doorstep from time to time, and they don't ask too many questions. But I wouldn't be first on her list to call in an emotional crisis. We both know that."

"Then how did Franky know to give your number to her husband?"

"I don't know if Franky knows exactly what I do. I don't think she's ever thought about it. But she knows I'm a woman who knows people. A woman who gets things done." O'Keefe reached into another concealed pocket on her leggings and pulled out an old Nokia. "Still, she's one of the very few who have access to this."

"And James thought the same, did he? That you could get things done for him?"

O'Keefe shrugged. "Just like his wife, he didn't ask many questions. But I gave him the answers he needed, and that was enough."

"Why use an unregistered phone?" Ivy asked. "Why not just use your business phone?"

"Habit, I suppose. A new phone for every client allows me to leave my other clients at home. They're cheap as chips, anyway. Twenty quid. Nothing fancy."

"And nothing that can lead back to you?" George added, to which she shrugged nonchalantly.

"What about this time? When did he call you about meeting on Tuesday?"

"Early on Tuesday morning. He sounded upset. Said he needed to meet straight away."

"And he didn't tell you why? He just said it was urgent?"

"Like I said."

"Was it about Sabina Anter?"

She shook her head. "No, that much I do know. It was personal, not business. He's not the type to get worked up over business affairs." She heard herself, and then corrected her statement. "At least he wasn't the type."

"It's okay," George told her. "But something's bothering me. You bought the phone on Monday, yet you said that he called you on Tuesday."

"S'right," she said. "I didn't buy the phone for him, specifically. I bought it for my next client. I was in town. I used my last phone for my last client, so I bought a new one. It's not rocket science."

George laughed at the little suffix to her explanation. "No. No, it's not rocket science, is it?"

"Look, he said he'd only tell me what it was about in person. And that I couldn't tell anyone."

"Not even Franky?"

She looked up at them, and all sarcasm and charm vanished, replaced by a darkness to her features that revealed her years in the shadows on her face.

"*Especially* not Franky," she said, and she signed the cross like a good Catholic. "God rest his soul."

CHAPTER FORTY-NINE

"The way I see it," George said, "there are two possibilities."

They stared out of the windscreen, watching an old man wheel his black bin back into his garage. The collection must have come by when they were inside O'Keefe's house. The old man watched them suspiciously as they watched him, his eyes narrowed with a sour look on his face as though he'd just swallowed a spoonful of vinegar. The engine was off. They didn't yet know where to go next.

"Either the murders are linked," he continued, "or the murders are separate. The killer only intended to kill James DeSilver that morning, but Lily saw something she shouldn't have, so they killed her too."

"So she witnessed the murder of her best friend," Ivy said, "then went on with her hike?"

"I'm not saying she witnessed his murder," George said. "That would be impossible anyway. The women were already hiking when James DeSilver was killed. I'm saying she saw or knew *something*. Something that the killer knew she would be able to link back to them."

"That sounds like the same thing to me," Ivy said. "Either way, the murders are linked."

"Yes, but linked to what?" He paused, ruminating. "We've been assuming that the case against Sabina Anter connects to the murders. But we have to follow the evidence, and the evidence tells us it wasn't her. It couldn't have been. So what if Lily and James's murders had nothing to do with Sabina? Where does that leave us?"

"Then why did James DeSilver hire the same PI he used on the software case?"

George shrugged. "Because he trusted her," he said. "Like O'Keefe said, they'd known each other a long time. Plus, they'd already worked together. He knew she was discreet. She was professional. She got results."

"Even if those results were against his wife? Her friend?"

"Even if," George said, nodding at the house from which, no doubt, they were being surveilled. "That's a woman who puts her duty before all else. Anyone can see that."

"So the question remains," Ivy said. "Why did James DeSilver hire a PI? And why tell that PI to not tell his wife about it, specifically?"

"I think that's obvious, don't you?"

"He was looking into Franky." Ivy nodded. "But why?"

"You heard what O'Keefe said," he replied. "Franky wanted to get back to herself. James was weighing her down. I expect he could feel that, don't you? Perhaps he sensed she was planning something."

"Planning what?"

"Planning the very events that played out this week, Ivy."

"So he was too late?"

"Or perhaps she acted early. Maybe she found out he was going to meet O'Keefe, so she had to act fast. Remember what Pip said? James DeSilver's murder was not premeditated. She acted in the moment. Out of desperation."

Ivy shook her head. "But it's impossible, guv. Franky was already hiking by the time James was killed, remember? Sure, she could've killed Lily. God knows she had enough of a motive. All she had to do was wait for the right moment for the fog to roll in. But James? She couldn't have killed him."

"No, she couldn't," George said, turning to Ivy, a new thought popping into his head, a theory that could explain how one person had to have been in so many places at once. "She couldn't have done it alone."

At that moment, startling them both, George's phone rang throughout the car's loudspeaker, Byrne's name glowing on the screen.

"Byrne," George said, clicking the green button to accept the call, "what have you got?"

"Guv, I just wanted to inform you that Sabina Anter has been handed over to the CID. They said they'll take it from here," he said.

"Good," George replied. "Actually, Byrne."

"Guv?"

"What are they charging her with?"

"Handling stolen goods to start with," he replied. "He seems to think HMRC will want a slice of the pie, though."

I need a favour. I need you to ask him to hold off for the time being."

"Guv?"

"Think about it," George said. "The moment CID rock up at Wolds Grove with their size eleven boots, they'll shut the place down."

"Right?"

"And we've asked Franky DeSilver and her friends to stay put," he explained. "If CIS shut the place down, we'll be chasing them all over the country with every question we have."

"Right, got it," Byrne said. "Also, Maguire wants a word."

"Put him on," George said. "And Byrne?"

"Yes, guv?"

"Good job."

Ivy had the distinct impression that George was performing some sort of damage control throughout the team, rebuilding the egos that her leadership had smashed to pieces.

"Guv," came Maguire's Irish growl over the line, not too dissimilar to O'Keefe's.

"Morning, Maguire. What's up?"

"Well, I've been doing some digging like you asked, looking into Lily's friendship group, trying to find any signs of conflict on social media."

"And?"

"Nada."

"Nothing?"

"Bugger all," he said, and Ivy rolled her eyes. "Ruby's got the CCTV, too, by the way, that shows Bob dropping Toby off in Walesby on Tuesday morning. Campbell's going through it now to double-check the timings. The village high street only has one camera, but it's enough. And Ruby's got access to half their phones already. But even those messages are all rainbows and daisies. It's not an act, guv. They genuinely do all love each other."

"Give me a friendship group without drama, Maguire," George said, "and I'll give you a snowy day in July."

"Well, you know what they're saying about global warming, guv."

"Just keep looking, Maguire," Ivy cut in. "There's bound to be something for us to dig into."

"I know, I know," he said. "But look, there is one thing. It's not a conflict, as such, but more a slight change in trends. In the last few years, their messages have grown increasingly sparse. More like a Happy Birthday and Merry Christmas here and there, maybe a few photos, but nothing half as pally as they've presented in the last few days. Until recently, they seemed more like old friends who were fading away from each other."

"Then what changed?"

"Jordan Hughes."

"Lily's husband?"

"Yes," Maguire said. "He died, and they suddenly all got back in contact with Lily, checking in on her, asking about funeral arrangements, you know how it is."

"Actually, I do," George said, no doubt remembering how his recently dialled list had changed drastically in the last few weeks. When Ivy's father died, friends she barely remembered had come out of the woodwork, half-recognised faces, those she'd forgotten she used to be close to, had turned up to stand by her side in the most difficult of times. Just in the same way, regular faces, like Tim in George's time of need, stepped away because he was uncomfortable with death and grief. Some friends, it turned out, just couldn't face the darkness and were only there for the good times.

"Aye, right. Sorry, guv."

"No bother," George said. "So you think that's what brought them all back together?"

"It seems like it. See, that's the thing. It got me thinking." Ivy and George shared a worried glance. When Maguire got thinking on his own, unsupervised, it had, more than once, led to trouble. "They're all part of this friendship group, right? The nine of them including Jordan. And then, within six months, *three* of them die. That's a third. Thirty per cent. We've only been considering Lily and James's death as connected. But don't you think it's a bit strange that a wife dies only *six months* after her husband?"

"Sure," George said slowly. "But Jordan's death was an accident."

"But was it?"

George and Ivy stared at each other. "What are you trying to say?"

"I'm telling you, guv, that I got in touch with the team that handled Jordan Hughes's case. It was called in as a road traffic accident but was quickly passed on to a Major Crimes team in the Met."

George sat up in his seat. "What? Why?"

"Because it was suspicious as hell. No clear cause for the crash. The road was empty, with no sudden turns or skid marks to suggest that he avoided something or had to brake suddenly."

"Then why wasn't Lily's name flagged if her husband was a victim?"

"Because he wasn't a victim for certain. They don't know exactly what happened. The investigation was left open."

George turned the ignition on and put the car into drive.

"Maguire?" he said, then performed a three-point turn in the middle of Meadow Drive, handling the wheel like a young police officer with nothing to lose. Ivy put on her seatbelt.

"Yes, guv?"

"First of all, good job. No..." he said, pulling onto the main road in such a way that caused Ivy to grab the handle above her door. "*Brilliant* job."

"Thank you, guv."

"Second of all, find out absolutely everything you can about Jordan Hughes's death." George put his foot down, and through the window, the gold and verdant fields blurred like a smudged watercolour. "Get ready for a briefing. We're on our way."

CHAPTER FIFTY

The team had been gathered, the whiteboard had been flipped, and a single name had been written in the middle of it — a name that had become lost, forgotten, or worse, overlooked.

"Jordan Hughes," George said, pointing to the name in the centre of the board. "What do we know about him?"

"An oncologist at St Paul's Hospital," Ruby said, flicking through her notepad. "He was a consultant who'd worked there since graduating in 2001."

"He met his wife, Lily Hughes, in 2012 at a prostate cancer fundraising event, where she was a sponsorship manager," Campbell said. "Some fancy gig at the Royal Albert Hall. According to a colleague that I spoke to at Jordan's hospital, they'd danced all night together and been inseparable ever since. They were married for twelve years until..."

"Until Jordan died in a car accident six months ago," Byrne picked up, and George couldn't help but admire the seamless choreography of their briefing. On their best days, the team showed real promise. Nurturing that so that it became a daily habit was a challenge he had yet to overcome. "According to the report, he was driving down Rushett Lane in South London when his car came off the road and hit a tree. No witnesses, but someone drove past a few minutes later and found him. He was pronounced dead at the scene."

"However, what was initially believed to be a tragic road accident was quickly passed on to major crimes," Maguire continued, picking up where Byrne had stopped. "There were signs of an impact on the rear bumper, as though someone had run into him. It was a semi-rural road without cameras. But some witnesses claim to have seen a car driving recklessly along that road not long before, which suggested it might have been a hit and run."

O'Hara cleared her throat to add to the summary.

"The Met looked into it but struggled to find much evidence to go on. There were plenty of cars nearby, but none with owners with any motive against killing Jordan Hughes. And if it *was* an accidental hit and run, then there was no way of telling who did it."

"But here's where it gets interesting," Maguire said, saving the ending for himself. It was, after all, his big find. "One of the cars investigated nearby belonged to someone we know."

"Let me guess..." George said.

"Franky DeSilver?" Ivy answered for him.

Maguire clicked his fingers at her and winked— a bold move that she ignored and prayed he wouldn't repeat. "Franky DeSilver's car was seen in the area, but as I said, they were unable to find any connection or any motive that might mean she would've run down Jordan Hughes."

"Was she questioned?"

"She was, but it seems that her and her husband were away in the States somewhere. He had some kind of work conference or something, so the investigating team put it down to a mix-up."

"So nobody suspected Franky?"

"They didn't get that far."

"There's something else you should know," Campbell said.

"Go on."

"Jordan wasn't driving *his* car when he was killed," she said slowly, highlighting its importance with her deliberate word choice. "His car was in the garage having an MOT. He was driving his wife's car. *Lily's* car."

George nodded. He knew exactly the point she was trying to make. "So it's plausible that somebody tried to run her off the road," he said, "not knowing that it was him driving?"

"Exactly."

George looked around at his team, who stared up at him and the whiteboard with serious, focused expressions.

"Well, you've had a busy morning, haven't you?" he said, and with a sudden swing of his arm, flipping the board back over. They all leaned back with the movement and settled their eyes on the list of suspects on the other side. But George didn't bother going through every name on their list. Instead, he went straight to Franky DeSilver's.

"Now it's our turn to share," he said, looking at Ivy to take over.

"Maeve O'Keefe, or Posy as she's known..." Ruby closed her eyes and sighed in defeat, and George grinned at her as Ivy continued, "was indeed a PI hired by James DeSilver," she began, as George tapped Franky's name, circling it while Ivy spoke, getting closer and closer until he landed right upon it, spiralling into the name like a penny drop. "They were meant to meet on Tuesday morning, but DeSilver never showed. We have reason to believe that he was looking into his wife, Franky."

"Do you think he suspected that she killed Jordan?" asked Byrne.

"How could she if they were in America?"

"Have you ever been to a medical conference?" George asked, to which the entire team shook their heads. "They are as dull as paint for anybody not medically minded anyway. It's plausible that she flew back. It's not like they were short of a few quid, and her husband wouldn't have even known she was missing."

"Jesus, that's quite the red eye," Maguire said.

"It's simple," George said. "And simplicity is, as you will learn, very often the answer. Who checked to see if she had made any flights between her scheduled trips?"

Maguire puffed his cheeks and shook his head. "I mean, I could ask the Met, but—"

"They didn't," George said. "Why would they? They probably saw the tickets, and maybe if one of them was diligent enough, they spoke to the Home Office and cross-checked the tickets with border control. Who would have checked to see if she had made two flights in between?"

"I can look into it," Ruby suggested.

"Do," George replied.

"So, are we to assume that Franky DeSilver is our lead suspect?" O'Hara asked.

"We can't know for certain," George replied. "O'Keefe said that James was very secretive, but he made one thing clear. She was not allowed to tell Franky that they were meeting. So," he said, focusing on the team, "the questions I pose to you are these. Why did DeSilver want to meet O'Keefe *that* morning? Why so urgently? Why did he arrange a holiday with his friends? What changed? What happened on Monday night or Tuesday morning to make it so vital that he saw her straight away? Jordan has been dead for six months. So why now?"

The team said nothing.

"If you don't have answers for me, find them," George continued. "Or at least write down the questions because I have many more for you. I want a deep dive into Franky DeSilver. How does she spend her time? Where does she go? What jobs has she had? Since when has she suspected her husband and best friend of having an affair? And if she has been planning something, why act now? What drove her to act irrationally?"

"Perhaps the kiss was just too much," Campbell offered. "Even if Franky had known about the... connection between James and

Lily for months, even years, it seems to have lain dormant until Monday night. That's when James actually acted on it. Then Violet embarrassed Franky in front of her friends, screaming about Lily having an affair and slapping her in the face for it. It must've been humiliating. That's what broke her. *That's* what pushed her over the edge." She paused. "So to speak."

"Good," George said. "Now, find me the evidence for that theory." He addressed the team as a whole. "Divide the tasks up as you see fit, but, Maguire, you keep finding everything you can about Jordan Hughes's accident. Let's go over this one more time." Again, he tapped Franky's name. "Motive for killing James DeSilver?" he asked the room.

"General resentment at the marriage," Ivy said. "Plus the possible affair."

"Motive for killing Lily Hughes?" continued George.

"Again, possibly for having an affair with her husband," Campbell replied. "And now we know she might have already tried six months earlier."

"And alibi for both?"

"She was hiking when James DeSilver was killed," Byrne said. "She couldn't have killed him."

"Not alone, she couldn't," he said cryptically. "And for Lily Hughes?"

"She and Cecelia were the only ones who weren't alone in the fog," Maguire said. "They're each other's alibis."

"And we followed up on that, did we?"

The team looked at each other guiltily.

"Aside from the initial statements we took in which Cecelia confirmed that they were together in the fog?" Byrne asked. "No, guv. We haven't made a point of it."

George put the lid back on the marker and placed the pen on the whiteboard's magnetic shelf.

"Well, let's rectify that, shall we?" he said, turning to the two most promising members of his team. "Byrne, Campbell?"

"Guv?" Byrne said.

"Call me when you get to Wolds Grove," he said, as the pieces of the puzzle his mind had been toying with began falling into place.

"Campbell," Ivy said, before the pair could leave.

"Sarge?"

"Don't forget your zip ties," she said. "If Franky knows we're onto her, who knows what she'll do."

"You want us to arrest her?"

"I want you to have Cecelia Adams reconfirm her initial statement," George said. "If she can't, or if she refuses to..." He looked at the pair, and despite them being more than capable of bringing Franky DeSilver in, he felt the burden of responsibility for them. "Well, let's just see what happens, shall we? You never know, she might just turn herself in."

CHAPTER FIFTY-ONE

"Is that them?" came Cecelia's cry as soon as Bob pulled back the yurt's entrance. "Let them in because I sure as hell want a word."

Bob offered them a grimace by way of an apology or perhaps a warning, then let Byrne and Campbell inside. The couple's room had escalated from slightly untidy to resembling a teenager's bedroom. Their suitcase was hidden beneath a mound of dirty clothes, coffee cup rings stained the pristine furniture, and the bamboo waste bin in the corner overflowed with crisp packets and plastic bottles.

Immediately, Cecelia accosted them with a packet of instant noodles in her hand.

"I've been eating these for a week," she said, shaking the chicken noodles and pointing at the kettle in the corner. "At least we could have a complimentary breakfast until you closed the whole bloody place down."

"We haven't closed anything down—"

"I don't give a rat's arse who did what. I want to know *why* we are being kept imprisoned instead of being allowed to go home."

"As I have explained, Mrs Adams, you are not being held prisoner," Byrne said flatly. "We are investigating the murders of two of your friends—"

"I haven't seen my children in a week," she hissed, her voice breaking. "After all we've been through, after all that's happened, I just want to hold them tight. Can't you understand that?"

"I *can* understand that, yes," he said, "but what I can't understand is why you would purposefully obstruct our investigation."

"Obstruct? What on earth are you talking about? We've done everything you asked."

"We have reason to believe that you haven't been entirely honest with us, Mrs Adams," Campbell said, her voice low and dangerous.

"What?" Bob whispered, coming to stand beside his wife, who let the noodle package fall limply by her side. "Are you accusing her of lying?"

"Perhaps we should sit down," Byrne offered.

"No, we'll stay standing. If you're accusing my wife of lying, then I want to know why."

"Fine," he said, turning to Cecelia. "Mrs Adams, you told us that you and Franky were alone in the fog on the morning that Lily died. That you stayed together until it cleared. But that's not true, is it?"

"We were," she said, her voice weak, but from emotion or the strain of lying, Byrne couldn't be sure. "We *were* together."

"For the whole time? From the second fog rolled in to the second it lifted, you were by Franky's side?"

She gaped soundlessly, then said, "Well, I...."

"Before you speak, Mrs Adams," Campbell said, her voice softer but no less dangerous, "remember that what you say now will affect you and your family for the rest of your life."

Cecelia stared at her for a long moment, no doubt allowing herself to visualise hypothetical futures to a few moments of life, if only in her mind.

"Perhaps not the *whole* time," she whispered eventually.

Her husband's mouth fell open, and he sat down beside her. "What do you mean, love?"

She sniffed. "I mean, there was maybe a minute, two at the most, when we were separated. She was close, I think. But the fog was so thick. I just assumed she was standing there. I couldn't see her, and she couldn't see me." She looked up at them. "I can't say for certain."

Bob sprung onto his feet and began pacing the room.

"*Jesus*, Cecelia," he snapped. "Why didn't you tell me?"

"Franky was the one who said we were together," she said, her voice growing as though it knew where it stood in an argument with her husband and strengthened with the familiarity of it. "She said it from the beginning, and I just... agreed. I didn't lie. Not really."

"Agreeing to a false truth is lying, my love," Bob said, and Byrne admired his turn of phrase.

"Why did you keep it from us, Mrs Adams?" he asked.

"I didn't mean to," she whispered. "I was just following Franky's lead. I assumed she had a good reason. Anyway, by the time the fog cleared, she *was* standing next to me. It was an assumption that she'd been just a few feet away the whole time, but it wasn't really a lie. I can't say for certain whether she was there or not."

"Then why didn't you tell us that?"

She shook her head and then buried it into her hands. Through her fingers, they heard, "I don't know."

"You can't jeopardise our family for your friends, Cecelia," Bob said, slamming his palm against the yurt post in the middle of the room. "I can't believe you would lie to the police to protect *her*?"

Cecelia slowly looked up from her hands and stared straight at her husband. "I would kill for that woman, Bob," she said, and he threw his head back in despair.

"Great," he said. "Great thing to say during a bloody *murder investigation* to two detectives, Cecelia. Real nice."

"I mean, I didn't..." she said, turning to Byrne suddenly, her eyes glazed with tears. "I just mean..." She took a deep breath. "Franky DeSilver is a good woman, a great woman. I've known her for years. She saved me."

"Lord, here we go," Bob muttered from the other side of the room.

"She did! You weren't there. You don't know what I was like. I was miserable," she explained to them. "Depressed. Franky was the only one there for me. The only one at work who took the time to get to know me. We became friends. She made my life worth living again."

"That's touching," Campbell said. "But it doesn't make a—"

"That's what I'm trying to tell you," Cecelia said, her eyes wide, on the verge of manic. "Franky would never hurt a soul. If she lied and said she was with me in the fog the whole time, she had her reasons."

"Yes, Mrs Adams," Campbell said dryly. "I can quite believe that."

"If you care about your friends as deeply as you claim to, you'll want the best for them," Byrne said, offering Cecelia Adams a level of patience that she didn't deserve. He felt sure that, in Campbell's eyes, they ought to have arrested her for providing a false statement. "You'll help us find out what happened, for everyone's sake."

Cecelia nodded and sank back down onto the bed. Bob continued pacing, his frustration at his wife emanating throughout the atmosphere of the room.

"Now, tell me," Byrne continued. "Did you hear anything in the fog? Anything that might suggest that Franky walked away? Did you hear the sound of footsteps?"

"No," she said quickly.

"Tell the truth, Cecelia," Bob warned.

"I am!" she yelled at him, then turned back to Byrne. "The fog was like a...a vacuum. I couldn't hear anything. I was disorientated."

"Is there anything else that you've kept from us?" asked Campbell. "Anything that we should know? Anything you haven't told us about Franky, James or Lily? This is important, Mrs Adams. These are people's lives." She crouched to meet her at eye level. "The lives of those you love."

She looked into Campbell's eyes, chestnut meeting chestnut, each waiting to see who would blink first.

It was Cecelia.

"There's one thing," she whispered. "Now, I didn't lie about it," she said pointedly, glancing between them and her husband. "I just didn't tell anybody. I didn't know if it was important."

"You didn't know if what was important?" Campbell asked as Bob slowly walked over to stare down at his wife with disapproval.

"I overheard something." She gulped. "On Tuesday morning, before everyone was up and dressed, before we met for breakfast."

"What was it?"

"It was just a conversation I heard. I didn't think much of it at the time, but now... I think it meant something. Like they knew they were in danger or something."

"Who, Mrs Adams?" asked Byrne. "Who did you hear talking?"

She looked up at him with puddle-like eyes. "James and Lily."

"They knew they were in danger?" asked Bob quietly.

Campbell leaned forward, her breath held as tight as a drum. "What makes you think that?"

"They said they were looking into something. I don't know what it was."

"What exactly happened?"

She cleared her throat and blinked as though struggling to remember. "I woke up that morning, Tuesday morning, with the sunrise. See, I'm used to the kids running in to jump on us. Bob can sleep through anything. He was there, snoring like a bear next to me." At this, Bob tutted and turned away. "But I couldn't get back to sleep, so I popped outside for some air, and that's when I heard it."

"What did you hear?"

"Voices," she said. "And footsteps."

"Where did you hear them?"

"Outside. I know it's a big field, but you can hear everything. The sound carries. You can hear footsteps going past the tent and voices, even if they're whispered."

"So you followed the sound?"

"Yes," she said. "Their voices were hushed."

"It was early in the morning," Byrne said. "They were probably being polite."

"No. No, it was like they weren't just trying not to wake people. They didn't want to be heard at all. I followed them. I couldn't help myself." She shrugged. So many of her gestures appeared childish, as though she was unaware of the consequences of her actions. "What can I say? I'm curious."

"What did you hear?" asked Byrne. "What was said? Who was it?"

Cecelia went to speak, then stopped herself. Her words caught like a ragged breath in the throat. She looked between them all slowly, from Campbell to Byrne to her husband, and then, like a shy child, she curled into herself and shut down.

"I'd rather not say."

Bob turned and smacked the yurt pole for the second time with the palm of his hand. "For Christ's sake," he yelled.

"Can't you just ask someone else?" Cecelia said, her voice childlike and feeble. "I'm sure someone else heard it."

"What do you mean?"

"There was someone else there," she said. "I saw their silhouette behind one of the tents. They were listening, just like me."

"Who was it?"

"I didn't see who."

"Cecelia, why didn't you tell us all this before?"

"Because..." Cecelia shook her head, and, at last, a tear fell from her brimming eyes. "They mentioned Franky. I knew how it looked." She turned her crazed, tearful stare on Byrne and Campbell. "I knew you lot would paint her like some kind of monster or something for a murder I know that she can't possibly have done."

Byrne straightened. "What makes you so sure?"

"I know her," she choked. "I love her."

"Even those we love can do monstrous things, Mrs Adams," he said. "It's time for you to tell us the truth. For Lily. For James."

But Cecelia shook her head.

"For God's sake, love," Bob said, kneeling beside his wife. "Just tell them what you know so that we can go home. So we can finally see the kids." He grabbed her hand like a desperate man. "Do it for them." He kissed her wedding ring. "Do it for us."

Finally, Cecelia looked at her husband and placed a loving hand on his cheek, rubbing his skin as though their love was new.

"Alright," she whispered and turned to Byrne. "Alright, I'll tell you." She paused, gathering herself. "It was something like—"

"No," Byrne said harshly. "*Something like* isn't good enough, Mrs Adams." He walked across the room and grabbed the two armchairs by the entrance, one for himself and one for Campbell, so they could sit down and pay proper attention to her story. "Tell us exactly what happened."

CHAPTER FIFTY-TWO

She had expected to find Lily and James outside the tent. Their voices had sounded so close, as though they'd been standing at the foot of her bed, whispering, so nearby, just on the verge of her dreams. But when she pulled open the yurt door, the glorious sunrise met her on the threshold, alone. Its long, glimmering rays stretched across the field, creating patterns on the grass between the yurts. Stretching her aching back, Cecelia glanced back at her sleeping husband, then stepped outside to enjoy the peaceful sunrise, something she hadn't enjoyed for many years. Birds sang in the trees, not in melodies, but in short, sharp chirps, like the sound of a car's key fob.

She followed the noise to the trees at the edge of the field, not far from her and Bob's yurt, listening for more birds, for the rustle of nocturnal creatures heading to their nests, and if she was honest with herself, because she was curious to hear those voices again.

And hear them, she did.

They were hushed and whispered, hisses that carried on the gentle morning breeze.

Bob would have called her nosey, but she called it curiosity. It was her curiosity that led her further into the trees, and it was her curiosity that led her to the little spot where nobody could see her, crouching behind the trunk of a large oak, straining to listen.

"Did you get my message?" the woman hissed.

Lily, Cecelia thought, and she frowned.

"Of course I did," a second voice replied. It was male and most definitely James.

"Jesus," Cecelia whispered to herself.

"Did you delete it? Like I said?"

"Yes, it's deleted."

Cecelia chanced a peek around the trunk and found James and Lily lit by one of those delightful rays of morning sun, their faces aglow, highlighting the worry etched into their furrowed brows and sleepless eyes.

"This can't be true, can it?" She'd never heard the type of fear that shook James's voice from a grown man. It was raw and reminded her of her children's voices at the end of her bed, in the middle of the night, a child afraid of the darkness.

Lily handed James what looked to be a business card. "Call them yourself if you don't believe me."

He shook his head in denial but took it from her. "I believe you," he said, gazing at her with a longing in his eyes. "When did you even have time to work all this out?"

"I've been up all night, James. I knew something wasn't adding up. Like I told you, it stayed on my mind. I thought about it over and over and over again, and I followed every hypothetical theory until I came to one that finally made sense of everything that's happened."

"Lily..." he said sadly.

Cecelia's friend stared into the sun rising over the Wolds, her face illuminated.

"You know, I've known all these months since he died that something was wrong," she said. "I kept asking God why. Why? Why? Why do this to me? And now I know, at last. It wasn't some freak accident. It wasn't God who took him from me. Because *this* is why Jordan died, isn't it?" She tapped the card James still held in his hand. Then Lily said something that was not a question but a statement, a truth, a declaration of fact, one that made Cecelia's blood run cold. "He was killed."

Cecelia's gasp was masked by the morning breeze rustling the tree canopy. She turned back to the protection of the trunk, her chest rising and falling in fear, her mind playing the words over and over. What were they talking about? Jordan wasn't killed, was he? It wasn't possible. It couldn't be. He was a good man, a doctor, a regular go-to-work and feed-your-family, take your-wife-on-holiday kind of chap. A friend. A good friend. But a murder victim?

Impossible.

"Lil, I'm so sorry," James said, and when Cecelia looked back, he was holding her in his arms, murmuring into her hair. "He must have worked it out already." Outrageously, James laughed, stepped back, and held Lily by the shoulders, but it seemed his laughter settled her tears. She wiped them away. "He always was smarter than all of us." He sighed and shook his head. "Jordan got caught up in all this. And he shouldn't have. I'm so sorry."

Lily's face crumpled, and she sobbed once more into his arms while heavy tears dropped down James's face. Cecelia couldn't believe what she was seeing. She'd only seen James cry once before, in all her years of knowing him, just once, and that was at Jordan's funeral.

"We can't let it happen again," Lily said eventually, a new resolve in her voice.

"No," said James, pulling away. "We won't. I'll sort this out."

"How?" she sniffed.

"I know someone who can help."

"What kind of someone?"

"Someone who can... help us. Someone who can look into this so that we don't have to."

Lily studied his face as though searching a puzzle for clues. "Not Posy?" she said eventually.

James didn't reply.

"I don't know, James. Maybe we should just go to the police?" Lily said. "Maybe they can help."

"What, like they did last time? They couldn't even tell that Jordan's death was a murder, let alone solve it."

"But Posy..." Lily shook her head and gripped James's hands in desperation. "Do you trust her?"

"She's a professional, Lily," James insisted, nodding. "She'll do what's right. She won't tell anyone."

Lily gulped down her tears and along with it, it seemed, her doubt. "Even Franky?"

"Especially Franky."

She nodded, giving into James's will, her shoulders slumping like a great weight had been taken from them.

"So what now?"

"Sit tight," James said, looking down at the hands he clutched in his own. "Just pretend everything's normal. Stay together when you're hiking, okay? And whatever you do, don't say anything that'll make Franky suspicious." Lily looked up at him darkly. "You know what she's like."

"James, if this is true, it changes everything."

"I know." He let go of her hands and nodded towards the yurts. "Go on now," he said. "Before they all wake up."

But she didn't move. She gazed up at him in nothing short of awe.

It was then that Cecelia saw it from the corner of her eye, the human form lurking behind Lily's yurt. It was a silhouette of a figure, as elusive as quicksilver, impossible to tell how long whoever it was had been standing there, listening, just as Cecelia had been: hearing everything. And as a spectre, as Lily and James's conversation came to an end, it grew smaller and faded until it was gone.

"Be safe," Lily said, rousing Cecelia from the intruder.

"You too."

Cecelia turned back to her old friends and watched them standing in the glow of their last sunrise, looking into each other's eyes, those vital words on the tips of their tongues, where they remained unspoken, undeclared, and banished. The oh-so-true confession that should have been confessed, not only that morning but so many decades ago, a lifetime ago, two marriages ago, was lost to the peace. James and Lily communicated all they could only in a slow release of each other's fingers and then went their separate ways, alone, sharing an over-the-shoulder glance or two, without ever having said what had needed so long ago to be said:

I love you.

CHAPTER FIFTY-THREE

"Bring her in," George said over the phone. "We've got more than enough to go on. If she wasn't with Cecelia in the fog, there goes her alibi for Lily Hughes. Along with her car being spotted in the area when Jordan died, that gives us all we need. She's got MMO up to her neck. Bring Franky DeSilver in."

"Yes, guv," Campbell said.

She and Byrne stood beside the copse of trees beyond Bob and Cecelia's yurt, out of earshot, not far from where Cecelia's story had taken place. In fact, she could identify the large oak behind which Cecelia had probably hidden.

"But only for the murder of Lily Hughes, hear?" George continued. "It's impossible that Franky could've killed James DeSilver without help, and the Jordan Hughes investigation doesn't belong to us. Not yet, at any rate," he added determinedly. "But we can outline the evidence against her killing Lily, so that will get us somewhere, at least. We can hold her on remand while we work out what happened to DeSilver."

"Yes, guv," Campbell repeated, but the guv wasn't listening.

Over the line, Campbell heard him allocating tasks to Ruby, O'Hara, and Maguire about outlining evidence and preparing for an interview. Meanwhile, Byrne had wandered over to the other side of Lily Hughes's tent, no doubt looking for signs that someone had stood there listening to an early-morning conversation on Tuesday morning, testing Cecelia's story. But it added up. Even without the long sun rays, his silhouette was clear when he crouched behind the yurt.

"Campbell," George said on the phone, "are you still there?"

"Yes, guv."

"Well, go," he said. "We're getting ready. Bring her straight to the station."

"Yes, guv," she said one last time and ended the call. She walked over to Byrne, who was kneeling on the ground, touching the grass. "Any footprints?" she asked sarcastically. "A rogue hair or cigarette butt? Better still, a vial with a 'Franky DeSilver DNA' label on it?"

He grinned up at her and stood up. "No such luck."

"But at least it finally makes sense now," Campbell said quietly, suddenly very aware of how sound travelled in that field, "the urgency of it. She was right here, listening. She knew Lily and James were onto her. Franky *had* to kill James that morning *before* he spoke to Posy O'Keefe. Before O'Keefe started looking into Jordan's death and discovered the truth."

"She killed her own husband," Byrne said, shaking his head. "Just to cover her tracks."

"Well, she'd tried to kill Lily already, remember? It was only by accident that Jordan died instead. I'd guess she was planning to kill James for his betrayal sooner or later, anyway."

"What did the guv say?"

"He wants us to bring her in," she said. "Come on. You can have this one."

Together, they rounded the corner of Lily Hughes's tent and directly into the path of the Entwhistles, who, as always, were walking hand in hand.

"Good morning, officers," Toby said, masking his surprise with a chipper demeanour. "How are you doing today? Are we any closer to going home?"

His boyish charm, however, had little effect on Campbell.

"We're looking for Franky DeSilver," she said flatly. "I don't suppose you know where she is?"

Marie nodded at a yurt two yurts away. "She hasn't left that room in four days," she said, then looked between the detectives with a sudden worried stare. "Why do you ask?"

Toby interpreted the focus in their eyes, and his smile faded.

"I think that's obvious, don't you, love?" he murmured, and Campbell did her best to appear impassive.

"You can't seriously think that Franky did this?" Marie huffed as if the whole thing was a joke.

"The investigation is still underway," Byrne said, clearly hoping to de-escalate.

"She wouldn't hurt a fly, let alone her two favourite people in the world."

"You know what? Everyone seems so sure Franky couldn't have done this," Campbell said. "Why is that?"

"Because we know her."

"If you know her so well, tell me this. How was her relationship with Lily's husband, Jordan?"

Marie gaped.

"Why are you asking about Jordan?" asked Toby.

"Was there ever any conflict?"

"No, of course not," Marie said. "They were friends."

"Good friends?"

"As good as any of us," Marie said, shrugging. "We all loved Jordan. We loved him and Lily as a couple. They were great together."

"Do you think that Jordan knew about Lily and James's affair?"

Marie threw up her hands in despair. "They *weren't* having an affair," she said. "I know you would like their relationship to be neat and tidy — and depraved! But it was complicated. They were loyal to their partners. They were happy as friends."

"Then why did they kiss on Monday night?" asked Byrne.

"Because we all drank about ten glasses of wine," Marie said. "It happens. It doesn't *mean* anything."

At this, Toby looked at his wife's profile with a hard stare, and Campbell felt sure she was witnessing the first simmers of doubt in their short marriage, the first little bubbles of suspicion that could easily rise to a boiling point if given the right stoking.

Oh, it happens, does it?

"You can't arrest Franky," Marie continued, ignoring her husband's jealous eyes. "You just can't. She didn't do this. It would kill her."

"How are you so sure, Mrs Entwistle?" Campbell asked. "Is there something you'd like to share?"

"Of course not, I just..."

"Then excuse us," Byrne said, and he and Campbell pushed past the couple heading towards Franky DeSilver's tent.

"Why would she have done it?" Marie cried after them. "Why would she murder the people she loved? It makes no sense."

"Well, to be fair, love," Toby said, "she probably wasn't going to see them again after Tuesday."

Campbell and Byrne stopped in their tracks and turned around.

"What do you mean?" asked Marie, glaring at her husband.

"Well, if they were going to run away—"

"Toby, what are you talking about?"

"They said so on Monday night," he said, looking at her as though she were confused. Or crazy. "Remember? That conversation we overheard after dinner. They said they were going to run away together."

A deep, knotted frown formed on Marie's face. "No, they didn't."

Toby laughed her poor memory off. "They did. We heard them."

"I didn't hear them say anything like that."

He laughed again and threw an arm over her shoulder. "Oh, you hear what you want to hear. They were your two best friends. You don't like the thought of them betraying Franky like that, but the truth is the truth." He glanced up at Byrne and Campbell and shrugged. "That's what we heard."

Marie looked long and hard at her husband's chiselled profile, then turned back to Byrne and Campbell, her face dazed and confused, as though she was trying to recall a dream. She could well have been lying. After all, why would she tell them a piece of information that gave her best friend even more motive to kill Lily and James?

Campbell caught her stare, which was lost behind a memory.

"Then why didn't you mention—"

Before she could finish her question, Bob sprinted around the corner of his yurt as fast as a man of Bob's stature could sprint. "Did you see them?" he asked breathlessly.

Byrne stepped forward. "Who?"

Bob clutched his waist and wincing, rubbing away a stitch. "I knew we shouldn't have stayed here," he said. "We don't even have doors on these bloody tents, let alone locks."

"Mr Adams," Campbell said, "is everything okay?"

"No, it's bloody not. I wanted to go for a drive," he said, "after you lot had upset my wife. I wanted to clear my head."

"So?"

"So," he spat, "someone's nicked my bloody car."

"What?" asked Toby.

"It's gone. My keys, too. They must've taken them from our tent."

"When?"

"I don't know," he said. "I haven't driven it since yesterday. When we were sleeping, for all I know."

Byrne and Campbell looked at each other, the same thought crossing their mind at once, and they both ran towards Franky DeSilver's tent. Without knocking on the post, they yanked back the canvas and burst inside.

It was empty.

"Franky?" Byrne called, checking the bathroom and returning, shaking his head, while Campbell checked for signs of a struggle. But there were none. "Mrs DeSilver?"

"She's not here," Campbell said, as something caught her eye. She stepped over to the corner of the room and carefully held the glossy rectangular card up to the light. It was a flash of purple against neutral tones and a light in the dark.

Byrne walked over slowly, his guard up. "What is it?"

"What does it look like?" Campbell said, turning the little piece of card between her fingers. "Get the guv on the phone."

CHAPTER FIFTY-FOUR

"Gone?" George said. "What do you mean gone?"

The incident room was quiet. Most of the officers were out on duty, and the few left over were busy with paperwork. So, when George put the call on loudspeaker and waved the team over, the team could clearly hear Campbell speaking. Ivy even caught a few whistles of birdsong in the background.

"I mean, Franky DeSilver isn't in her yurt," Campbell replied urgently. "Coincidentally, Bob Adams' car is also missing."

"Ruby," George said, pointing at her with a long finger. "ANPR on Bob Adams's car. Maguire, get all units on the lookout. Go."

"Guv," they replied, and Ruby immediately began tapping on her keyboard while Maguire picked up his desk phone to call downstairs.

"Byrne, Campbell, let's get ahead of this. Franky DeSilver knows we've found her out. She knows that we're asking after her. Where would she go?"

"On the run, guv," came Byrne's rather useless reply.

"She's got nothing," George continued, "only what she brought on holiday with her."

"Bob's car was just seen on the B1225 South," Ruby interrupted. "Mobile unit passed it a few minutes ago."

"B1225 South," he repeated. "Where does that go?"

"Stenigot," Byrne said. "She's going home, guv. It's twenty-five minutes from here. Maybe she needs cash or her passport."

"She's not there yet," George said. "Byrne, Campbell, head over to the DeSilver house. Catch up with her. I'll send Maguire and O'Hara too. We're closer. It's fifteen minutes from here, ten with the blues on."

At this, Maguire and O'Hara rushed into action, grabbing their coats from the back of their chairs.

"Do you think that's necessary, guv?" asked Byrne.

"Franky DeSilver has killed two people," George replied. "The game's up. There's no knowing what she'll do."

"Guv," Campbell said, "there's something else you should know. We found something in DeSilver's room."

"What is it?"

"A card."

"What kind of card?"

"A business card for a cancer support group in London. There's a number."

"Send us a photo of it," George said, then added. "Make sure Ruby sees it."

"Do you think it could be important?"

"Why would Franky have a card for a support group?" asked Ivy, and for a moment, George had the answer jumbled up in his mind, but before he could piece it together, the clarity faded. He left the question hanging in the air.

He turned to the PCs and clapped once. "Come on, let's move."

"Yes, guv," O'Hara said, buttoning her coat.

"We'll call you from the car," Maguire said into the phone to Byrne and Campbell. "Let's coordinate this."

And with George's final nod, they rushed across the room, ready to jump into action. Whether or not their eagerness was a good thing, Ivy had yet to be sure. It had led them into trouble in the past. But George clearly didn't have time to consider that right now.

"What about you, guv?" asked Ruby.

"I want answers," he said. "I want every one of those friends in one room and a single, straight narrative. No more lies. No more conflicting tales. No more skipped stories. Ivy, we're going to the Grove." He twirled his coat around his shoulders, ready to rush out of the room without a second thought. "Let's go," he said, strolling past her towards the door. "Grab your coat."

"Wait!" Ivy yelled, and like a thunderclap at a festival, her voice brought everything to a standstill.

George turned to face her as though he'd half-forgotten she was there. O'Hara and Maguire stopped in their tracks. Even Ruby had ceased her typing.

"Ivy?" George had let his collar stay the way his coat had fallen — jauntily, at an angle. Ivy stood motionless in the middle of their little whiteboard area. "What's wrong?" he asked.

"It's too neat," she whispered, looking up at him. "I feel like we're playing right into her hands." She shook her head, trying to narrow down the flood of information they'd gathered in the last few days into a single faucet. "There's something I'm not remembering," she said. "Something just on the edge of my memory, but I can't connect it all. I need time to think."

"We don't have time to think," he replied.

"You said it yourself, guv. Franky couldn't have done this alone."

"So?"

"So she must've been in on it with someone. Someone else has got her back."

"Ivy—"

"There's more than we think there is. And I don't think we

should rush into anything else until we know exactly what we're dealing with. Until we know what's going on."

"*Anyone* could've killed James DeSilver while Franky was hiking," George said. "She's friends with a private investigator who has access to a dozen people who could've done the job for the right money. The point is we can bring her in for Lily's murder, which is more than enough to go on for now. And if we don't act *right now*, then she's going to get away. She knows the game is up. She's on the run. We need to follow her, Ivy."

"I feel like that's exactly what she wants us to do."

"So?"

"So, how do we know it's not a trap?"

"Even if it is, Ivy, what are we meant to do? Just sit here and let her get away?"

"If we just had more time—"

"But we don't."

Ivy shook her head. Her ears rang with important information she couldn't quite hear. "There's something I'm missing, I know it."

"So what do you want to do, Ivy?" George asked.

"Just take a step back. Consider our options."

"So stay here and do what? Gather more evidence? Write some more names on the bloody board?"

"I don't know, I..."

Her voice faded out like a dying candle. She didn't have answers, nothing solid, anyway. Just shadows of answers, floating at the back of her thoughts, elusive, slipping through her fingers like desert sand.

"No, Ivy," George said slowly, his face softening. "I'm really asking you." He walked over to her and placed his large hand on her shoulder. "It's your investigation," he whispered.

She looked up at him. "What do you mean?"

"You started it," he said. "Now finish it. We'll do what you say. Won't we?" He turned to the team, Ruby, Maguire, and O'Hara in person, who nodded in agreement. Then, he looked over at the phone, which emanated Byrne's voice.

"Yes, guv," he said. "What do you want us to do, sarge?"

George turned back to face her. "Ivy?"

She felt the energy of each of their instincts, the resolve in Byrne and Campbell's voice and the focus in the eyes she could meet around the room. Maguire and O'Hara bounced on the balls of their feet, ready to act. And even though Ivy's heart thumped with a certainty that her instinct was the one to follow, she had to admit that she was outnumbered. Six to one. Ivy was not a betting woman, but if she was to become one, she knew it was wise to follow the odds: to trust the instincts of the many over the one.

She knew that's what George would have done.

"Byrne, Campbell, head to Franky's house," she ordered. "Maguire and O'Hara will meet you there." And on her word, they continued their rush out of the room. "Ruby, keep tracking Bob's car for now. Then look into that support group."

"Yes, sarge," the numerous voices sounded in harmony.

"Guv," she said, turning to the man she admired the most, who grinned at her as though she'd passed a test she didn't know she had taken. "You can drive."

CHAPTER FIFTY-FIVE

It wasn't often that George sped. He was a slow but sure kind of driver, except when the occasion or his mood called for it. It wasn't often, either, that George overtook other drivers, not being a reckless man or in enough of a hurry to risk his life. But today, it seemed, was an exception. The winding lanes had always reminded Ivy of a ribbon thrown to the floor, its curves random and tight at unexpected intervals, as though discarded onto a map.

"So what's the plan?" he asked Ivy, who, in the blurry chaos, collated her thoughts, the details, the stories she had heard over the last few days, from Bob, from Marie, from Violet, from Cecelia. Something itched at her mind, an irritation.

"You were right," she said. "We need all those friends in one place, where they can't present conflicting stories. Either Franky DeSilver was working with someone, or her friends are lying about them all being together on the hike. Perhaps she *did* have the opportunity to get to James and the others are covering for her. We need to break their stories down. We need to expose the weaknesses."

"It's not ideal," George said, "to be relying so heavily on unreliable witness statements."

"You can say that again," Ivy said, rubbing her forehead. "I've missed something. Something that seemed insignificant at the time, but I can't put my finger on it." She slammed the dashboard. "I feel bad now," she muttered, "for being so critical of Maguire when he had forgotten about seeing Anter at the crime scene."

"Don't overthink it. Just go where your mind wants you to go. Whose story was it? Which one does your instinct lead you to?"

She couldn't be sure when she answered that it was the right one, but she said, "Marie. It was Marie's account. When she told us the story about overhearing James and Lily on Monday night just before their kiss."

"What exactly did she tell you? From beginning to end?"

"That she and Toby were hiding in the trees, and they heard—"

"No, go back," George said. "Before then. What were they doing in the trees?"

She raised her eyebrows and gave him a look. He glanced over when she didn't reply and read everything he needed to know in her expression alone. "Oh," he said and gave a little chuckle. "After the dinner, wasn't it?"

"Yes. Toby was... congratulating Marie for telling her friends about her illness. He said they should celebrate life while they still could."

George chuckled again. "A classic Carpe Diem argument," he said. "Goes back centuries, you know. Poets like Marvell used it to convince women to lose their virginity by reminding them that life is short. *And yonder all before us lie deserts of vast eternity. Thy beauty shall no more be found, nor, in thy marble vault, shall sound my echoing song, then worms shall try that long-preserved virginity—*"

"Guv," Ivy said, rousing him from what could have been a lengthy monologue.

"Right," he said. "Sorry. What part of James and Lily's conversation did they overhear? What was said, exactly?"

Ivy closed her eyes. The blurred, rushing fields didn't help. They only made her dizzy.

"They were talking about their disbelief, their sadness that Marie was going to die," Ivy said slowly. "Just like Jordan. Lily was crying."

"Because of Marie? Or because of Jordan?"

"Neither," Ivy said, the memory coming back in shallow waves as though the tide was coming in. George's prompts helped. "That was the thing. James said that Lily didn't cry when she was sad. That she only cried when she was scared. It didn't mean much when I heard it, but now..."

Her mind, busied with the memory and what it all meant, held her attention hostage to the rush of fields and trees as George aptly overtook a tractor. "And what was she scared about?" he asked.

"I don't know. She said..."

"Ivy, you need to put the pieces together."

"She said that Marie's case reminded her of something."

"Her cancer, you mean?" he asked, to which she nodded.

"A case that Jordan had worked on," Ivy said, "where the patient, rather than undergo the horrors of treatment for a few more miserable years, had decided to stop their treatment."

"And this made Lily scared?" George asked.

"Yes. I mean, that's what she said in Marie's story."

George turned onto the main road that would take them north through the centre of the Wolds, where he could put his foot down. "But why?"

Ivy shook her head. Any sense of accomplishment she'd found from locating that thought was lost to the overwhelming nature of its meaning. But before she could consider it further, George's phone rang throughout the car like an alarm clock waking her from a dream and sending those fragments of thoughts scattering into the shadows.

"Campbell," George said as soon as he answered, "Are you at the house? Have you got her?"

"No," Campbell said urgently. "She's not here."

"Damn it," George muttered. "Is the car still there?"

"No, it's gone, too. She must have run in and out. We weren't that far behind her."

"Fetching her passport, maybe?" he suggested.

"Actually, no, guv," Campbell replied. "We did a sweep of the house. They have this big wine cellar and bar room."

"Lucky them," George said.

"We found a gun cabinet, guv," she said, and the worry was evident in her tone.

"You're sure it's a gun cabinet?" George asked.

"He said he had guns," Ivy added. "One of them mentioned it."

"It's unlocked," Campbell said. "As though she didn't even have the time to close it behind her."

"Or she didn't care about leaving it open," George added. "Don't tell me a gun is missing."

"There were a few empty slots and chains hanging loose."

"Chains?" he said. "Plural?"

"Yes, guv. It looks like James DeSilver was the type of man to go all in when he moved up here. He's got a whole shooting set up."

"How many guns are missing?"

"Could be three. Hard to say. We have no way of knowing if the slots were filled. Worst case scenario, three."

"Best case?" Ivy asked.

"Best case is none," George said. "But I'm not hopeful."

"What do we do, guv?" Campbell asked.

"Are Maguire and O'Hara there?"

"They've just arrived."

"This could turn into a major event," he said. "Stay there. Call in some uniformed officers for backup and have them stay there. I want the house locked down. Call the station and have the Armed Response Team on standby, too. I do not want any of you to intercept. Is that clear? If she comes back, the first sign of a weapon, you back off and radio in."

"Guv," she said by way of confirmation.

"I'll call Ruby and let you know as soon as we have a location. We can't have a killer driving around with three bloody shotguns in the back of a stolen car."

"No, guv, we can't."

George ended the call, and, with one hand on the wheel, he swerved around a camper van and navigated to Ruby's number on the dashboard screen. It was all Ivy could do to hold on for dear life.

"Ruby, she's not at the house," he said as soon as she answered.

"Hold on, guv," she replied, and over the line, they heard the sound of her long fingernails on the plastic keys. "ANPR picked up the number plate going north along the B1225," she said. "She's going back the way she came."

"She's heading back to the Grove," George mused aloud.

"That was quick," Ivy said.

"She can't be that far ahead of you," Ruby said. "Do you want me to send some uniformed support?"

"Not yet," George said. "I want to get it under control. Campbell is at the DeSilver house. She found an empty gun cabinet. We think DeSilver has three bloody guns with her, so expect some calls and keep her calm, will you?"

"Three? Jesus. What does she need with three?"

"I guess we'll find out," George said, turning into Spring View. "Get Armed Response on standby. I don't want them engaged until we know for sure. The last thing I want is the full circus. This could be nothing for all we know."

"You can't do this on your own, guv," she said, displaying a parental-like firmness Ivy hadn't heard from Ruby before. "I'm calling downstairs to see if they can spare a few bodies. Wait for them to arrive, okay? Okay, guv?"

"Alright," he said, resigning to the fact that Ruby was becoming the team's mother. "But keep them at bay. I do not want them steaming into play before I have things under control."

"Understood," Ruby said.

She switched lines, and the call went quiet for a moment.

They rounded a corner, and dead ahead of them in the distance, the Grove's brown yurts eased into view. She glanced across at George, noting the furrowed brow, which some may have interpreted as stress, but she knew better. It was the focus. A focus she hadn't seen on that face of his for a long time. But whatever joy she sought from her old friend's rehabilitation was short-lived when something beyond him, beyond the car and the hedgerow, caught her eye.

"There," she said, unable to articulate the thought in an instant.

"What?" he replied, slowing a little.

"Up there," she said, pointing up at the old rundown house that he had described as a stain on the otherwise immaculate property. "That's Bob's car?"

Immediately, George made a left-hand turn onto the road up to Sabina's house, narrowly avoiding the drainage ditch that ran alongside the fields. He hurled the car up the hill, small stones clattering like firecrackers against the floor pan until they skidded to a halt outside the old house. Completely ignoring Ruby's advice, they both climbed out without a second thought but clung to their car doors as they took in the scene.

Ruby came back on the line.

"Guv, I'm sorry. I've lost the car. It should have been through the next camera by now—"

"It's okay," George said, distracted by the looming house with all its angles and those darker-than-dark windows.

"I've got an alert set up—"

"Where's Sabina Anter?" George asked quietly as Ivy paced slowly around Bob's car and peered through the windows. She glanced back at him, shaking her head to indicate that there was no sign of Franky.

"You're there?" Ruby said over the line, connecting the dots for herself.

"For our sins, yes," he muttered in response. "Where is she? Is she still in custody?"

"She was bailed, guv," she said, then her voice carried on the evening breeze. "They couldn't hold her any longer, not for handling stolen goods. CID are building the case against her. She'll be summoned to court in a few weeks..."

Ivy let Ruby's voice fade as she opened the stolen car's boot, half-anticipating to make a gruesome discovery as she searched through the few possessions. An old cagoule, a pair of boots, and a six-pack of water in addition to the bags of what looks like picnic blankets and camping equipment.

"I see," George said, humouring Ruby. It was another of those differences, Ivy thought. Where she would have spoken to Ruby when the day was over, he had the composure to wait for her to finish, to let her have her moment.

"By the way, guv, I made a call to the support group on that business card..."

Ivy crouched to get a closer look at the ground in front of the house, leaving Ruby to George. She didn't have to be Katy South-well to recognise the signs of a scuffle. Deep heel marks through the torn grass indicated that someone had been dragged to the doorstep from the car. Alongside the drag lines were footprints evident in the mud, many pairs of varying sizes — fresh and heavy, as though they'd needed a firm standing, and very recently.

Ivy stood straight and turned to catch George's attention. As Ruby spoke, his eyes widened with the truth. But before he could relay any information to Ivy, there came a loud, sickening click. The kind of click that, even unidentified, commanded attention, like the snap of a broken bone or the click of a pressure switch.

Or the hammer of a loaded gun.

"Hang up the phone, Inspector Larson."

"Guv?" Ruby called out, her voice clear over the car's speakers. "Guv, are you there? Can you hear me?"

In front of her, George stopped still. Ivy did the same, her body frozen, although her insides hummed with adrenaline, her heart pummelling, and her blood pumping. They turned as one, Ivy only a second behind George, doing exactly as he did, following his lead. He held his hands up slowly, and Ivy followed suit.

"I said end the call," their assailant persisted.

"I'll call you back, Ruby," George said, with no sign of a quiver in his tone. "Something's come up."

"Right," she replied, a little unsure of herself. "I'll get it all typed up, shall I?"

George locked onto those two reddened eyes before him, while Ivy focused on the end of the shotgun's barrel.

"Thank you, Ruby," George said, and they heard the call end, leaving a deathly silence for him to capture everybody's attention. "You're making a big mistake."

"No," they replied. "No, you see, of all the decisions I've ever made, this one is right. It feels right. I've never been surer of anything in my life."

"Too many people have died," Ivy said, chancing a void in the tension to pull the attention from George. "Enough blood has been spilled. You don't have to do this."

They took a step back, putting distance between themselves and George before turning the gun on Ivy.

"That's where you're wrong. I *do* have to do this, and there's more blood to spill," they replied, and Ivy let her eyes wander along the length of the gun to the eye that stared along the length of the barrel at her. For a moment, she could have sworn she saw that ink-dark pupil expand, then retract as the eye narrowed, and they muttered a single chilling command. "Inside now."

CHAPTER FIFTY-SIX

"Move!" The order was almost militant in tone. With the shotgun nestled into the small of George's back, they were led up the old concrete steps to the front door. "It's not locked. There's nothing to steal."

The gun was used to nudge George further inside, and he heard the door close and the bolt slide into place. Perhaps it was nerves or plain old inexperience, but she was wrong to focus on him, leaving Ivy to walk freely by his side. She was the one that needed watching. She was the one with youth on her side. George only hoped that neither of them made any rash movements.

Just like last time, the smell of mould offended his senses, and he marvelled at both the historic significance of the house and the state of decay it had fallen into. And just like last time, it took only a few steps to move through the living room and into the kitchen.

Ivy gasped at the sight before them, whereas George, with every step, was piecing the investigation together. He saw the whiteboard in his mind's eye, the conversations they'd had in the incident room played out, and the statements he had read were right there before his eyes.

And now, Sabina Anter was seated at her kitchen table, her eyes wide at George and Ivy being led in at gunpoint. Behind her, with the second shotgun trained on Anter's back, was Violet.

"You're wrong," George said, and he took a deep breath before turning to face the gun, which was immediately raised and pressed into his chest. "You've got this all wrong, Franky. You need to stop—"

A single shot rang out, reverberating off the tiled walls and floor.

Immediately, he grimaced. He clutched at his chest, his mind a blur of life, of regrets, and joy, and hope, and love, and... Grace.

Grace, he thought, picturing her face. Picturing how, if there was a heaven, he would hold her in his arms once more.

But the seconds passed, and the fingers that groped at his chest were dry, and the pain he had expected to hit him like an avalanche didn't come.

He stared down at his hands, at his chest, and then at Franky, whose gun was still trained on him, and she studied him curiously. George turned to find Violet breaching her shotgun to slide another cartridge into the chamber. The high-pitched whine cascaded through the octaves, from soprano to the dull tenor hum.

"Over there," Franky said, gesturing to the far side of the kitchen with the shotgun. "Away from the door."

He was dumbfounded. It had felt like minutes. Minutes of experiencing death.

But far from being elated, he felt cheated. Cheated from the death he had welcomed. Cheated from the onslaught of pain and cheated from being with her again. From being with Grace.

"Did you hear what I just said?" Franky hissed.

"Franky, this is—"

Violet's shotgun snapped closed, and Franky glared at him, daring him to argue.

"The next shot won't be aimed at the ceiling," Violet said, her angry tone now perfectly at home in the midst of conflict.

Placing himself in front of Ivy, he edged her towards the far corner of the room, eyeing her roving eye as it settled on the kettle: the only available weapon to hand.

He opened his mouth to speak, but Franky raised her weapon to her shoulder, her feet finding that solid stance almost naturally.

"With all respect, Inspector, you've had your turn. You've had a week," she said. "You've got nowhere. Now it's our turn."

"You don't get a turn," he replied, far harsher than his situation afforded.

"You didn't know her," Franky said. "You didn't know Lily. You didn't know James and sure as hell didn't know Jordan."

"This is not a matter of taking turns," George said, and he found himself staring at Sabina Anter on the old wooden chair in the centre of the room, a puddle glistening in the dim evening light on the floor beneath her. "For Christ's sake, look at her. She's terrified, Franky."

"I knew you'd come for me eventually," Franky whispered, her voice hoarse and pained. She stood with her rear foot planted to absorb the potential shot, her solid stance belying her more feminine attributes — her long, blonde hair that, despite the circumstance, appeared styled, and her clothing that hugged her figure, offering a glimpse into the lithe strength that lay underneath.

Still, she pulled the stock into her shoulder as though it belonged there, and a single, manicured finger curled around the trigger as lightly as a violinist might grip their bow. She exhaled slow and steady, confident as though she'd been taught exactly how to use the deadly weapon cradled in her arms.

"This isn't the way to go about this," George said, gesturing at Ivy. "Let her go."

"Guv—"

"No," Franky snapped, and the shotgun's big round eye glared at her briefly before returning to George. Then, as if it were a game, and she was making her final move, she moved the gun onto Sabina Anter.

"Everything points to me, Inspector," Franky said. "It was just a matter of time—"

"If you want to talk, then let's talk," he said. "But put the guns down. Both of you. This needn't go any further. Put them down, and we'll talk. We can be reasonable—"

"Don't insult me," Franky yelled. "James and...*her.* I know, alright. I know. The kiss, I know. And as for being with Cecelia in the fog that morning, she's too honest for her own good. I knew it wouldn't take too long for you to put it all together. What did you call it, eliminating the suspects? Eliminating all of us. It couldn't have been Violet. She was way out on her own up front. It couldn't have been any of our husbands, could it? One of them was at the market, one of them was at home, I suppose the others were eating roast bloody beef and going wee wee wee all the way home, were they?"

"Franky, look—"

"No, you look," she said, taking a step towards Sabina and raising the barrel to point at her head. "I've lost everything. You think prison scares me? Eh? Do you think I'm afraid of being locked up?" She shook her head. "It doesn't. Do you know what scares me? Do you know what I've been thinking about ever since you told me about James?"

Her nostrils flared, and her finger tensed on the trigger.

George eyed her, then eyed the gun and raised his chin in defiance.

"Being alone," he said, hearing his voice crack. "You're afraid of being alone. Of spending your entire life in the arms of somebody you thought you knew. Of coming home to find that they're not there. Of remembering the past and all those things you did together and wondering if he loved you as you loved him."

His words were softly spoken, yet they moved her as if they

were a tangible force. She stepped back, almost laughing the truth from her mind.

"What do you know about it?" she said, and for the first time, there was emotion in her voice.

"I know that you're remembering the last time you were together. You can see it now, can't you?" He said, tapping at his temple with an index finger. "You can see it in here. You're staring into James's eyes. He's staring back, but his expression isn't as you recall it. There's a doubt there."

"You know nothing—"

"You're seeing what your mind wants you to see, Franky. You're tormenting yourself. Of course, he loved you."

As he spoke, those final few moments with Grace eased into the forefront of his mind. If he were to go, then he would want her here. He would go with her.

His reasoned tone had tamed the mood as a wild stallion might succumb to a tenacious hand.

He glanced down at Sabina, who was pale with fright, and almost choking on her own tears.

"Look at her, Franky. She didn't do this," he said. "I don't know how you came to this conclusion, but I can prove to you that she couldn't have been there when James died, and she certainly couldn't have been there when Lily died."

Franky stared at Anter, her gun still raised, but her finger loose now.

There were voices outside, and for a moment, George thought that Ruby's uniformed support might just be on time for once. But Franky seemed unfazed at the growing voices, and Violet glanced calmly out of the window as the kitchen door burst open and a handful of bodies fell into the room.

Each one of them stopped in their track: Bob, Marie, Toby, and Cecelia.

"What the bloody hell's going on, Franky?" Bob said as a mother might question a child who had drawn on the walls. He eyed the shotgun she brandished. "Is there something you want to tell us?"

The mind is a curious thing, George mused to himself as Franky's lips formed a cruel smile. Amid the chaos of thoughts, hate, and pain she was enduring, there was space for such a devilish scheme to bear fruit.

She stared at him, and he saw it, the truth, as if it were written in those dark eyes.

"You planned this," he said. "You're not going to kill her, are you? You don't think she killed them any more than I do."

Slowly, Franky raised her shotgun, keeping it pointed at the ceiling, ready to drop in a beat of her broken heart. She turned to Violet, the silent one to George's left, who retrieved the third shotgun from the pantry to her side.

"Can someone tell me what on earth is going on?" Toby said. "What's with the guns? Franky? Violet?"

But neither of the women replied. Instead, Violet held the spare weapon up in offering.

"Cecelia," she said.

"What?" Bob said as his wife stepped forward. "Babe? Babe, what are you doing?" Cecelia, the most timid of them all, accepted the shotgun, and she joined the ranks. Three scorned women, three loaded shotguns, and three terrified friends. "Cecelia put that down. What the bloody hell are you doing? This is ridiculous. We're supposed to be having dinner to remember James and Lily, not bloody pointing guns at—"

"One of you killed Lily," Franky announced, and Bob's words faded along with any hope his expression had held. She let the shotgun fall into place against her shoulder, and her back foot braced to absorb the recoil as the muzzle lined up with Toby's head.

"Franky, no," Marie said, and she lurched forward but was halted by Violet's weapon, which was aimed directly at her chest. With the two guns trained on two of the suspects, both Franky and Violet glanced sideways at Cecelia, who closed her eyes, muttered something like a prayer to herself, and raised her own weapon, aiming from her hip directly at her husband.

"Cecelia?"

"I can't live," Franky began, cutting his protest off, "knowing that one of you is responsible for all of this. I would rather die than let you walk free. I would rather rot in a cell knowing that my husband's killer is dead."

"Franky," George said, sensing the time for intervention expiring like the last few grains of sand slipping through the timer's narrow funnel. "You are out of control. There's nothing to gain from this. Is this what James would have wanted? Is it?"

At the mention of her husband's name, the shotgun wavered, but she steadied it with a deep breath.

"There are three of them, Franky," he pleaded. "Two of them are innocent. They're your friends, for God's sake."

"Cecelia?" Ivy started, preying on the weaker of the trio. "Come on, see sense. You'll spend your life in prison. Do you know what that means?"

"Don't listen to her, Cecelia," Violet said. "In two minutes, this will all be over."

"No, in two minutes, this will not all be over," George added. "In two minutes, you'll have three more dead bodies to deal with. This won't be over until you're all in your eighties. Then what? Freedom? How does that solve anything?"

"I'll sleep at night," Franky hissed.

"You won't sleep a wink, Franky," he replied. "You would lay awake all night listening to the drug addicts whining and crying to be put out of their misery. You'll listen to the weak and the vulnerable, like Cecelia here, being taunted and coerced into tying her bedsheets together and slipping a makeshift noose around her neck. You'll listen to the sound of cell doors crashing open in the middle of the night and prisoners being dragged from their cells to the infirmary to be sedated." He swallowed nothing but stale and mouldy air, and then inhaled to bring his temper under control. "In two minutes, you'll have signed your own death warrants. You'll all be dead," he said. "And a fat lot of good that'll do you."

"Well, then, I suppose it's down to you, Inspector," Franky said, raising her head from the breach.

"To do what, Franky?" he said, knowing the answer before he'd even asked the question.

"To save two lives," she whispered. "You know who did it, don't you? You've worked it out."

"I have a theory," he replied softly, and in his peripheral vision, Ivy turned to stare at him bemused.

"Is it me?" Franky asked, to which, after a few short moments to be sure, he shook his head.

She gestured at the two women by her side.

"Cecelia or Violet?"

He lowered his head and sighed, seeing no way out. Eventually, he shook his head and met her stare. "No."

The room was deathly silent. Sabina Anter sat wide eyed, too petrified to move. Ivy stood poised to pounce. The three women brandished their weapons, the weight of which was apparent in their wavering grips.

And the three terrified individuals who remained stood aghast. Toby clung to a sobbing Marie while Bob did his best to distance himself from the pair.

"Are you asking me to sign somebody's death warrant?" George asked quietly and calmly.

"I'm asking you to save two people's lives," she replied. She hesitated, then reached out and placed a hand on top of Violet's shotgun, coaxing her to lower the weapon. A little bemused, Violet did as requested, and in response to an encouraging nod from Franky, Cecelia followed suit. "There," Franky said. "I've saved two lives." She raised her weapon once more, aiming blindly at the threesome before her. "Your turn, Inspector."

CHAPTER FIFTY-SEVEN

"Ivy," George said, and he nodded at the two, now redundant shotguns. She took the hint, and both Violet and Cecelia handed them over without argument, shame etched on their faces.

"This was your plan all along, wasn't it, Franky?" George said, seeing the truth unravel in her eyes. "You never intended for them to kill anybody. It was all hype. You just wanted them to be scared." He pointed at the threesome, who cowered each time her wavering weapon passed across them. "You wanted them to be as scared as you are."

"I want them to show courage," Franky snapped. "I want whoever did this to step forward." She waved a hand at them. "Look at them. Two of them are terrified and most likely will never forgive me. Well, that's just fine by me. I don't need forgiveness where I'm going. I won't need friends. I won't need little bloody holidays walking in the Wolds with wet bloody feet and a different bed every night. I'll have one bed and four walls, and on that wall, I'll have a picture of my husband. That's all I need."

"You make it sound easy."

"It is easy," she said. "It is. Because you know what, I'm already dead. I died with James. The real me. The me this lot all know. She's gone. She's as dead as a dodo. And this?" She waved her trigger hand over herself, like a young girl presenting a new outfit. "This is nothing but scraps. The remains of Franky. The gristly bit that nobody wants. The bits that get stuck in your teeth, that's all this is. Prison? It's nothing compared to living like this."

"You're wrong, Franky," George told her. "You're wrong. Trust me, I've been there."

"Don't bore me with your tales of woe, Inspector Larson," she said, her tone cold and bitter. "That only works once."

"You callous little—" he began, but she brought the shotgun up to her shoulder once more. "I'll do all three if I have to."

"Franky," Marie called out and silenced when the gun trained on her.

"Starting with her," Franky said, and she took two steps forward until the gun's muzzle was less than six feet from Marie's face. "She was there when it all happened, wasn't she? She was there cowering by a tree. Oh, she has cancer, does she? She's dying? I'll bet you haven't heard that one before, Inspector, eh?"

"Don't do this, Franky," George yelled. "Put the gun down before it's too late—"

"Eliminate them, Inspector. That's what you do, isn't it? That's what you told us. You eliminate those closest to the victim." She turned to eye George, her face a picture of scorn. "So eliminate them."

"I cannot hand out a death sentence," he argued.

"But you are. Don't you see it? You're killing two innocent people. You might not pull the trigger, but you'll be as responsible as me." George was silenced. There was no retort. She was too far away for either Ivy or him to get to her, especially with the two other guns in the room. "The question is, Inspector," she hissed back at him. "Could *you* handle prison?" He said nothing, numbed at her words. "I didn't think so." She turned her face from him, rested her cheek on the breach, and her finger curled around the trigger.

"No," Marie said, shying away from the barrel that followed her every move. She tried to hide behind Toby, whose limits of love were apparent when he pushed her away to remove himself from the line of fire. "Toby? Help me."

"That's right, help her, Toby," Franky said. "Put an arm around her, why don't you. Two birds with one stone, and all that." Again, Toby distanced himself from his wife, a look of sheer panic on his face and a dark patch growing at his groin. "Looks like we're doing this the hard way," Franky announced, turning the gun on Toby, "Whose first, eh? Tobes?" She swung the gun around at Bob. "How about you, big fella? Nothing to say? You're normally full of advice. What's the matter with you? Guilt got ya, has it?"

"Stop," George yelled, and the melee silenced in a heartbeat. Franky turned her head enough to see him, an eyebrow raised in question. "Just stop this," he said again. "If you're scraps, then God knows what I am. I'm not the man I used to be. I know that much. I'm not a man who walks with his head held high anymore, safe in the knowledge that my loving wife is at home waiting for me. I failed her. I failed my wife. And I have to live with that. Every day, I have to look in the bloody mirror and see myself alive when she's dead. I failed her. I should have gone first. She was the angel. She was the one who deserved to live. But every day, I wore her down. Every day, I deal with this." He gestured at the room, the guns and the tears and the urine and the fear. "Every day, she had to listen to me. Every day, I weighed her down, venting, releasing, unloading, whatever you want to call it. I did that to her. I'm the reason she lost her bloody mind. I'm the reason that for the last God knows how many years of her life, she didn't know who the bloody hell I was." He cleared his throat and rejected Ivy's sympathetic touch. "You want to do this? he said to Franky. "You want to eliminate them? Then let's do it. Because like you, I'm scraps. I'm the gristly bit that nobody wants. The carcass. And I have absolutely nothing to lose."

Franky eyed him with suspicion, and then finally, after a quick glance at Violet, she took a step back.

"The floor is yours," she said, lowering the weapon, and George took a tentative step forward.

"Guv?" Ivy started, but he dismissed her immediately with an irritated wave of his hand.

He moved to the far side of the room, away from Ivy, away from them all. At the table before him, Sabina Anter peered up at him. To his left, the three individuals whose lives hung in the balance stared open-mouthed. To his right was Franky, and beyond her were Violet and Cecelia.

And opposite him, shaking her head in utter disbelief, was Ivy.

"It starts with an MMO," he began, his eyes fixed on Ivy's as if the clocks had been turned back to her first day in major crimes, and he was explaining the basics again. "Means, motive, and opportunity. Should we fail to find any one of those things, then the suspect is eliminated from our enquiries. Only when we find all three do we proceed with our investigation. In short, that person becomes a person of interest."

"Start with her," Franky said, nodding at Marie.

"Franky?" Marie whined. "What on earth—?"

"Well, she was found closest to Lily's body, so we can assume opportunity," George said, matching Franky's cold tone.

"I was ill. I was having a turn—"

"I mean, if the diagnosis is genuine—"

"Of course, it's bloody genuine—"

"Then we could surmise that her mind wasn't as...stable as it otherwise would have been."

"I didn't do anything," Marie shouted, backing against the wall behind her. "I wouldn't. Franky, you know me—"

"And then there's Bob," George continued, silencing Marie, who was clearly suffering from the contradiction in emotions as the possibility of her friend taking the brunt of Franky's vengeance would save her own skin. "No alibi as such. He was good friends with Jordan, though. It's possible he could have harboured a grudge."

"You what?" Bob said. "This is a joke, right?"

"He's certainly capable of strangling Lily and causing the damage to James's face. I mean, it's feasible that Marie could have strangled Lily, but could she have done that to James?" He shook his head. "No. No, I don't think so."

"See?" Marie said to Franky. "See, it couldn't have been me."

"Unless, of course, she had help," George continued. "You see, collectively, they had the means, the motive, and the opportunity to not only murder Lily and James but Jordan as well."

"You can't be serious," Bob said.

"All this time, we've been trying to eliminate the three of them. As individuals, they either had the means and the motive but not the opportunity, or they had the opportunity and the means but no motive. No reason why." He cleared his throat, considering his next words very carefully. "But as a collective? As a collective, they have all three."

"Then all of them die," Franky said, heaving the gun to her shoulder.

"The problem is, Franky," George said. "You've two cartridges in that shotgun and three suspects." He nodded at the threesome. "What are you going to do, Franky?"

The revelation seemed to rock Franky, and she took a step back as if to consider her options. The threesome, perhaps sensing an opportunity, spread out across the kitchen's back wall. Marie reached for Toby's hand, and he held the tips of her fingers. Tears streamed down his face, and the colour drained from Marie's face. Bob, however, showed little emotion. It was as if he had resigned himself to his fate and stared at his shamed wife with nothing short of pity.

"You're lying," Franky said, turning the gun on him. "You're bloody lying. You think I won't do this?"

"You wanted to be the judge, trial, and executioner, Franky. Nobody said it would be easy."

"It can't have been all three of them," she spat.

"No?"

"It can't be," she said, doubting herself.

"Not so straightforward now, is it?" He forced a beaming grin, hoping it broke through the dark clouds.

"You know it wasn't all three of them. Who was it? Tell me, Inspector. You can save lives here."

"I've given you all I care to give, young lady," he said, letting that smile fade to reveal the contempt he felt.

But Franky wasn't to be beaten. She turned on her heels, swung the gun around and aimed directly at Ivy's head.

"What about now, Inspector?" Franky said. "Maybe this will convince you."

She eased the muzzle under Ivy's chin, forcing her head back. Ivy's chest rose and fell in double time as she sought to keep control of her emotions. At her side, she slowly extended an arm toward the two shotguns she had rested against the kitchen cupboards, but Franky saw the move and kicked them away. For a terrible moment, George thought one of them might go off, but they scattered across the terracotta tiles, out of everybody's reach.

"Stay calm, Ivy," George told her. "She's not going to pull the trigger. She's using you, just like she used Sabina, and just like she used everybody in here. She's scared, that's all."

Ivy said nothing. With her head tilted back, she peered along the length of the gun at Franky.

"Somebody needs to die," Franky said, then raised her voice to a scream to drive the point home. "Somebody needs to pay. My husband is dead. He's dead."

"Guv!" Ivy called out. "If this is it—"

"This is not it, Ivy," he told her.

"But if it is—"

"Stop talking," Franky shouted.

"The kids," Ivy continued. "Tell them. Tell them, will you?"

"I said, shut up," Franky said, forcing the muzzle into her jaw so that Ivy stared up at the ceiling.

"It was me," a voice said amidst the chorus of ragged breaths and thumping hearts. Every pair of eyes in that room turned towards the kitchen wall, where Marie took a step forward. "I'm dying anyway," she said, shaking her head.

"Marie, no," Toby urged, his voice childlike in tone and pitch. "No, you don't have to do this."

"Think about what you're saying, Marie," Franky urged. "Don't think just because it's you that I won't do this. Somebody has to pay. My husband is dead."

Marie took another step forward, daring Franky to react. Ivy tensed, ready to make her move the moment the gun was removed from under her chin. Marie crouched and gripped one of the shotguns by the barrel, dragging the heavy weapon towards her as she stood.

"What are you doing, Marie?" Franky said.

"You don't have to do this, Franky," she replied. Her hands trembled as she manoeuvred the shotgun into place, the muzzle beneath her own chin, and her arms extended to the trigger.

"God, Marie, no," Toby cried while everyone looked on in fear.

"If somebody has to die, then let it be me," she said quietly, her eyes fixed on Franky's. "God knows my life is over, anyway."

"Marie, no," Franky called out, but it was too late. Marie's slender thumb tensed across the trigger.

"Live," she said, and she pulled.

CHAPTER FIFTY-EIGHT

The room waited for that terrible sound to reverberate off the walls. For the spray of blood and bone and for the inevitable slump of Marie's body, as gravity took hold.

But the only sound they all heard was harmless.

Click.

There was no spray of blood and bone and no slumping of Marie's lifeless body.

Click.

She pulled at the second trigger. Then, she frantically tried them both, her face bright red with fear, dread and every emotion under the dying sun.

The time that passes could be measured in seconds. Two or three. Five at the most. But an eternity rolled by as the reality of what had happened became evident like a reel of slow-motion video. But the silence was short-lived as Ivy saw her chance. She shoved the muzzle from under her chin with one hand and, with her free hand, reached for Franky, who, in the sudden terror, pulled at the trigger, blasting a hole nine inches across in the kitchen window. Cracks formed and the pane of old glass tumbled from the frame as Ivy dug her heels in and wrestled Franky across the room and into the wall beside George.

George gripped the end of the shotgun with both hands, and as Ivy kicked Franky's legs away, he tore it free from her hands, immediately opening the breach to remove the one live cartridge. He tossed the gun to one side into the living room and the cartridge through the broken window.

"Franky DeSilver, I am arresting you for the attempted murders of..." he looked about him at the pale faces. "Pretty much everyone in this room. You do not have to say anything, but it may harm your defence if you do not mention, when questioned, something which you later rely on in court. Anything you do say may be given in evidence." Ivy tugged a zip tie from the little pouch on her belt. "Do you understand me, Franky?"

She was face down with her head to one side and her arms pulled behind her back, but she eyed him with nothing short of hostility.

"Go to hell," she hissed, then grimaced as Ivy added weight to the knee in her back.

George laughed, and then eased himself to the floor beside her, where he leaned against the wall as if it was Grace beside him and they were at the beach, staring out at the North Sea.

"You forget," he said quietly. "I'm already in hell." He let that little nugget sink in and watched as Toby consoled his wife, and Cecelia approached Bob cautiously, unsure of where she stood since pointing a gun at him. "You were never in any danger, Bob," George called, nodding at the gun in Marie's hands. "Cecelia's gun was never loaded. Franky made sure of that, didn't you?"

Franky closed her eyes, unable to face the truth that inside the bitter shell, the remnants of a heart existed. Cecelia closed in on him, and despite his lack of embrace, she held him, a silent beg for forgiveness.

The empty shotgun lay at Marie's feet, and she stood numb, while a sobbing Toby rested his head on her shoulder.

Violet had dropped to the floor. She sat cross-legged, her head resting on the cupboard behind her, and her eyes closed to the drama, seeking solace in the darkness all people carry for such times.

"What happens now?" Bob asked, still cold to his wife's touch. But at least he hadn't pushed her away. They'd be okay, George thought, given enough time.

"Well, that's down to you all," George replied. "We can wait for our colleagues to arrive and continue our investigation, or we can do it right now, right here."

"But you said you thought it was us three."

"He was lying," Franky hissed from beside George, which George confirmed with a nod of acceptance. "He was trying to buy time. That's why I didn't pull the bloody trigger."

"Well, I know it wasn't me," Bob said. "I say we do this now. It's gone on for too long. I just want it over. I don't know if I can ever forget these past few days, but I'll try. I'll move on."

"Does everybody feel the same way?" George asked, to which he received a few mumbles and more than a few nods. "I should add that despite my reason for meeting you all, I have to say, never before have I seen such love between friends."

"Love?" Violet said, mocking the comment.

"That's right," George told her. "Love. You see, the thing we've been battling since day one is the lies you've all told."

"I haven't lied," she said.

"You haven't been entirely honest, though. You withheld information," he said. "That's as good as lying. But while you all thought your dishonesty would protect a friend, a spouse, a sister-in-law," he continued, looking at each of them in turn. "You've only served to make this twice as difficult as it should have been. Now, I'm not so pious as to claim perfection. I should have seen it. I should have brought you all together a long time ago. If anyone of you lies, then the rest of you would have said so before either Sergeant Hart or I could have worked it out."

"How do we do this?" Bob asked. "I mean, we're all here. We can answer any questions you have. Nobody can lie."

"Well, we begin with a confession," George replied. "A confession from me: I made a mistake." He looked at Ivy, whose face saddened by his admission. "I should have listened to advice. I pursued the murders of Lily and James when the whole time I should have focused on Jordan."

"What?" Toby said. "Jordan? That was six months ago."

"If there's one thing I've learned in my career, if you can call it that, it's that it takes a lot for somebody to murder a person. The films you see on the TV might portray almost everyone as having the ability to snuff the life from another, but the reality is that few of us can stomach it. Few of us have what it takes: one in a thousand, maybe, perhaps, even less. So for three of you to work together to do all of this..." he shook his head and rephrased his statement. "The chances of three friends all possessing that single critical attribute are so remote, it's not even worth considering. No. No, this began with Jordan. In fact, it began while Jordan was still alive. It began the night that Franky's car was used to run him off the road."

"What?" she hissed at him. "Jordan? I didn't bloody kill Jordan—"

"Oh, I know it wasn't you, Franky," he said. "You don't have what it takes. You don't have that critical attribute. If you did have it, then you'd have shot half the people in this room, and we'd be having a very different conversation. No, all that can be put down to an emotional outburst. The weight of grief on your shoulders, that's all that was. They were never in any danger. Nor was Sergeant Hart. You just used *their* fear to ease your own."

"But it was her car?" Bob said. "You just said it was her car."

"Franky?" Violet said softly. "Franky, is this true?"

"We weren't even in the country," Franky argued from the floor. "We were in New York. James had been invited to an investor's conference."

"Then why was your car in the area?" Bob asked with a curious frown. "This is a joke. You had the bloody gall to accuse us, and all this time—"

"I wasn't even there, Bob. I was three thousand miles away."

"I think the question we need to be asking ourselves," George cut in, silencing them all, "is why would Franky want to hurt Jordan?"

"The motive," Toby said, to which George nodded.

"Why? Come on, you all knew Jordan. You know Franky better than I do. What motive could she possibly have had?"

Bob shook his head, and when George turned to Violet, she too shrugged.

"So, if Franky wasn't in the country, yet her car was captured on camera at the time of the accident, then who could have been driving the car?"

Franky closed her eyes and let her face rest on the cold tile.

"We did," Marie said so quietly that George almost didn't hear her. "We were housesitting while they were away."

CHAPTER FIFTY-NINE

"Marie?" Toby said, his tone more of a warning than curious.

"We liked it there," she continued. "It was near Richmond Park, and we live in a tiny little flat, so it was nice to get out for the week. So we took the chance to housesit for them."

"We?" George asked.

"Me," she said and slowly stood up, stepping beyond her husband's reach, "and Toby." Then she leant against the kitchen's back door, her chest rising and falling with visible exertion as though she was spiralling into panic. "Franky said we could use her car."

"*Marie*," Toby whispered urgently, his eyes focused on his wife. "Marie, look at me. Don't let them do this to us. Don't let them get inside your head."

"The car keys were in the drawer near the front door," she said as if recalling a memory. "It must have been you—"

"Marie, listen to yourself," Toby said as she withdrew from his embrace. "Remember getting coffee at that little Italian place? And walking through the park every morning? Remember the deer with the wonky antler that we called Jeff?" He smiled at the memory, and a long, heavy tear fell down Marie's face. "Do you think I made all that up? How? How could I make up my love for you?"

But Marie had pressed against the kitchen door, as far from him as she could get.

"The day Jordan died," he continued, "that's when we watched the sunset on Richmond Hill. Remember? It was so beautiful, so clear but cloudy, and the whole sky turned pink. You think I met you there just after I murdered your best friend's husband? You think I could have done that? Me?" He laughed, a short, shaky laugh that reminded George of a ripple in a shallow pool. "Don't be crazy, love." He looked about the room. "This is insane."

"I'm not crazy," Marie whispered as if convincing herself of the truth. "Blind, perhaps—"

"Why then? Why would I do that? Why would I hurt somebody?"

"Well, that's what I've been trying to figure out," George cut in. "See, I knew that whoever was responsible for Jordan's death must have been responsible for James' and Lily's murders. I had to link them. Without that link, I had nothing."

"Well, then you have nothing, Inspector," Toby said. "You can't have. Because there is no link."

George smiled patiently. Often, in these scenarios, it was best to listen. The truth would out. Although sometimes, it needed a little luring.

"Marie?" He said, and slowly, she tore her eyes from the man she thought she knew and peered fearfully at George. "Marie, tell me how you two met." He gestured at Toby. "Where was it?"

"Sorry?"

"How did you come to know each other?" he asked.

"This is ridiculous," Toby spat.

"Erm, a coffee shop," she said. "In London."

"London?"

"St Pauls," she added, and he waited for her to embellish the story he had been told already. "I was having a coffee, reading my book, and he..." she paused for thought, then looked back up. "He approached me. We were reading the same book."

"The same book?"

She nodded.

"A crime thriller. I can't remember the title. It was a Kevin Banner book. His latest one, I think."

"And Toby was reading it too, was he?"

She nodded again.

"So you had a common ground to talk about, did you?"

"Is this really necessary," Toby said with a huff.

"Marie?" George said, ignoring the interruption.

She nodded once more.

"I suppose we did."

"And did you have anything else in common?" he asked.

"Our relationship has nothing to do with anybody else, least of all you, Inspector—"

"His wife had died," she continued as if a thread of thought had presented itself, and she clung to the end with her mind, unravelling it slowly. "It was cancer."

"Cancer?" George said. "What type of cancer, exactly."

"This has gone far enough," Toby said.

"Oh, shut up," Bob snapped at him, daring to close the gap between them, placing himself between Marie and her husband. "We just want this to be over."

"Don't you think I want that, too—?"

"It was pancreatic," Marie said, raising her voice to be heard over the men, who silenced almost immediately. Toby rolled his eyes and shook his head.

"Same as you, I believe," George said, and she agreed.

"That's why I was there. The erm, support group. It's near to the cafe," she said, and lowered her head. "It can be quite exhausting, you know? Sharing my news, my feelings, and my darkest thoughts with people who, even though I barely knew them, I knew they were experiencing the same. You share, and you listen. That's what you do. You relate. The things I couldn't bring myself to admit, others did. And you relate. It's exhausting. So, I used to sit in the coffee shop. I used to read to escape. That's all. I just wanted to forget about what I'd heard. Just for a while."

"And then Toby came along?" George said.

"Yes," she said. "Yes, he did. He was a light in the darkness. I just found out that I could talk to him. Not about the illness but about life. He was a good listener."

"I love you," Toby announced. "I've loved you from that very first day—"

"Marie, I want to ask you a question, and you don't have to answer it if you don't feel up to it, okay?" George said, to which she peered up at him through bloodshot eyes. "The decision you made—"

"Oh, come off it," Toby cut in.

"The decision you made," George continued, "to stop the treatment. Was that decision entirely your own?"

"This is ridiculous,' Toby said, a terrified laugh emerging from his thinned lips. "You can't honestly believe—"

"It was my decision," Marie said, cutting him off. "It was entirely my decision. It's my life. I get to decide. Nobody else."

"I see," George replied. "But I imagine you talked it through with your husband."

"Of course," she said. "We discussed what the next few months would look like both with and without the treatment. He'd been through it all before, so..." her voice trailed off, and her eyes wandered to an empty corner. Then, slowly, she turned to face her husband.

"I believe that he let you think it was your decision," George said, and from his pocket, he withdrew his phone and browsed to the latest message, which was an image of a business card, purple on one side. "This is the link I've been looking for."

He held up the phone so she could read the name printed in a bold rounded font.

"That's my support group," she said. "How did you—"

"We found it in Franky's yurt," George explained. "Well, our colleagues did, anyway. It was one of those tiny details that either added weight to the theory that Franky was responsible for all of this or was insignificant. In which case, why would she have it?" He grinned. "But of course, you didn't have it, did you, Franky?"

From the floor, she shook her head as best she could.

"Never seen it before."

"No. No, of course not. That's because it was James who had it. He must have dropped it at some point," George said. "Which leads me backwards. Why would James have a business card for a cancer support group?" George pushed himself up to his feet and dusted his trousers off with a few wipes of his sullied hands. "That's when I remembered something Sergeant Hart said. Something about Lily remembering a case that Jordan had worked on. A patient had stopped their treatment. It's not uncommon, but I asked my researcher to look into it, and while it's not uncommon, it's not exactly common. Not common enough for one man to be married three times, and every single one of those wives elect to stop cancer treatment."

"What?" Toby said, almost choking on his own words.

"Cecelia, you said you overheard Lily and James talking one night."

"Me?"

"That's what you told my colleagues, isn't it? You said that you saw Lily pass James what looked like a business card, and she said that he should call them if he didn't believe her."

"Well, yes, I did, but—"

"And am I right when I say that you also claimed to see somebody behind the tent? Or, you saw their silhouette, at least."

She nodded. "I did, yes."

"But you didn't know who it was?"

She shook her head, eyes wide. "No. No, I never saw who."

George nodded his thanks and took a deep breath.

"My researcher called the support group. They refused to provide a list of names of cancer patients—"

"Bloody right, too," Toby said.

"But they were willing to confirm two names that we provided them," George continued. "Georgina Shaw was one of those names, Toby. Your first wife."

Toby shook his head.

"How dare you—"

"And Lyndsey Wilson," George added. "Your second wife. Both of whom died of pancreatic cancer. Both of whom, like Marie here, attended the support group at St Pauls."

"You can't be serious—"

"It is my belief, Toby, that your first wife elected to stop her treatment of her own accord." Toby shook his head, his lips pulled back in disgust. "And you, rightly so, grieved as any husband might." George said. "And then the money came. The insurance. On the death of your first wife, the insurance company cleared your mortgage and left you with a lump sum of one hundred thousand pounds."

"You low-life scum—" Violet started, but George hadn't finished.

"I believe that when that money had all gone, you saw an easy way to a life beyond your means. You'd seen the victims at the support group. You'd heard their tales of woe, no doubt, from Georgina. How hard was it for you to latch onto one? Make a connection. Relate to her, much as you did with Marie."

Marie dropped her head into her hands, and Bob dragged her towards where he and Cecelia were standing so that the two of them could hold her as George made the final announcement.

"Two hundred and fifty thousand pounds," George said. "That

was the second pay out. "For Lyndsey's death: a quarter of a million pounds. Is that what she was worth?"

"You know nothing—"

"Marie," George said, his tone angry and riled. She peered out from Cecelia and Bob's embrace. "I trust you have your estate in order."

She closed her eyes, took a few breaths through her open mouth, and then licked her lips.

"We changed our wills last month," she said.

"To a single beneficiary?" George asked, to which she nodded.

"To Toby. He gets everything." She wore a look George had seen a thousand times; the look of somebody who had fallen for a scam, lost money, lost possessions. But she had lost everything. She had lost her life.

"This is rubbish," Toby said. "I'm the victim here. Can't you see that? I've lost people I loved. I don't care about the money."

"Toby, you have failed to provide an account of your where-abouts during the time that James and Lily were murdered. Until now, we've had no motive. No reason to pursue you as a person of interest."

"Until now? What, you think that because I had to watch the people I loved die, that I now have a motive?"

"Jordan was onto you, wasn't he?" George said. He spoke quietly, forcing everybody to listen hard. This was the crux of the investigation. This was his theory laid bare. "Jordan knew what you were up to. Georgina was a patient of his."

"So?"

"As was Lyndsey," George finished. "He voiced his concerns to Lily. He didn't give any names, of course. But he voiced them, nonetheless. And that was enough. Lily carried that burden, sharing her feelings and anxieties with the one person she could trust."

"James," Franky said, to which George nodded.

"Yes. There was no affair, just a harmless schoolboy crush. We all have them. He loved you, Franky. You can be sure of that," he said. "But when Lily shared the news with James, little did she know that she had just sealed their fates." He stared at Toby, who, with nowhere else to turn, stared back in shame. "They had to die."

The room was silent.

George imagined each of the friends doubting every single word they had shared, every memory they had created. Yet every eye in the room was on Toby, who pleaded with them. He stared at them all in turn, searching for one ally-just one.

"Marie?" he whined. "Marie, believe me. He's wrong. He's got it all wrong."

But it was when she turned her back on him and buried her face into Cecelia's shoulders that Toby saw his only recourse. He lunged for the shotgun in the middle of the room. Marie had dropped Cecelia's empty shotgun by her feet, and George had tossed Franky's into the living room, which left Violet's. And George had seen her reload it.

"No," George started, and before he could take a single step, Ivy was on her feet and shouldered Toby to the ground. Despite her small frame, she twisted his arms behind his back with ease and used her last zip-tie to secure him.

She peered back at George, who gave her the nod. She deserved the credit, after all.

"Toby Entwistle, I am arresting you on suspicion of the murders of Lily Hughes, James DeSilver, and Jordan Hughes. You do not have to say anything, but it may harm your defence if you fail to mention something you later rely on in court. Anything you do say may be given in evidence. Do you understand?" He said nothing, and she gave his arms little tweak. "I said, do you understand?"

"Yes, yes," he said, writhing in agony.

Ivy shoved herself off him, and stood, just as the room seemed to look to George for answers.

"What now?" Bob asked. "What do we do?"

"Now? That's easy," George said, easing himself into one of the old wooden chairs beside Sabina. He rested his hand on her forearm and gave her a sympathetic smile before addressing the room. "Consider yourselves eliminated. Go home, and as Marie quite rightly said..." George looked at them all in turn, finishing on Ivy. "Live your lives."

CHAPTER SIXTY

There was nothing unusual about seeing more than a dozen service vehicles with their flashing blues lighting the evening. The last rays of sun glowed orange on the horizon, but if it wasn't for the blue lights and the tripods that CSI had set up, they would have been in pitch darkness. In the distance, the yurts stood like white pimples against the dark backdrop, and George could just about make out the few figures who were packing their belongings and preparing to leave.

"I can't believe you didn't call us, guv," Byrne said. They were standing outside the old run-down house in a spot where they wouldn't be in the way. One Crime Scene Investigator was photographing the broken glass on the grass from where Franky's shotgun had damn near taken Ivy's head off. Three more investigators were inside, no doubt collating every shred of evidence to support the reports that George and Ivy would no doubt be writing up that weekend.

"Is the place secure?" George asked.

"Officers on both entrances, Franky DeSilver and Toby Entwhistle are en-route to the station, and CID have arranged accommodation for Sabina Anter," Campbell said. "I think you'll have some explaining to do when you see your mate in CID. You basically handed him a charge for handling stolen goods and lumbered the responsibility onto him."

George grinned. "He would have done the same to me," he said. "What about the friends?"

"They're staying local," Ivy said. "They'll travel down to London in the morning."

George shook his head. "What a mess. You know, in all my years of police work, I don't think I ever came across anything like this. You think you've cracked it. You think that surely you've seen it all and that from here on in, you'll know how to handle a situation. But Christ almighty, that one will go down in history. My history, anyway. If ever I write my memoirs."

"That's good," Ivy added. "Don't want you getting bored, guv."

"You mean you don't want me to retire?"

"That's not what I said."

"But that's what you meant," he told her. "Anyway, you can handle it. If I retired tomorrow, you'd be okay."

"Me?"

"No, not you singular," he said. "You, the team. The lot of you. You don't need me anymore."

"Guv?"

"It's okay, I'm not going anywhere," he said. "It's just nice to know that when the time comes, you'll be okay."

"What makes you say that?" Campbell asked.

"What makes me say that? Well, Sergeant Hart was the one who wanted to look into Jordan's death. Had we done that, then perhaps none of this would have happened. "Perhaps we would have made the connection to Toby and the cancer support group earlier."

"I don't think that was a mistake on your behalf, guv," Byrne said. "I mean, not one of them told us the truth, not entirely, anyway."

"Oh, it was a mistake, alright,' George told him. "Not my first, and it sure as hell won't be my last." He peered around at the three bemused faces. "What? We all make them. We can't be expected to get things right every single time. There's six of us, and we had nearly a dozen paths to take. The important thing is that we have the killer in custody and no more lives were lost. I call that a win."

"Right," Byrne said, and George caught a bemused expression passing between the three of them.

"Speaking of mistakes," George continued. "Where's Maguire and O'Hara?"

"Bin duty," Ivy said.

"Bin duty?"

"I figured that we'll need every shred of evidence to build the case for the CPS. Now we know it was Toby, we're going to need a lot more to make the charges stick."

"Such as?"

"Gloves," a voice called out in the darkness, unmistakably Irish. Maguire and O'Hara emerged from the gloom, carrying a single clear plastic bag.

"Gloves?" George said, eyeing the contents. There was indeed a pair of gloves inside, the type one might wear on a dog walk or to the shops on a winter's morning. "Where were they?"

"Bins," Maguire replied. "We reckon Toby Entwhistle dumped them when he came back to the Grove. By rights, the bins should have been emptied by now, but this place has been shut down."

"And you think there'll be DNA or something on them, do you?" George asked Ivy.

"If they're his, then they'll have his DNA on them."

"It's not his DNA we're interested in though, is it? If the CPS are going to accept them as evidence, they'll want to know they are linked to the crime. I mean, he's not a complete half-wit. He's probably washed them in a stream or something."

"There's that," she admitted. "But then, why else would a pair of gloves that belonged to him be in the bin? Seems odd, doesn't it?"

"Right," he said. "Right, if you say so, then on your head be it. Anything else?"

"We've got a few uniforms packing his belongings into boxes, but I'm not putting much faith into it. We might get lucky with his clothing. If it was him who killed James DeSilver, then his clothing must have a few drops of blood on. You saw the state of his face, right?"

"So, nothing concrete, then?"

"Nothing concrete, no," she said.

"Is there anything in all of this that you do have faith in?" George asked. "Aside from a pair of old gloves and some clothes that may or may not contain traces of DeSilver's blood."

"Yes, actually," she replied, nodding for the four young officers to follow her. "You, guv."

"Me? You can't box me up and send me to the CPS, you know?" he called after them as they left him alone in the dark. "Where are you going, anyway?"

"To the station to get Ruby," she called back, then turned and took a few backward steps to keep pace with the others. "I thought I'd buy the team a round of drinks. I think we've earned it, don't you?" He nodded and laughed, but it was short-lived. "Coming?"

"I'll meet you there," he replied, turning to take in the sight of the old house one more time. "There's a couple of things I'd like to finish off."

"You're not going to blow us off, are you?" she asked. She had stopped at the limits of the tripod lights, and every other second, a blue light washed over her. She was ethereal, in George's mind, at least.

"Guv?" she called one more time, and he waited for her to continue. "We're going to need more, you know? If we're going to build a solid case against him."

He laughed and hoped she could see his smile.

"Have Maguire rewind that video a little further," he said.

"Sorry?"

"We know he left the campsite with Bob, and we know James left before them."

"Right, so...?"

"Just go," he told her. "Enjoy yourselves."

She hesitated. The not knowing would drive her mad, but he hadn't the energy to go into detail. Not now.

"Live our lives, you mean?" she replied as she turned away before he could respond, and jogged a few paces to catch up with the team.

"Yes," he muttered to himself. "Live your lives. Probably the best advice I've ever given."

"Excuse me," somebody said, their voice familiar. He turned to find Marie Entwhistle standing close to the house, a little unsure of where to stand due to the little plastic flags the CSI team had planted to mark the evidence. "I..." she paused, abashed. "We were just leaving, and...well, I wanted to see you before I went."

"Stay there," he told her, and he took the safe route around the flags, then led her by the arm to where his car was parked. "How are you feeling?"

"Well, I..."

"Sorry, that was a poor question. Of course, you've been through a lot. You're going through a lot. You're understandably shaken."

"Actually, no," she said. "I don't know if it hasn't hit me yet, or if it ever will, but I feel surprisingly good. Free."

"Free?" he repeated. "You must be remarkably resilient."

"I..." she shook her head and stared at her feet as she dragged a semicircle into the gravel with her boot. "I didn't see it. I couldn't see what he was doing."

"Now, listen. You can't blame yourself for that. I didn't see it, either. That's how these people do what they do. That's how they get away with it."

"It was all my idea," she said. "I wanted to give him the house when I died. My money, what little investments I have. It was all going to him, and it was all my idea."

"Oh no," he said. "No, no, no. It was his idea. He planted the seeds. It's a long game, and it's based on trust. When he had your trust, he could do anything. A comment here and there, an idea that seemed unrelated. He was the architect. Of that, I have no doubt."

"Do you think he'll be found guilty?" she asked.

"Well, I can't answer that," he told her. "I'm neither the judge nor the jury."

"Or the executioner," she said, and the beginnings of a smile formed in the corners of her mouth. "I don't know how you did that. Did you really not know it was him?"

"Oh, I knew it was him, alright," he said. "The problem was that Franky had the evidence stacked against her. All I had was a theory based on circumstance. That is until you mentioned the housesitting thing. That's what brought it all together. When I heard you say that, and might I add, it was brave of you to do so. But when I heard it, I knew I could push the theory. I knew I could make sense of it."

"But he was in town. He told me he was in town when—"

"Oh, he was in town, all right. He said he was in town, and he was. He made sure the camera caught him to prove it. The thing is...this job. It's as much about what people don't say as what they do, if that makes sense."

"It does."

"He didn't buy anything, did he?"

She gave the question some thought, then shook her head.

"No, I don't think so, but then, I didn't ask."

George inhaled long and hard, then released the breath slowly.

"I believe he left the glampsite before James. I believe he

waited for him. He intercepted James before he could get to his meeting."

"Can you prove that?"

"We may be able to," he replied. "I hope we can, anyway. Once he was in town, he could have walked back to where you were all hiking. All he had to do was follow the tracker you were all using. It would have led him straight to Lily, even in the fog."

"But if he was caught on one camera, then surely he would be on others? I mean, it's not like he confessed or anything."

"Listen, Marie. If I have to get individual warrants to check every CCTV camera in Walesby, then I will. It's not a big place. It would be pretty hard to walk around there for over an hour and not go into any shops or cafe's."

"But you thought it was Franky?" she said. "Until then, you thought Franky had done it all."

"Let's just say I had conflicting thoughts," he said. "But yes. Franky was my primary suspect. I mean, she held a gun to my head, for God's sake. All the evidence pointed at her. Nothing pointed to Toby. Nothing concrete, anyway. I didn't hear him defending her during that ordeal, did you? The rest of you did."

Marie laughed a little, that smile daring to reveal more of itself.

"Will she be charged?"

George took a deep breath and led her further from the buildings, towards what he presumed was Bob's car waiting on the long driveway.

"I pride myself on doing the right thing," he said. "The legal system works to an extent, but it's not without its flaws." He stopped again at the midway point between the waiting car and the house. "Sometimes, the way I word a report can make a difference. Sometimes, it makes things worse for the individual in question."

"So you'll help her?"

"Is that what you want?" George asked. "After all she just put you through, you'd really want to help her?"

Marie shrugged.

"I don't know how I feel about her. A part of me wants her to rot in prison for a few years," she said. "But then, another part of me thinks that she did all that because of her love for James and Lily."

"And Jordan?"

"God, Jordan," she said. "I miss him, you know? He had his head screwed on. I won't live until I'm eighty, so why not just give Franky a hug and get on with life."

"Live it, you mean?" he said, to which she nodded, and the moment was cut short by Bob giving a polite toot of his horn.

"I've decided to resume my treatment," she said, and a laugh fell from her mouth as she dabbed at her eye with her sleeve."

"You have?"

She nodded again, beaming as a young woman might when telling her father he was going to be a grandfather.

"Oh, Marie," he said, wanting to wrap his arms around her. "That's the best news I've heard in... I don't know how long."

"I just..." she began, taking a few sideways steps towards the car. "I just wanted you to know that... well. It's because of you. You didn't give up on us. I owe it to Jordan, Lily, and James. And well, I owe it to you."

"You owe Sergeant Hart. She's the one who nearly had her head blown off."

"All of you," she said in summary. "I wanted you to know, that's all."

He watched her stroll back to the car and climb into the back seat. She lowered the window as Bob pulled away, and her words clung to his thoughts as she waved good-bye.

"Live life," he said to himself, nodding, as the red taillights disappeared around the corner. He turned and started toward his own car. But it was as he climbed in and started the engine that what she had really said became clear. It was the moments before she had held the shotgun to her own mouth that she had given her advice to everyone in the room, free, as only the condemned can. She hadn't told them to live life. She had simply uttered one word, and the meaning of that single syllable was far greater than entire books with hundreds of thousands of words could ever articulate.

He peered up at the rear-view mirror, seeing the old man in the reflection, and he offered that same advice.

"Live."

CHAPTER SIXTY-ONE

The beach had been Grace's favourite place. She had painted dozens of scenes in that place. From the water's edge, capturing the great expanse of nature, and from atop the dunes, where George now stood, with tall grasses growing around him that she used as the foreground and in the lower corners. There was one painting in particular that he recalled, that she painted long before the wind turbines had been installed out to sea.

"It's a vignette," she used to say. "It leads your eye to the focal point, which, in this case, is the sea."

"I'll take your word for it," he had told her, knowing better than to question her art. No, it was far better to simply enjoy it.

To his left was the small car park for beachgoers. Something was happening. A man and a woman were standing there while another man wrestled a woman on the shore ahead of them. He couldn't tell if they were play fighting or if something far more serious was taking place.

But today was not a day for intervention.

Today was a day for living.

"I remember your face the first time we came here," he said

aloud. "You were sad. Not at what you saw, no. No, you were sad because you thought that one day they might build here. You said that there would be amusements, coffee shops, and ice cream stands and that the beach would be covered in litter." He peered out at the scene before him, and it could have been that painting from thirty years or more ago. "Well, you were wrong about that," he told her. "It's not often I get to say that, Grace. But on that occasion, you were wrong. Nothing's changed. It's still your beach. It'll always be your beach. To me, anyway."

He smiled to himself and shuffled his feet, remembering that sound piece of advice he had so recently received.

"I'm..." he started but heard his voice tremble. He cleared his throat. He had to say it. He had to voice what was on his mind. It was the only way. "I... I'm going to leave you here, Grace," he said. "I'll never forget you. You're with me always. In my heart. You're in my heart, and you always have been. But, dear, I'm still here. I know I shouldn't be. I know I should be with you, but for the time being, I'm here. I have to live, Grace. That's the long and short of it." He took a deep breath and felt his chest quiver with the agony of what he was trying to do. "If I am to stay, then I need to live. And I can't live knowing that your journey hasn't finished. I can't keep you bottled up." He laughed to himself, and she would have, too. "Like a fine wine," he added for good measure. "I can't do it, Grace. This is where you belong. This is where you were the happiest."

He watched as the tall man that had been grappling with the woman on the shore, helped her back towards the car park, both of them sodden through.

"There are so many people out there, Grace. So many stories. So many... avenues for people to take. Chance meetings, rash decisions." He took another breath. "I... I'm glad I spent my life with you. I'm glad that, for the most part, we were on this journey together. I don't know how things would have turned out had I not met you. Maybe I would have been a baker or something, or maybe I would have moved abroad." He laughed again. "No, you're right. That would be far too daring, and I'd never get a decent cup of tea, would I. But I am glad, Grace. For everything. And thank you. Thank you for sharing your journey with me. It was... it was wonderful," he said, and his eyes filled with tears. "Every second of it. Even those last few years when we were apart. It was wonderful. Coming to see you, seeing your face. I wouldn't change a single thing."

He tore the lid from the urn in his hand before his emotions got the better of him, and he changed his mind.

"Go free," he said as he raised it in the air and let her fly on the breeze. "Go free, my dear."

It was as if the wind had been waiting on the far side of the dunes. The moment he upturned the urn, she was displaced, this way and that, as if she had been captive in that vessel and now faced the freedom she had earned.

He replaced the lid and held the urn at his side as Grace's ashes were carried to the far corners of the place she loved the most. "I'll be right behind you," he told her.

He hadn't taken but three steps when he saw her.

"Ivy," he said, a little startled. "I thought you were going to wait in the car."

"I..." she started. "I wanted to be close. Close enough to..."

"To what?"

"To catch you, should you fall," she said. "But far enough that you could speak freely. So that you could say goodbye."

"I see," he said. "Well, it's done. She's free."

"She is, guv," Ivy said, and she had a look in her eye that George recognised.

"What is it?"

She grimaced a little.

"Ivy?'

"Speaking of freedom, guv," she said. "Look, I know now's not a good time, but... but it's time. The estate agent wants the deposit on that place."

"You're going then, are you?" he said. "Well, you need your freedom, and I can't stop you."

"Guv?"

"You're young," he said. "You don't need to be holed up with an old codger like me."

"You are *not* an old codger."

"You need your freedom," he said, and he cast a glance along the length of the beach. "Like Grace."

"Guv, I wasn't referring to *my* freedom," she said. "I was talking about *your* freedom. I've taken advantage for far too long, so... so I'll be moving out."

"Does it scare you?" George asked.

"Moving out? No."

"Not moving out. Starting again. On your own. Without Jamie or the kids. Does that scare you?"

"Well, it didn't, but now you mention it."

"Stay," he told her before he had even given the idea some thought.

"What?"

"Stay," he said, and then laughed aloud, hearing how feeble he sounded. But he had started now, and there was little to gain from backtracking. So, he stood before her. He looked her in the eye and found whatever resolve he had left. "Stay with me. Save some money."

"Guv, you don't know what you're saying. I'll have the kids every other weekend, and..."

"I know what I'm saying," he told her. "I know what it means. I just..."

"Guv?" she said. "Guv, are you okay?"

"I... I want to live," he told her, nodding as if to reiterate the point. "I want to do as Marie Entwhistle suggested. I want to make Grace proud, and I want to see the team thrive. I want all of those things, Ivy. I want them so very much—"

"But?" she said, her head cocked to one side, sensing there was a caveat to his dreams.

"But..." he agreed, smiling for a moment, then setting it free. "But I can't do it alone."

The End.

SECRETS FROM THE GRAVE - PROLOGUE

It had been one of those blissful summer days that never ended. Oscar breathed in the Lincolnshire countryside, the petrichor waft of grass and wildflowers, trees and hedges, and streams and pools flowed through a version of Snipe Dales he hadn't seen for nearly a year. His favourite place was bathed in the soft orange glow of the dying sun, casting shadows from trees that swayed in the gentle breeze, like the ghosts of soldiers amidst the lush vegetation.

It had been the kind of afternoon that stretched on, later and later, as though apologising for the long, dark winter ahead. The sunlight seemed to linger only for them, sinking beneath the horizon as slowly as a peach into jelly. It was a gift. One that they shouldn't waste.

"Come *on*, Wesley," he yelled down the slope.

But Wesley didn't move. He was bent over on the narrow wooden bridge that spanned the stream, clutching a stitch in his side. At his feet, the roll of carpet they had found lay still and curved like a body.

Oscar looked past him to Louis, who grinned and rolled his eyes, then glanced up at the sunset.

"Come on, it's not far now," he said. "Let's just get it to the den so we can make a fire."

"It's alright for you," Wesley said, clearly in pain. "You're not carrying it."

"I carried the sofa," Oscar told him. "I'm not a bloody donkey."

"We've got marshmallows," Louis added, as a mother might attempt to tempt a small child.

Despite his concerns that they may have to abandon the carpet, Oscar's heart was full. It had been the first proper day of summer. The Snipe Dales had lain before them like their own private playground, and although the three boys could — and often did — enjoy the country park in all weathers, they could now lose entire days in it. Snipe Dales offered all the comforts of their parents' homes and all the adventure of the world beyond childhood: trees to climb, streams to wade in, springy grass to lie upon and stare up at the clouds...

What more could they need?

But everything ended eventually. Oscar knew that well enough by now. He watched the perfect day fade away, second by second, behind the trees, lowering behind one leaf and then disappearing behind the next, and those soldiers that swayed to and fro with the breeze, faded like a memory.

"Seriously, Wesley," he yelled down the slope, "can you hurry the—"

"It's *heavy!*" Wesley screamed back before Oscar could finish.

The retaliation had been on the tip of his tongue, just waiting for a trigger. Wesley was like that. He held it in and in and in — until he snapped. When they were younger, Oscar and Louis would test his patience by continuously poking him in the shoulder or pretending not to understand a joke, turning Wesley's crank over and over until he lashed out like a jack-in-the-box. In the last year or so, however, Wesley had grown more outward than upward, unlike Oscar, who'd grown tall and lean, and Louis, who'd somehow managed both, becoming an awkward bear of a teenager.

"Right, come on," Louis said when Wesley seemed to have recovered. "One, two…"

They shouldered the carpet like pallbearers, and with gritted teeth, they walked on shaky legs with dogged determination.

"I dragged it all the way from the carpark," Oscar defended as they reached the top.

"Yeah, downhill," spat Wesley between heavy breaths.

"It *is* bloody heavy," Louis said as they entered the trees and made their way up to the camp they had spent the day making.

He turned to Oscar as a removal man might. "Where do you want it?"

They had already built the foundations. Leafy branches strung together formed the walls, an old tent cover draped across them formed a makeshift roof, and all of it had built around the object that had inspired their project, the old stained, red sofa they had found abandoned in the car park. The carpet was the final finish to smooth over the loose sticks and ant nests. Of course, in a perfect world, they might not have chosen a gaudy, red, diamond-patterned carpet with gold fringe along the edges, but you have to work with what you've got when you're a teenager.

With a final heave, they dumped the carpet which landed with a heavy *thump* that scattered the nearby leaves.

"Oi! What are you lot doing?" The voice came at them like gunfire through the trees, and they all froze. "Get out of there."

Oscar peered through the trees, finding an old man on the footpath at the bottom of the hill, who held up a hand against the glare of the sunset as though to see them better. A long, loose raincoat hung off him, and a small, golden, curly-haired puppy bounced around his feet, curiously discovering what mud was and whether it was to his or her liking.

Oscar stepped forward. "What's it got to do with you?"

"You know this is a country park, don't you, son?"

"I said, what's it to you?"

"It's a nature reserve," the man continued, stepping off the footpath and into the trees, encroaching on their territory. "You can't dump all that here."

"*We* didn't bring it here, sir," Louis said, stepping up beside Oscar. "Someone dumped it in the car park. We're just..." He looked back at the den. "Recycling it."

"Well, you shouldn't play around in rubbish. Could have anything in it, you hear? Glass, knives. You should call the authorities if—"

But before he could finish, a large, thick stick landed at the old man's feet, causing his golden-haired puppy to whimper and scurry to safety behind its master's ankles. The man instinctively held his hands to his face, then scowled at the boy who had thrown it.

"What the *hell* are you doing?"

But Wesley bent down to grab another.

"Playing fetch with your dog," he yelled, readying himself to lob a huge tree branch like a discus thrower. "Hey, doggie — fetch this!"

But before he could let go, Oscar turned and grabbed his arm hard, allowing the old man to pick up his traumatised puppy. He backed off, shaking his head and muttering to himself, as he slinked off along the footpath back towards the car park, throwing jaded stares over his shoulder.

Oscar glared at his friend. "What's wrong with you?"

"What?" Wesley shrugged out of his grip. "Got rid of him, didn't it?"

Louis laughed in the way that someone does when they don't know how else to deal with tension. But Oscar was more familiar with conflict than Louis, whose parents didn't keep him awake every night with their screaming rows.

"You're a bloody psychopath sometimes, you know that?"

Wesley seemed to take it as a compliment and threw himself down on the red, stained sofa with an insufferable grin.

"Budge up," Louis said, sitting beside him and saving space for Oscar, who shook his head but joined them nonetheless.

The three boys shared the two-person sofa and watched the orange passage of time through the trees. Oscar was well aware that things must end — perfect days, toxic marriages, even childhoods. He was willing to fight. But he'd been learning recently that such things were beyond his control. He wriggled uncomfortably. The three boys sat so close together that Oscar could feel Louis's vibrations through his jeans pocket. Eventually, after a series of violent buzzes, Louis pulled out his phone and then groaned at the screen.

"Ah, biscuits," he said. "It's my mum."

Oscar's heart drained. "Can't you tell her you'll just be an hour? I thought we could stay a bit. Make a fire." He paused, then offered an idea that now sounded pathetic. "I bought marshmallows, remember?"

"I don't know, she's freaking out," Louis said, holding up a screen of notifications.

Oscar's phone hadn't buzzed once all day.

"Ah, come on," he said. "I mean, we could stay all night if we wanted."

"No thanks," Wesley scoffed, stretching. "I've got a roast dinner waiting at home."

But Louis held Oscar's gaze, reading his mind. "You've got to go home eventually, mate," he said quietly.

Oscar didn't reply. He just picked up the largest stick within reach and chucked it at the nearest tree, causing a chunk of bark to break off and fall to the ground.

"Come on," Louis said, jumping up and offering a hand. "We can come back tomorrow, yeah?"

"Fine," Oscar said eventually, allowing his oldest friend to pull him to his feet. He stretched and kicked out at the carpet. "Let's unroll this first, eh? A bit of air might get rid of the smell."

"Sure." Louis smiled. "You going to help?" he asked Wesley, who reluctantly dragged himself to his feet.

After trying to kick the carpet open, to little avail, the three boys knelt on the ground to push it instead.

"One, two, three," Louis said as though directing a rugby play, and they began rolling the carpet open, which turned over and over with the same sluggish drag as a flat tyre.

"Jesus," Wesley choked halfway through. "It *stinks*."

"So would you if you'd be left out in the rain," Oscar said breathlessly.

"Come to think of it, you do smell," Louis added, earning him a playful dead arm.

"It'll be alright tomorrow. The roof will keep it dry," Oscar said, hoping to coax them on.

They continued their battle with the carpet until Wesley suddenly stopped. Without his bulk, Oscar and Louis stood little chance.

He squinted into the trees, then sat back on his ankles.

"What is it now?" asked Oscar breathlessly.

"Did you see that?" Wesley said.

"See what?"

Oscar looked around the clearing, noticing nothing but the elongated shadows fading to merge with the ground.

"It's just a shadow, Wesley. Come on."

"Wait—"

Even Oscar noticed it that time, the flash of a dark shape through the trees and the accompanying sound of a murmur.

"It's just a dog walker or something," Louis said, though his voice had quietened. "Come on."

He returned to the task of unfurling the carpet, but Wesley and Louis were transfixed.

"Come on, you two," he said. "Let's just get it done and then get out of here if you're scared."

Oscar fell onto his backside, pressed his feet against the roll, and gave everything he had. He felt it give and fell onto his back to get his breath back with the exertion.

Wesley and Louis were silent.

"Some help you were," Oscar told them, groaning. He could have laid there all night. It wasn't the most comfortable he had ever been, but it was a far better prospect than going home.

"Oscar," Louis hissed.

"I'm staying here," he told them.

"Oscar!" Louis hissed again, with more urgency in his voice.

Oscar remained horizontal but raised his head to peer up at him. Both boys were staring at the carpet down at his feet.

"What?" he asked, shoving himself up onto one elbow to see what the fuss was about.

And then he saw it.

And the blood in his veins ran cold.

And the prospect of a perfect summer died with the final breath of the day's sun.

ALSO BY JACK CARTWRIGHT

The Deadly Wolds Murder Mysteries

When The Storm Dies

The Harder They Fall

Until Death Do Us Part

The Devil Inside Her

Secrets From The Grave

The Wild Fens Murder Mysteries

Secrets In Blood

One For Sorrow

In Cold Blood

Suffer In Silence

Dying To Tell

Never To Return

Lie Beside Me

Dance With Death

In Dead Water

One Deadly Night

Her Dying Mind

Into Death's Arms

No More Blood

Burden of Truth

Run From Evil

Deadly Little Secret

The DCI Cook Murder Mysteries

A Winter of Blood

A Secret to Die For

VIP READER CLUB

Your FREE ebook is waiting for you now.

Get your FREE copy of the prequel story to the Wild Fens Murder Mystery series, and learn how Freya came to give up everything she had to start a new life in Lincolnshire.

Visit www.jackcartwrightbooks.com to join the VIP Reader Club.

I'll see you there.

Jack Cartwright

A NOTE FROM THE AUTHOR

Locations are as important to the story as the characters are, sometimes even more so.

I have heard it said on many occasions that Lincolnshire is as much of a character in The Deadly Wolds series, as George is, or Ivy. That is mainly due to the fact that I visit the places used within my stories to see with my own eyes, breathe in the air, and to listen to the sounds.

However, there are times when I am compelled to create a fictional place within a real environment.

For example, in the story you have just read, the towns and villages mentioned are all real places. However, the houses that are described and the glampsite are entirely fictitious.

The reason I create fictional places is so that I can be sure not to cast any real location, setting, business, street, or feature in a negative light. Nobody wants to see their beloved home described as a scene for a murder, or any business portrayed as anything but excellent.

If any names of bonafide locations and businesses appear in my books, I ensure they bask in a positive light, because I truly believe that Lincolnshire has so much to offer and that these locations should be celebrated with vehemence.

I hope you agree.

Jack Cartwright

AUTHOR

AFTERWORD

Because reviews are critical to an author's career, if you have enjoyed this novel, you could do me a huge favour by leaving a review on Amazon.

Reviews allow other readers to find my books. Your help in leaving one would make a big difference to this author.

Thank you for taking the time to read *The Devil Inside Her*.

Best wishes,

Jack Cartwright
AUTHOR

COPYRIGHT